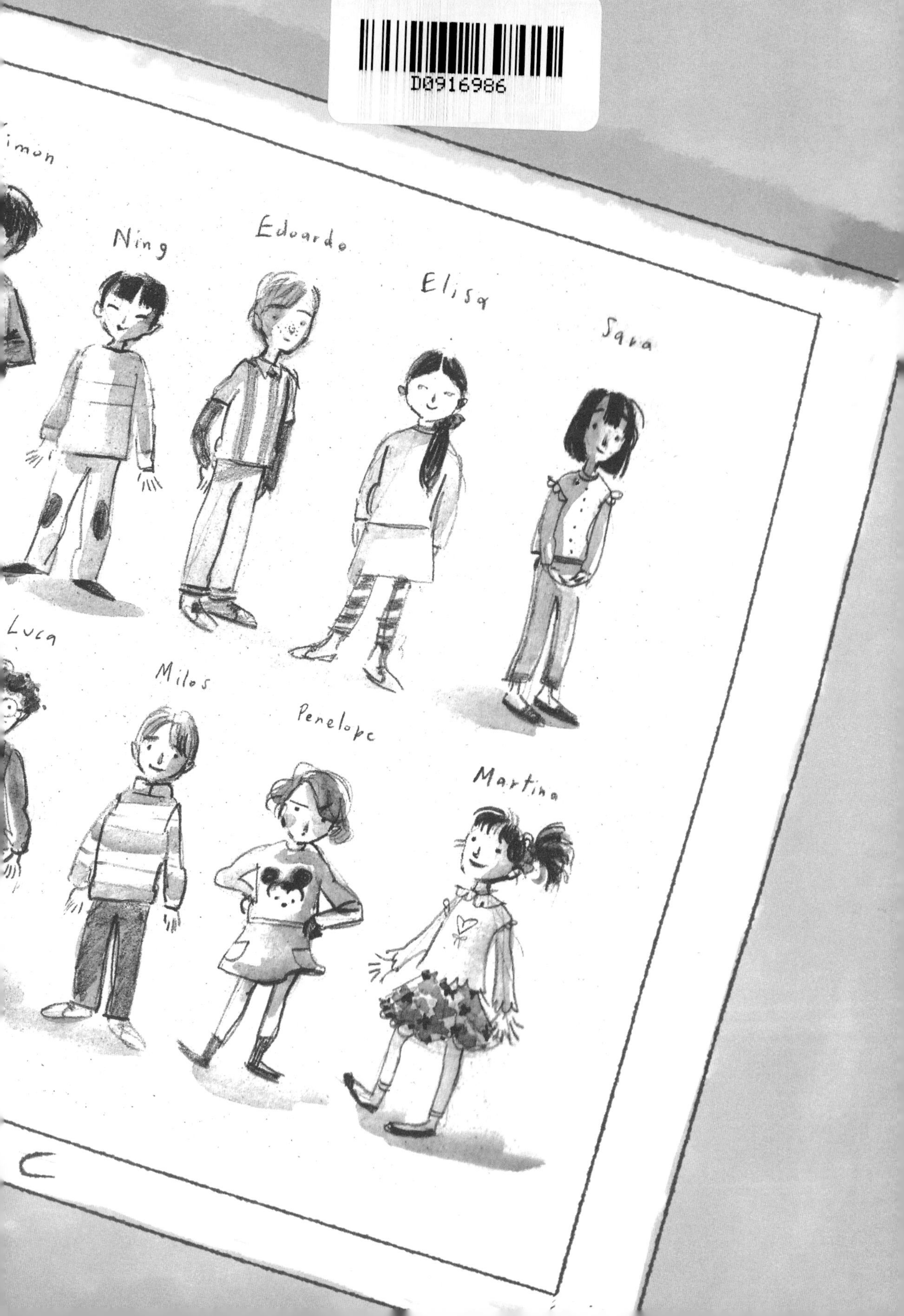
imon
Ning
Eduardo
Elisa
Sara
Luca
Milos
Penelope
Martina

Story by
BRIAN FRESCHI

Illustrated by
ILARIA URBINATI

DARK HORSE BOOKS

Lettering and Page Layout by
Officine Bolzoni
with a font based on Ilaria Urbinati's handwriting

Translated by
Carla Roncalli di Montorio

President and Publisher
Mike Richardson

Editor
Brett Israel

Assistant Editor
Sanjay Dharawat

Digital Art Technician
Samantha Hummer

Collection Designer
May Hijikuro

Special Thanks to Kari Torson *at Dark Horse Comics*

Neil Hankerson *Executive Vice President* Tom Weddle *Chief Financial Officer* Dale LaFountain *Chief Information Officer* Tim Wiesch *Vice President of Licensing* Matt Parkinson *Vice President of Marketing* Vanessa Todd-Holmes *Vice President of Production and Scheduling* Mark Bernardi *Vice President of Book Trade and Digital Sales* Randy Lahrman *Vice President of Product Development* Ken Lizzi *General Counsel* Dave Marshall *Editor in Chief* Davey Estrada *Editorial Director* Chris Warner *Senior Books Editor* Cary Grazzini *Director of Specialty Projects* Lia Ribacchi *Art Director* Matt Dryer *Director of Digital Art and Prepress* Michael Gombos *Senior Director of Licensed Publications* Kari Yadro *Director of Custom Programs* Kari Torson *Director of International Licensing*

Published by Dark Horse Books || A division of Dark Horse Comics LLC
10956 SE Main Street, Milwaukie, OR 97222

First edition: July 2022
Ebook ISBN 978-1-50672-675-5 || Hardcover ISBN 978-1-50672-672-4

10 9 8 7 6 5 4 3 2 1
Printed in China

MIX
Paper from responsible sources
FSC® C109093

Library of Congress Cataloging-in-Publication Data

Names: Freschi, Brian, 1993- author. | Urbinati, Ilaria, 1984- illustrator. | Roncalli di Montorio, Carla, translator.
Title: The vertical sea / story by Brian Freschi ; illustrated by Ilaria Urbinati ; [translated by Carla Roncalli di Montorio].
Other titles: Mare verticale. English
Description: First edition. | Milwaukie, OR : Dark Horse Books, 2022. | Summary: "With a good job as an elementary school teacher and a love for her partner, India's life seems ok at face value. However, with a chronic mental illness that causes her to have panic attacks regularly, each day can be a struggle. With the threat of having her class taken from her, the pressure is building, and India needs to face her problems head on and take action"-- Provided by publisher.
Identifiers: LCCN 2021055639 | ISBN 9781506726724 (hardcover) | ISBN 9781506726755 (ebook)
Subjects: LCGFT: Graphic novels.
Classification: LCC PN6767.F73 M3713 2022 | DDC 741.5/945--dc23/eng/20211118
LC record available at https://lccn.loc.gov/2021055639

To those who choose not to give in to an invisible fear,
but rather fight it and understand it every day,
each in their own special way.

—Brian & Ilaria

Inside my head
There always was an empty room for you
Oh, the times I brought it flowers
Oh, the times I saved it from monsters
Now, I live in it
And the monsters came with me.

—Michele Mari, *Cento poesie d'amore a
Ladyhawke* (Giulio Einaudi Editore)

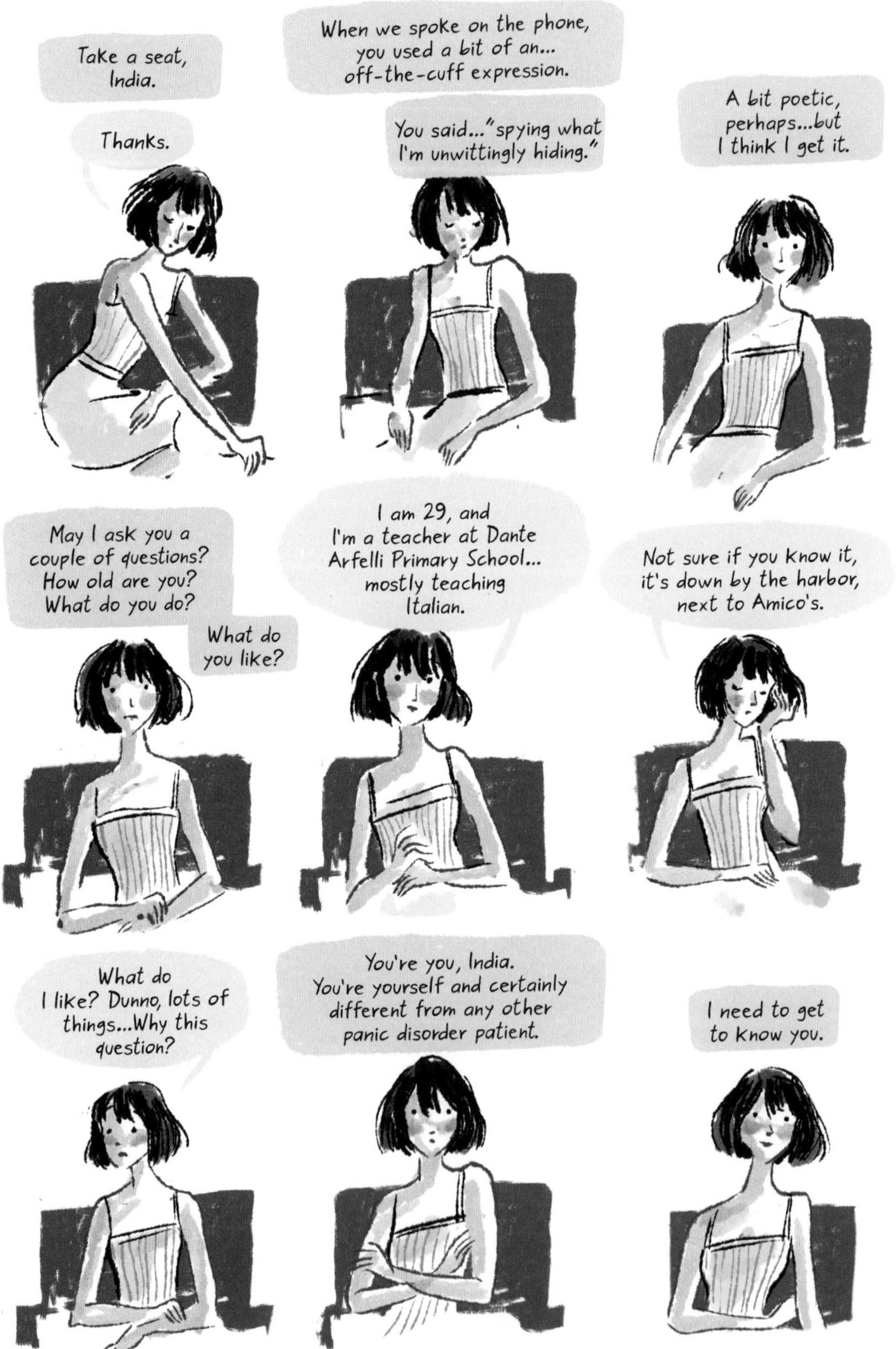
Take a seat, India.
Thanks.
When we spoke on the phone, you used a bit of an... off-the-cuff expression.
You said..."spying what I'm unwittingly hiding."
A bit poetic, perhaps...but I think I get it.
May I ask you a couple of questions? How old are you? What do you do?
What do you like?
I am 29, and I'm a teacher at Dante Arfelli Primary School... mostly teaching Italian.
Not sure if you know it, it's down by the harbor, next to Amico's.
What do I like? Dunno, lots of things...Why this question?
You're you, India. You're yourself and certainly different from any other panic disorder patient.
I need to get to know you.

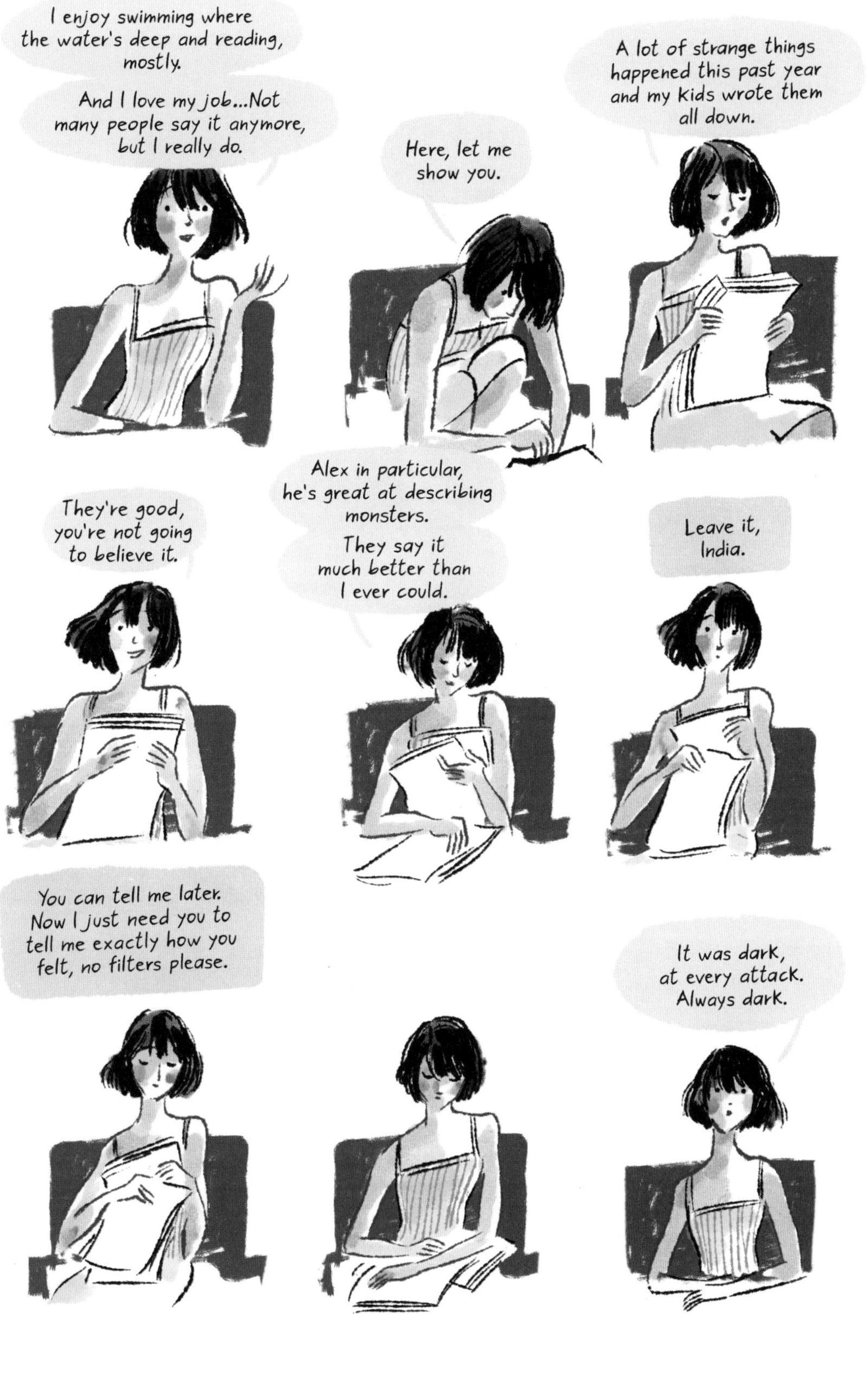
I enjoy swimming where the water's deep and reading, mostly.
And I love my job...Not many people say it anymore, but I really do.
Here, let me show you.
A lot of strange things happened this past year and my kids wrote them all down.
They're good, you're not going to believe it.
Alex in particular, he's great at describing monsters.
They say it much better than I ever could.
Leave it, India.
You can tell me later. Now I just need you to tell me exactly how you felt, no filters please.
It was dark, at every attack. Always dark.

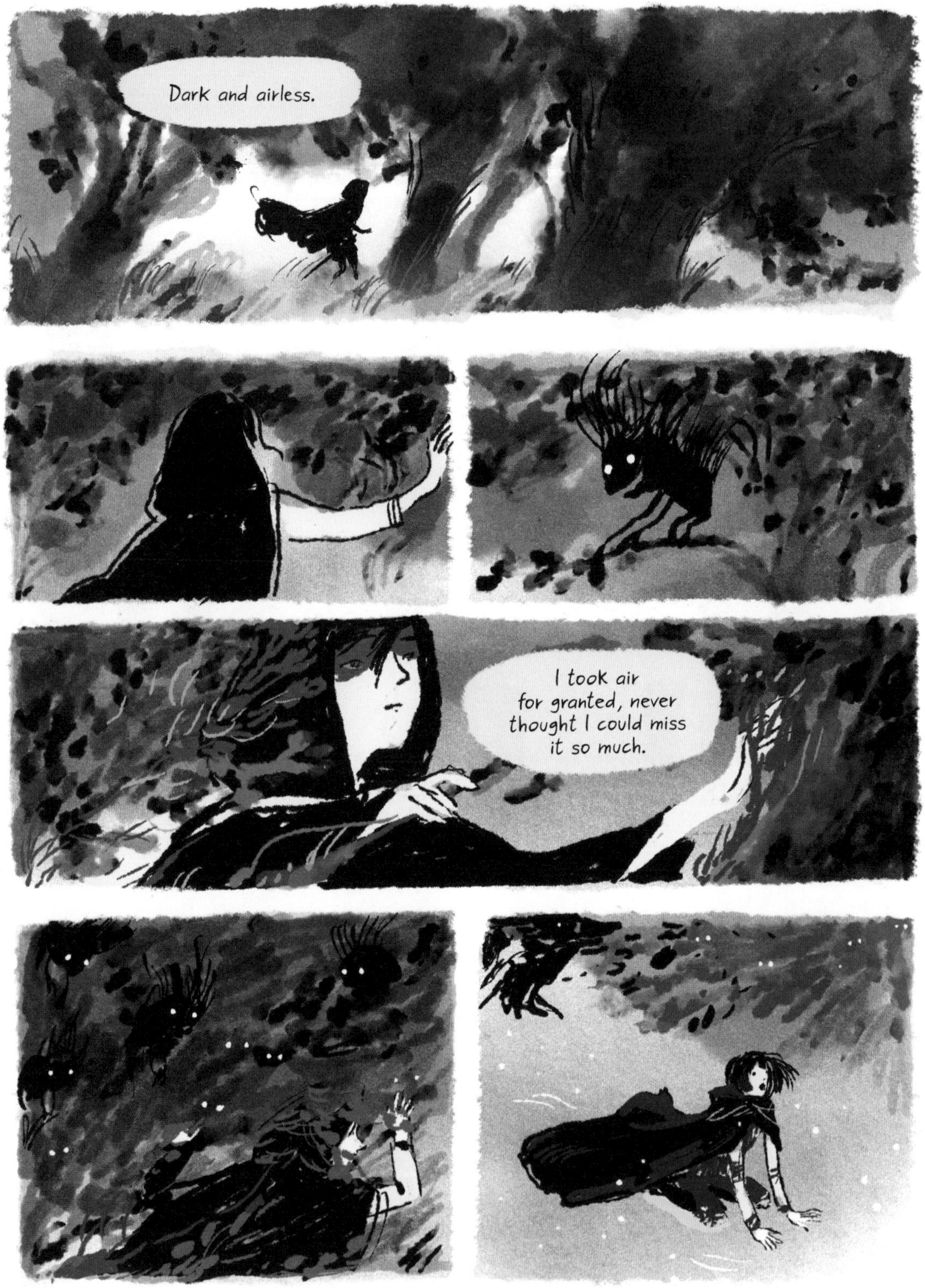
Dark and airless.
I took air for granted, never thought I could miss it so much.

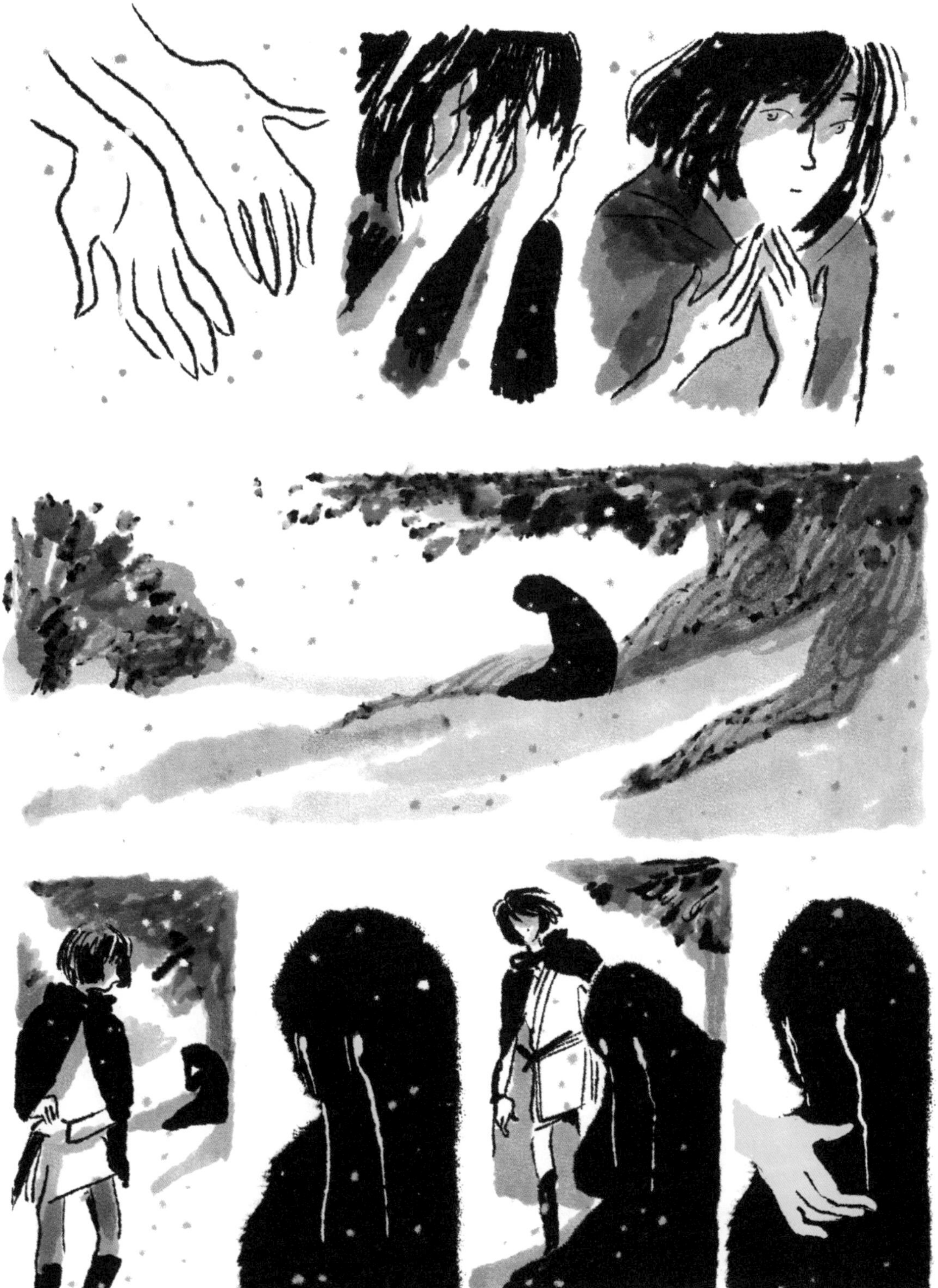

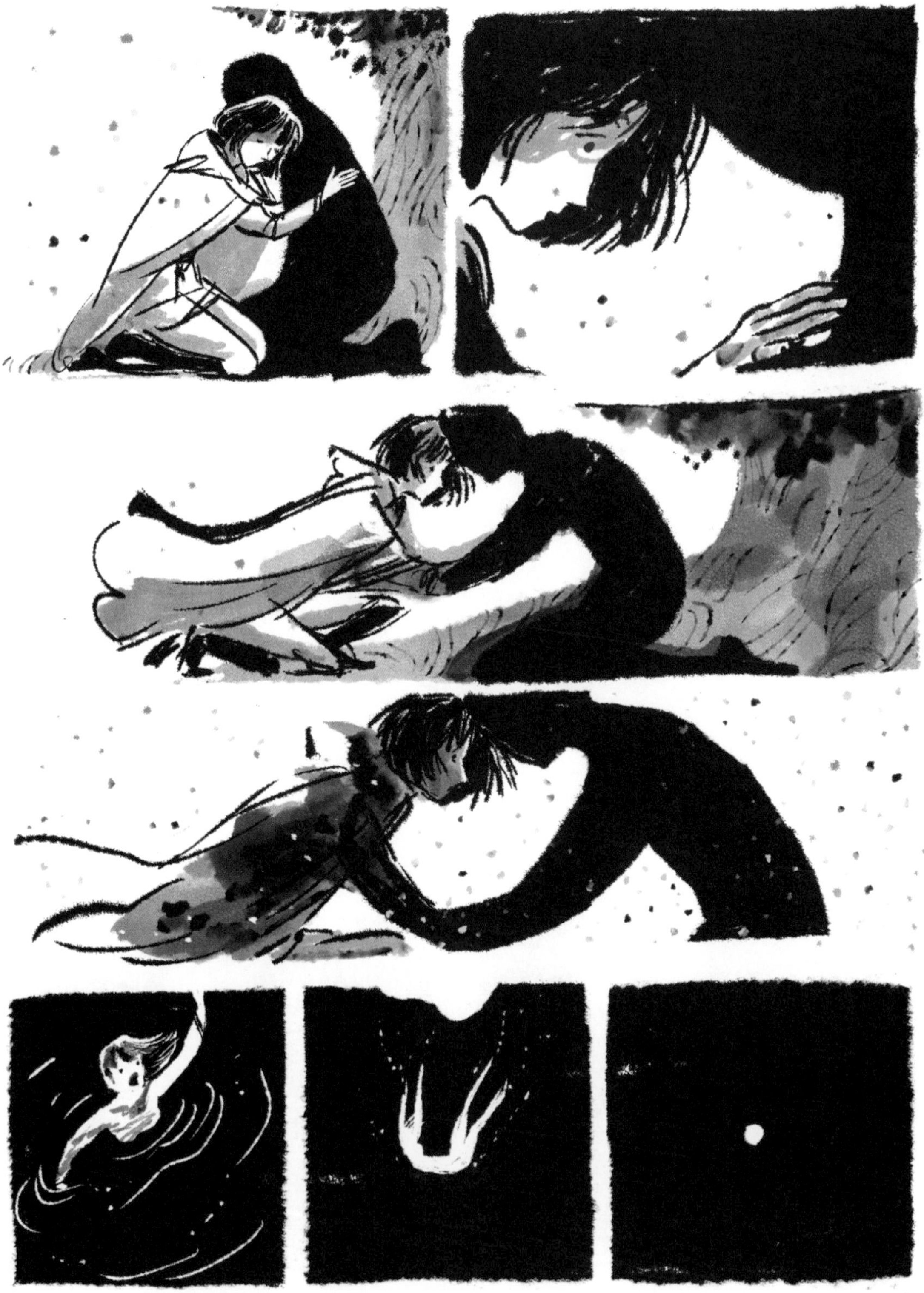

Chapter One

The land of
the gleaming
moon

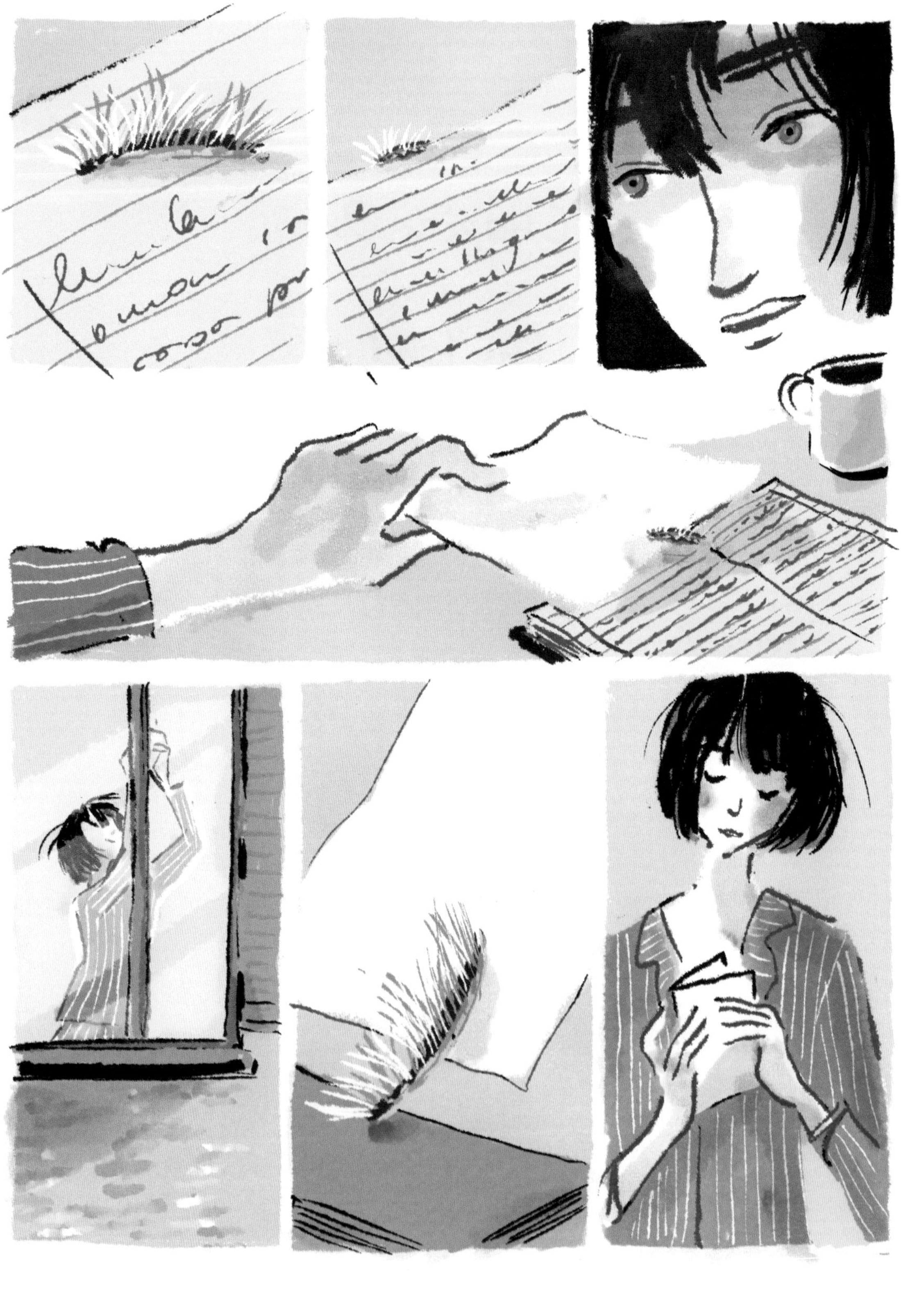

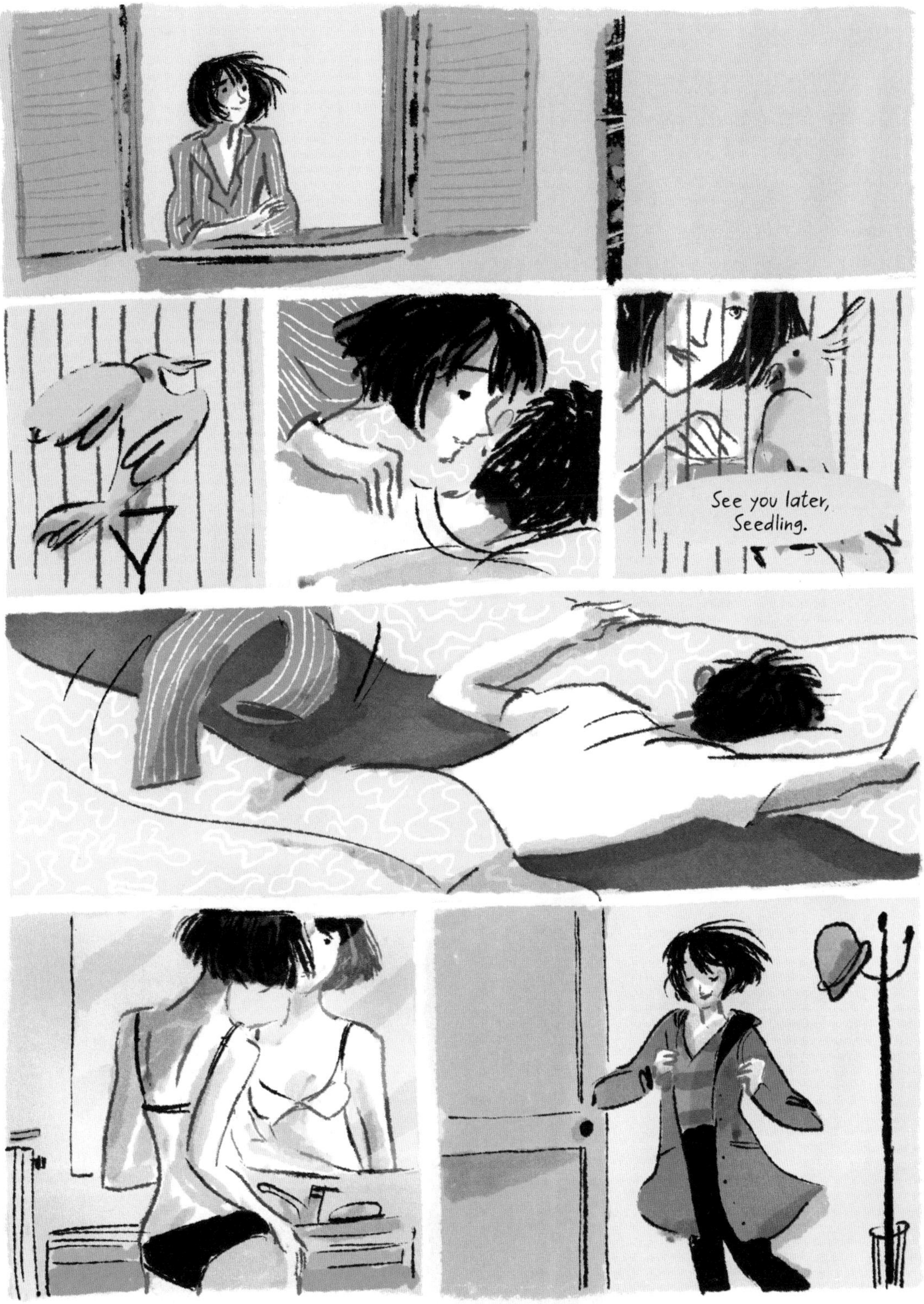
See you later,
Seedling.

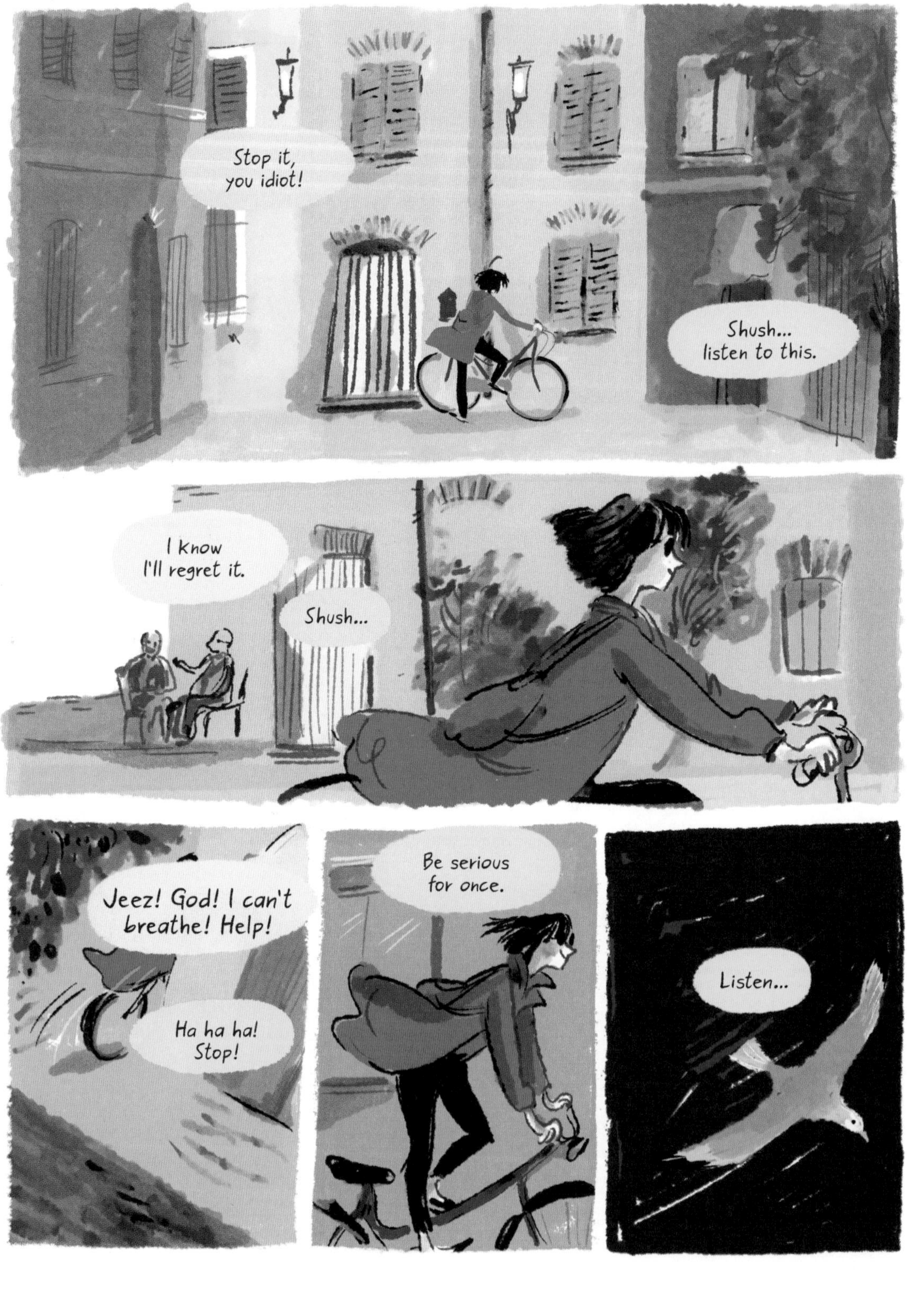
Stop it, you idiot!
Shush... listen to this.
I know I'll regret it.
Shush...
Jeez! God! I can't breathe! Help!
Ha ha ha! Stop!
Be serious for once.
Listen...

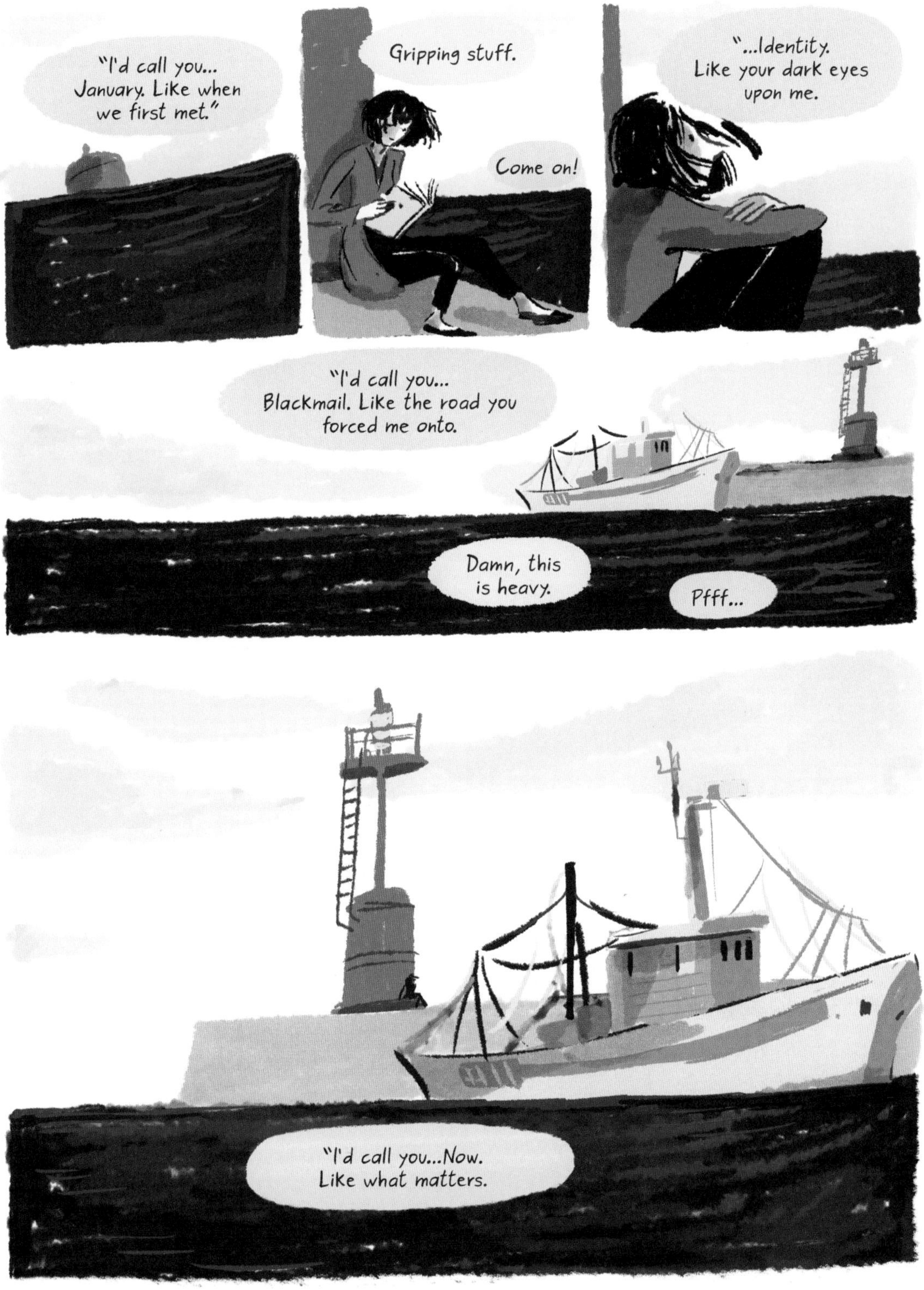
"I'd call you...
January. Like when
we first met."
Gripping stuff.
Come on!
"...Identity.
Like your dark eyes
upon me.
"I'd call you...
Blackmail. Like the road you
forced me onto.
Damn, this
is heavy.
Pfff...
"I'd call you...Now.
Like what matters.

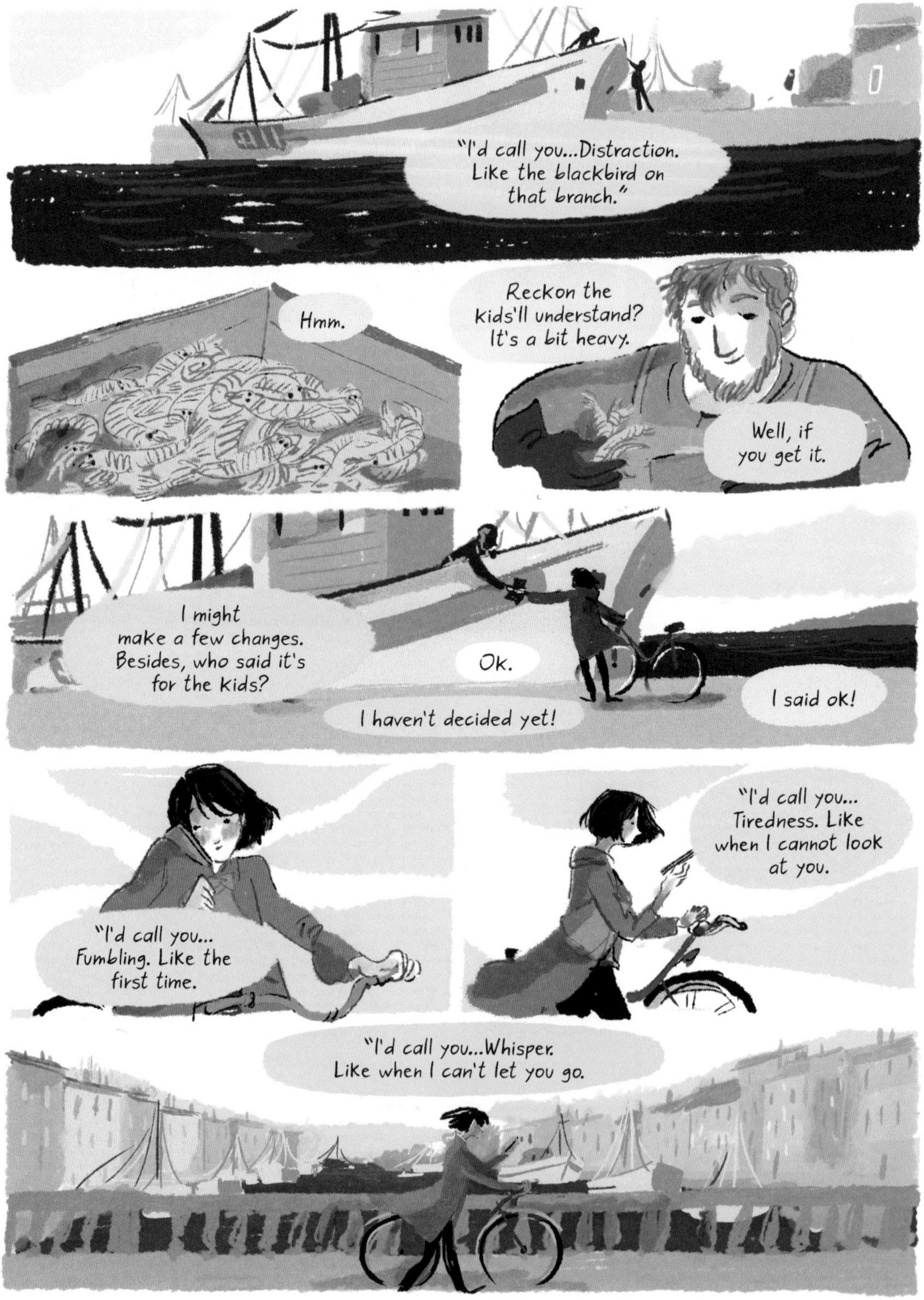
"I'd call you...Distraction. Like the blackbird on that branch."
Hmm.
Reckon the kids'll understand? It's a bit heavy.
Well, if you get it.
I might make a few changes. Besides, who said it's for the kids?
Ok.
I haven't decided yet!
I said ok!
"I'd call you... Fumbling. Like the first time.
"I'd call you... Tiredness. Like when I cannot look at you.
"I'd call you...Whisper. Like when I can't let you go.

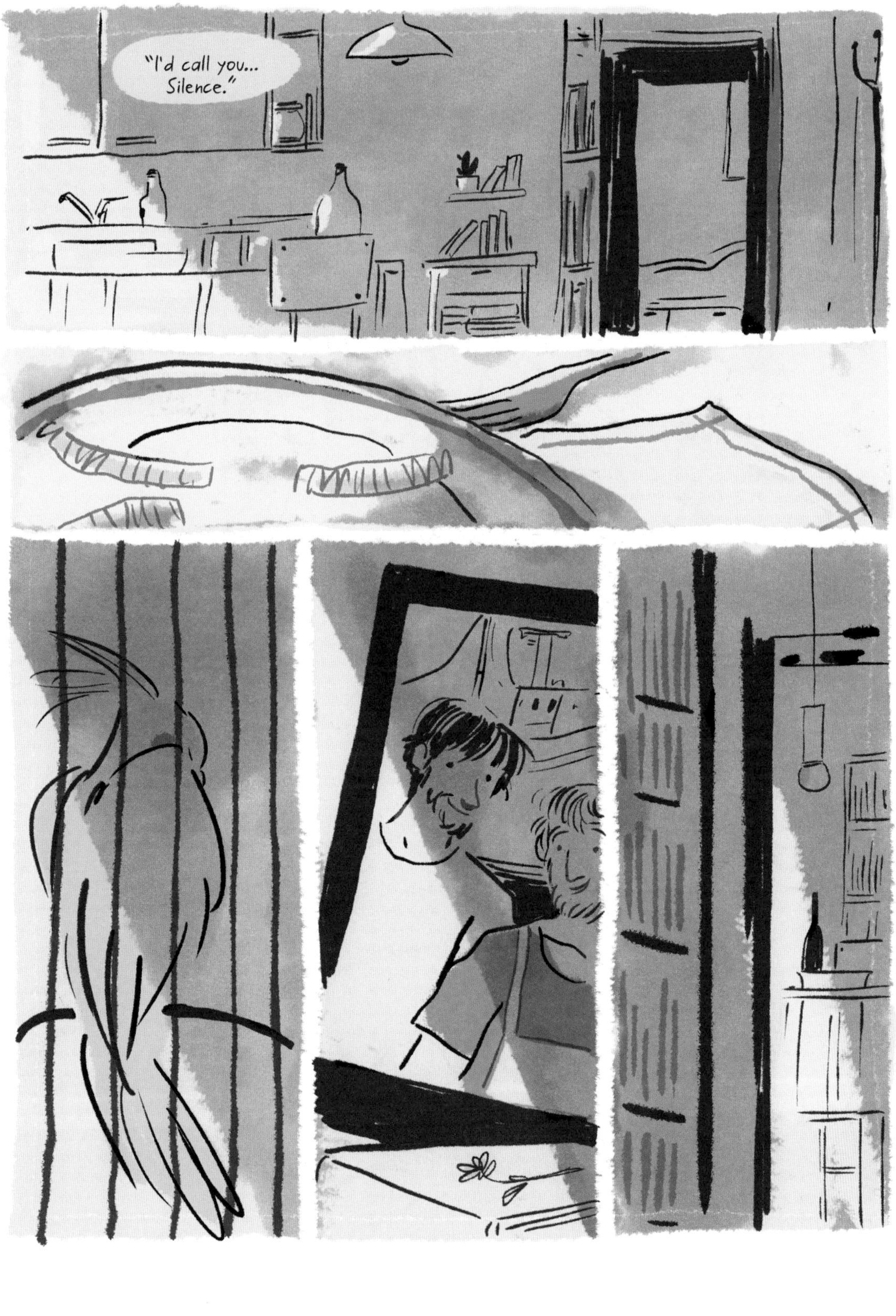
"I'd call you... Silence."

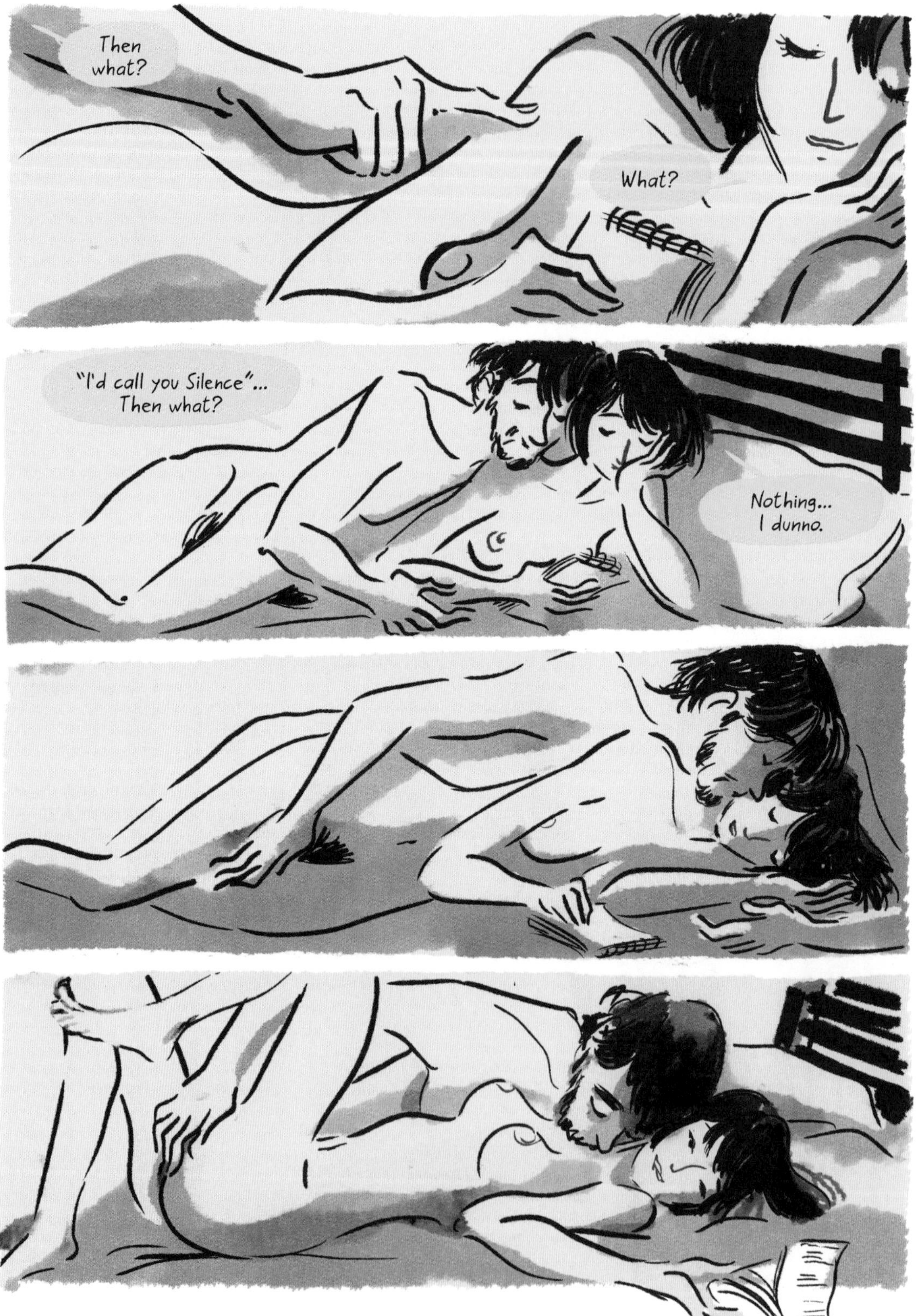
Then what?
What?
“I'd call you Silence”... Then what?
Nothing... I dunno.

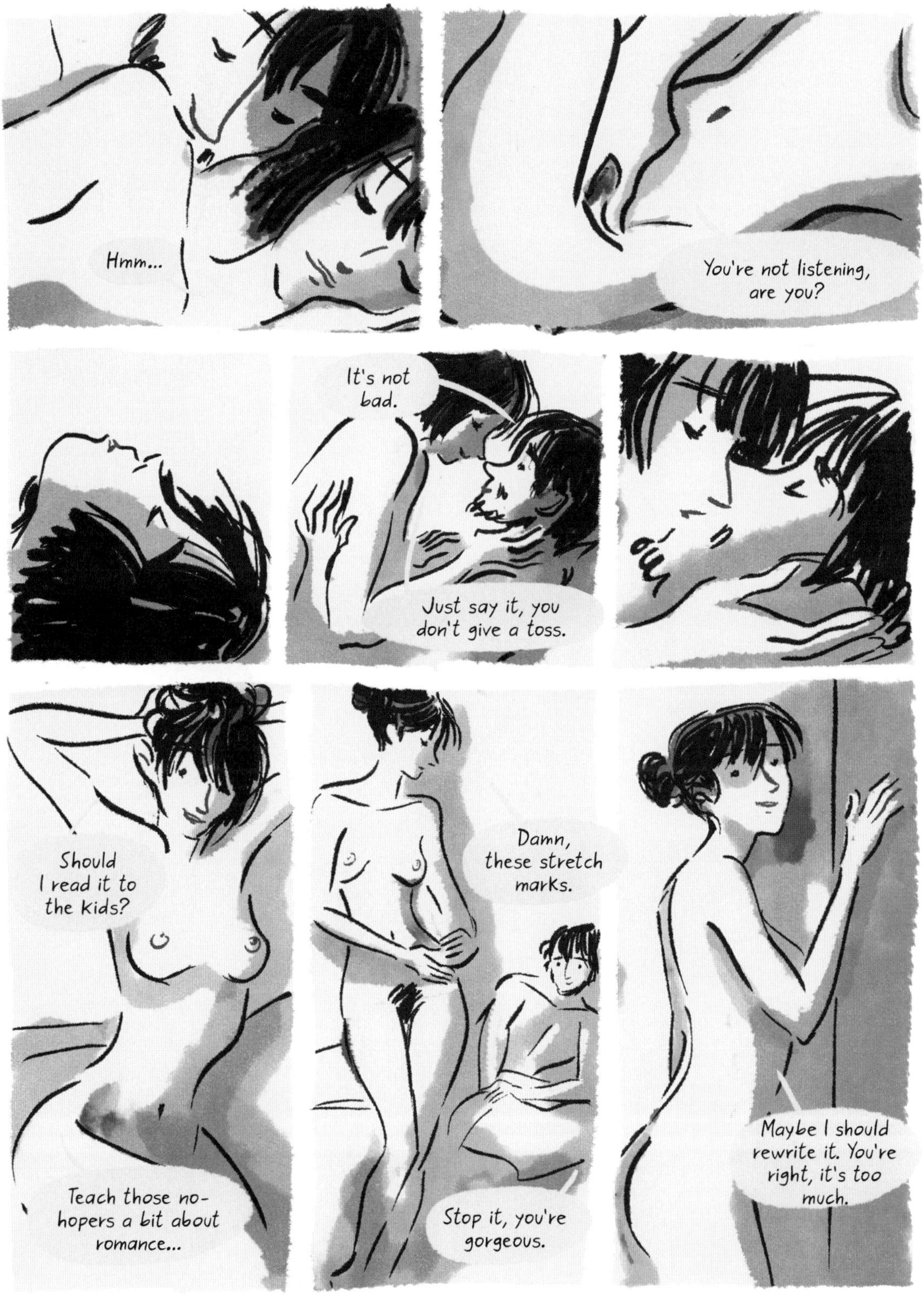
Hmm...
You're not listening, are you?
It's not bad.
Just say it, you don't give a toss.
Should I read it to the kids?
Teach those no-hopers a bit about romance...
Damn, these stretch marks.
Stop it, you're gorgeous.
Maybe I should rewrite it. You're right, it's too much.

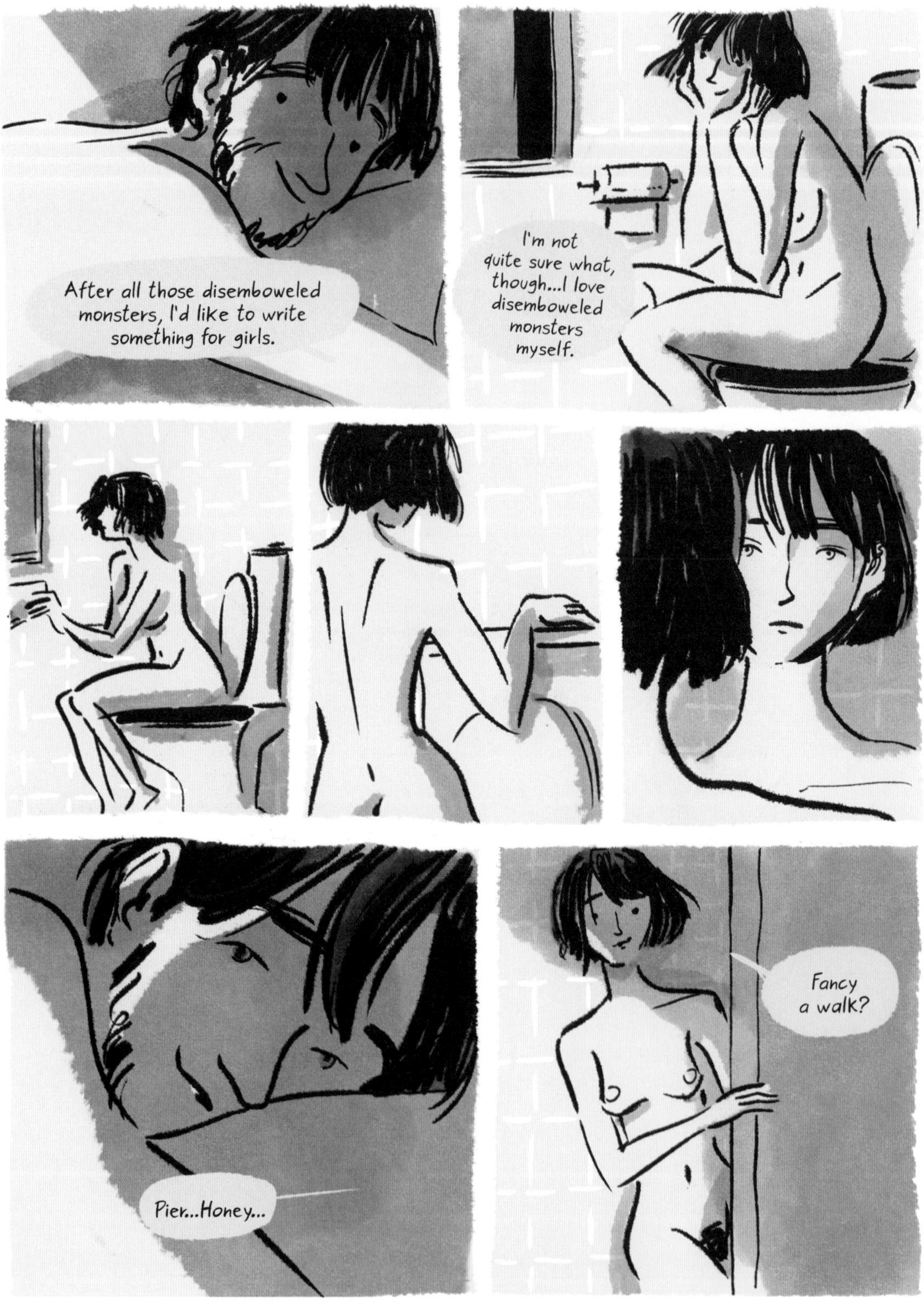
After all those disemboweled monsters, I'd like to write something for girls.
I'm not quite sure what, though...I love disemboweled monsters myself.
Pier...Honey...
Fancy a walk?

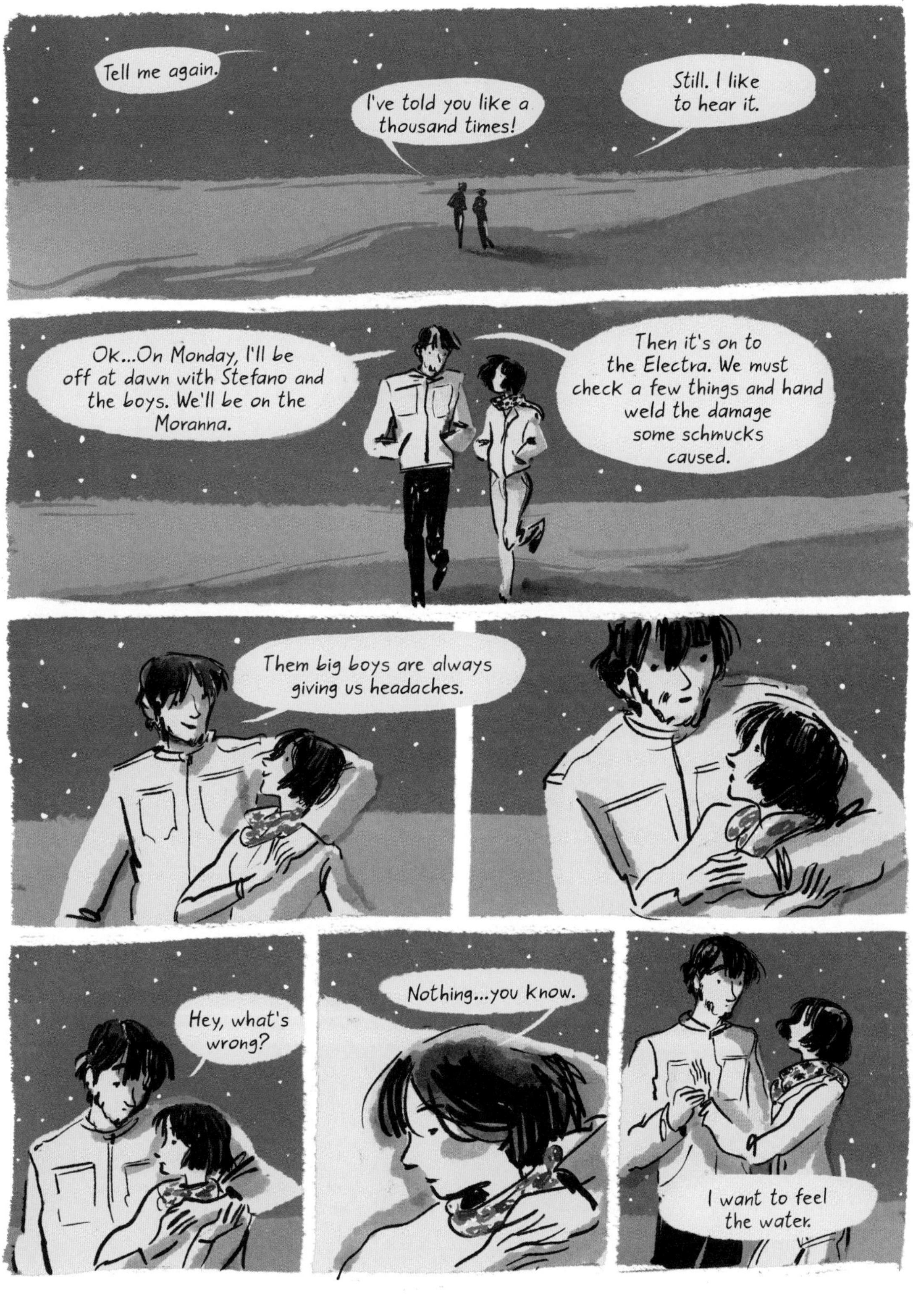
Tell me again.
I've told you like a thousand times!
Still. I like to hear it.
Ok...On Monday, I'll be off at dawn with Stefano and the boys. We'll be on the Moranna.
Then it's on to the Electra. We must check a few things and hand weld the damage some schmucks caused.
Them big boys are always giving us headaches.
Hey, what's wrong?
Nothing...you know.
I want to feel the water.

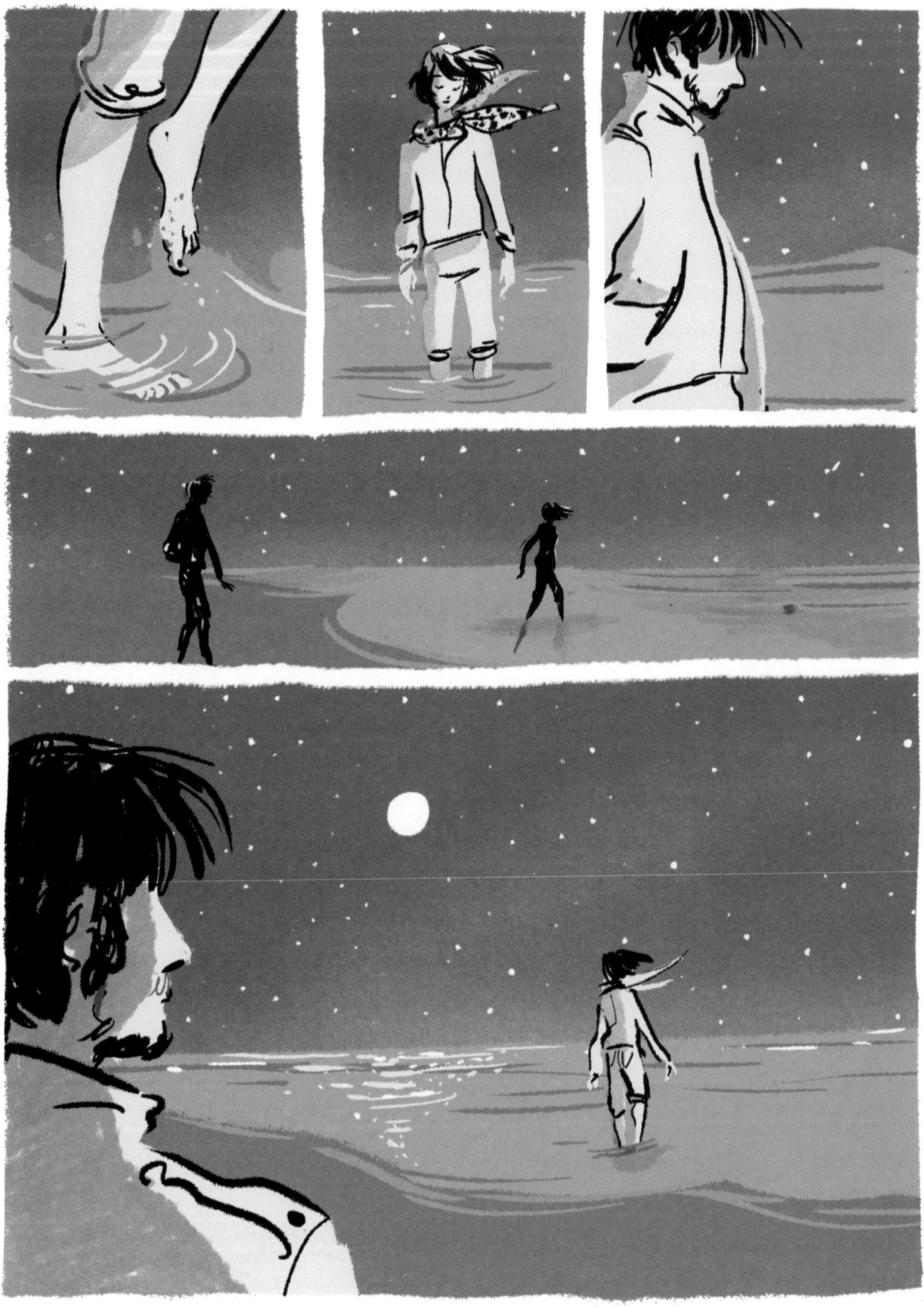

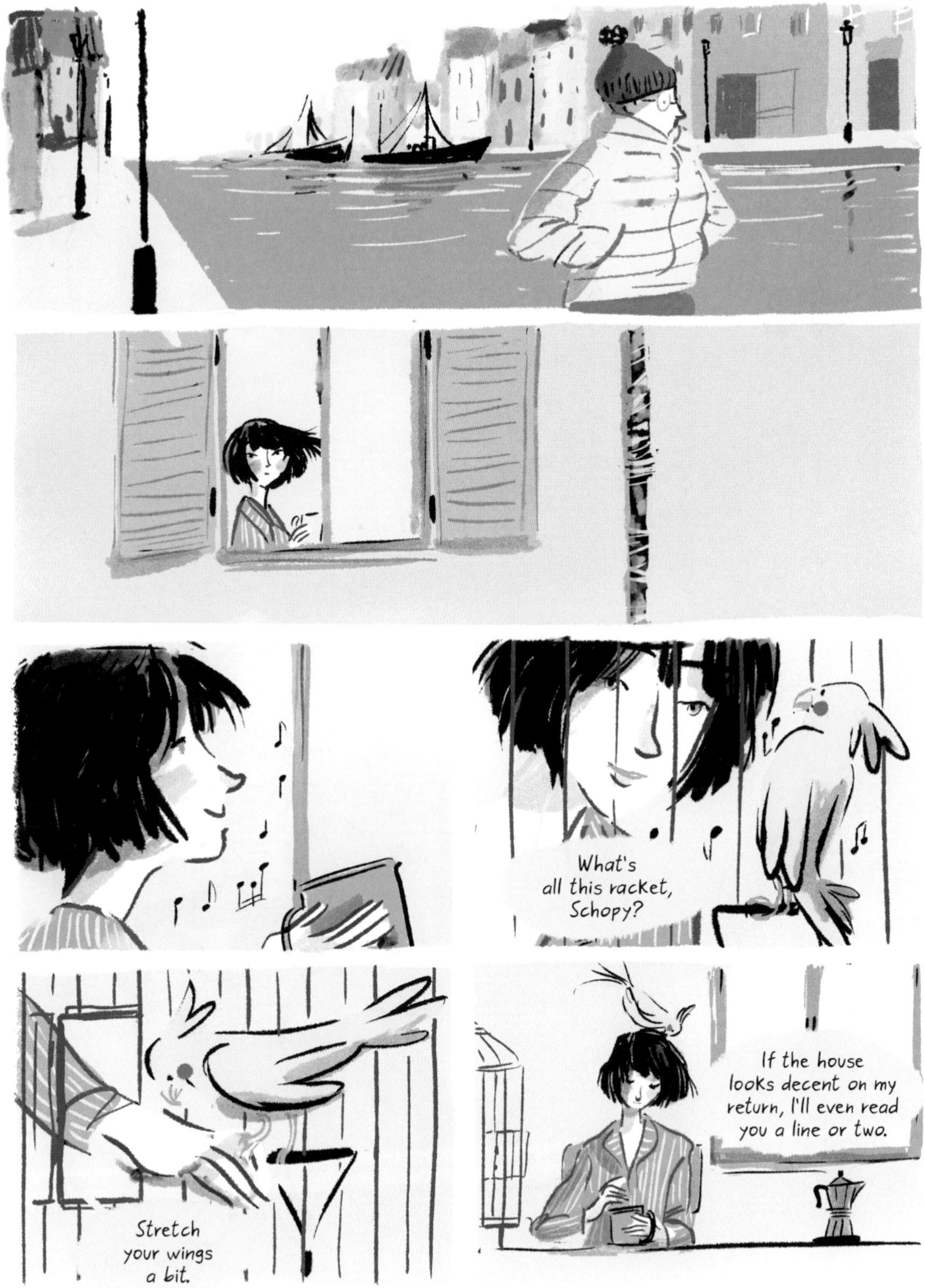
What's all this racket, Schopy?
Stretch your wings a bit.
If the house looks decent on my return, I'll even read you a line or two.

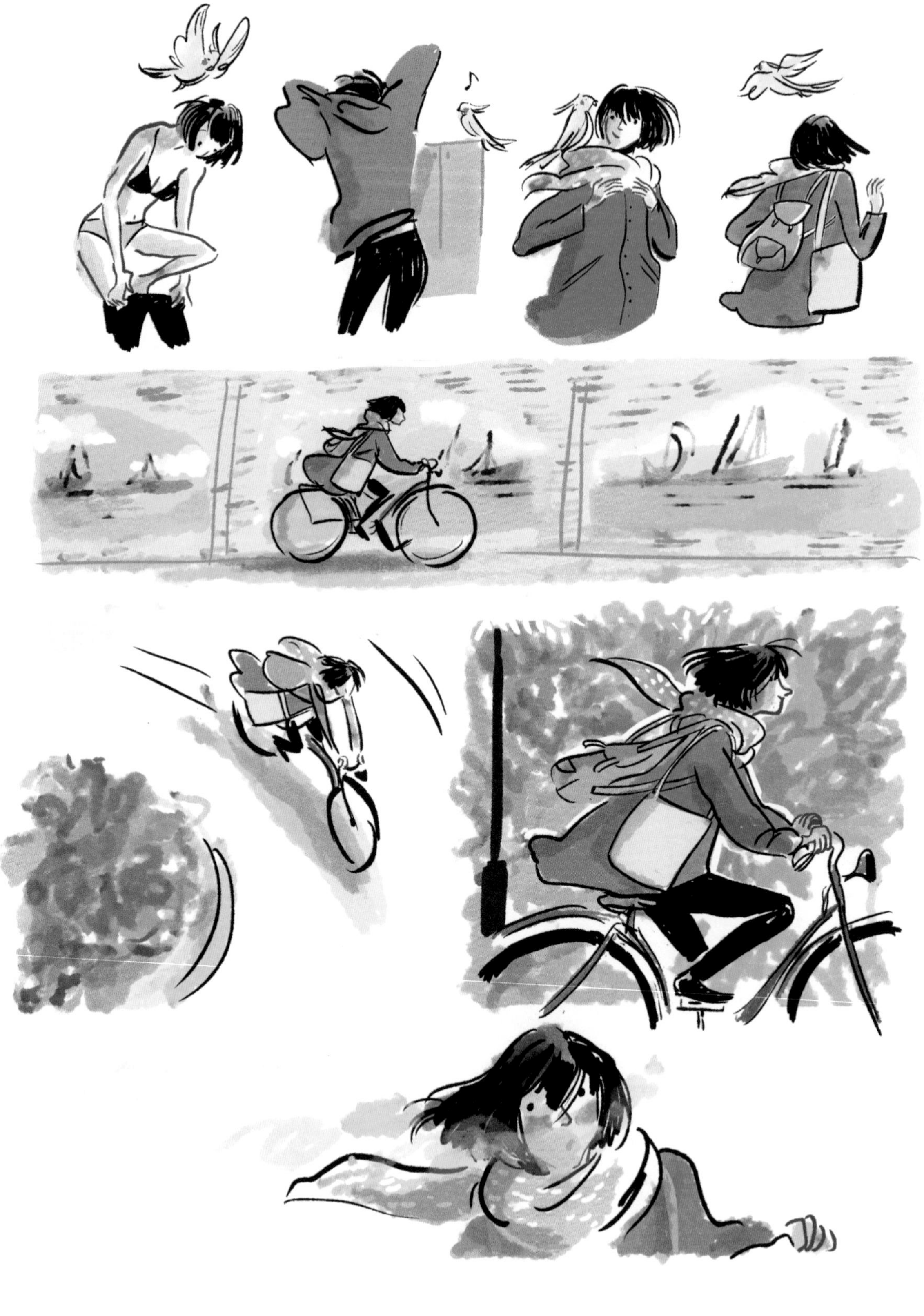

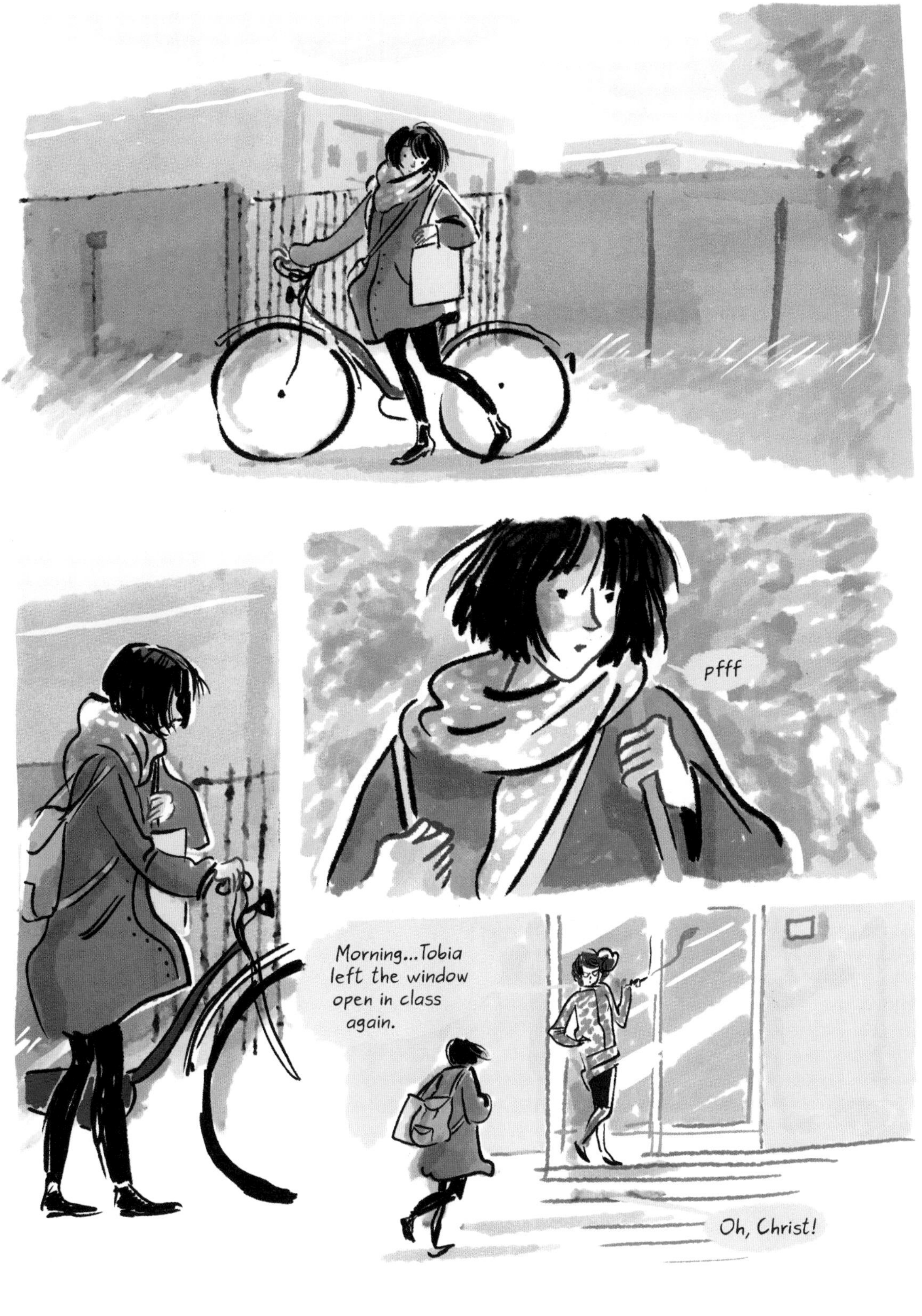
pfff
Morning...Tobia left the window open in class again.
Oh, Christ!

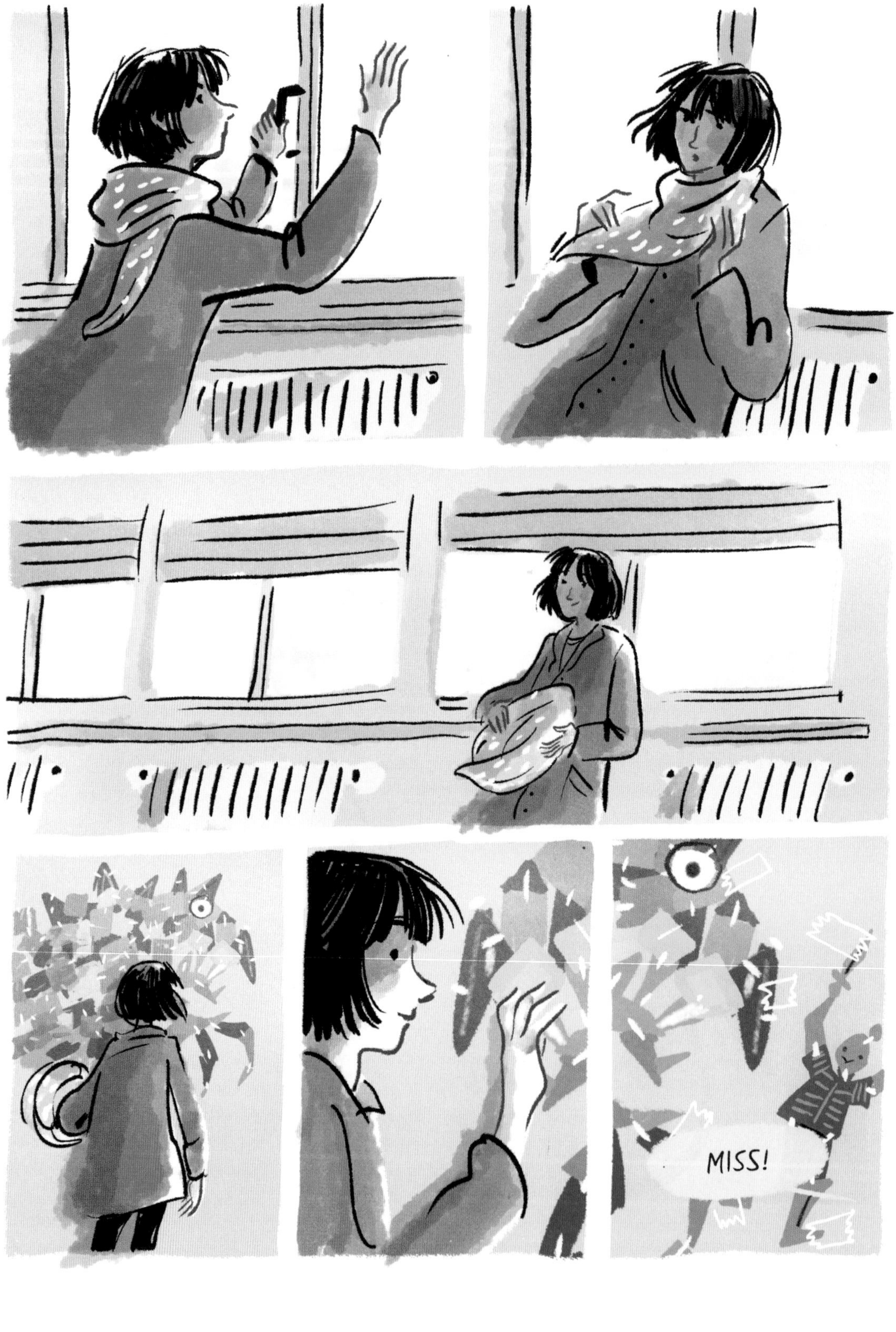
MISS!

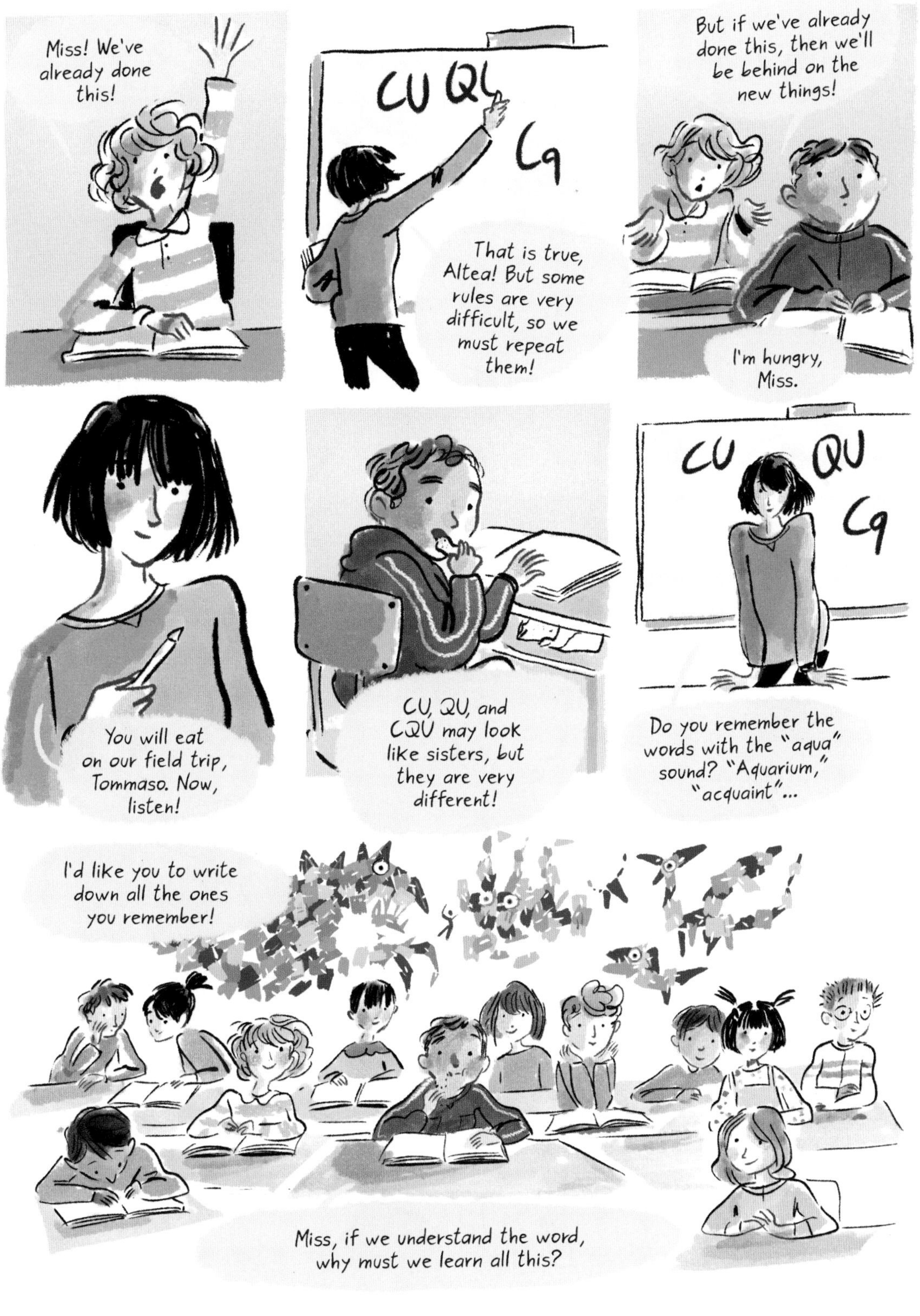
Miss! We've already done this!
CU QU
Cq
That is true, Altea! But some rules are very difficult, so we must repeat them!
But if we've already done this, then we'll be behind on the new things!
I'm hungry, Miss.
You will eat on our field trip, Tommaso. Now, listen!
CU, QU, and CQU may look like sisters, but they are very different!
CU
QU
Cq
Do you remember the words with the "aqua" sound? "Aquarium," "acquaint"...
I'd like you to write down all the ones you remember!
Miss, if we understand the word, why must we learn all this?

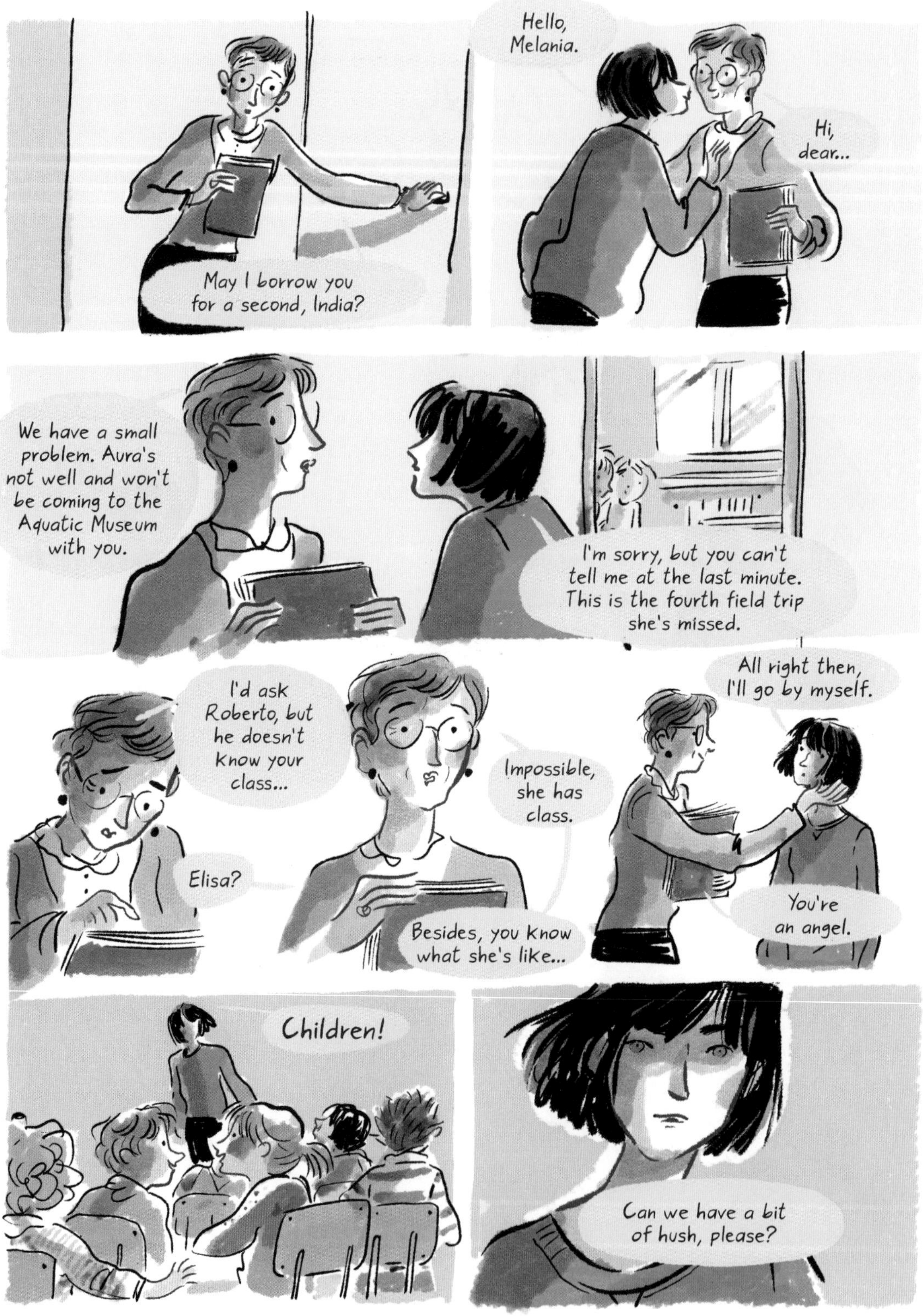
May I borrow you for a second, India?
Hello, Melania.
Hi, dear...
We have a small problem. Aura's not well and won't be coming to the Aquatic Museum with you.
I'm sorry, but you can't tell me at the last minute. This is the fourth field trip she's missed.
I'd ask Roberto, but he doesn't know your class...
Elisa?
Impossible, she has class.
Besides, you know what she's like...
All right then, I'll go by myself.
You're an angel.
Children!
Can we have a bit of hush, please?

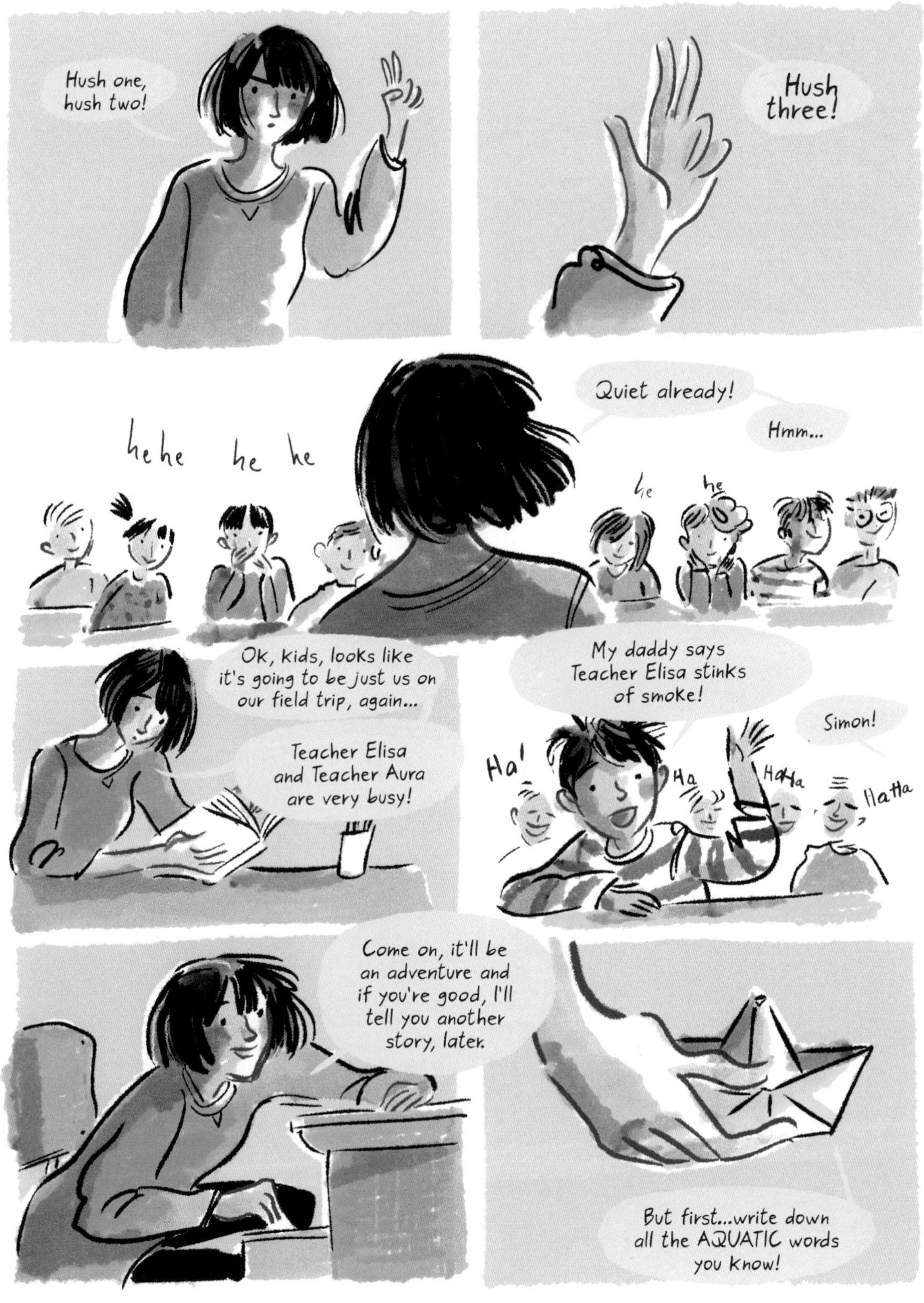
Hush one, hush two!
Hush three!
hehe he he
Quiet already!
Hmm...
he
he
Ok, kids, looks like it's going to be just us on our field trip, again...
Teacher Elisa and Teacher Aura are very busy!
My daddy says Teacher Elisa stinks of smoke!
Simon!
Ha!
Ha
HaHa
HaHa
Come on, it'll be an adventure and if you're good, I'll tell you another story, later.
But first...write down all the AQUATIC words you know!

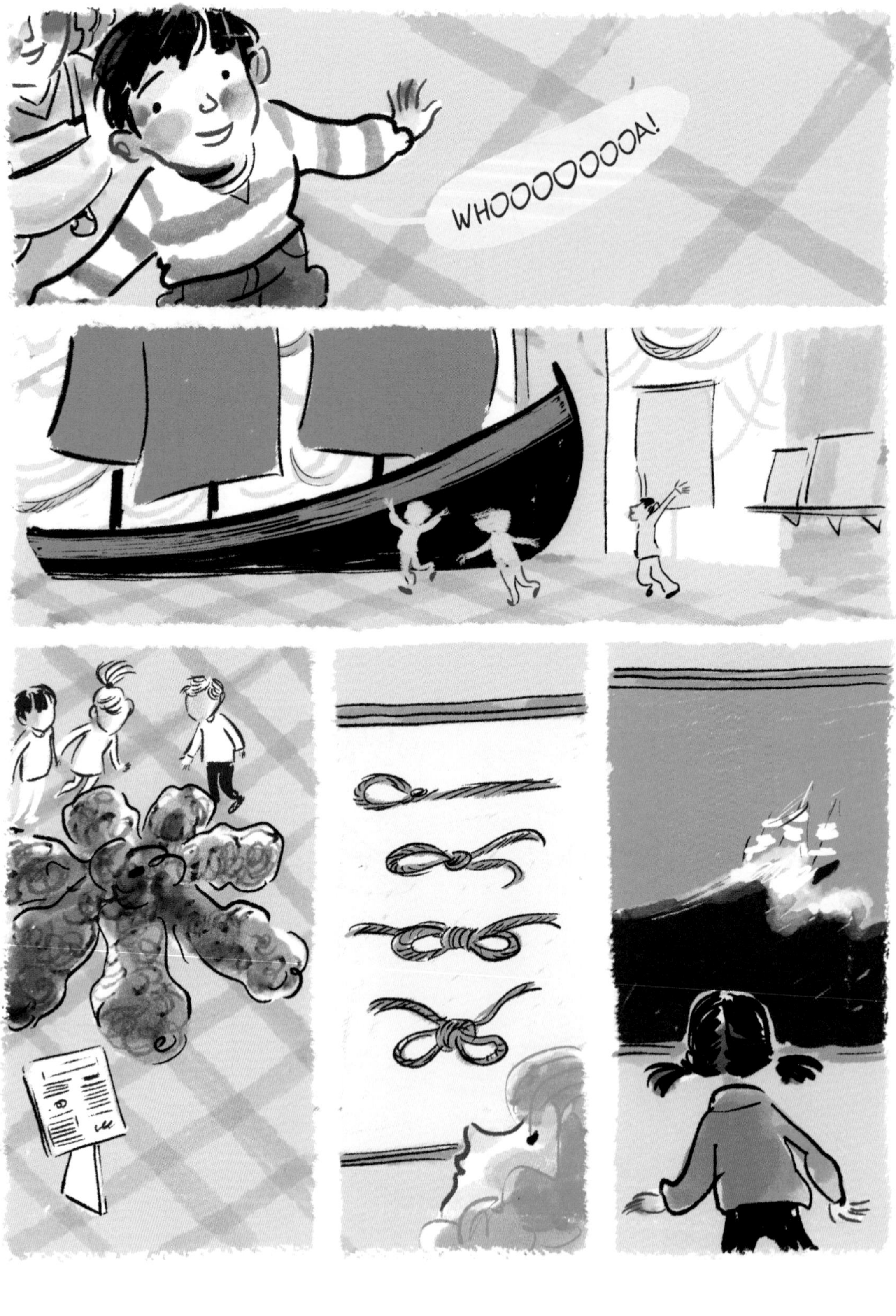
WHOOOOOOOA!

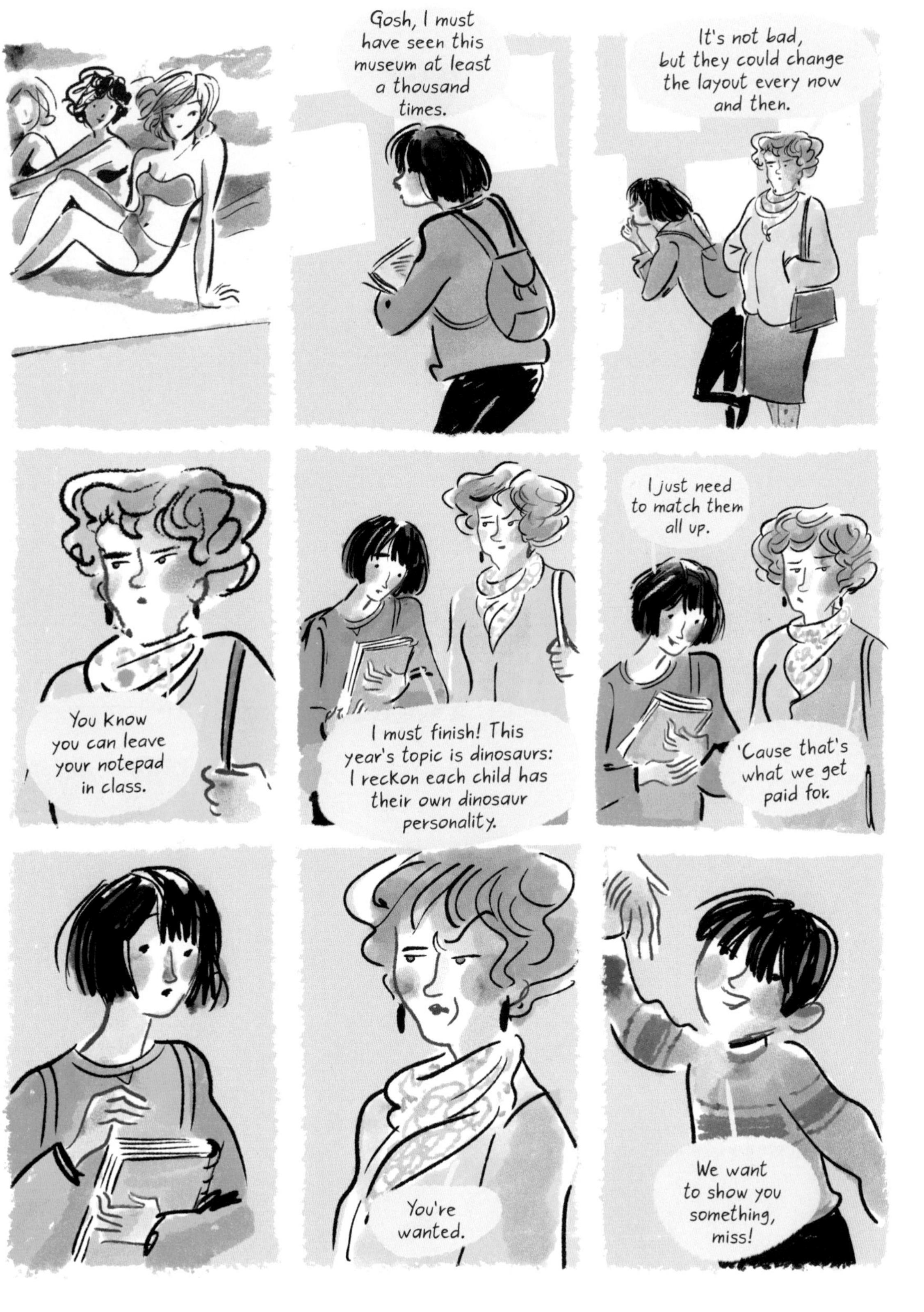
Gosh, I must have seen this museum at least a thousand times.
It's not bad, but they could change the layout every now and then.
You know you can leave your notepad in class.
I must finish! This year's topic is dinosaurs: I reckon each child has their own dinosaur personality.
I just need to match them all up.
'Cause that's what we get paid for.
You're wanted.
We want to show you something, miss!

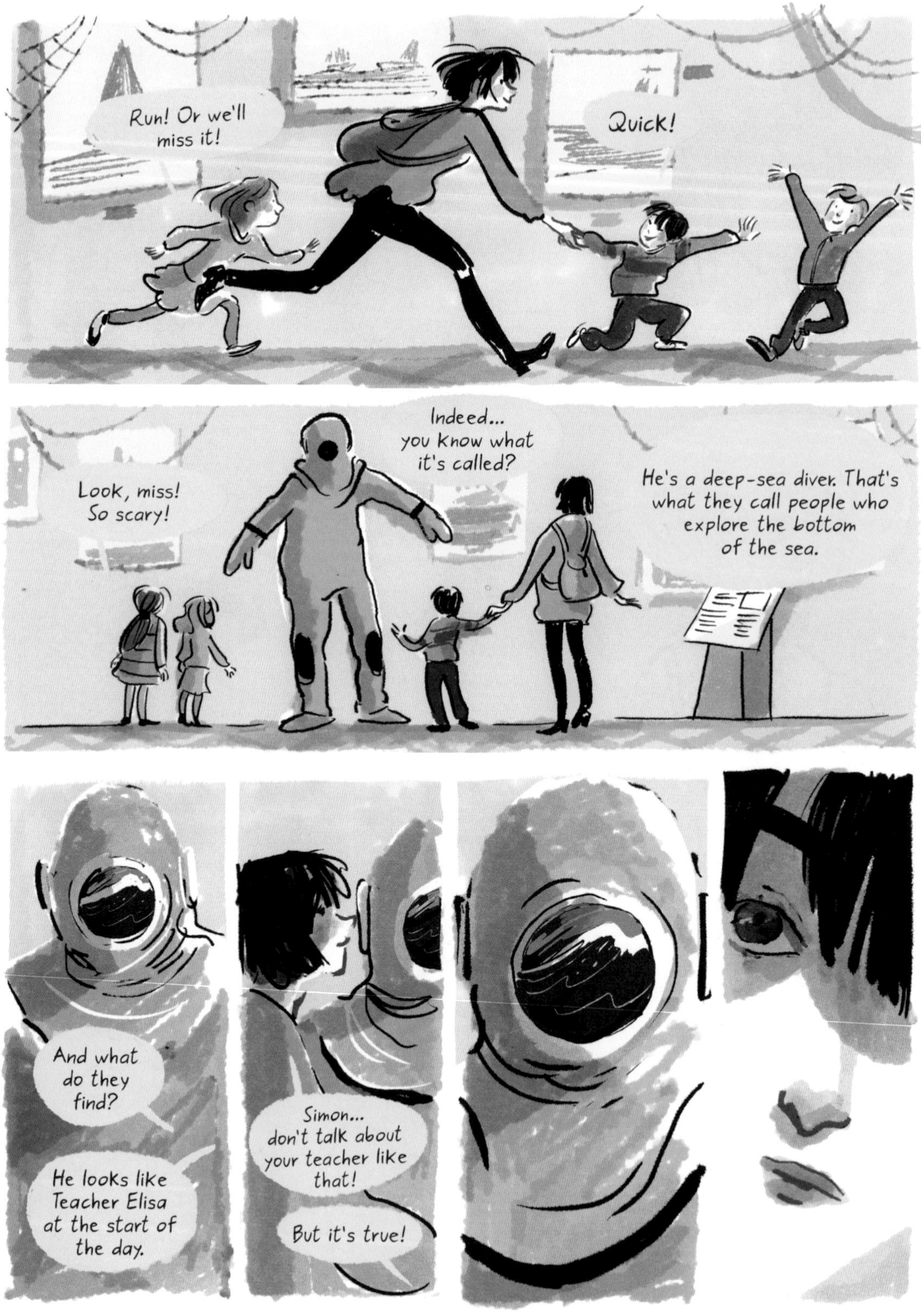
Run! Or we'll miss it!
Quick!
Look, miss! So scary!
Indeed... you know what it's called?
He's a deep-sea diver. That's what they call people who explore the bottom of the sea.
And what do they find?
He looks like Teacher Elisa at the start of the day.
Simon... don't talk about your teacher like that!
But it's true!

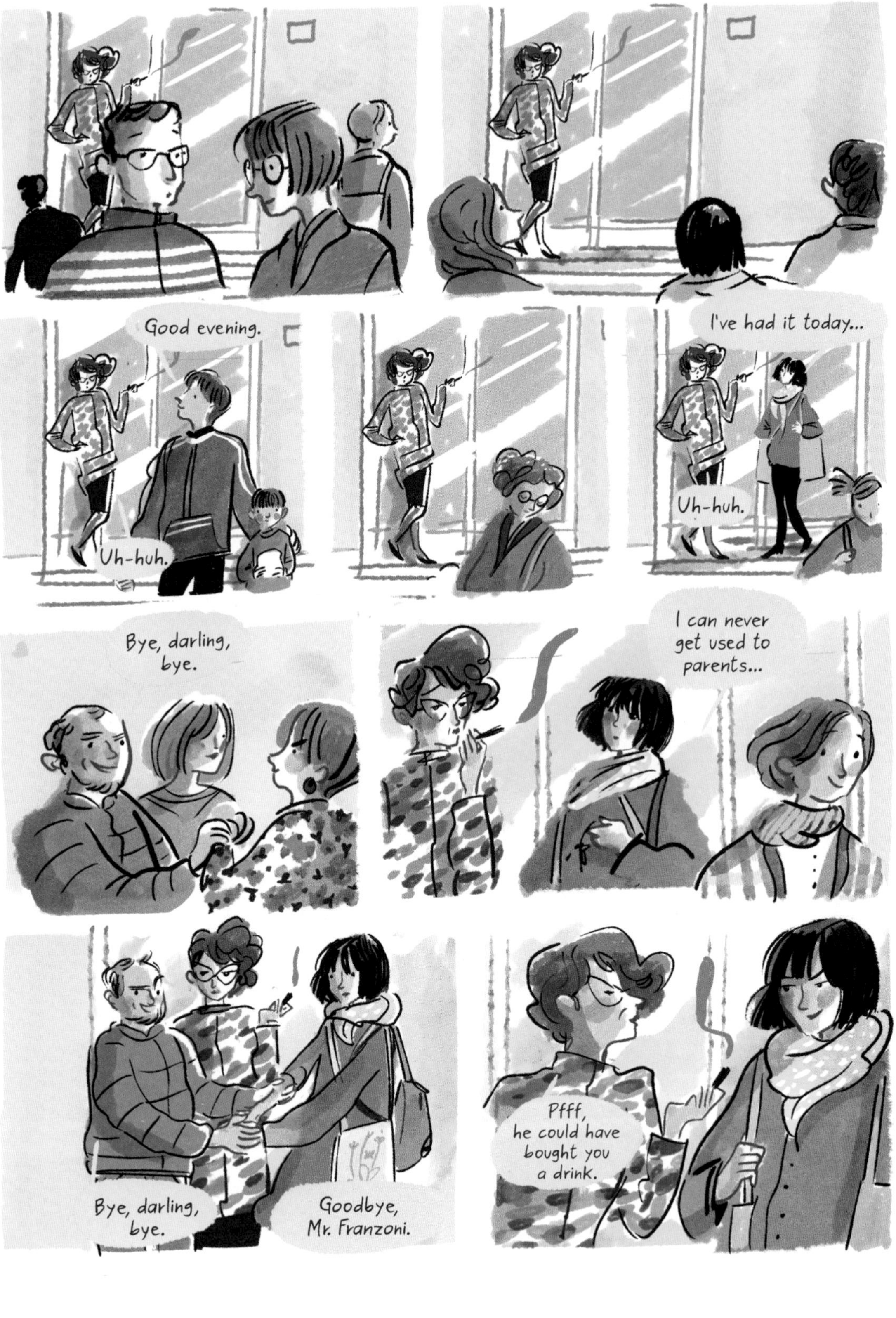
Good evening.
Uh-huh.
I've had it today...
Uh-huh.
Bye, darling, bye.
I can never get used to parents...
Bye, darling, bye.
Goodbye, Mr. Franzoni.
Pfff, he could have bought you a drink.

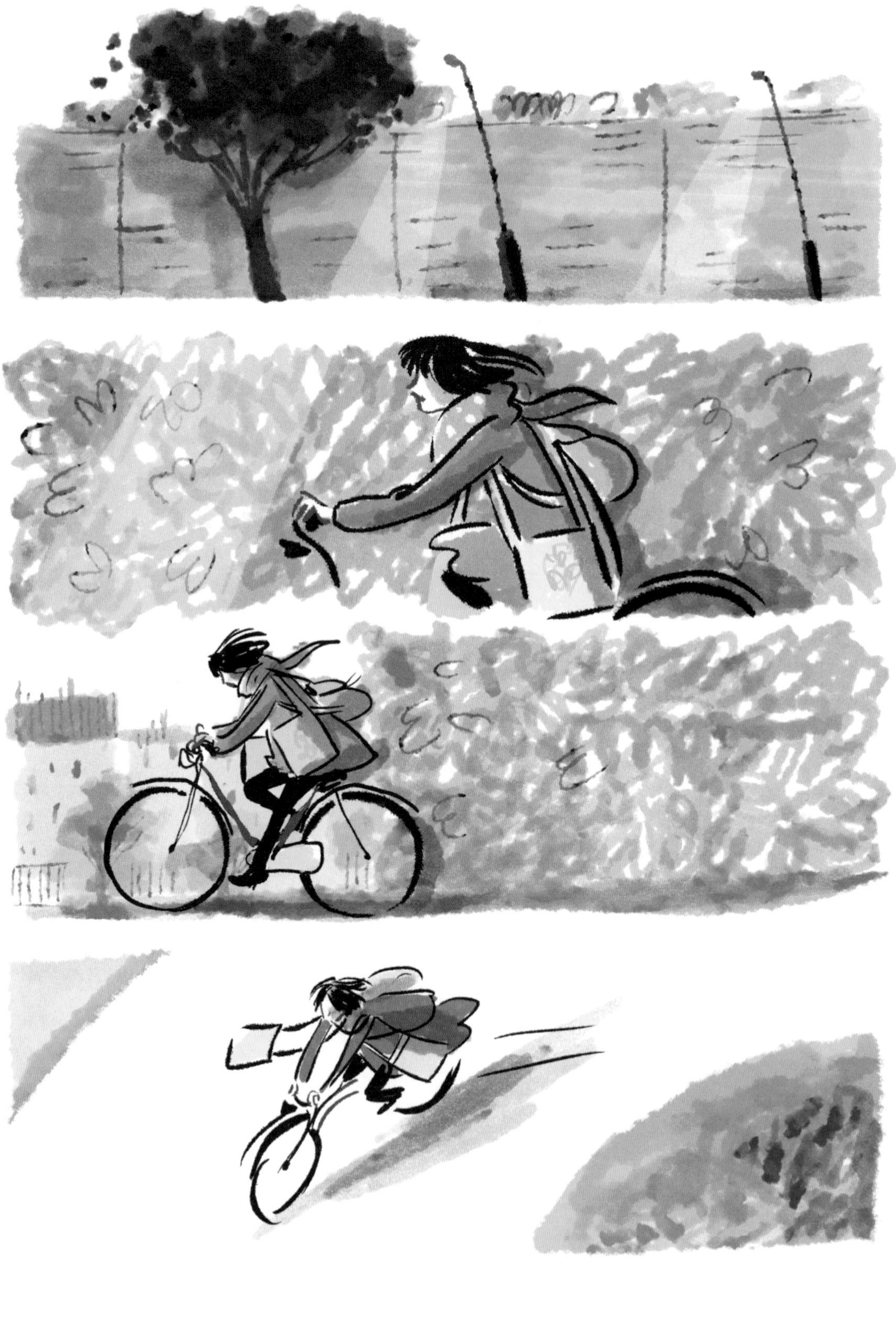

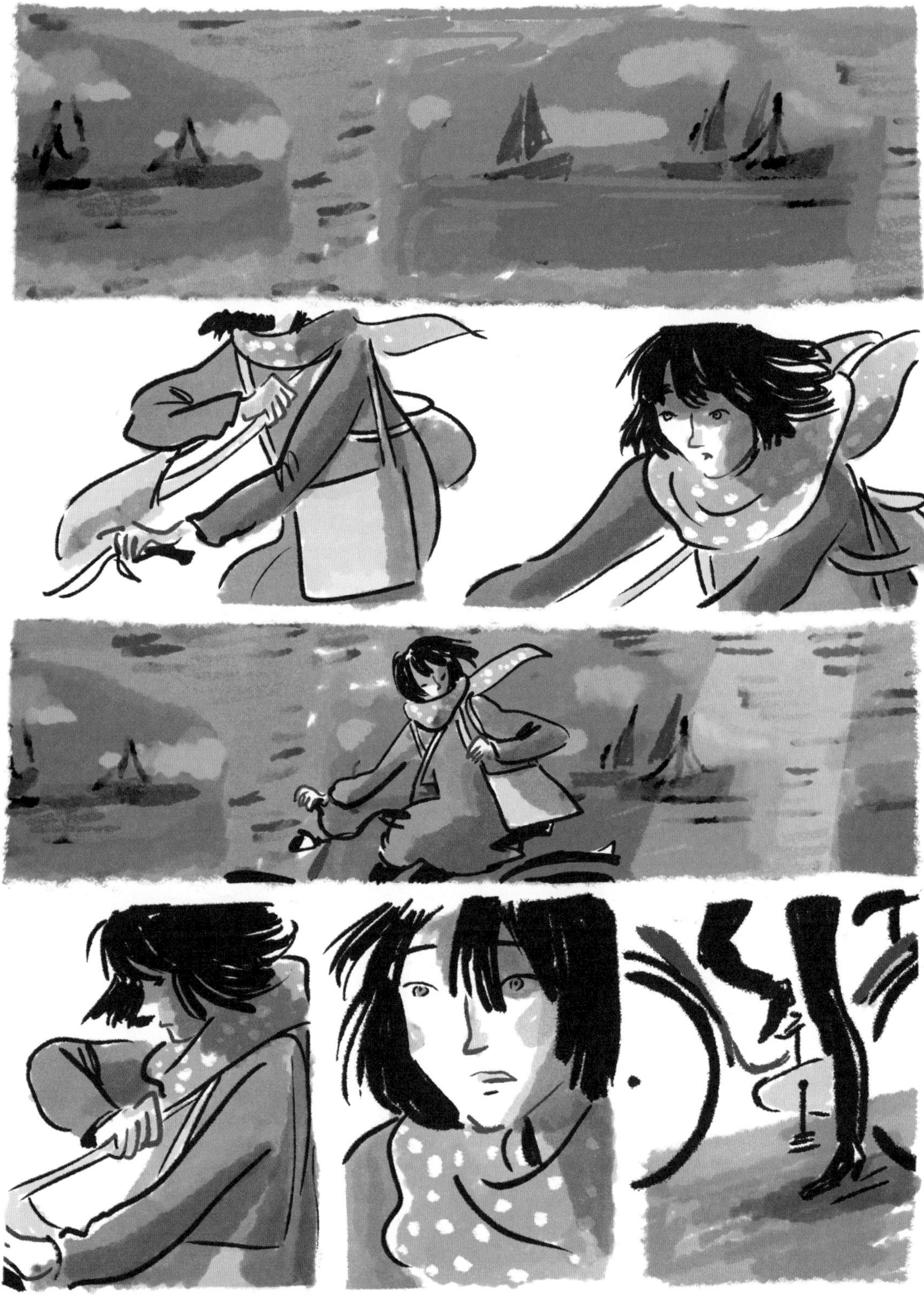

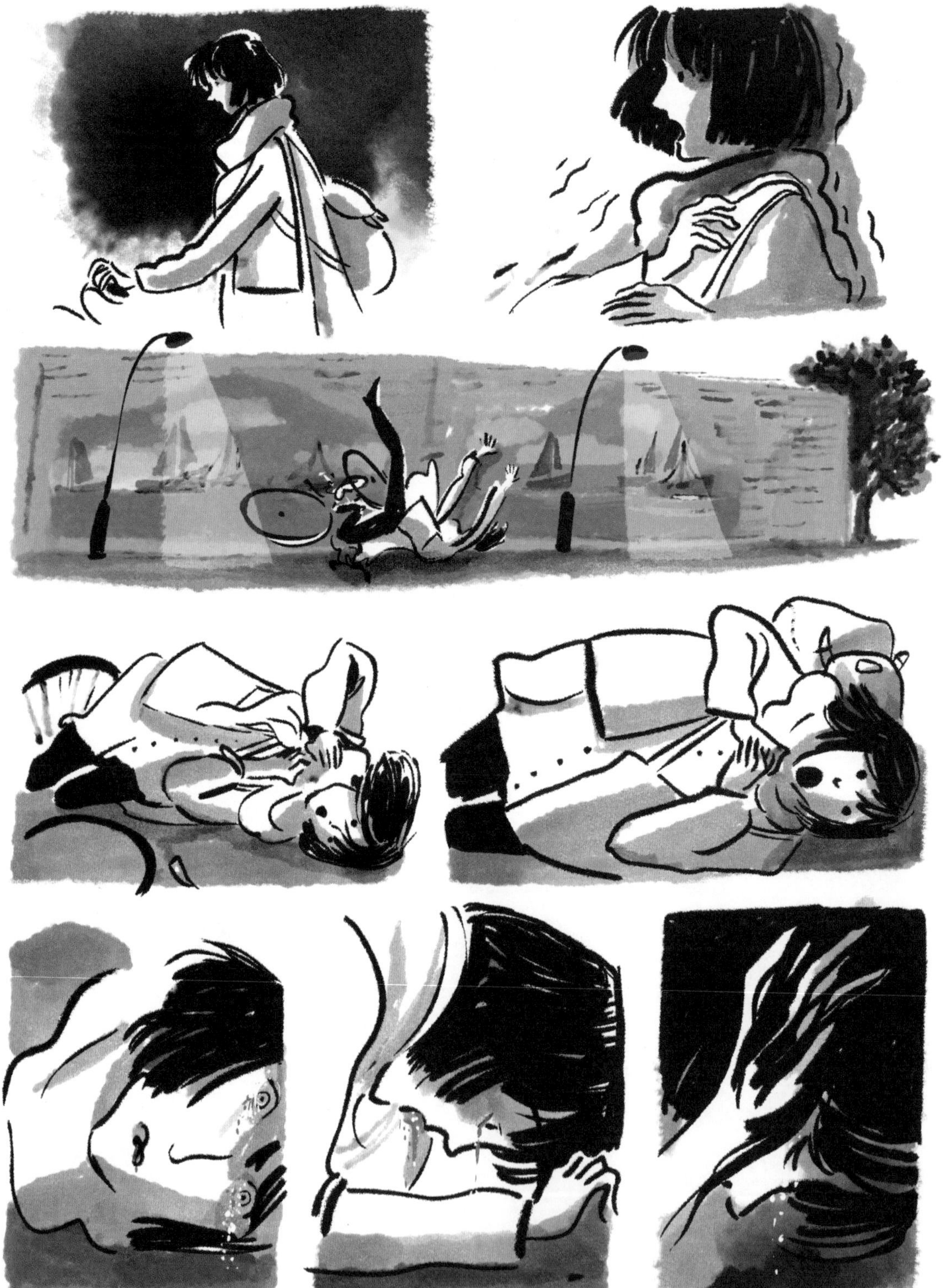

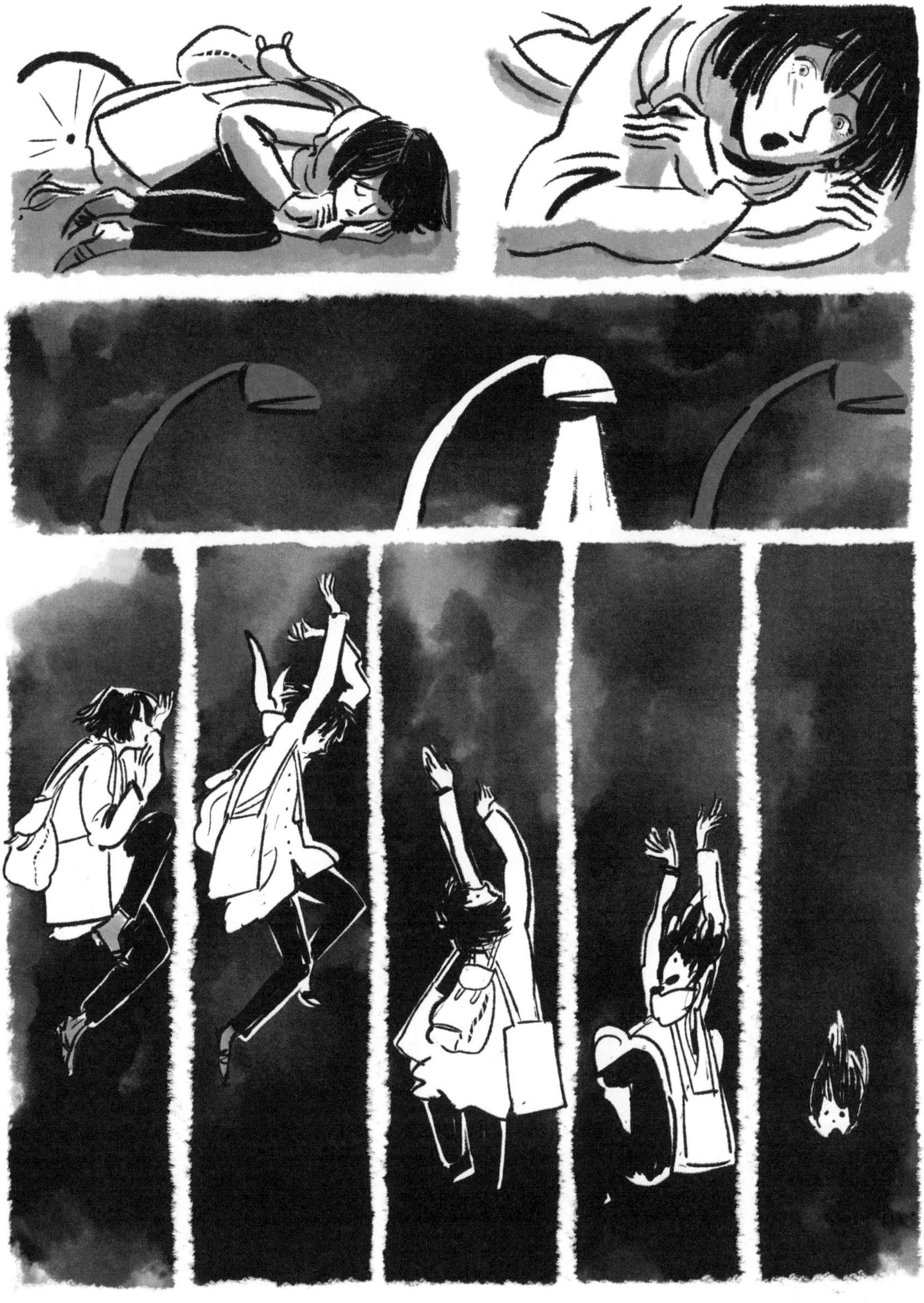

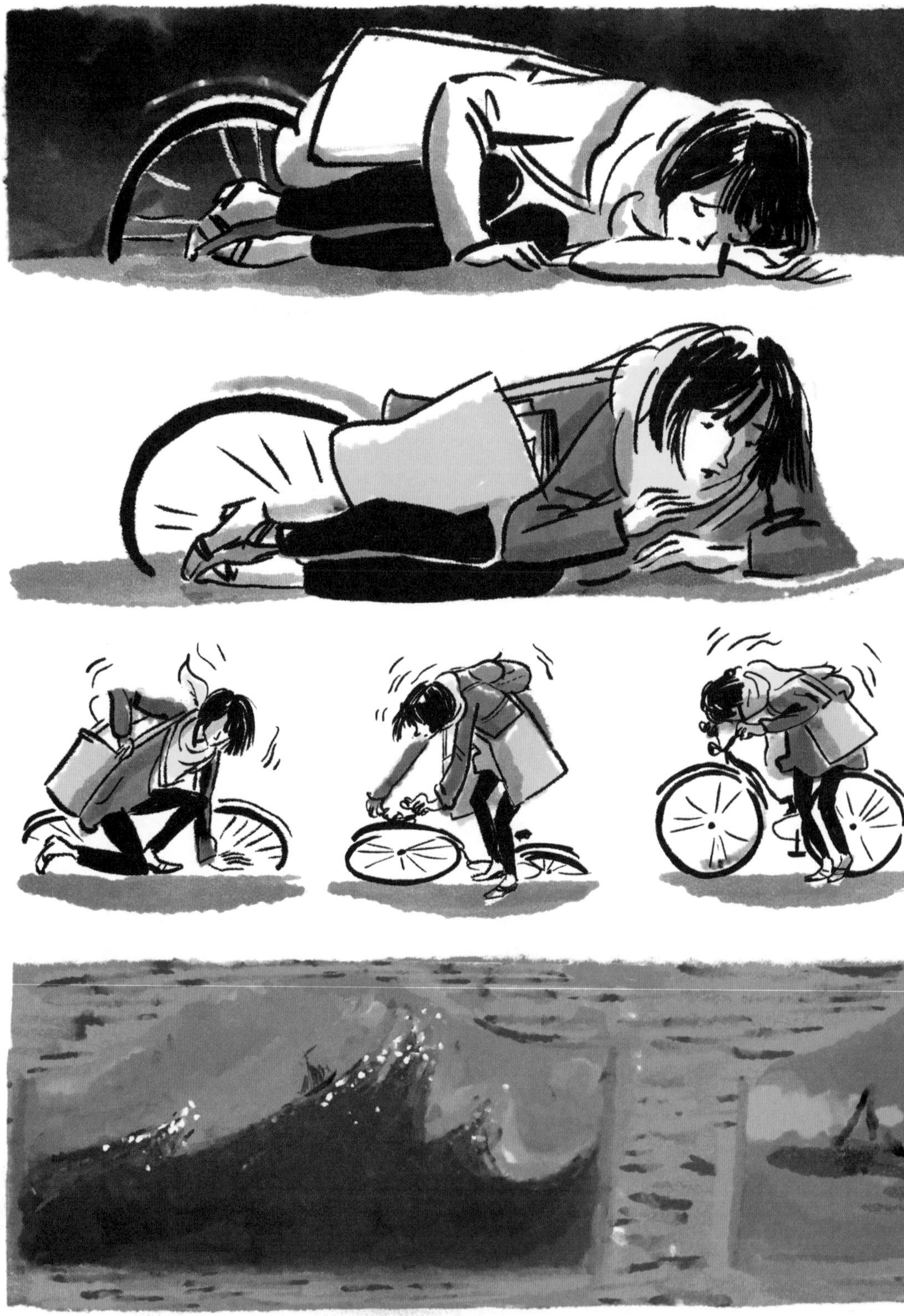

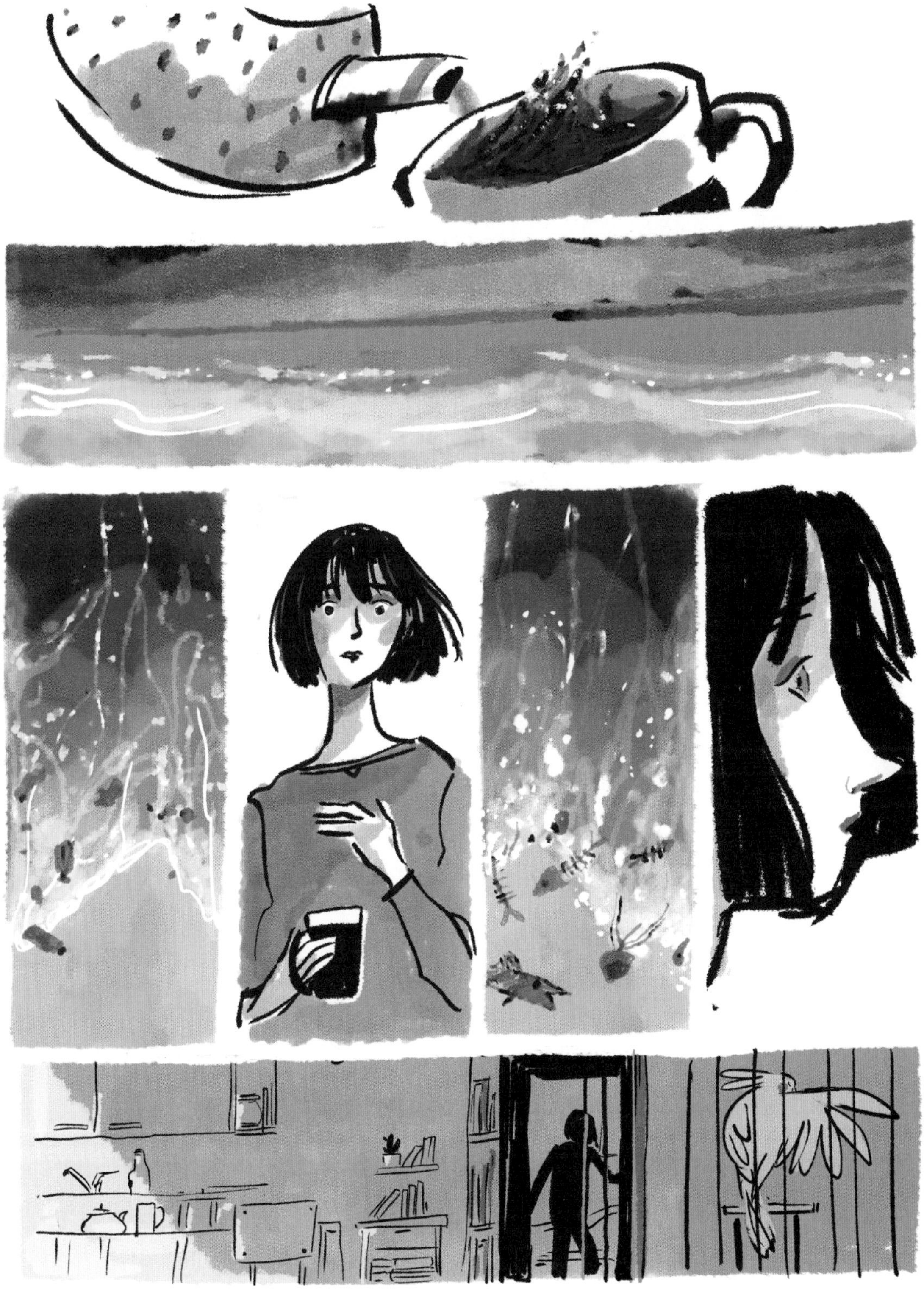

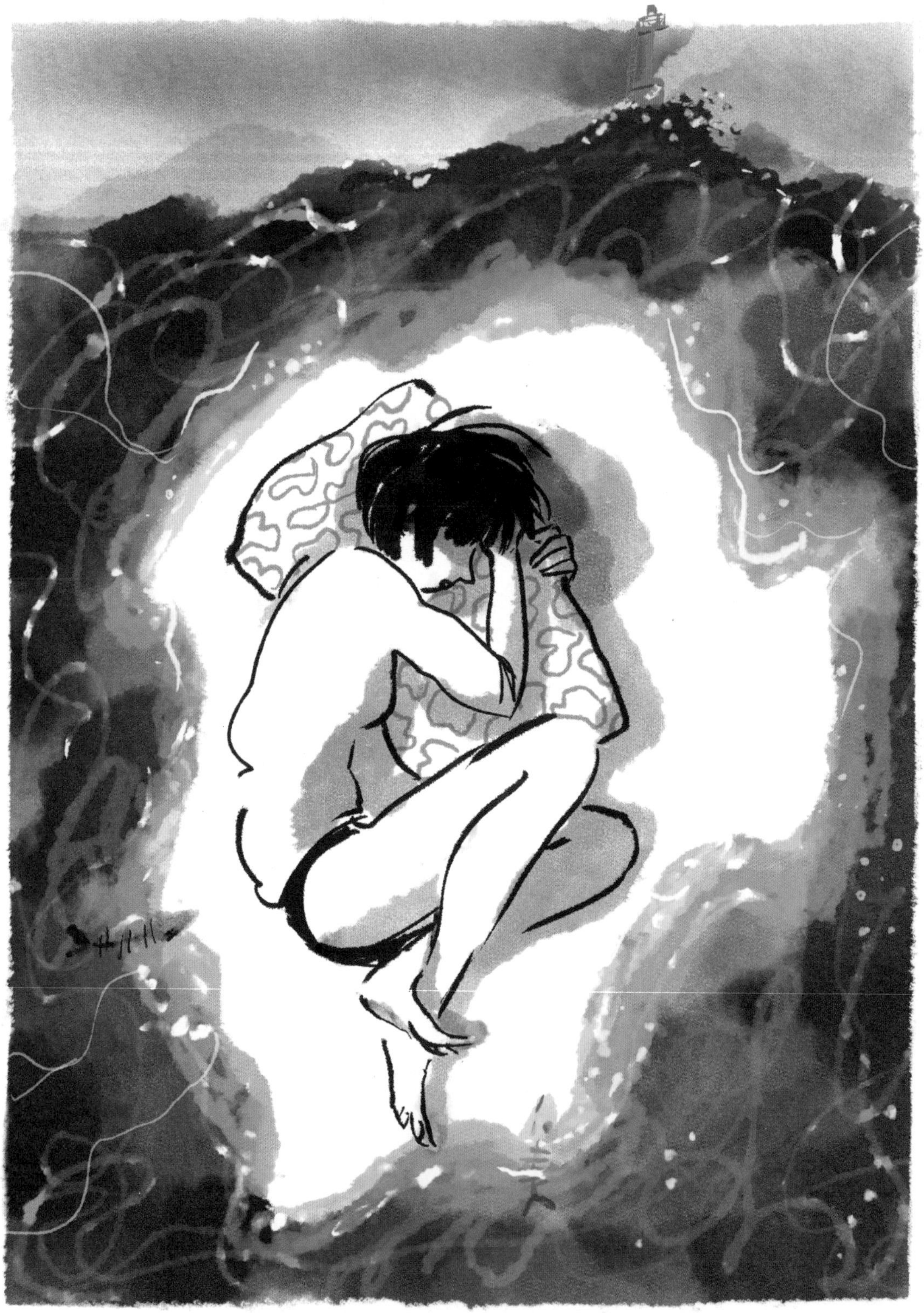

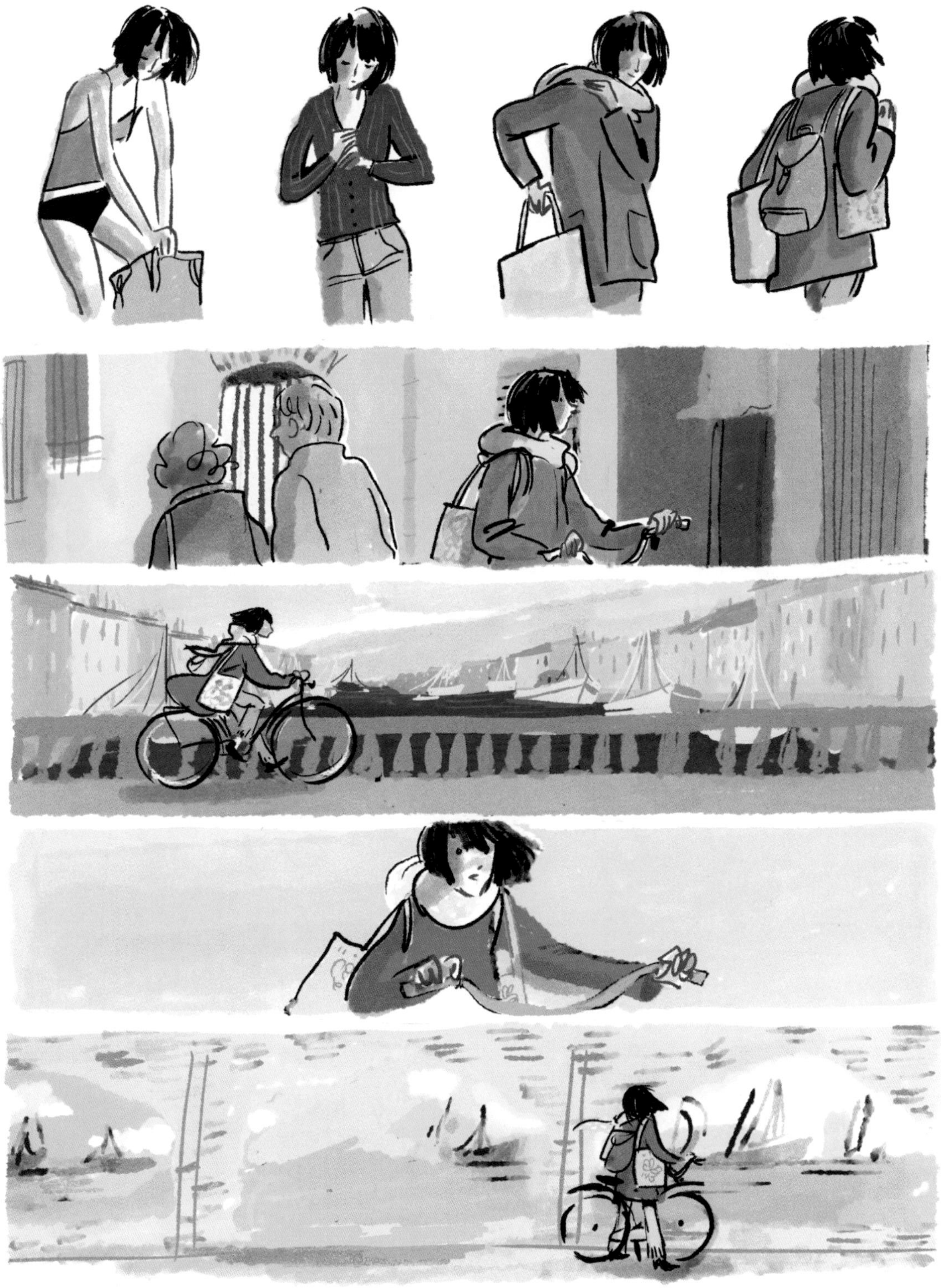

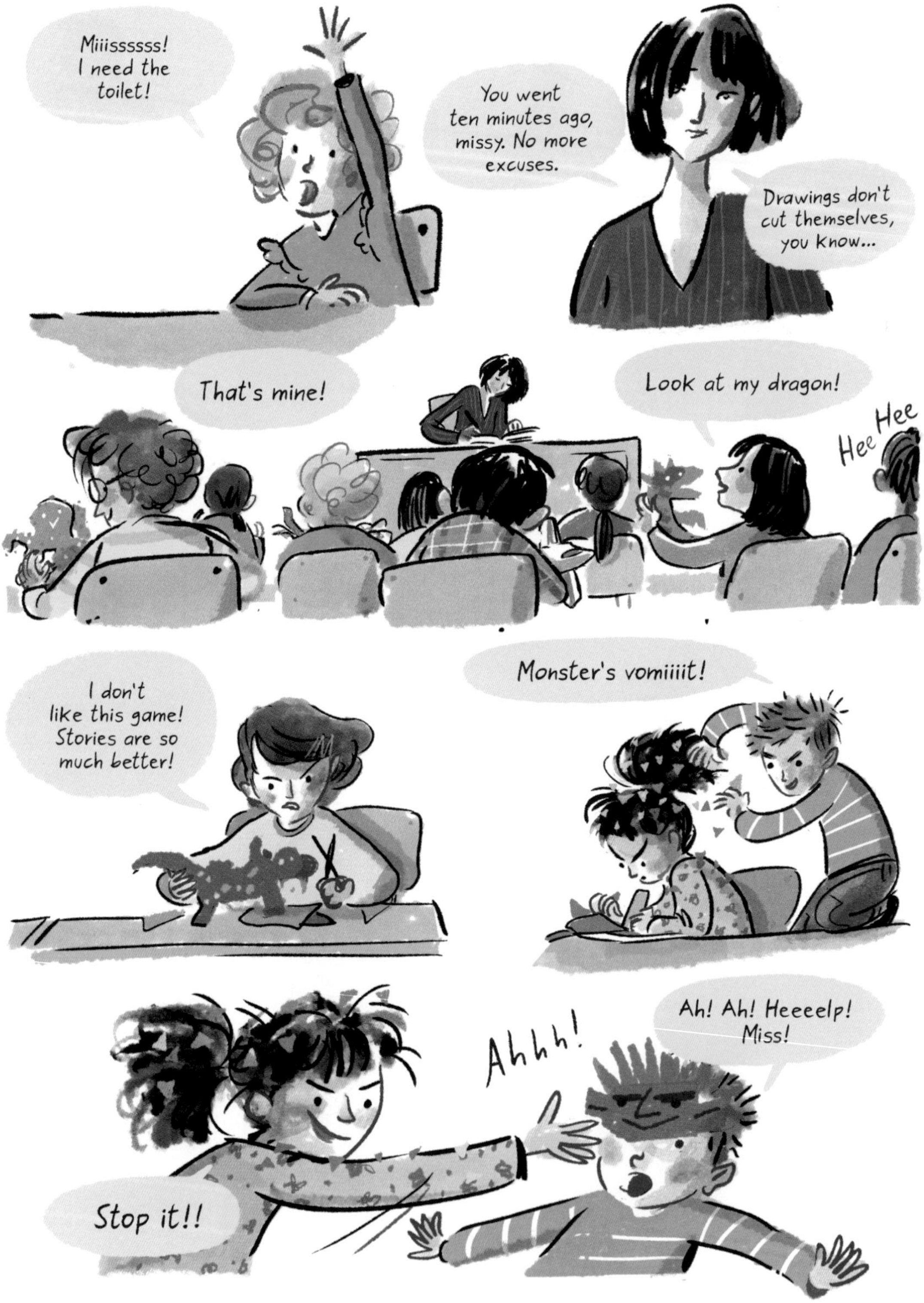
Miiissssss! I need the toilet!
You went ten minutes ago, missy. No more excuses.
Drawings don't cut themselves, you know...
That's mine!
Look at my dragon!
Hee Hee
I don't like this game! Stories are so much better!
Monster's vomiiiit!
Ahhh!
Ah! Ah! Heeeelp! Miss!
Stop it!!

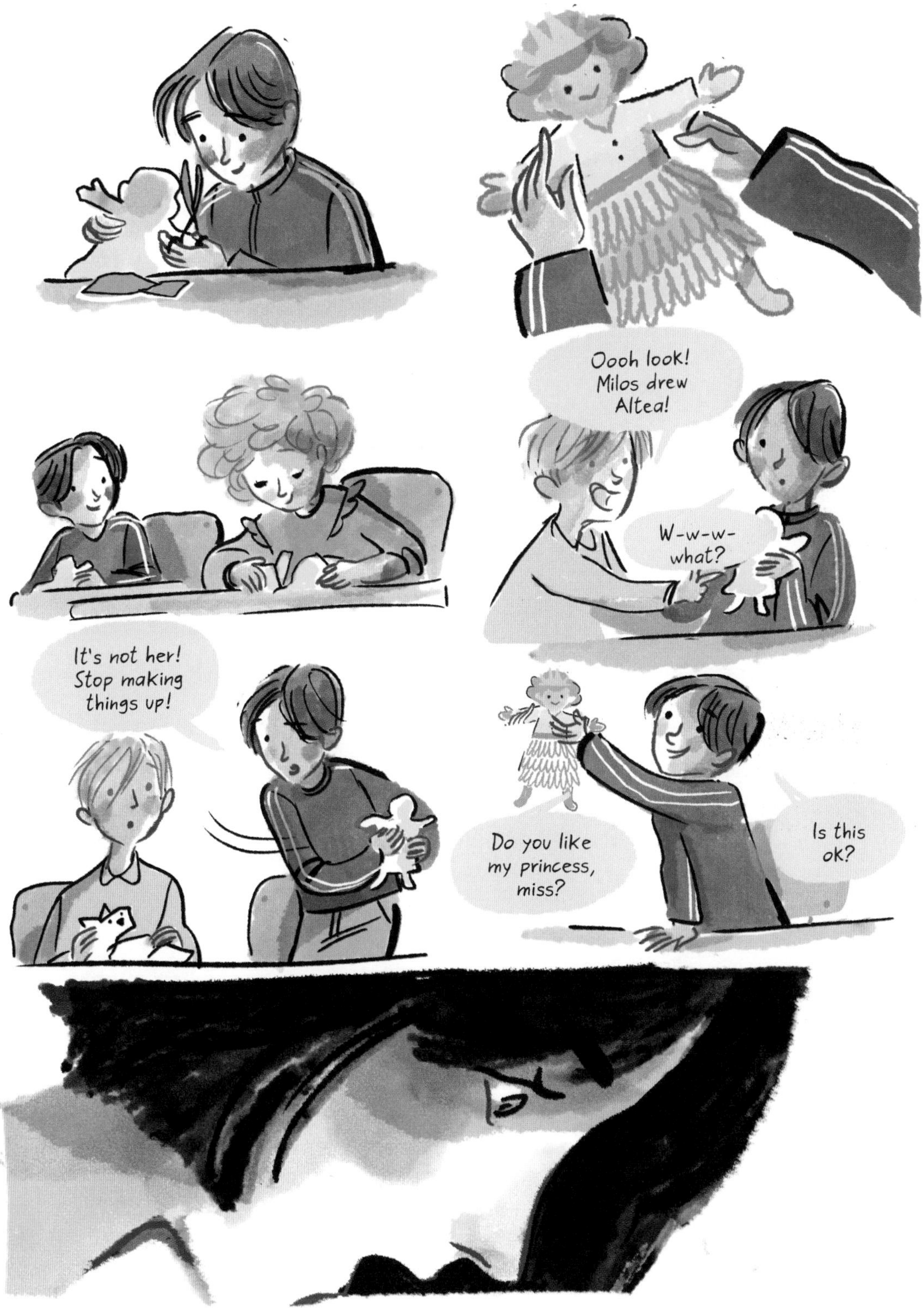
Oooh look! Milos drew Altea!
W-w-w-what?
It's not her! Stop making things up!
Do you like my princess, miss?
Is this ok?

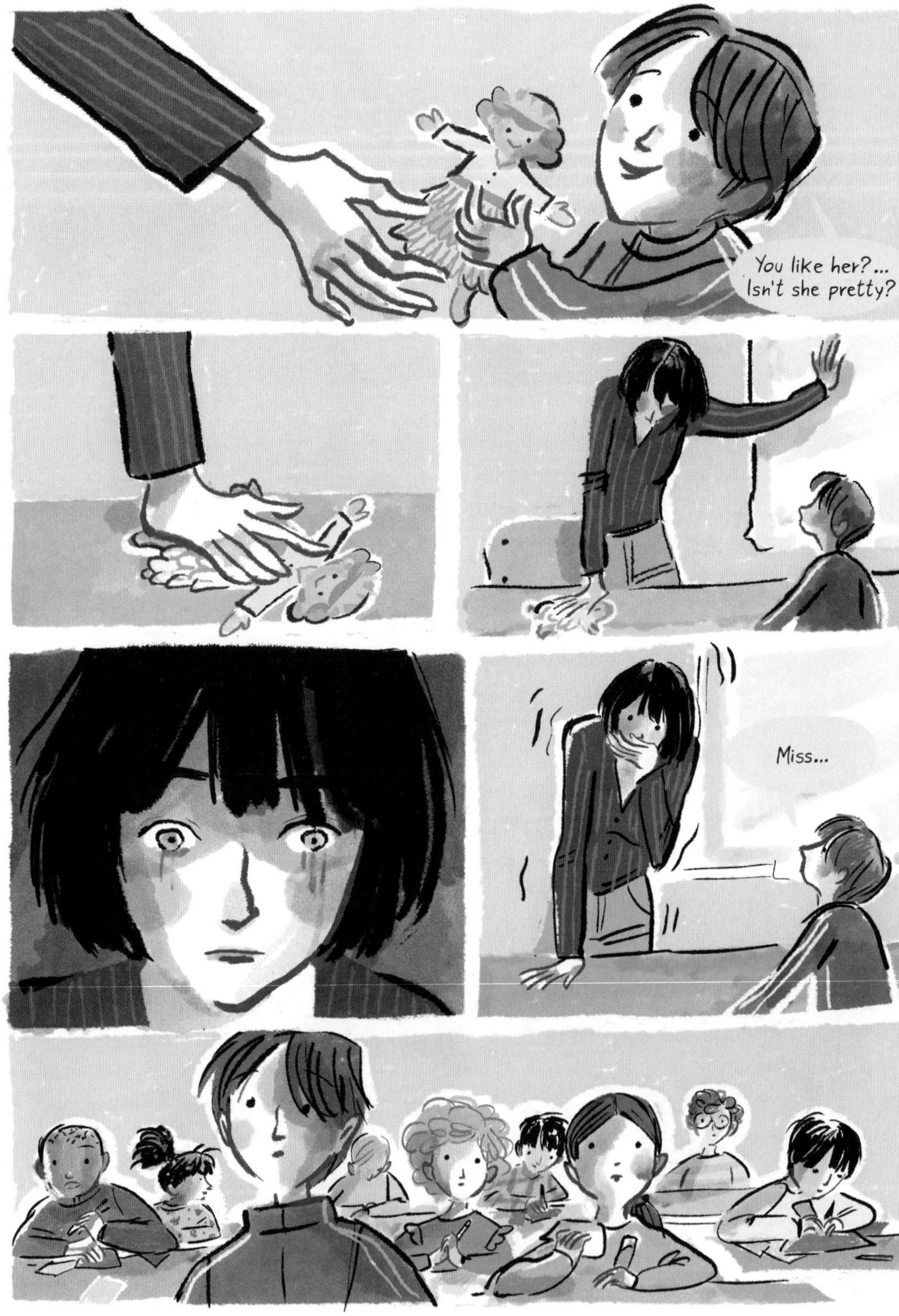
You like her?...
Isn't she pretty?
Miss...

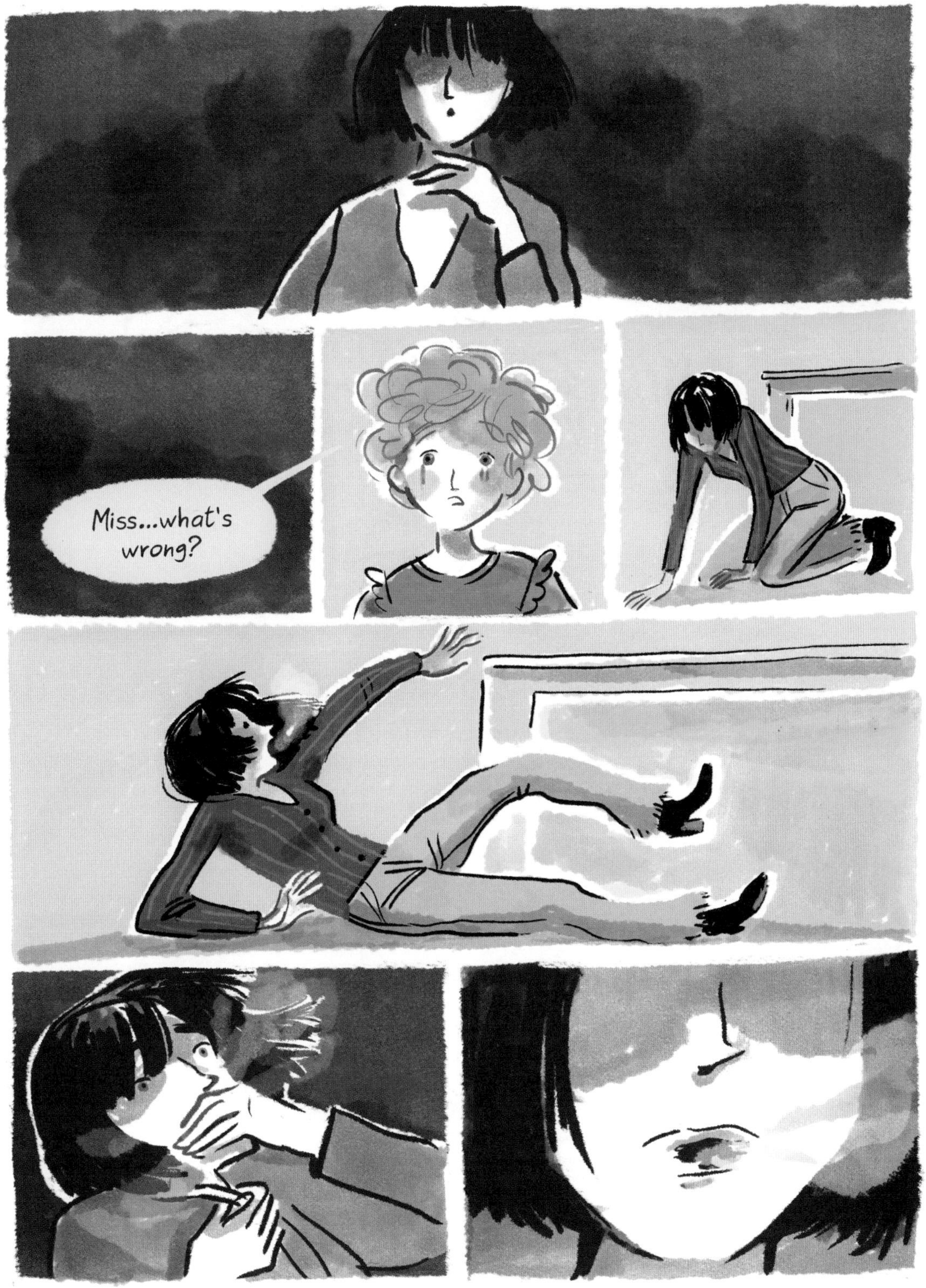
Miss...what's wrong?

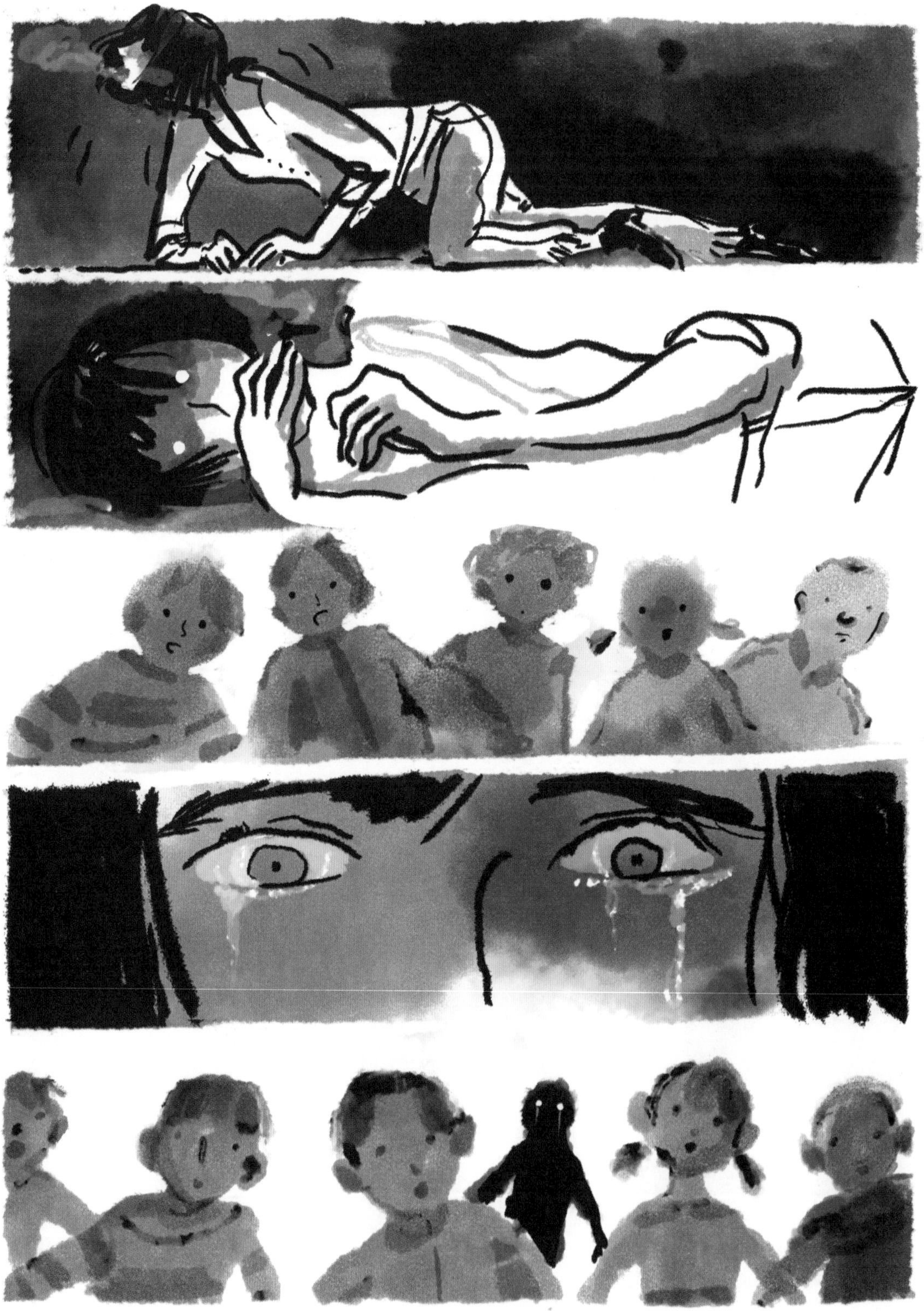

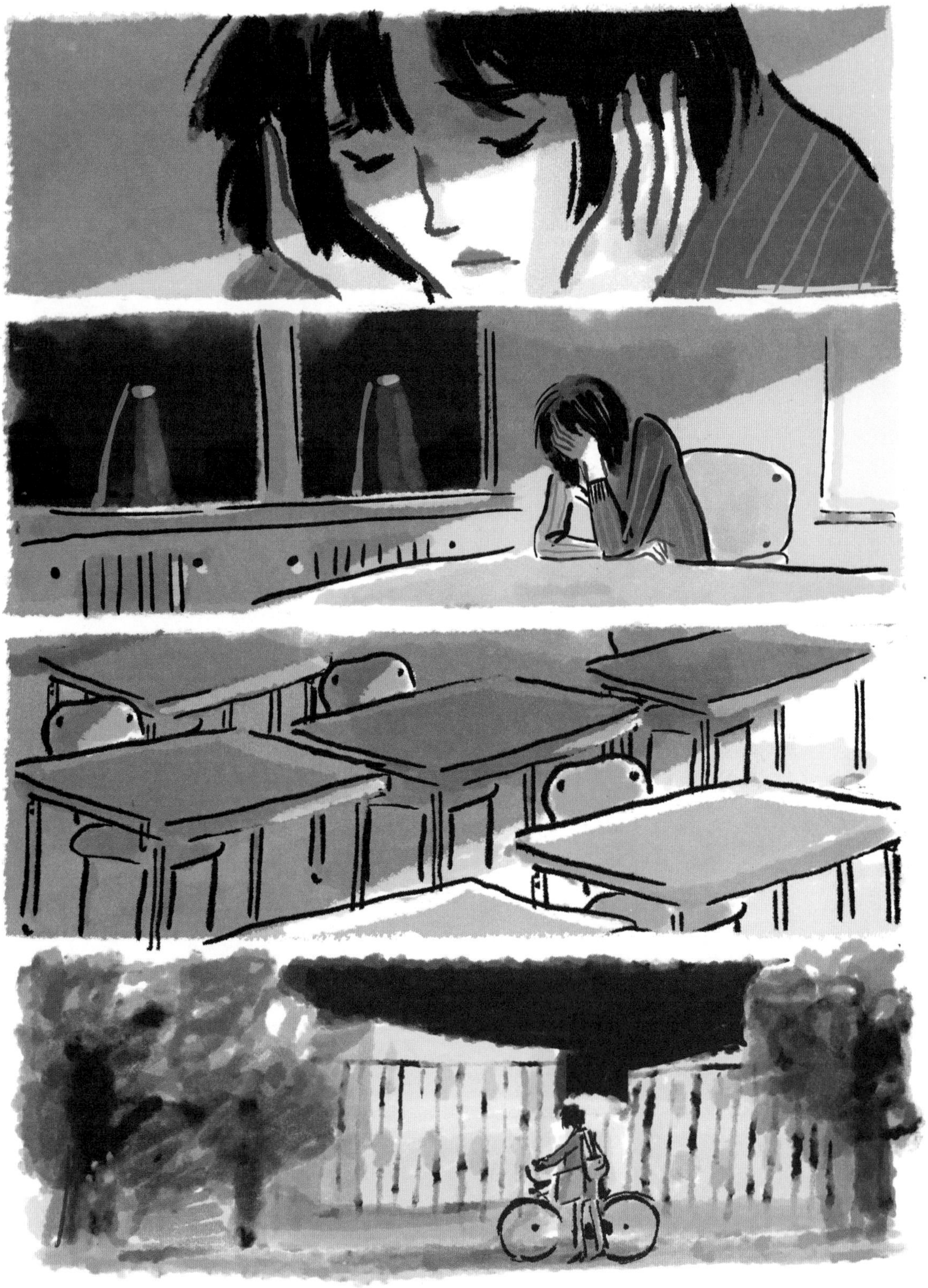

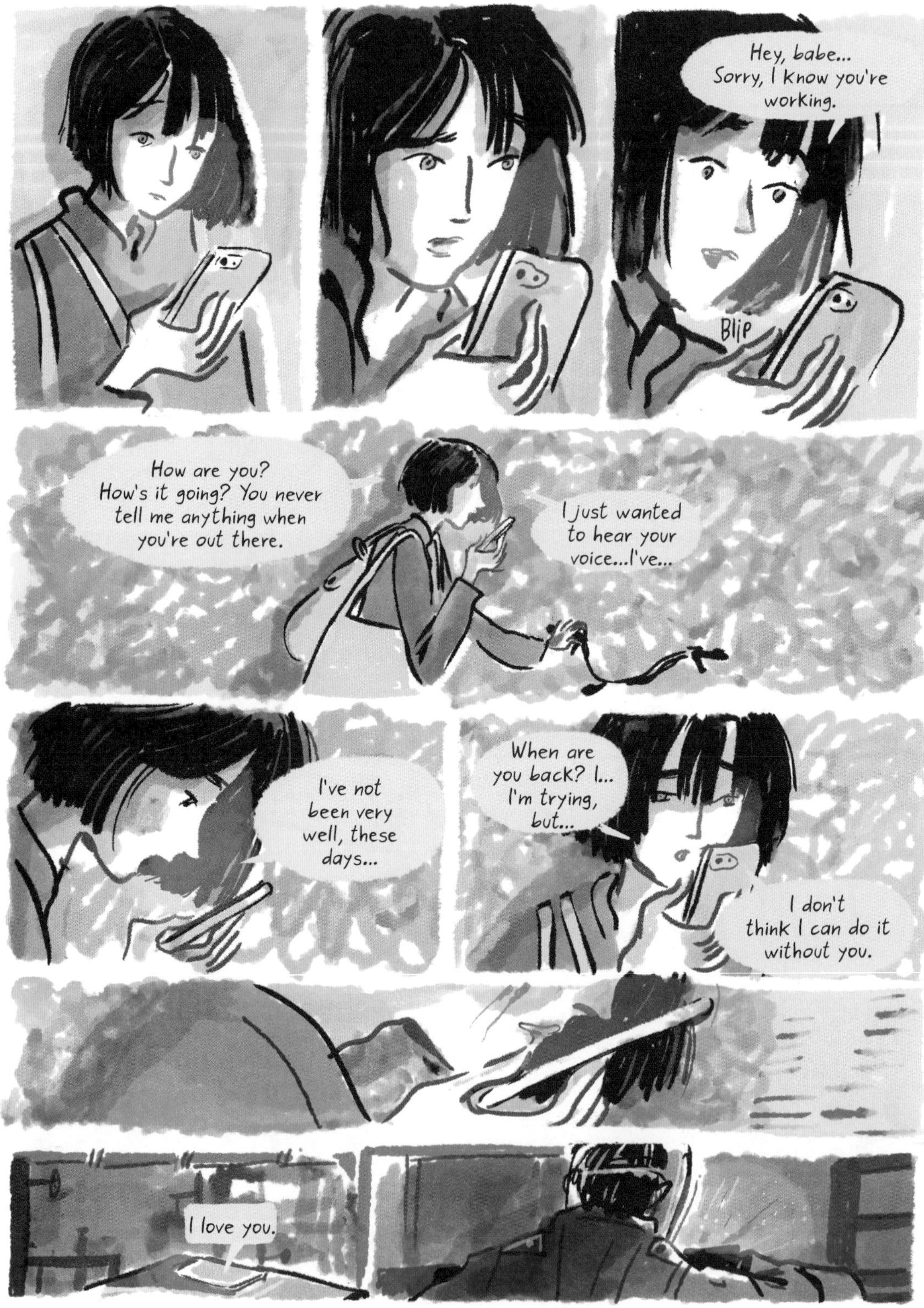
Hey, babe...
Sorry, I know you're working.
Blip
How are you?
How's it going? You never tell me anything when you're out there.
I just wanted to hear your voice...I've...
I've not been very well, these days...
When are you back? I...
I'm trying, but...
I don't think I can do it without you.
I love you.

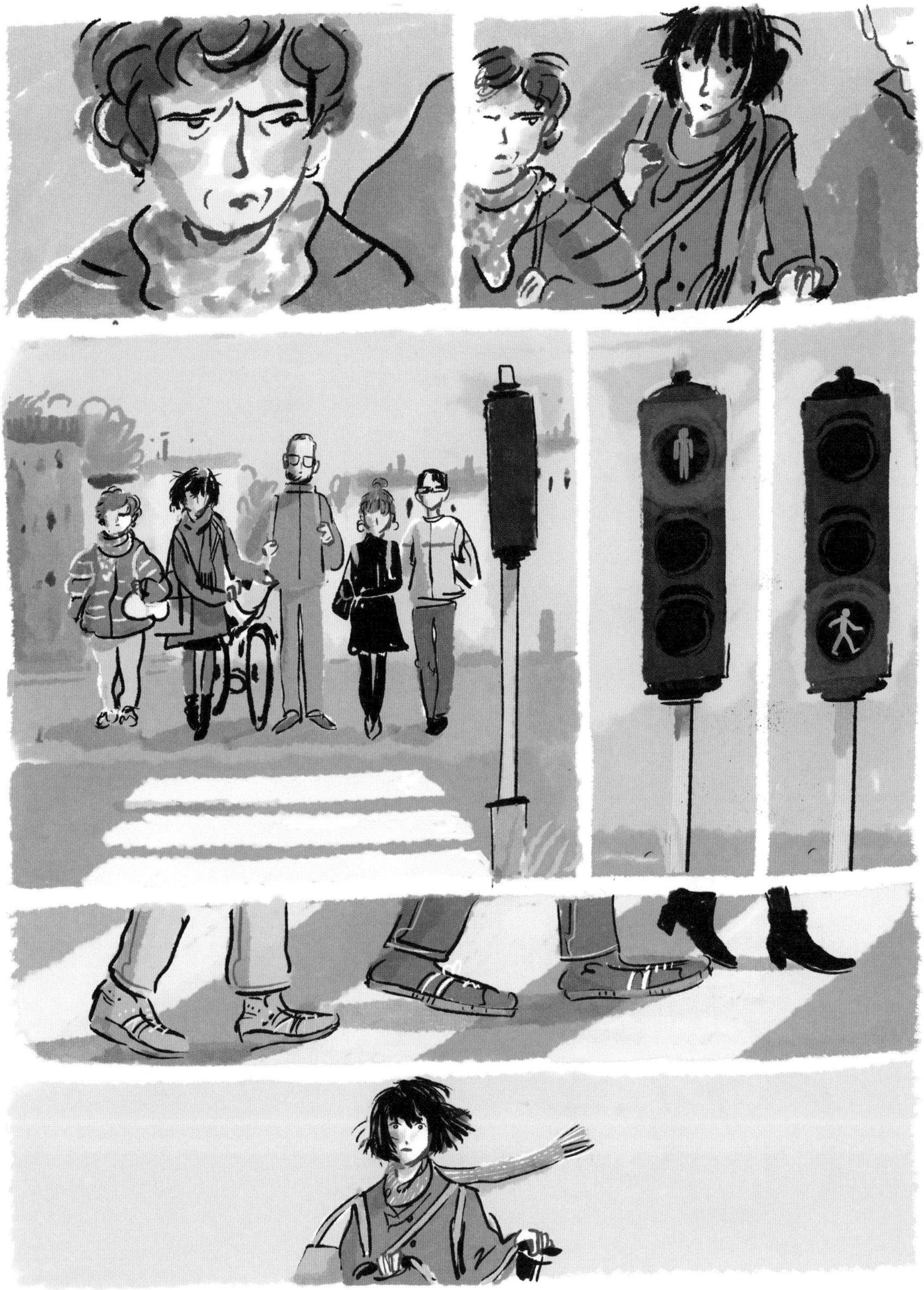

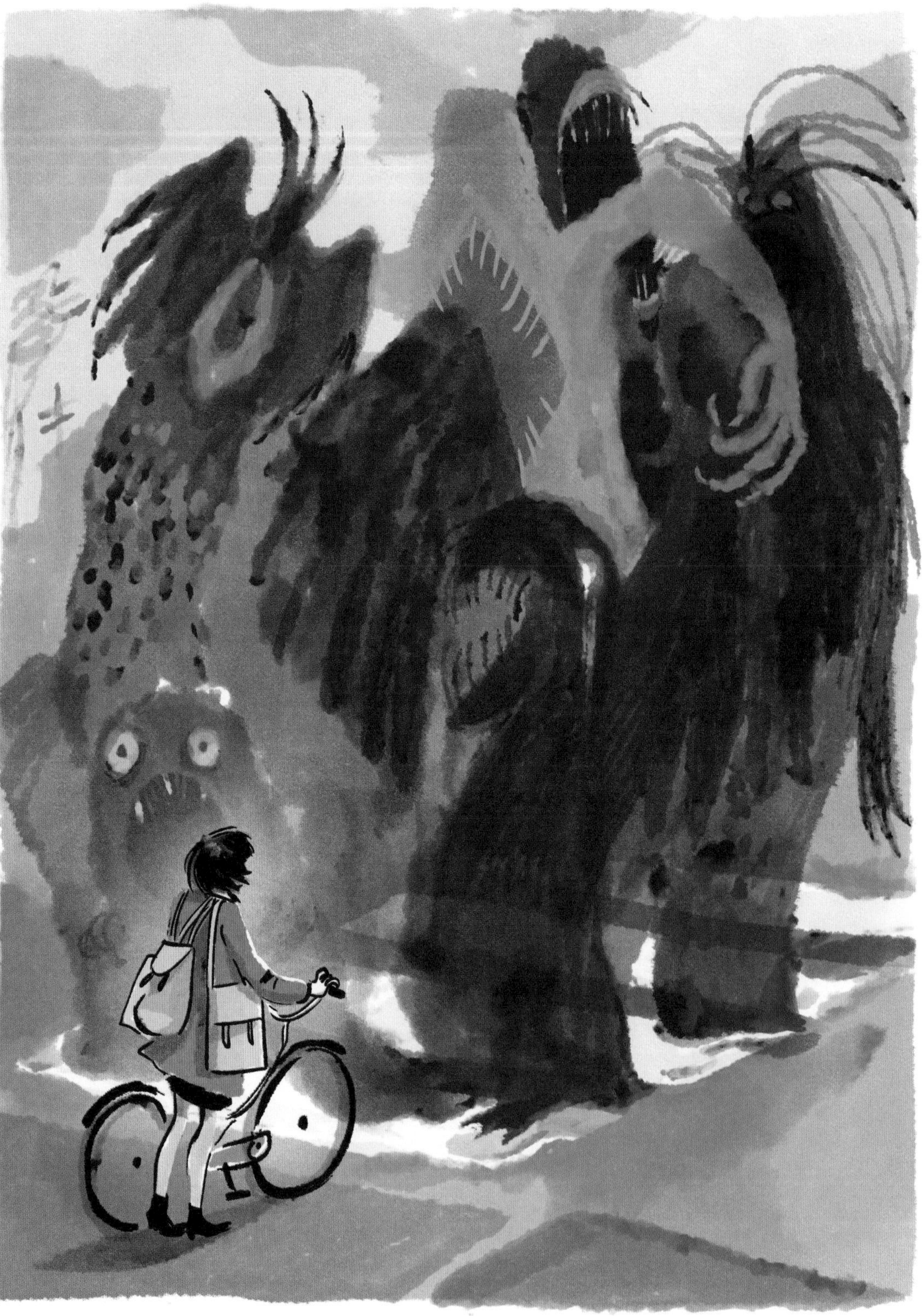

Chapter Two

Morning Light

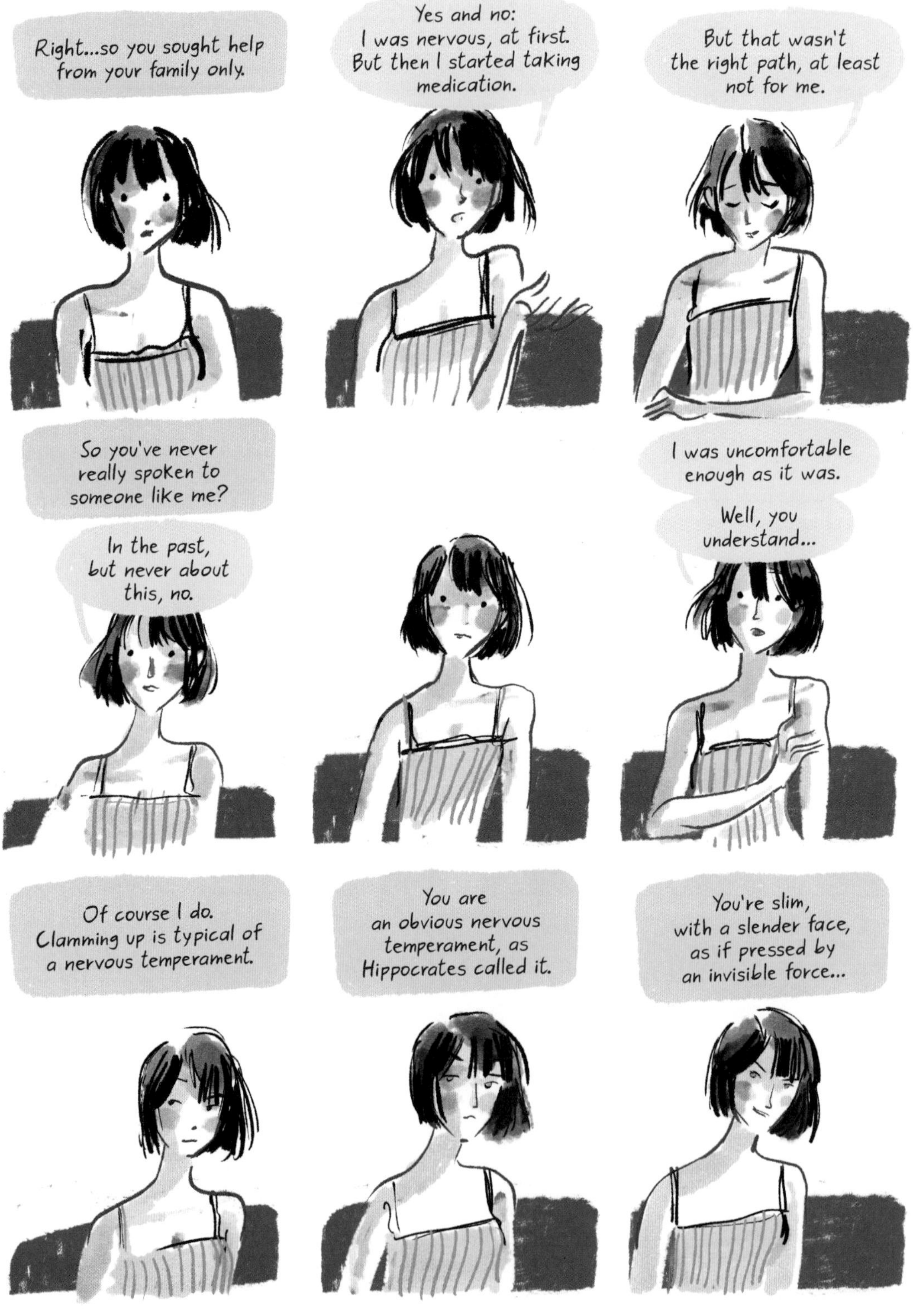
Right...so you sought help from your family only.
Yes and no: I was nervous, at first. But then I started taking medication.
But that wasn't the right path, at least not for me.
So you've never really spoken to someone like me?
In the past, but never about this, no.
I was uncomfortable enough as it was.
Well, you understand...
Of course I do. Clamming up is typical of a nervous temperament.
You are an obvious nervous temperament, as Hippocrates called it.
You're slim, with a slender face, as if pressed by an invisible force...

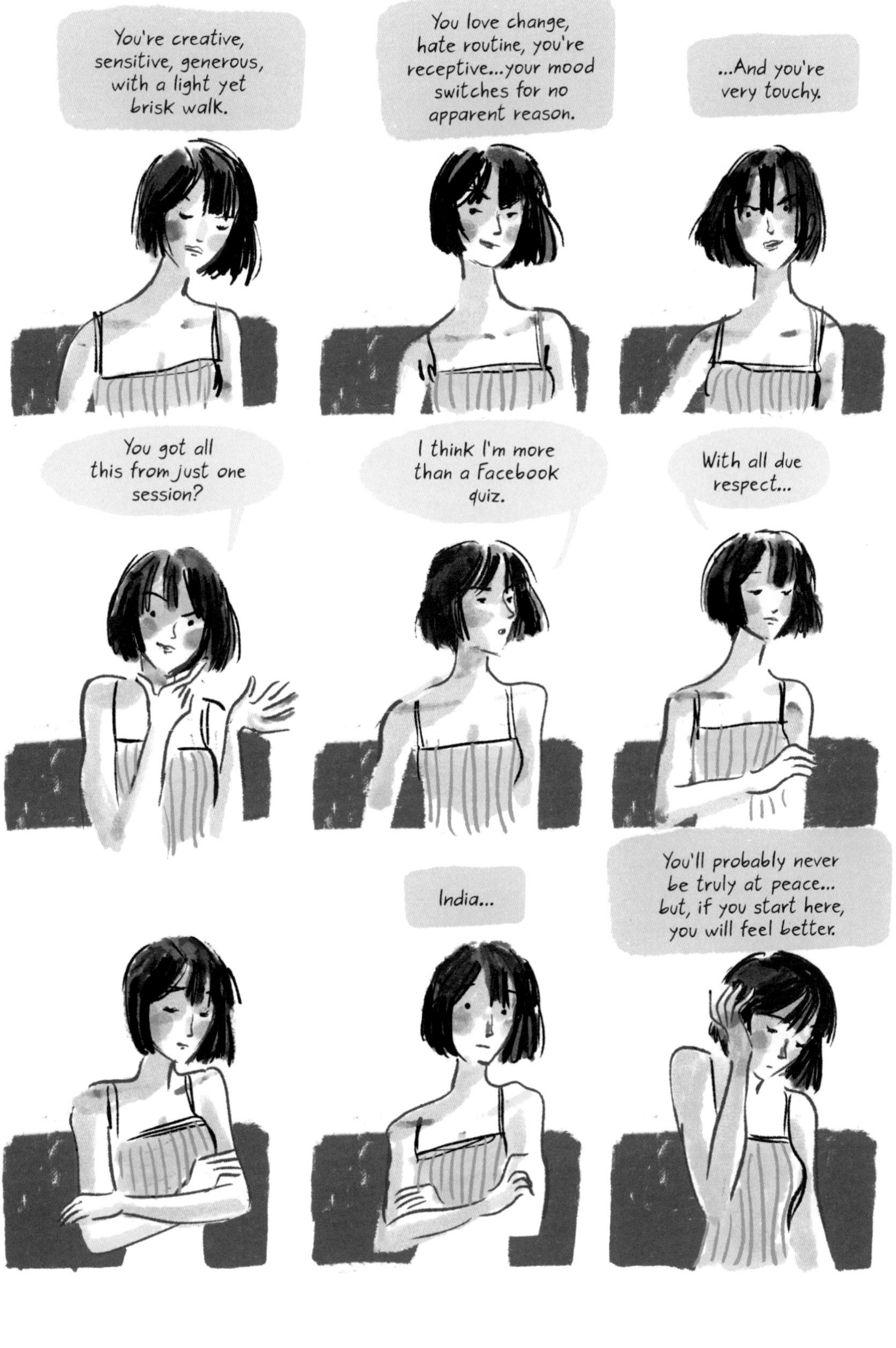
You're creative, sensitive, generous, with a light yet brisk walk.
You love change, hate routine, you're receptive...your mood switches for no apparent reason.
...And you're very touchy.
You got all this from just one session?
I think I'm more than a Facebook quiz.
With all due respect...
India...
You'll probably never be truly at peace... but, if you start here, you will feel better.

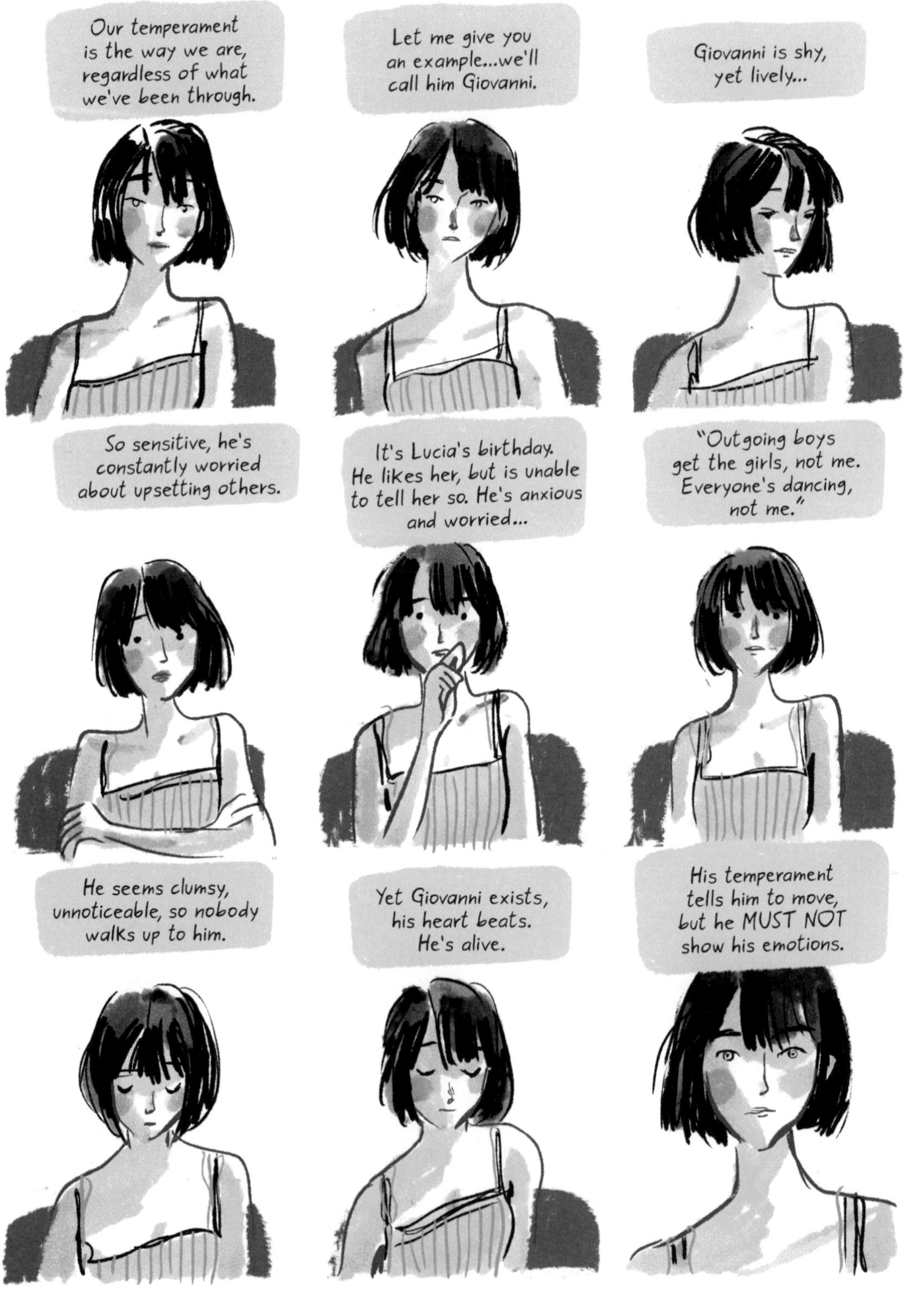
Our temperament is the way we are, regardless of what we've been through.
Let me give you an example...we'll call him Giovanni.
Giovanni is shy, yet lively...
So sensitive, he's constantly worried about upsetting others.
It's Lucia's birthday. He likes her, but is unable to tell her so. He's anxious and worried...
"Outgoing boys get the girls, not me. Everyone's dancing, not me."
He seems clumsy, unnoticeable, so nobody walks up to him.
Yet Giovanni exists, his heart beats. He's alive.
His temperament tells him to move, but he MUST NOT show his emotions.

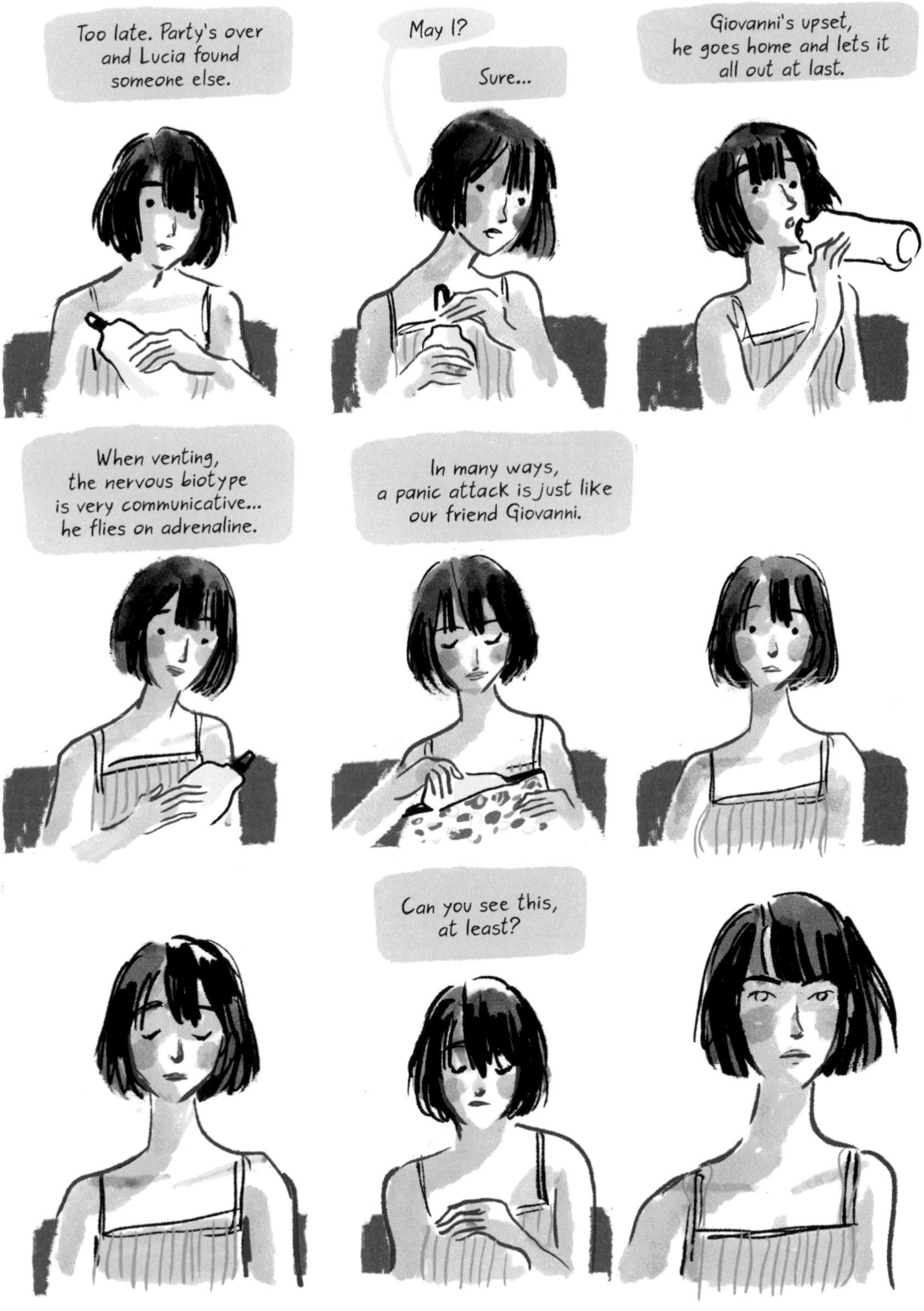
Too late. Party's over and Lucia found someone else.
May I?
Sure...
Giovanni's upset, he goes home and lets it all out at last.
When venting, the nervous biotype is very communicative... he flies on adrenaline.
In many ways, a panic attack is just like our friend Giovanni.
Can you see this, at least?

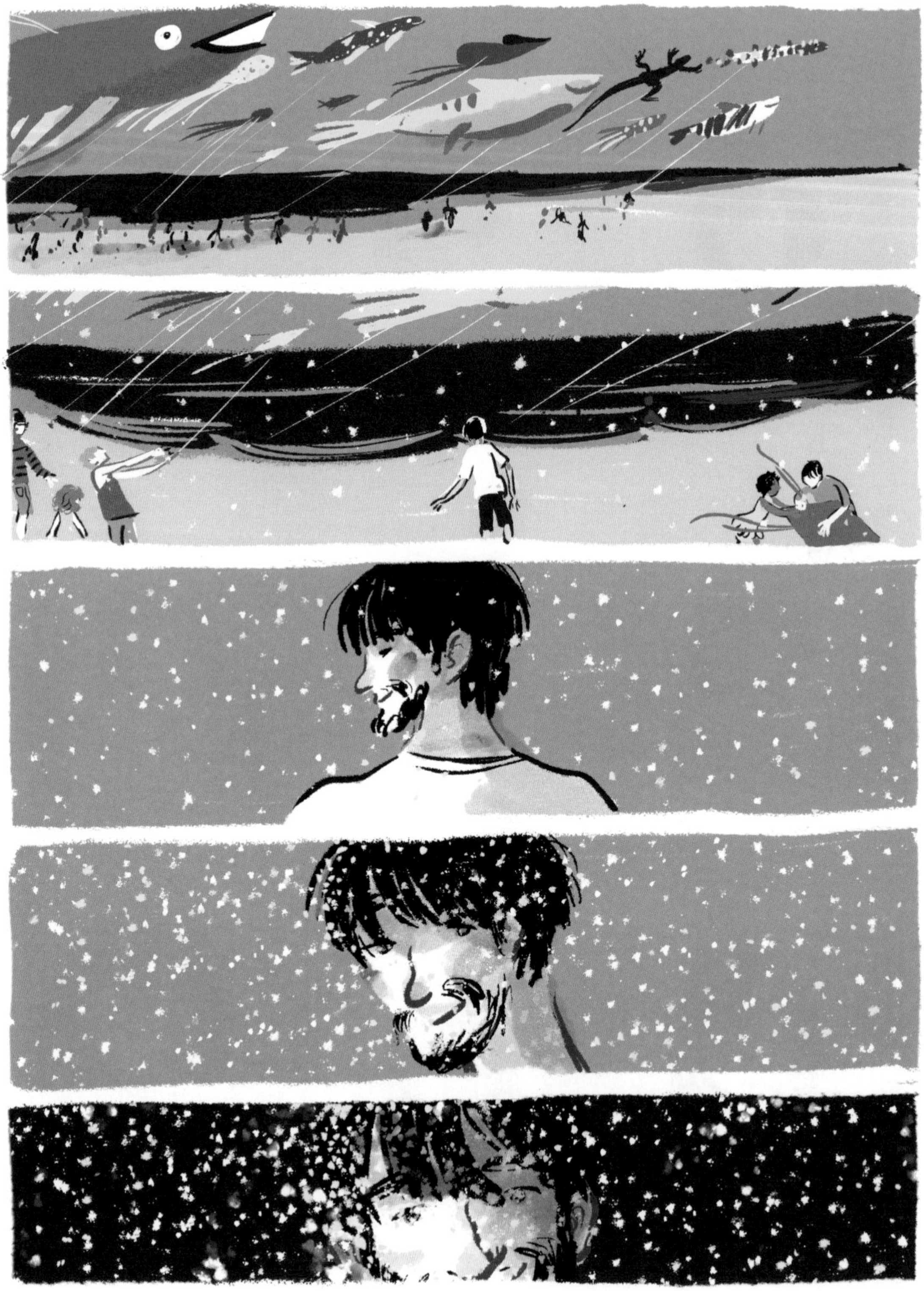

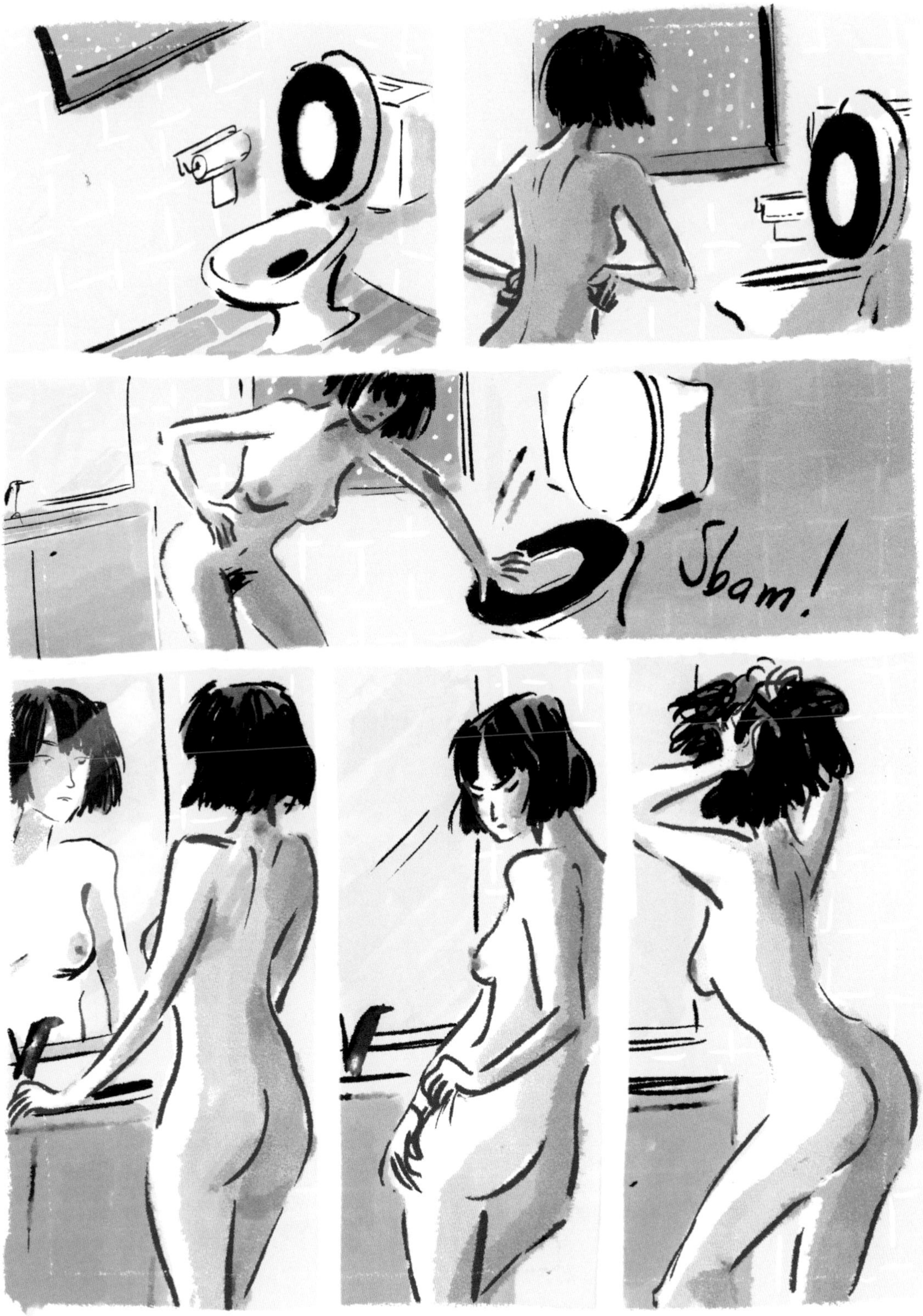
Sbam!

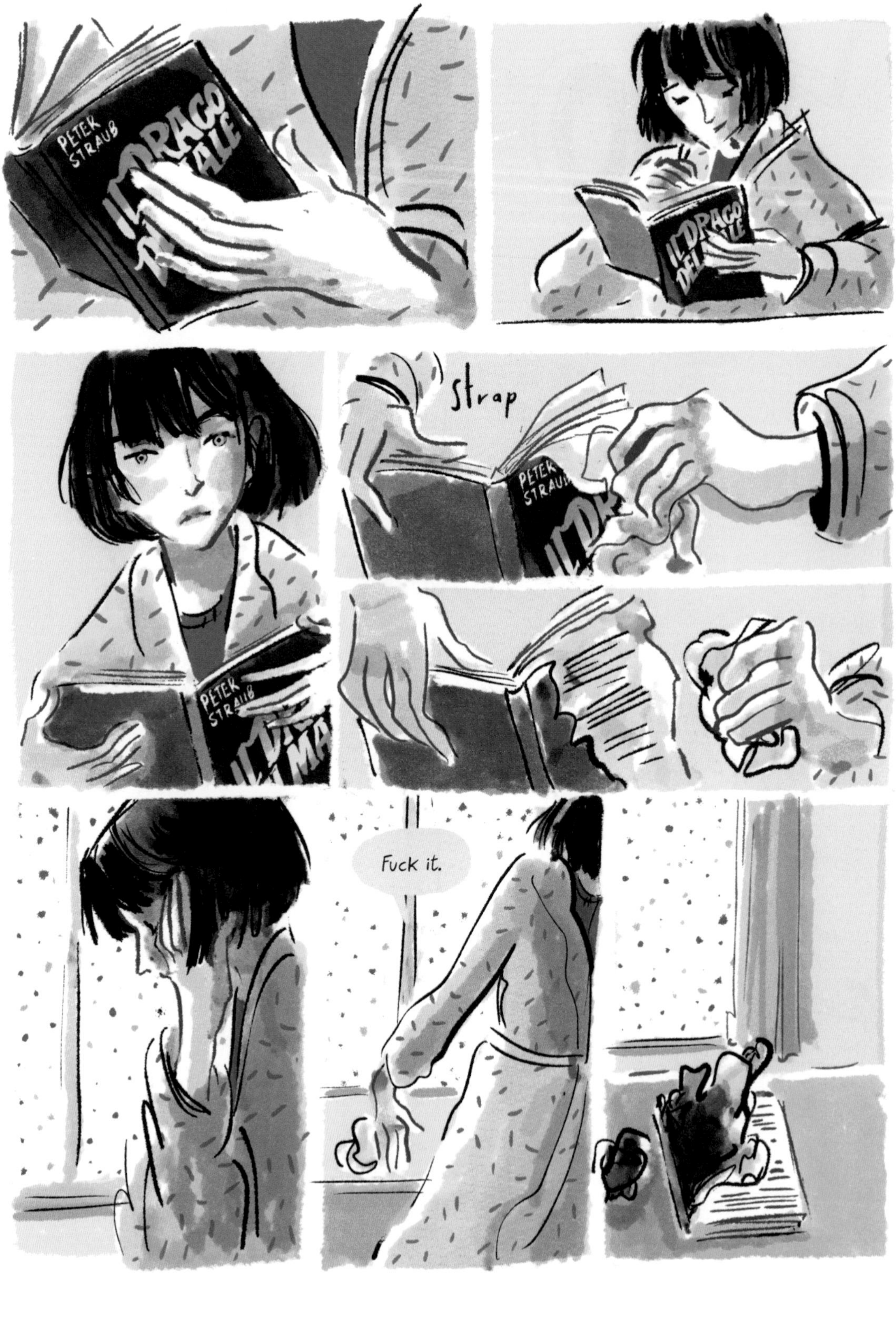
PETER STRAUB
Strap
Fuck it.

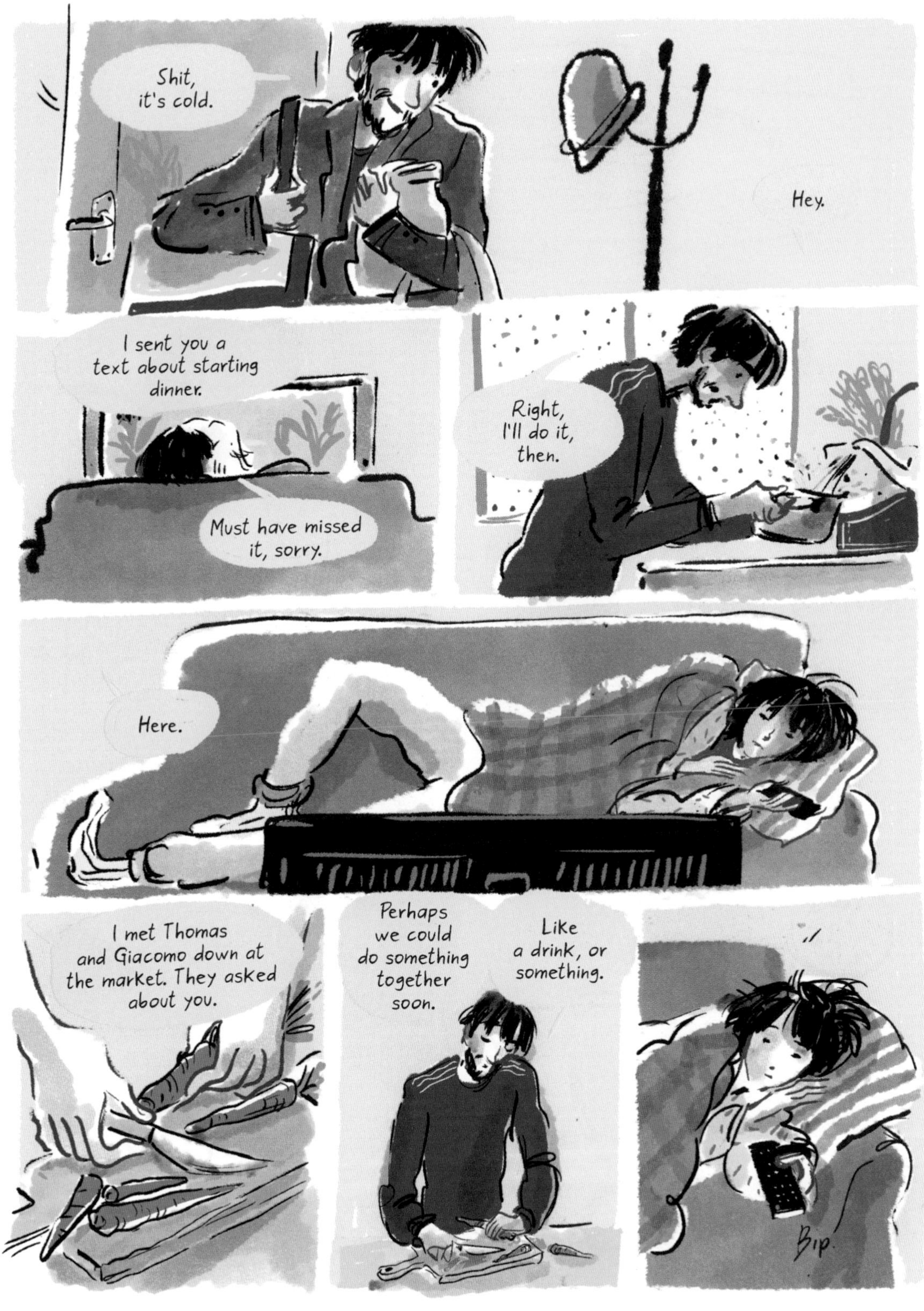
Shit, it's cold.
Hey.
I sent you a text about starting dinner.
Must have missed it, sorry.
Right, I'll do it, then.
Here.
I met Thomas and Giacomo down at the market. They asked about you.
Perhaps we could do something together soon.
Like a drink, or something.
Bip.

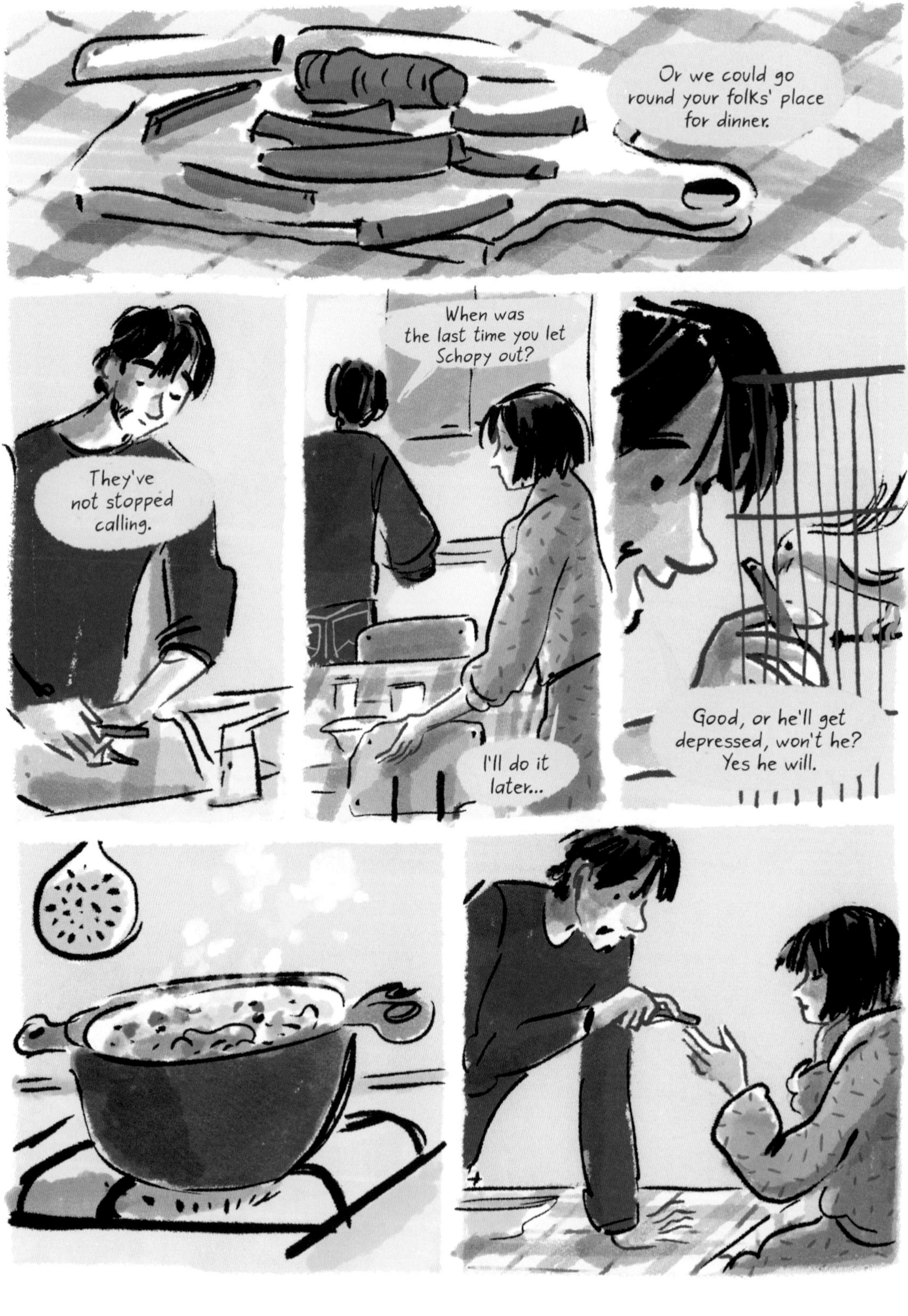
Or we could go round your folks' place for dinner.
They've not stopped calling.
When was the last time you let Schopy out?
I'll do it later...
Good, or he'll get depressed, won't he? Yes he will.

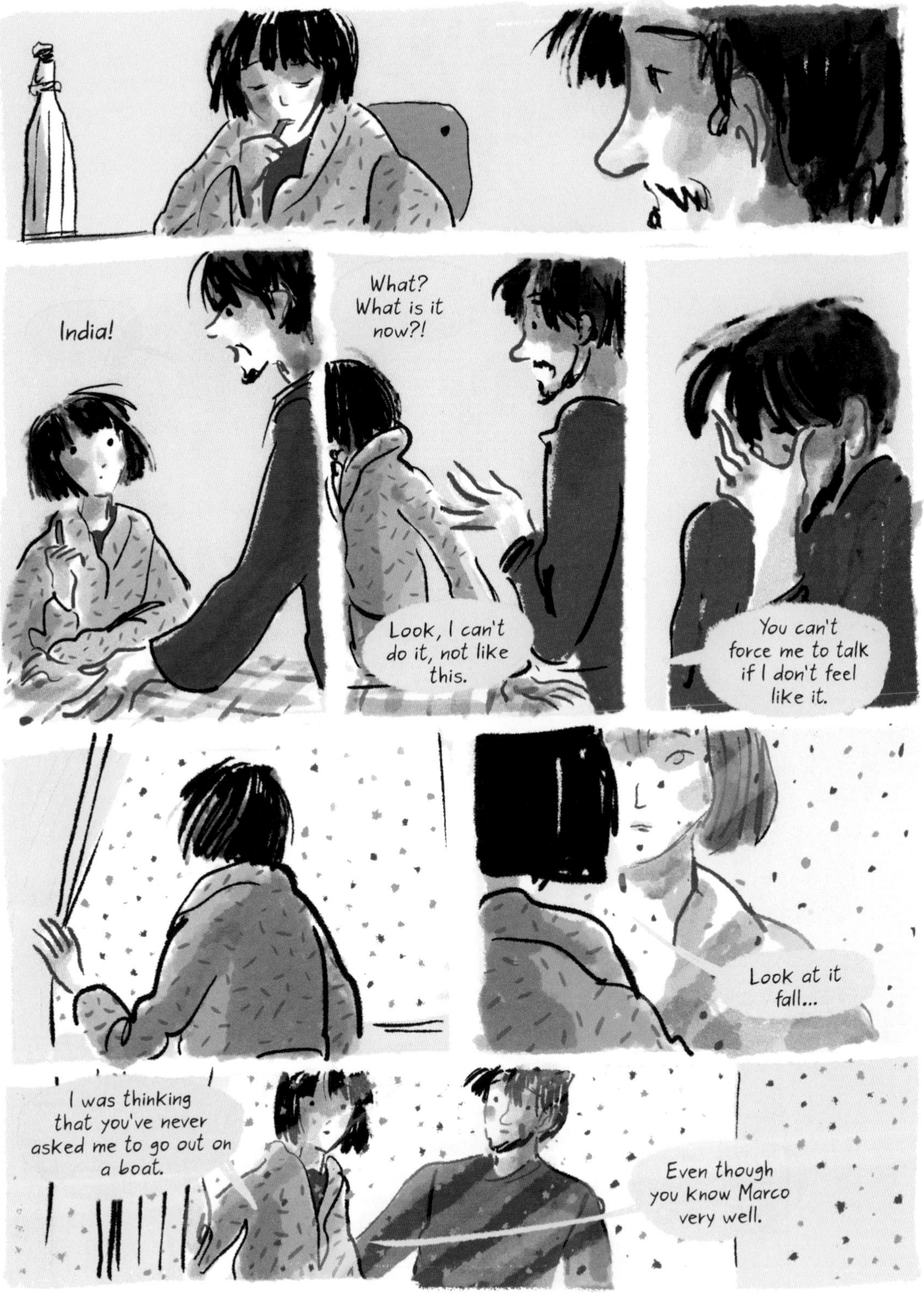
India!
What? What is it now?!
Look, I can't do it, not like this.
You can't force me to talk if I don't feel like it.
Look at it fall...
I was thinking that you've never asked me to go out on a boat.
Even though you know Marco very well.

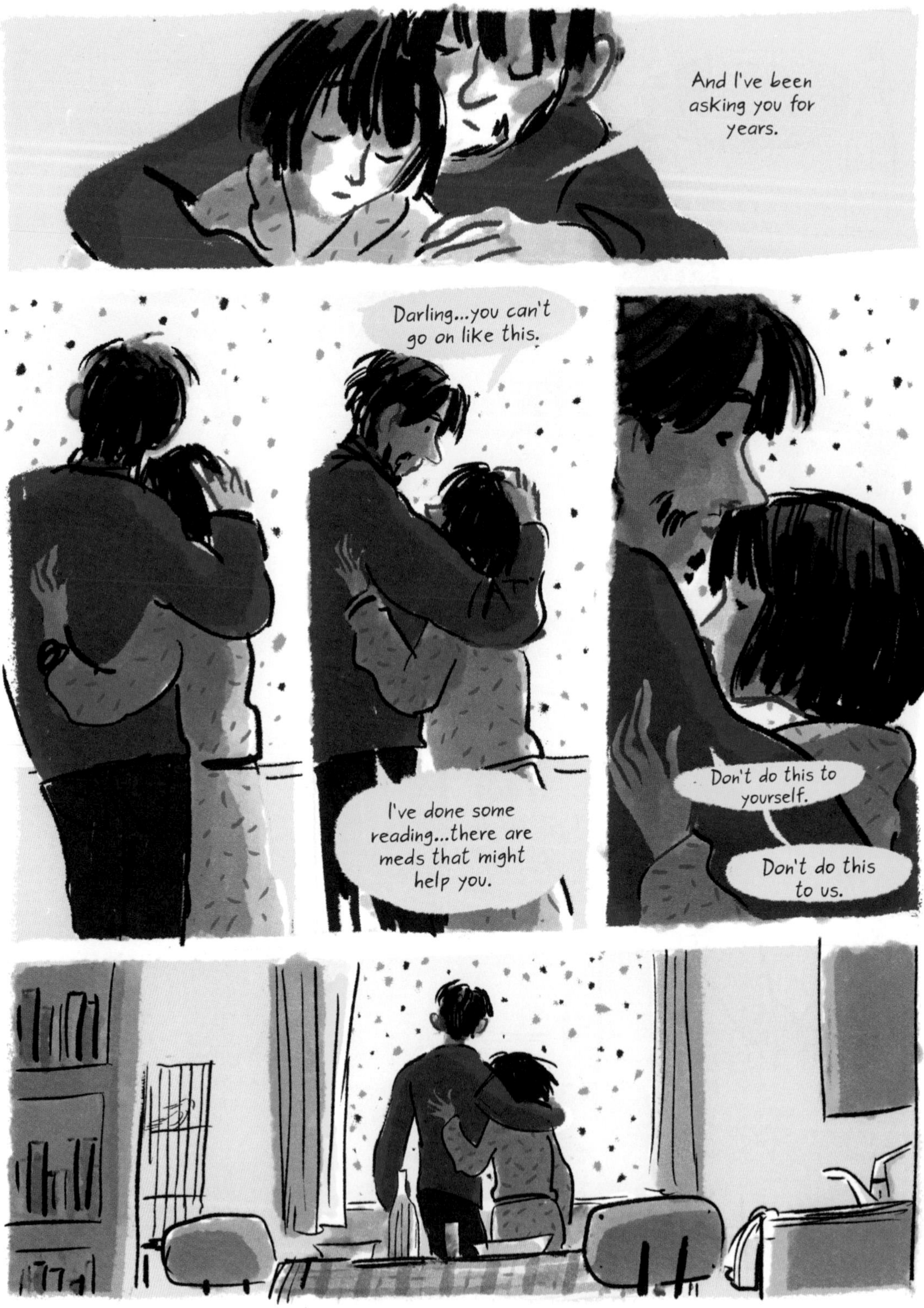
And I've been asking you for years.
Darling...you can't go on like this.
I've done some reading...there are meds that might help you.
Don't do this to yourself.
Don't do this to us.

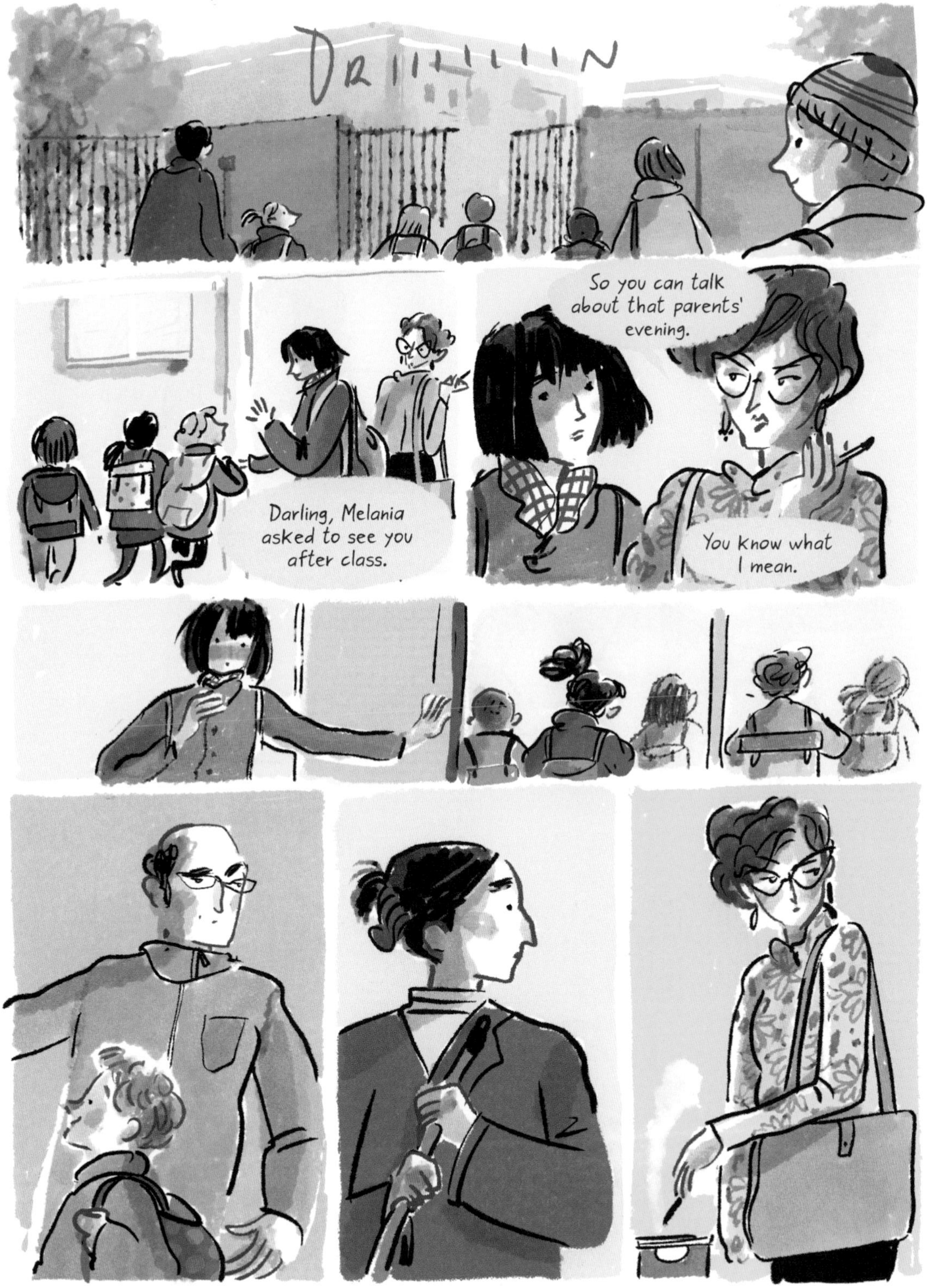
DRIIIIIIN
Darling, Melania asked to see you after class.
So you can talk about that parents' evening.
You know what I mean.

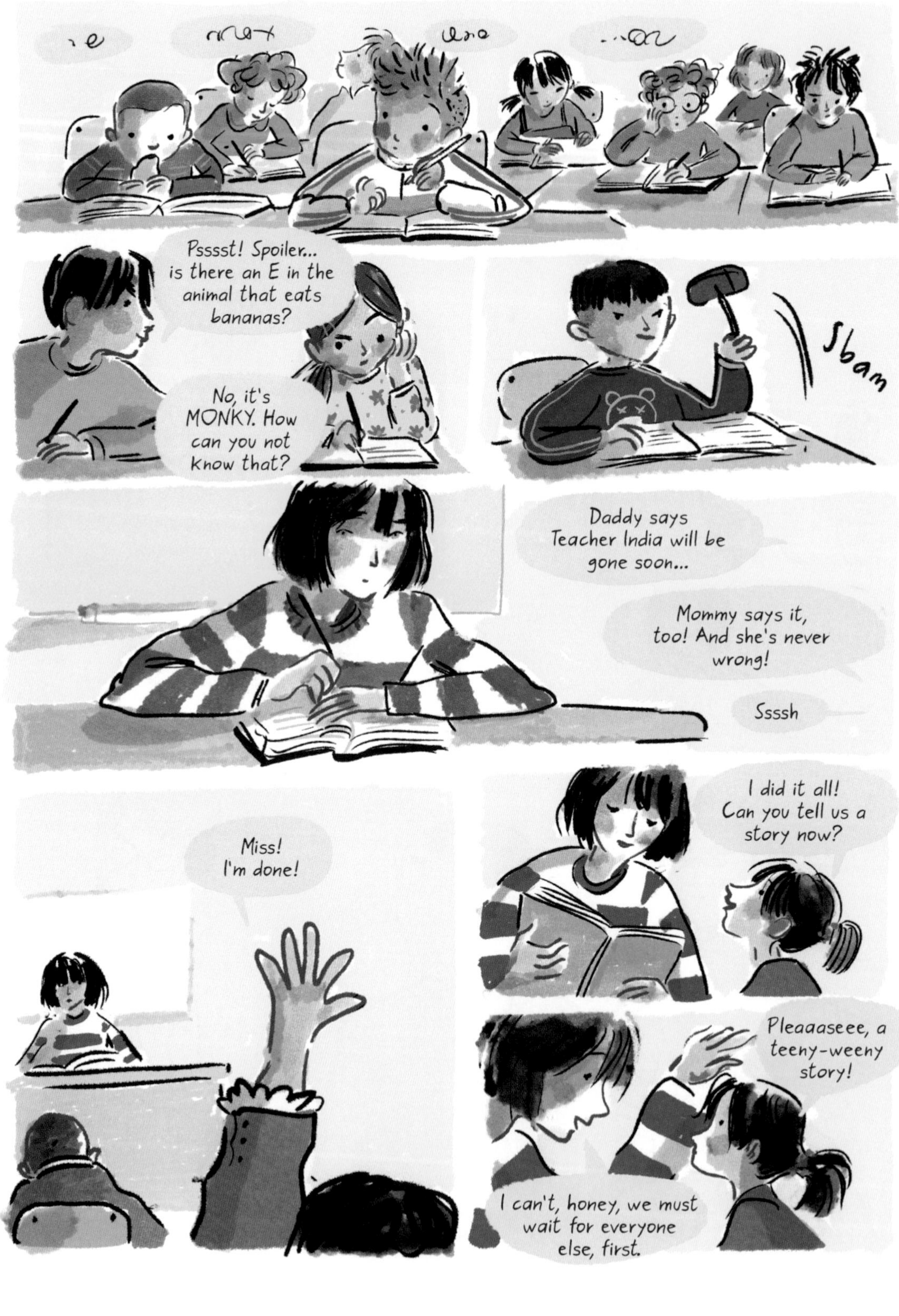
Pssst! Spoiler... is there an E in the animal that eats bananas?
No, it's MONKY. How can you not know that?
Sbam
Daddy says Teacher India will be gone soon...
Mommy says it, too! And she's never wrong!
Ssssh
Miss! I'm done!
I did it all! Can you tell us a story now?
Pleaaaseee, a teeny-weeny story!
I can't, honey, we must wait for everyone else, first.

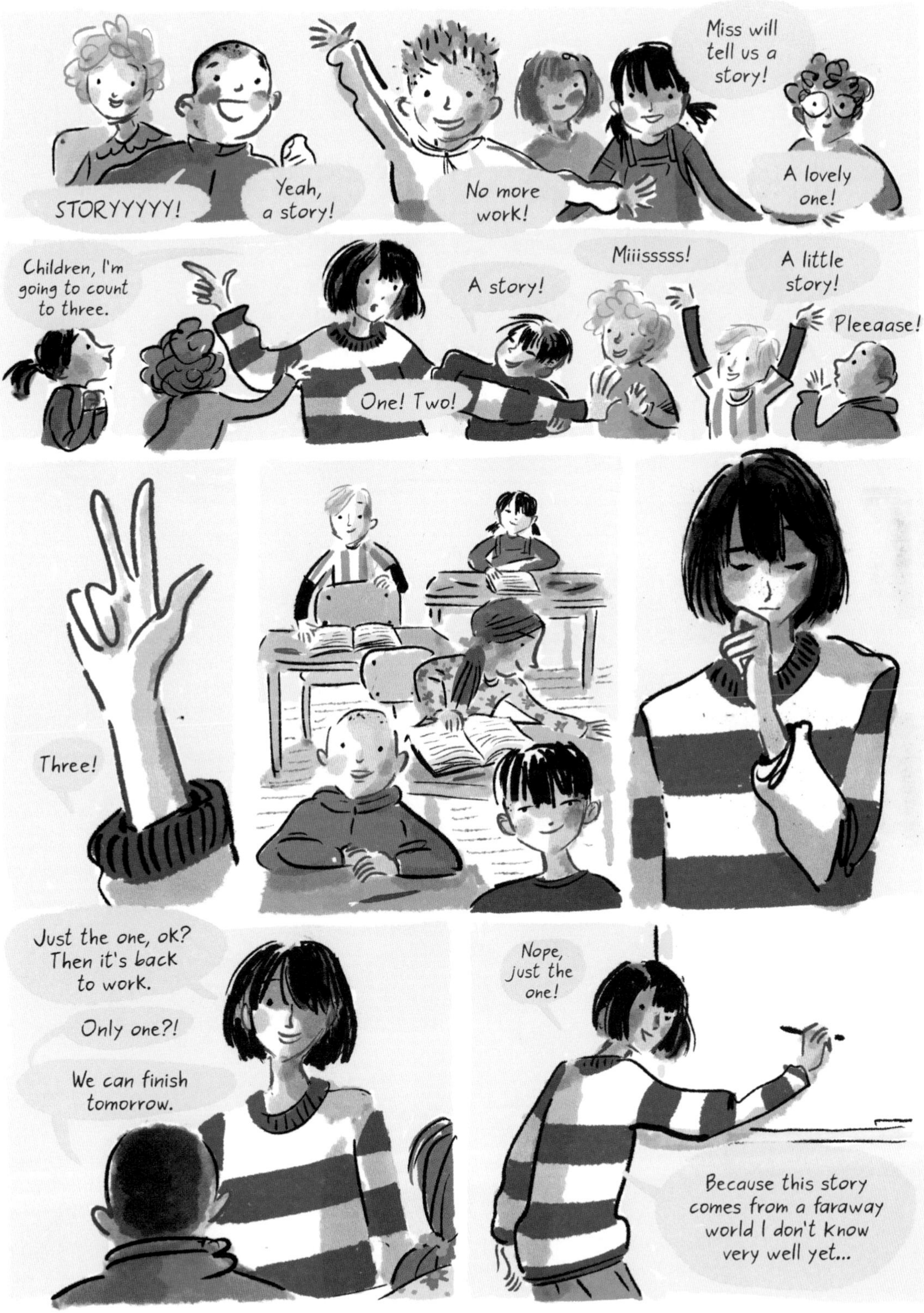
STORYYYYY!
Yeah, a story!
No more work!
Miss will tell us a story!
A lovely one!
Children, I'm going to count to three.
A story!
Miiissssss!
A little story!
Pleeaase!
One! Two!
Three!
Just the one, ok? Then it's back to work.
Only one?!
We can finish tomorrow.
Nope, just the one!
Because this story comes from a faraway world I don't know very well yet...

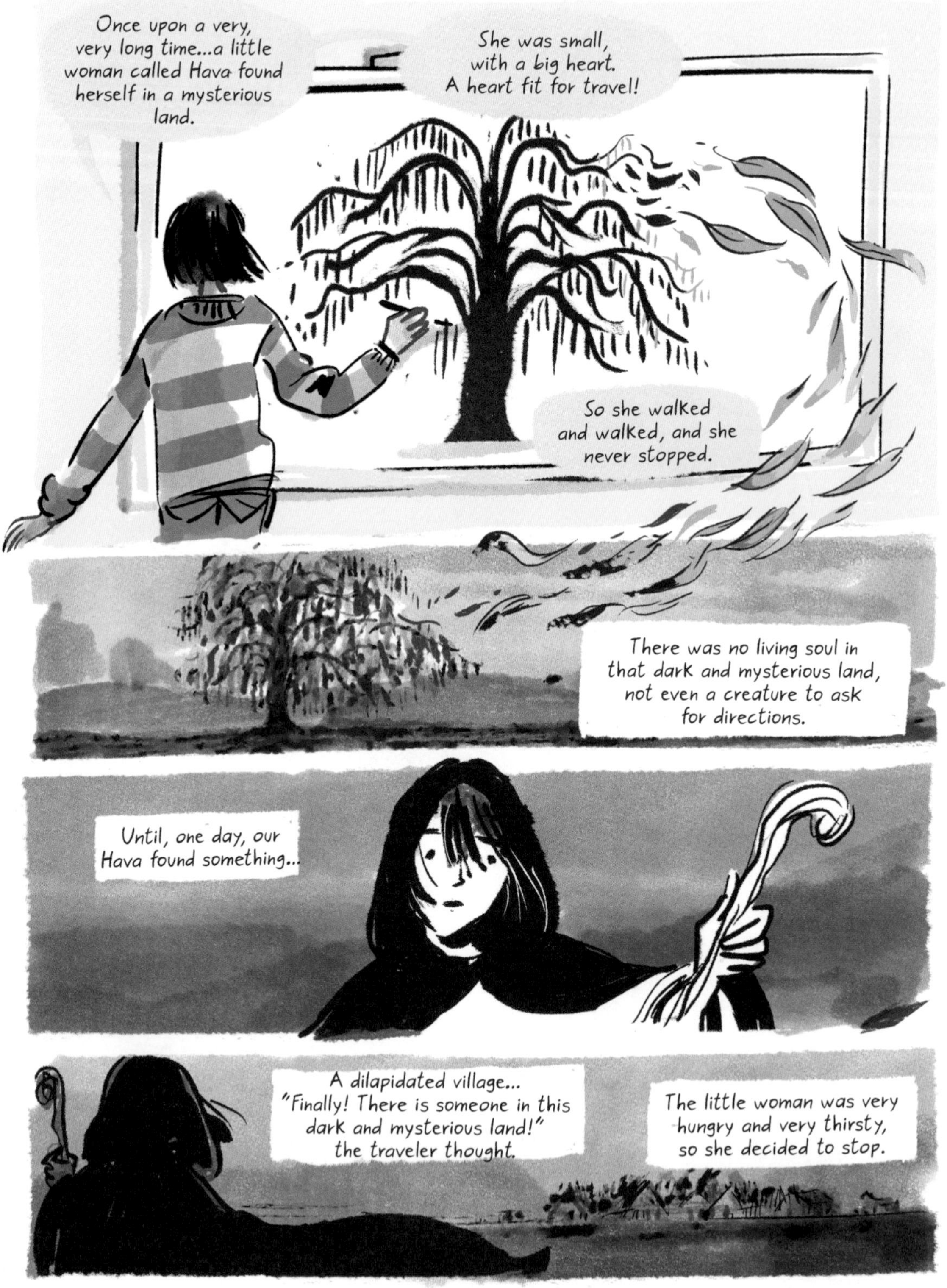
Once upon a very, very long time...a little woman called Hava found herself in a mysterious land.
She was small, with a big heart. A heart fit for travel!
So she walked and walked, and she never stopped.
There was no living soul in that dark and mysterious land, not even a creature to ask for directions.
Until, one day, our Hava found something...
A dilapidated village... "Finally! There is someone in this dark and mysterious land!" the traveler thought.
The little woman was very hungry and very thirsty, so she decided to stop.

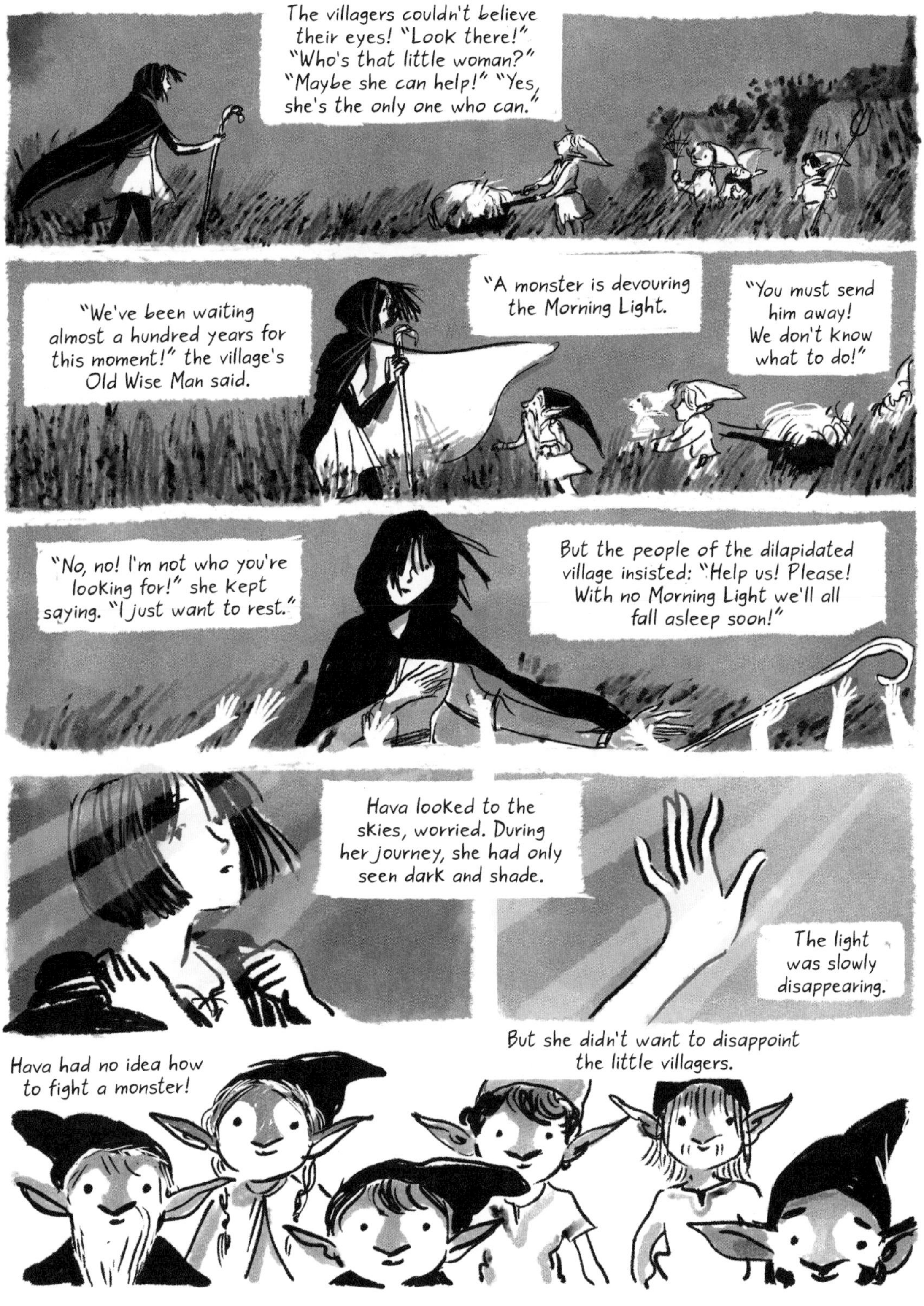

The villagers couldn't believe their eyes! "Look there!" "Who's that little woman?" "Maybe she can help!" "Yes, she's the only one who can."
"We've been waiting almost a hundred years for this moment!" the village's Old Wise Man said.
"A monster is devouring the Morning Light.
"You must send him away! We don't know what to do!"
"No, no! I'm not who you're looking for!" she kept saying. "I just want to rest."
But the people of the dilapidated village insisted: "Help us! Please! With no Morning Light we'll all fall asleep soon!"
Hava looked to the skies, worried. During her journey, she had only seen dark and shade.
The light was slowly disappearing.
Hava had no idea how to fight a monster!
But she didn't want to disappoint the little villagers.

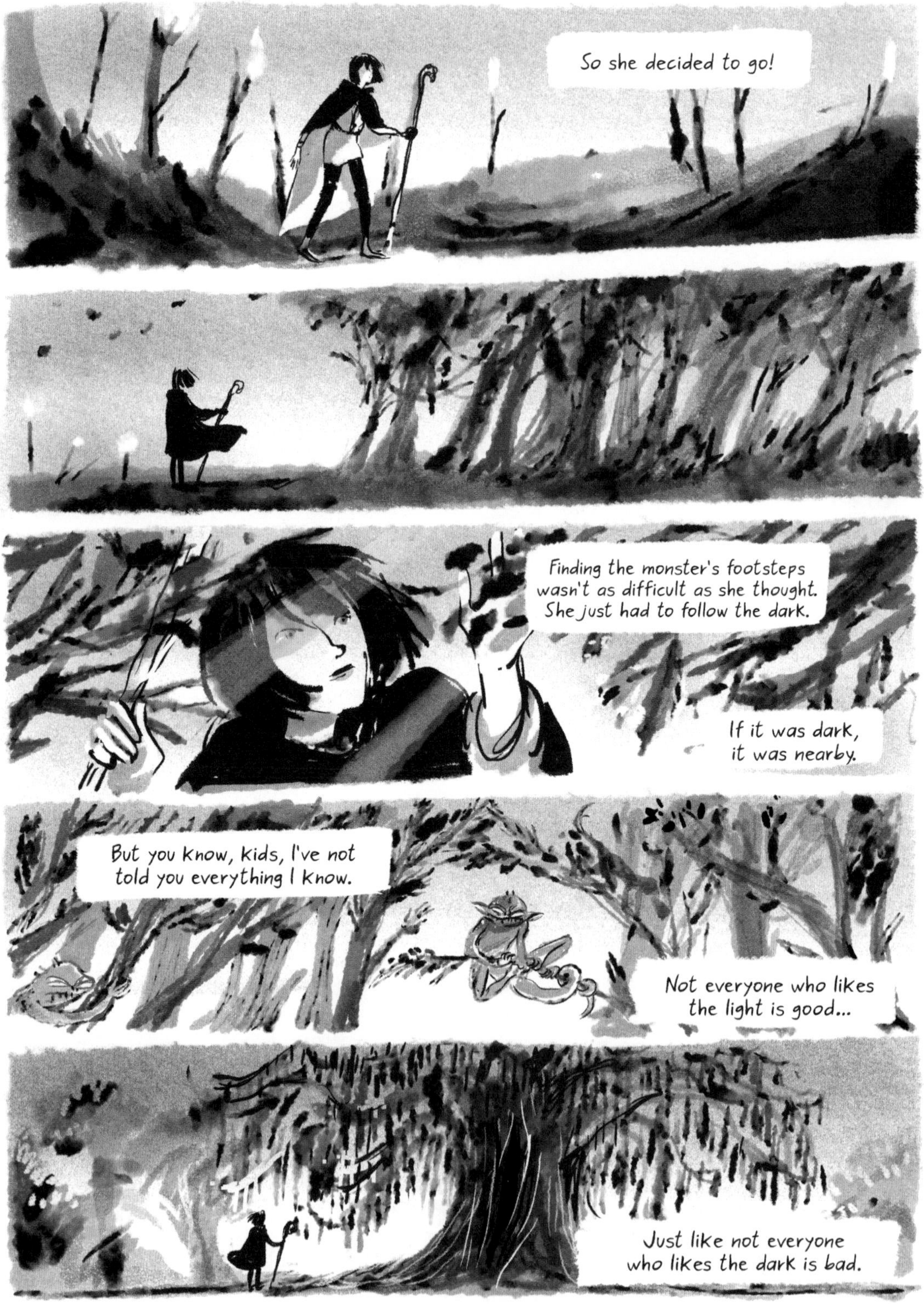
So she decided to go!
Finding the monster's footsteps wasn't as difficult as she thought. She just had to follow the dark.
If it was dark, it was nearby.
But you know, kids, I've not told you everything I know.
Not everyone who likes the light is good...
Just like not everyone who likes the dark is bad.

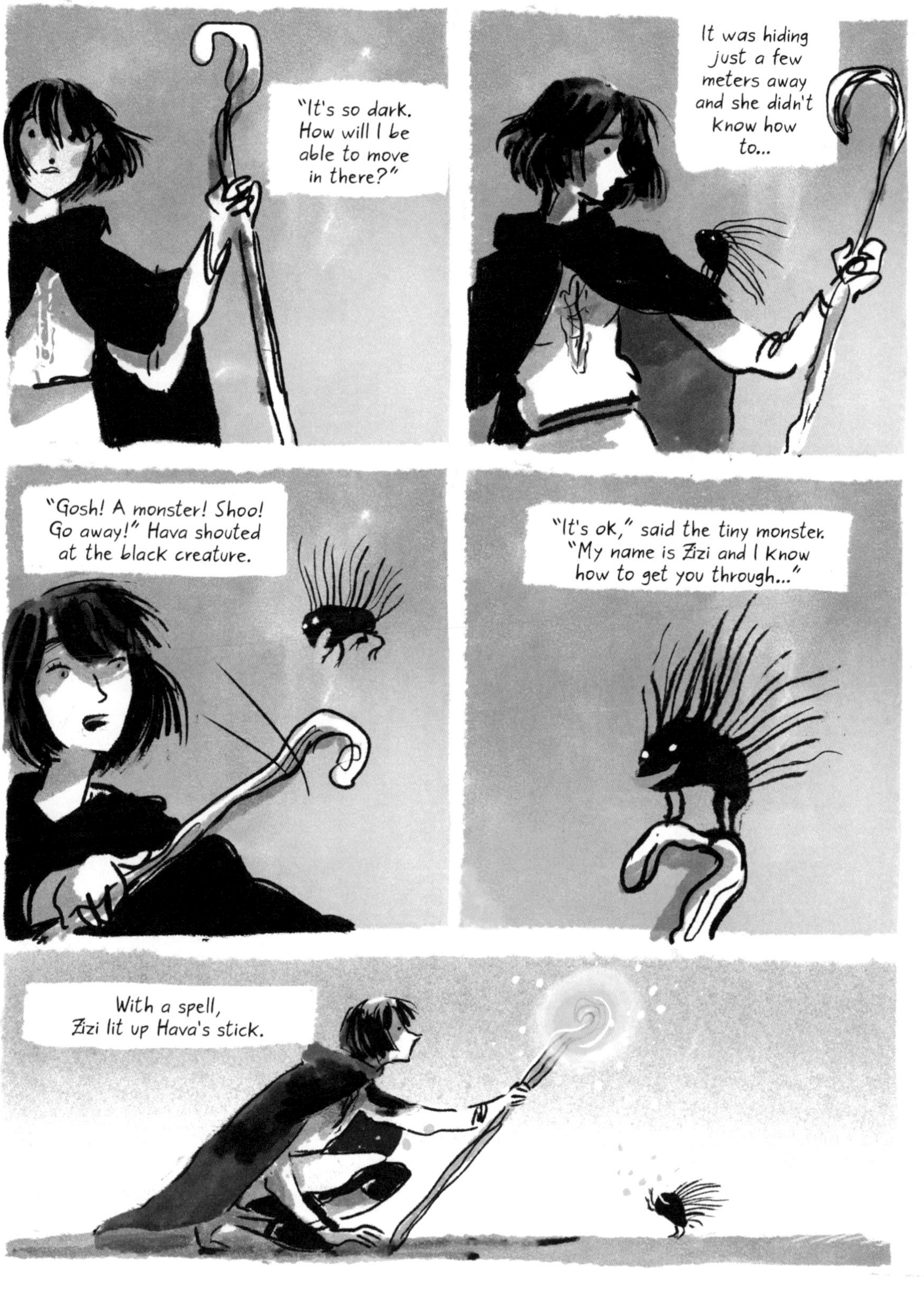
"It's so dark. How will I be able to move in there?"
It was hiding just a few meters away and she didn't know how to...
"Gosh! A monster! Shoo! Go away!" Hava shouted at the black creature.
"It's ok," said the tiny monster. "My name is Zizi and I know how to get you through..."
With a spell, Zizi lit up Hava's stick.

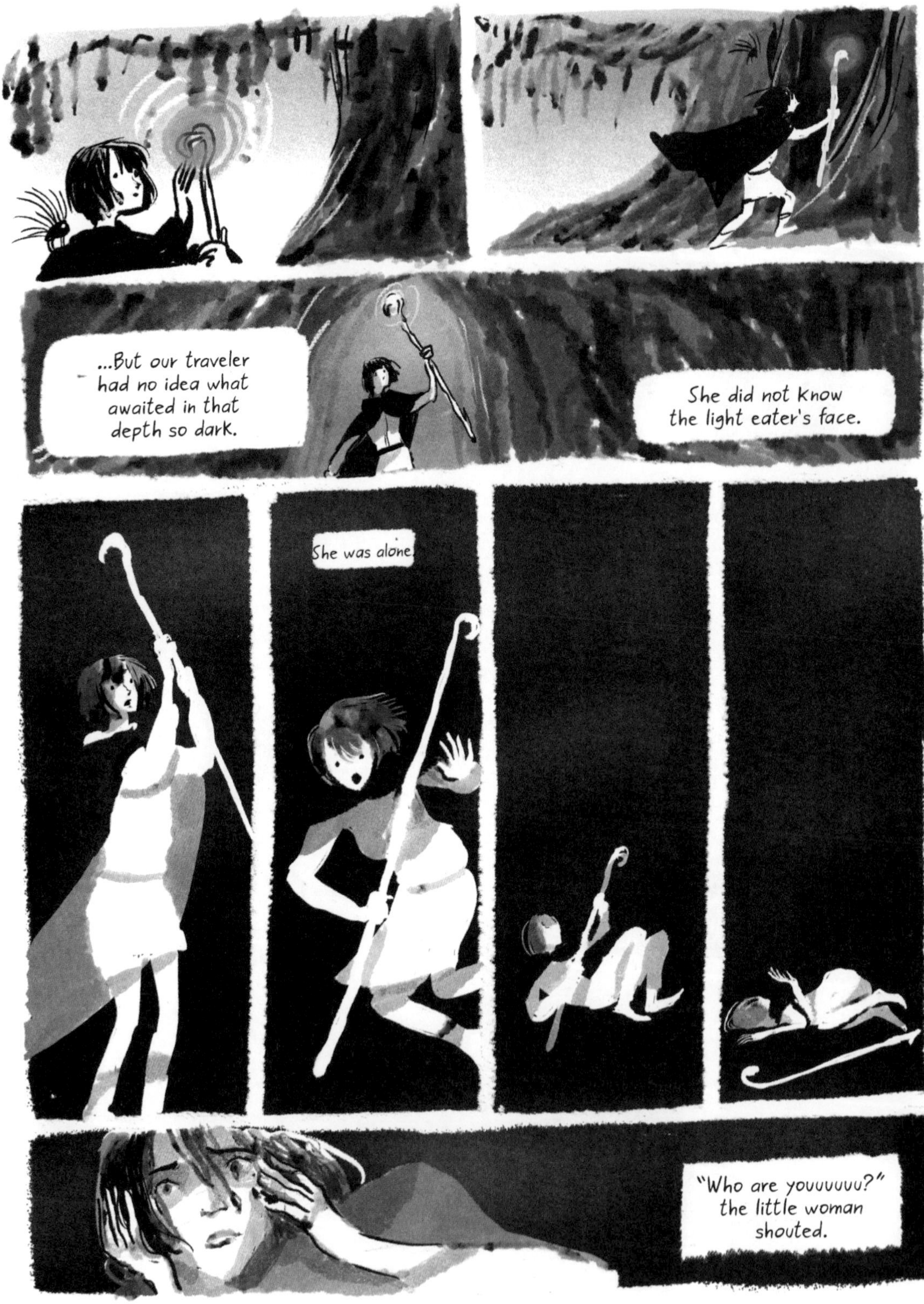

...But our traveler had no idea what awaited in that depth so dark.
She did not know the light eater's face.
She was alone.
"Who are youuuuuu?" the little woman shouted.

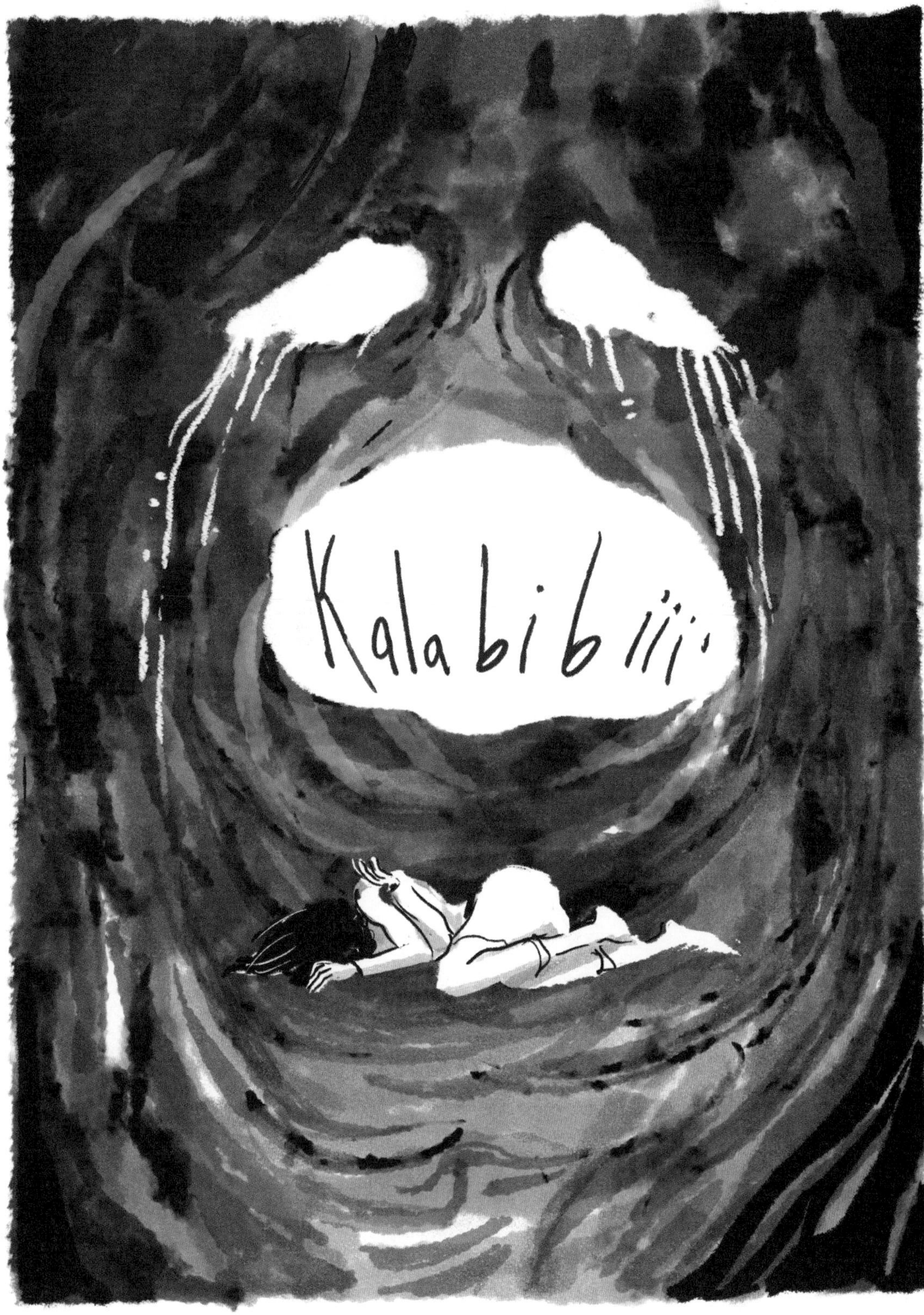
Kalabibiii

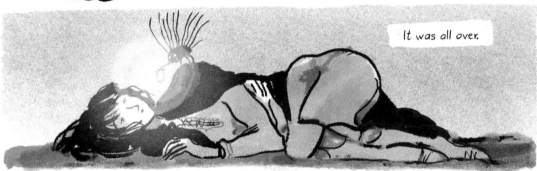

It was all over.

Kalabibi vanished in its own shadow, taking the Morning Light with it.

Where before lay the heart of the big tree, now there was just a hole.

A void that Hava would dream about for many, many nights to come.

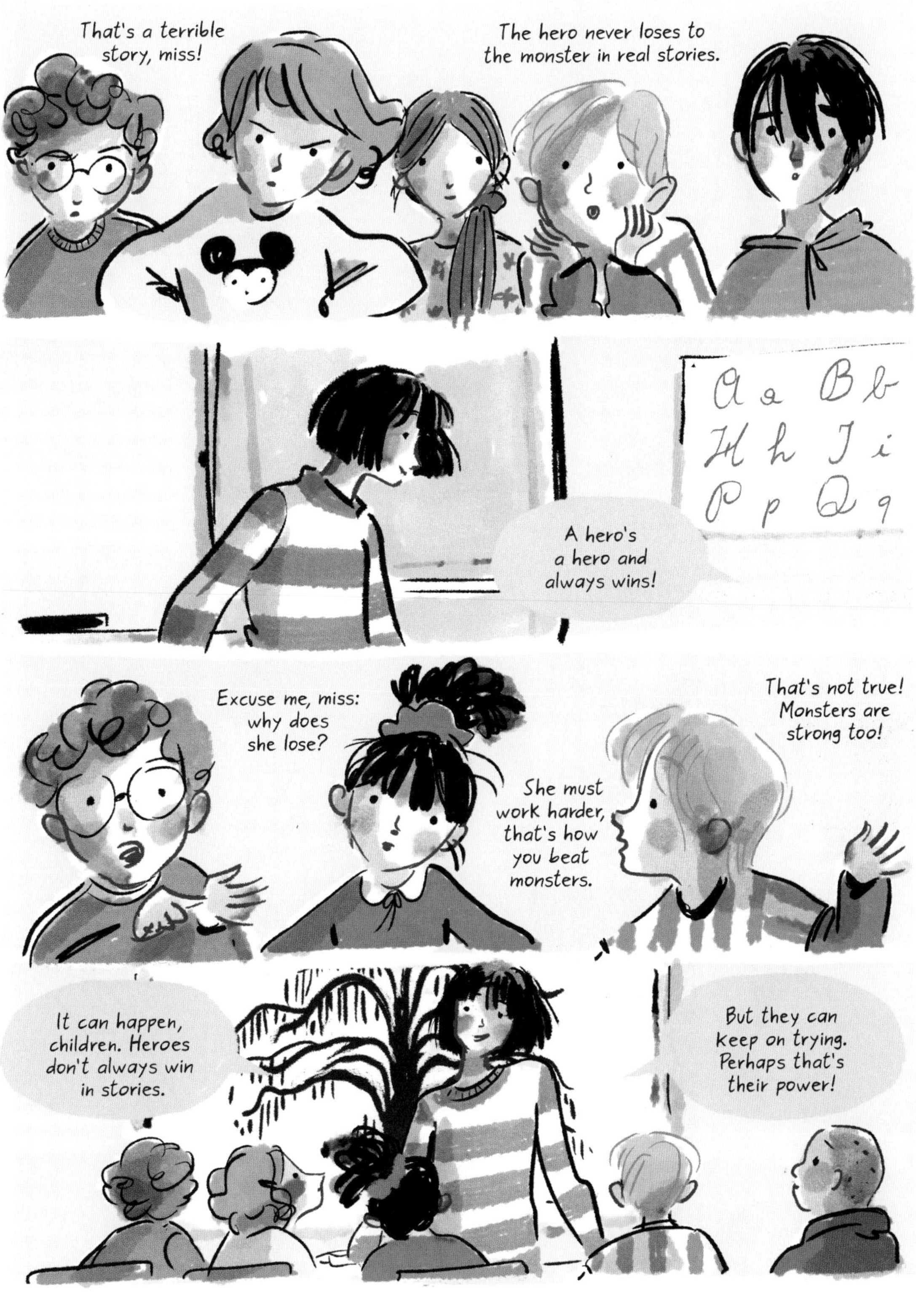
That's a terrible story, miss!
The hero never loses to the monster in real stories.
Aa Bb
Hh Ii
Pp Qq
A hero's a hero and always wins!
Excuse me, miss: why does she lose?
She must work harder, that's how you beat monsters.
That's not true! Monsters are strong too!
It can happen, children. Heroes don't always win in stories.
But they can keep on trying. Perhaps that's their power!

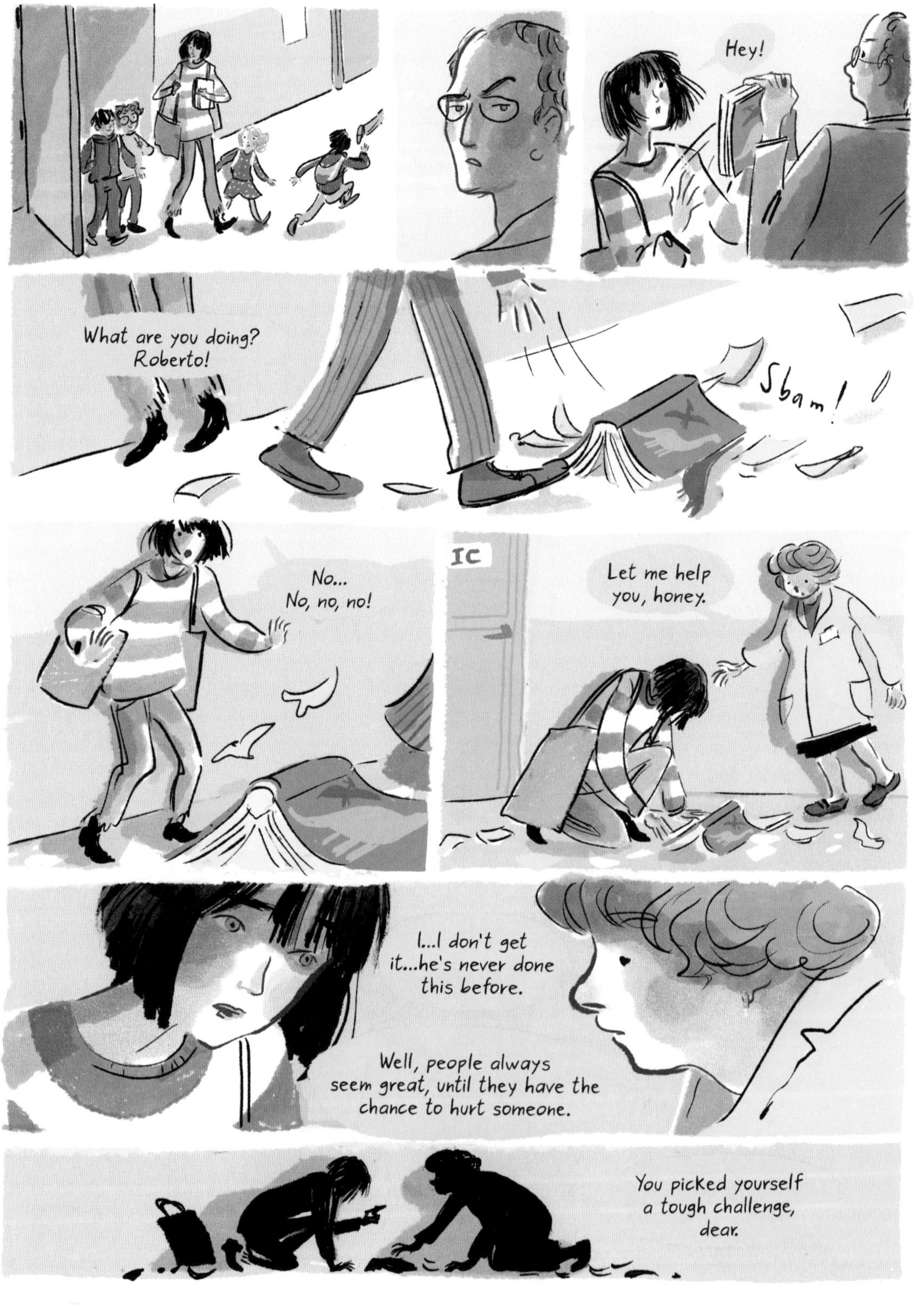
Hey!
What are you doing? Roberto!
Sbam!
No... No, no, no!
IC
Let me help you, honey.
I...I don't get it...he's never done this before.
Well, people always seem great, until they have the chance to hurt someone.
You picked yourself a tough challenge, dear.

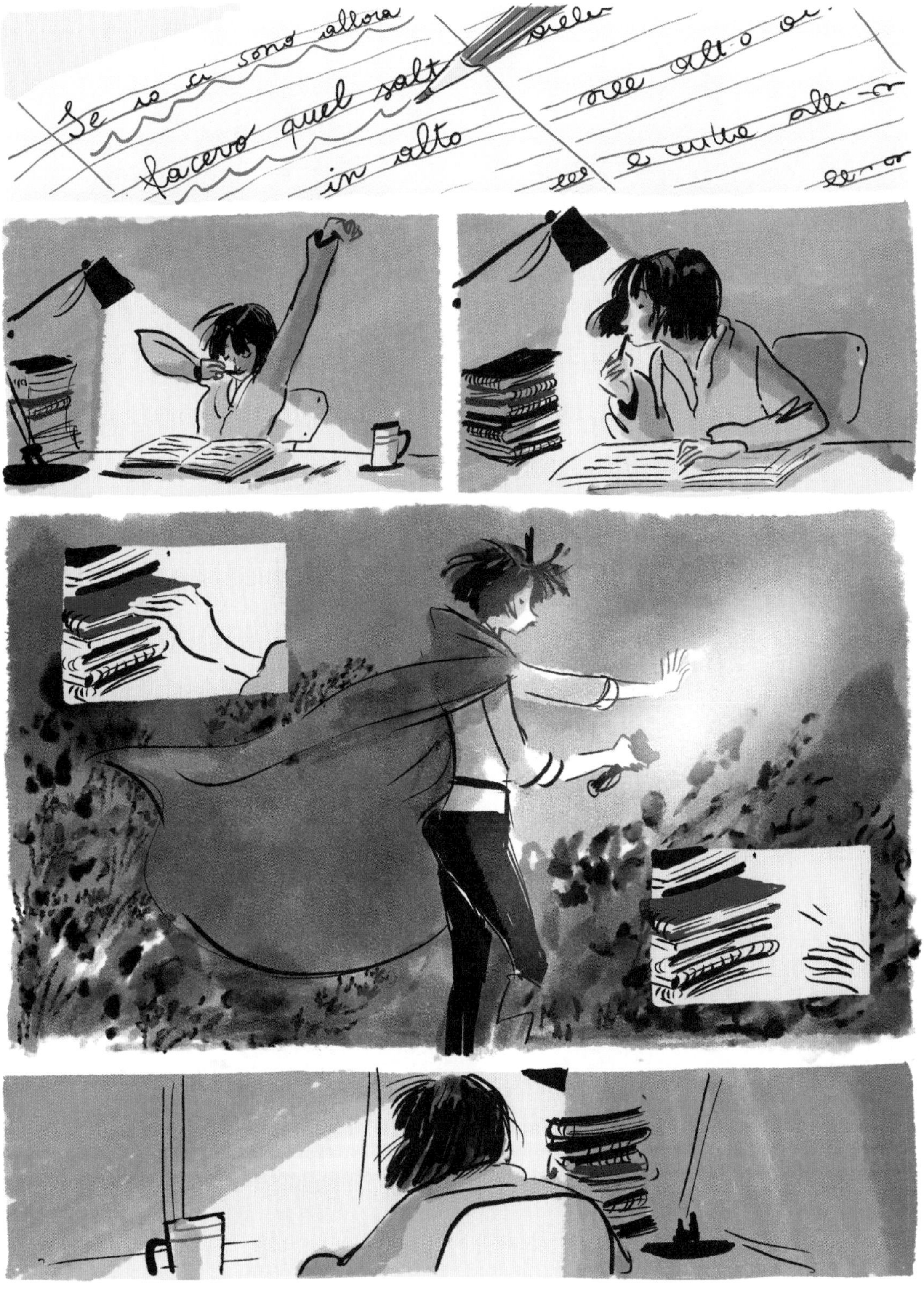
Se io ci sono allora
facevo quel salt
in alto

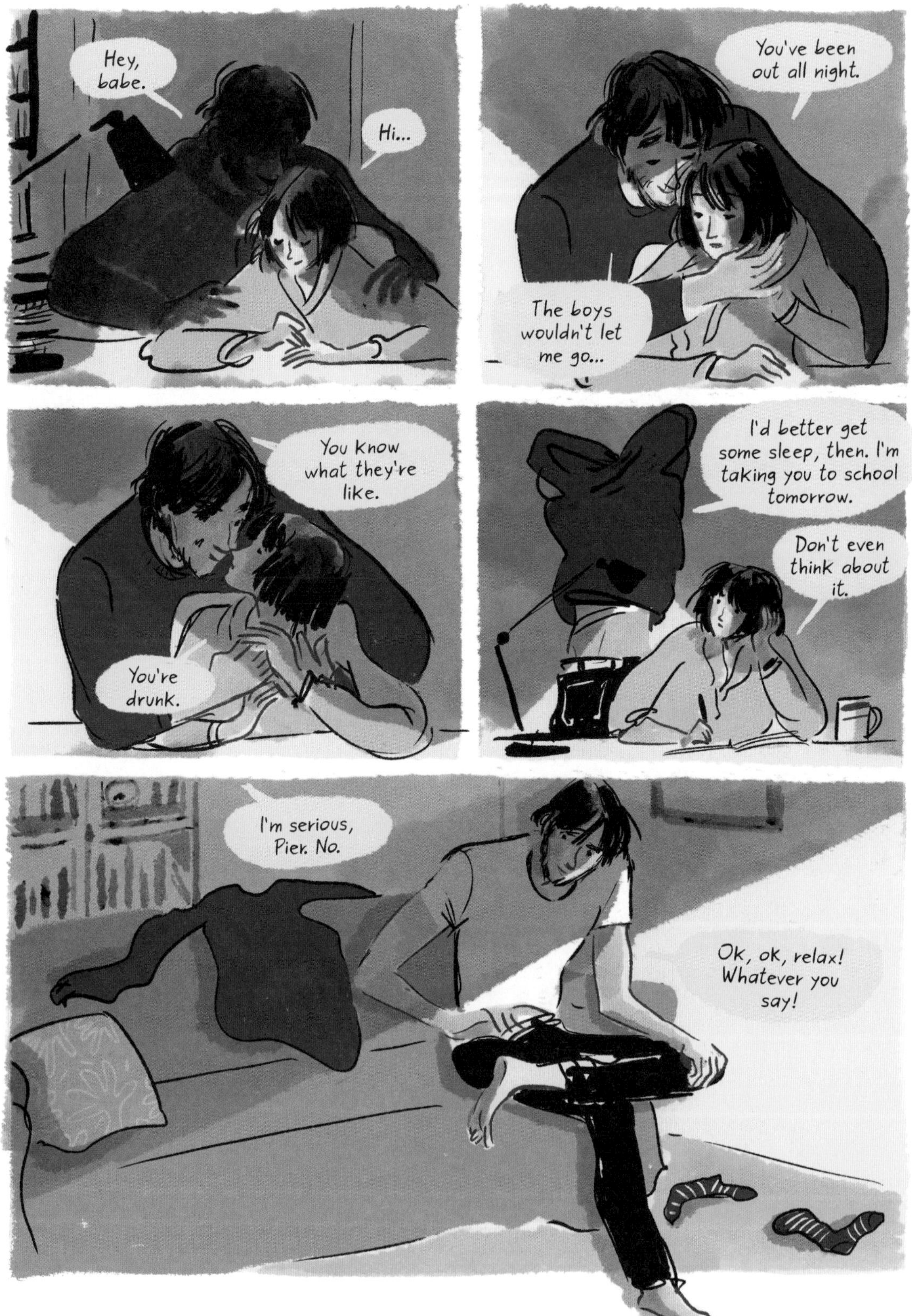
Hey, babe.
Hi...
You've been out all night.
The boys wouldn't let me go...
You know what they're like.
You're drunk.
I'd better get some sleep, then. I'm taking you to school tomorrow.
Don't even think about it.
I'm serious, Pier. No.
Ok, ok, relax! Whatever you say!

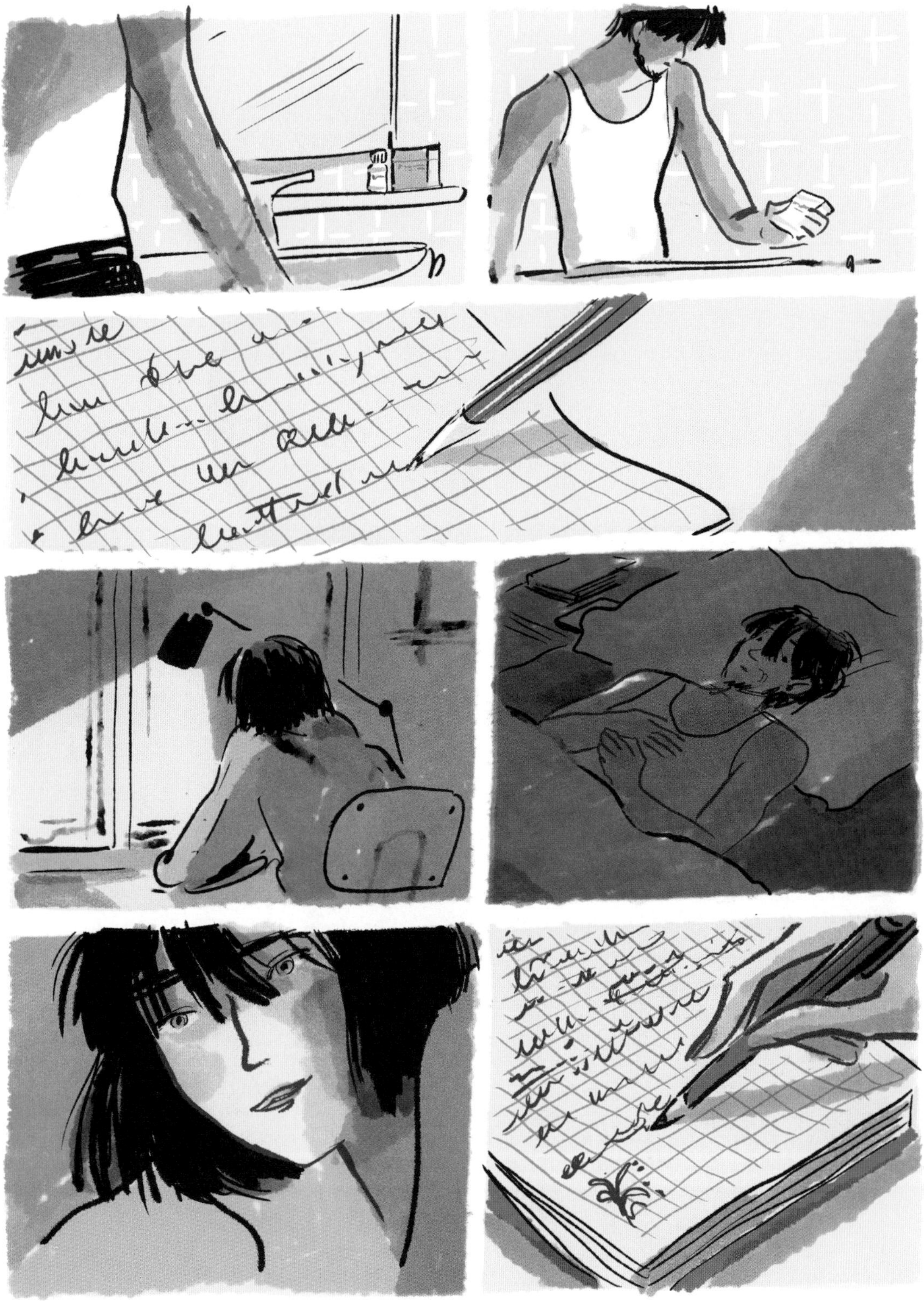

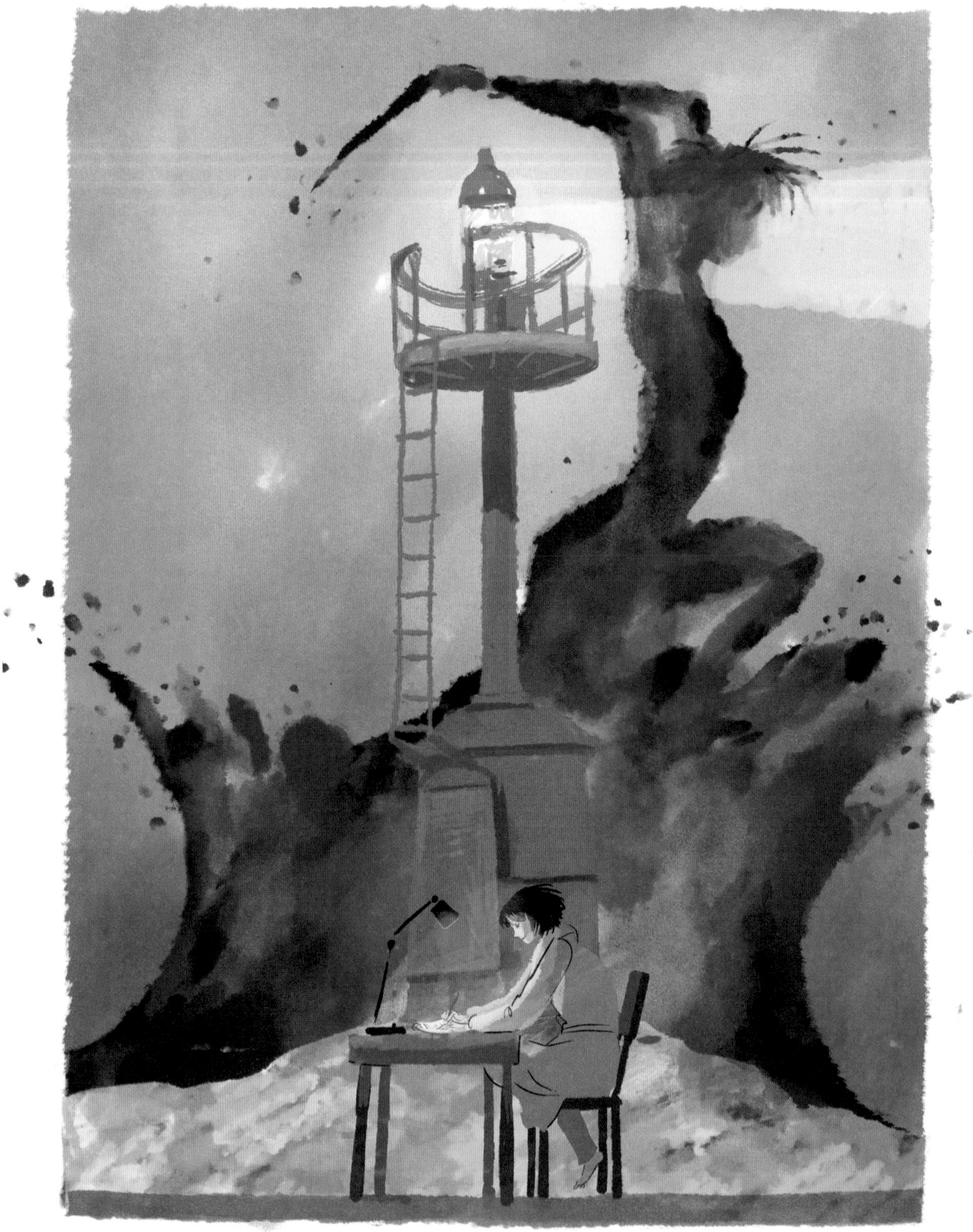

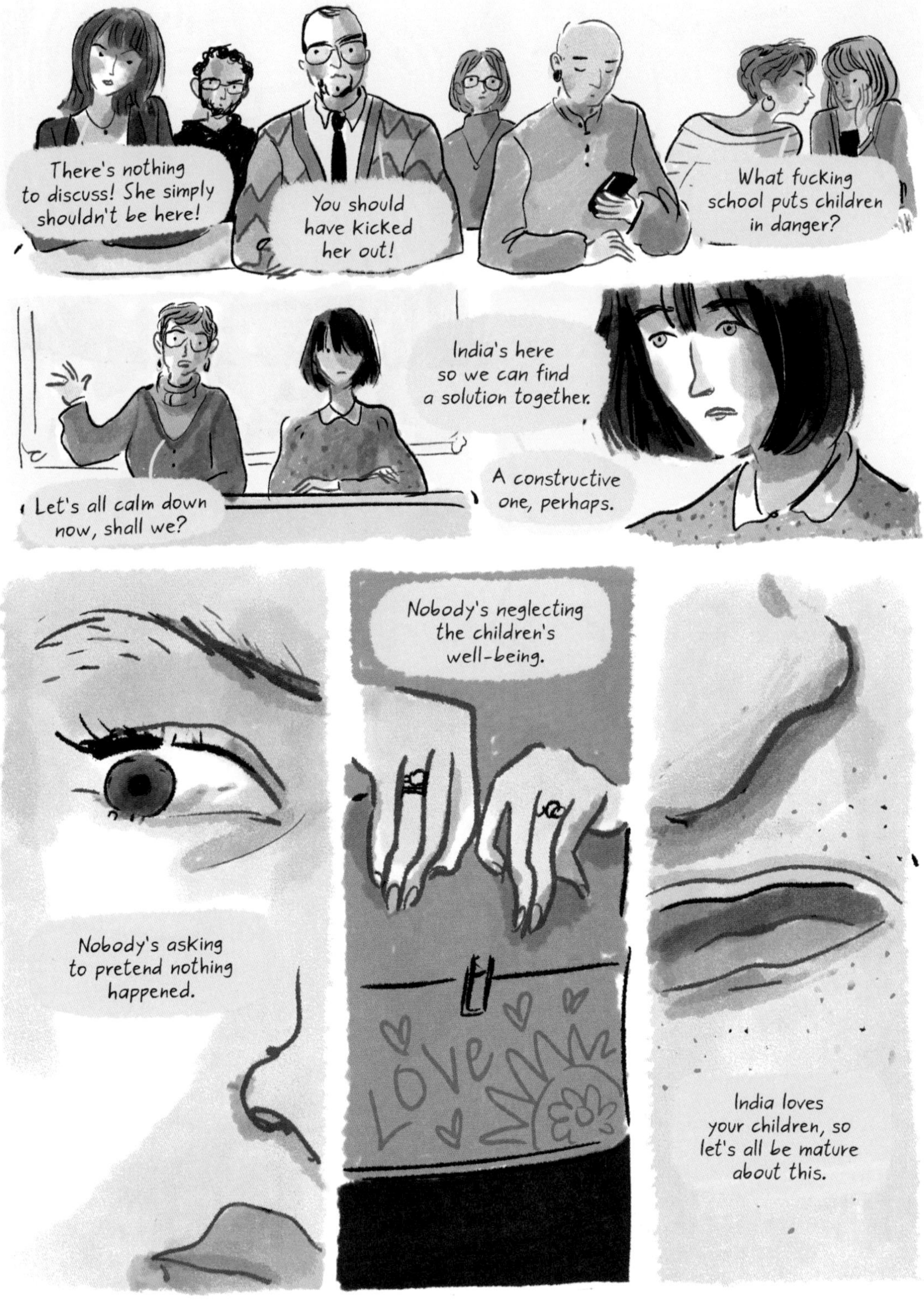
There's nothing to discuss! She simply shouldn't be here!
You should have kicked her out!
What fucking school puts children in danger?
Let's all calm down now, shall we?
India's here so we can find a solution together.
A constructive one, perhaps.
Nobody's asking to pretend nothing happened.
Nobody's neglecting the children's well-being.
LOVE
India loves your children, so let's all be mature about this.

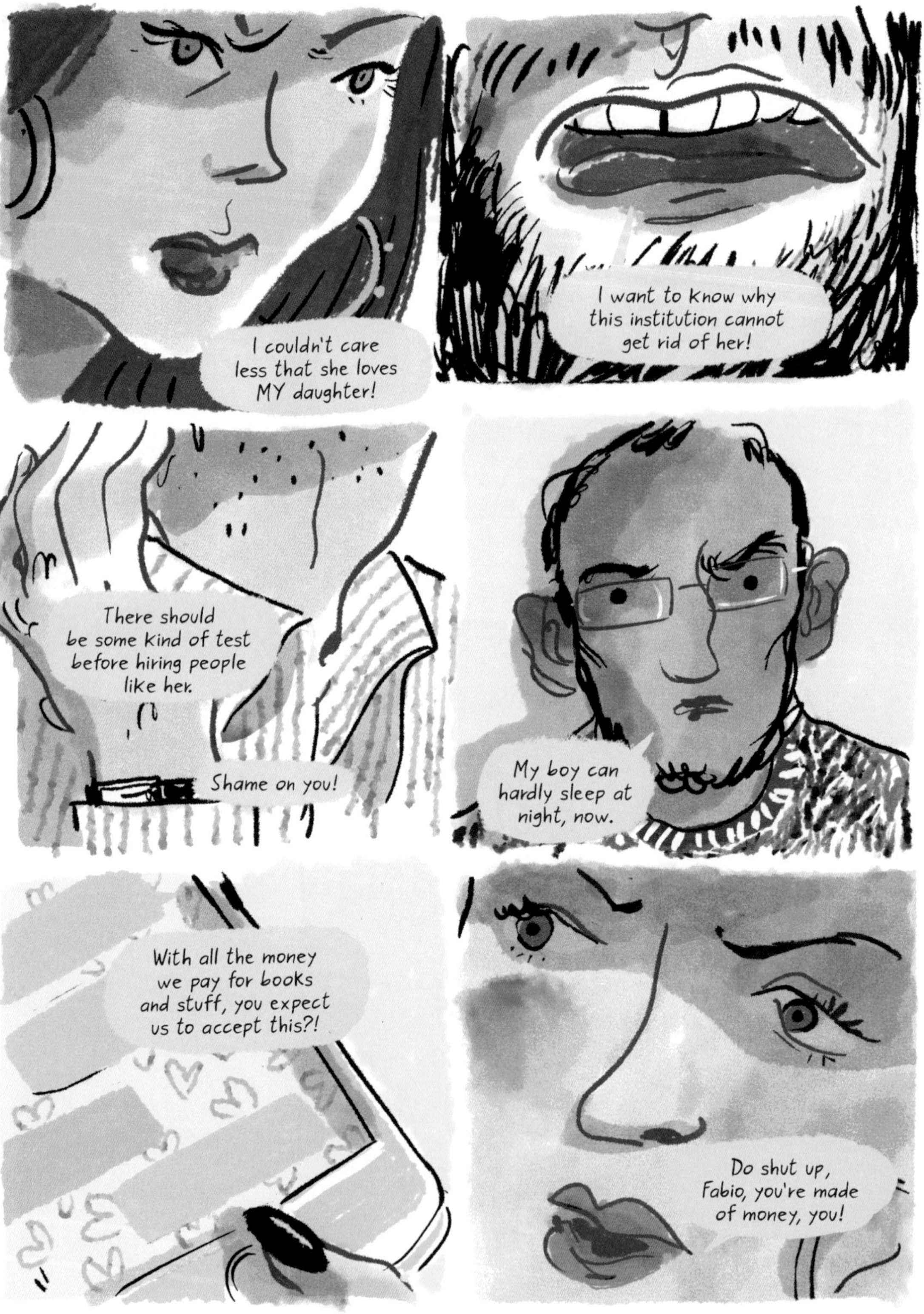
I couldn't care less that she loves MY daughter!
I want to know why this institution cannot get rid of her!
There should be some kind of test before hiring people like her.
Shame on you!
My boy can hardly sleep at night, now.
With all the money we pay for books and stuff, you expect us to accept this?!
Do shut up, Fabio, you're made of money, you!

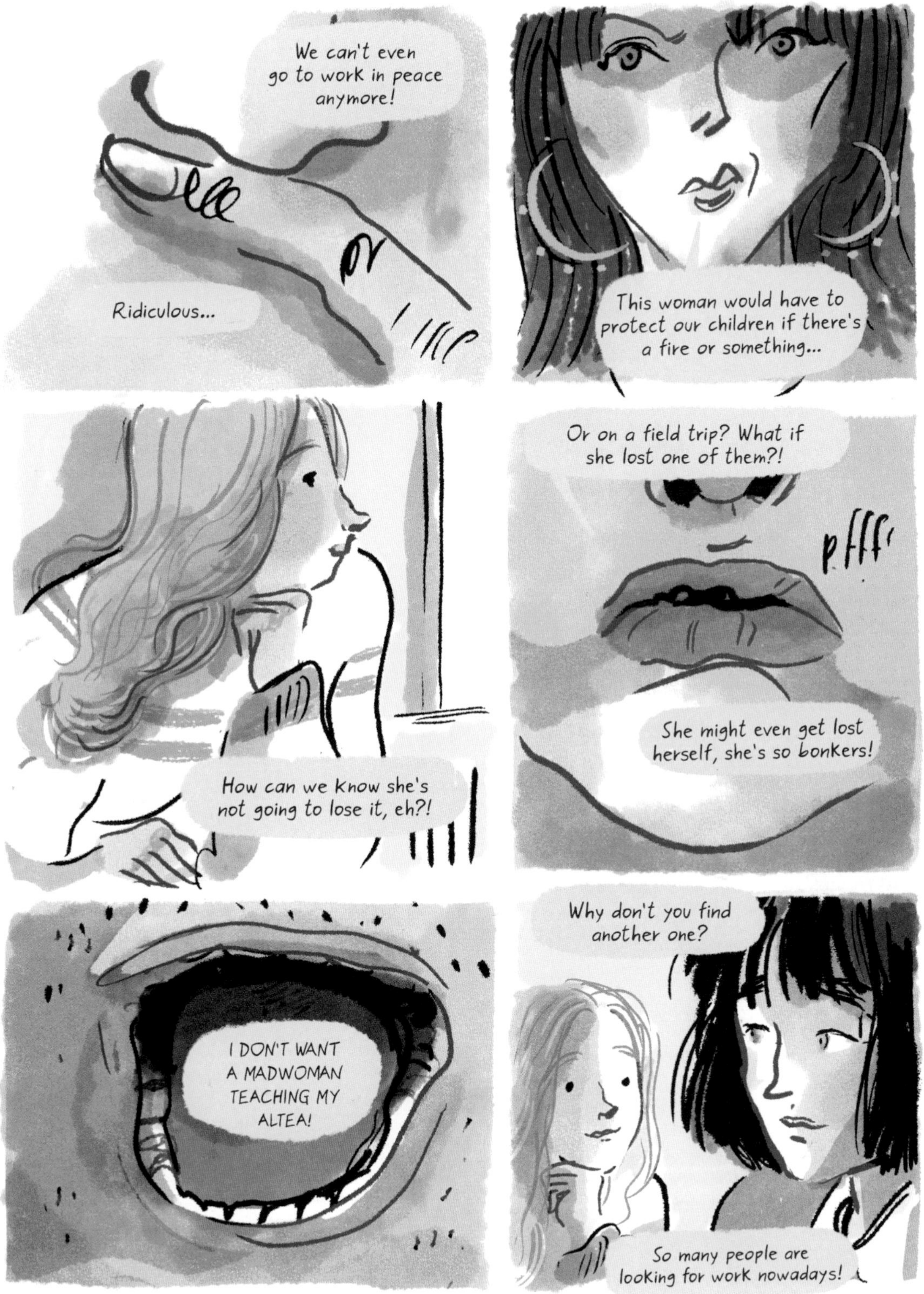
We can't even go to work in peace anymore!
Ridiculous...
This woman would have to protect our children if there's a fire or something...
How can we know she's not going to lose it, eh?!
Or on a field trip? What if she lost one of them?!
pfff
She might even get lost herself, she's so bonkers!
I DON'T WANT A MADWOMAN TEACHING MY ALTEA!
Why don't you find another one?
So many people are looking for work nowadays!

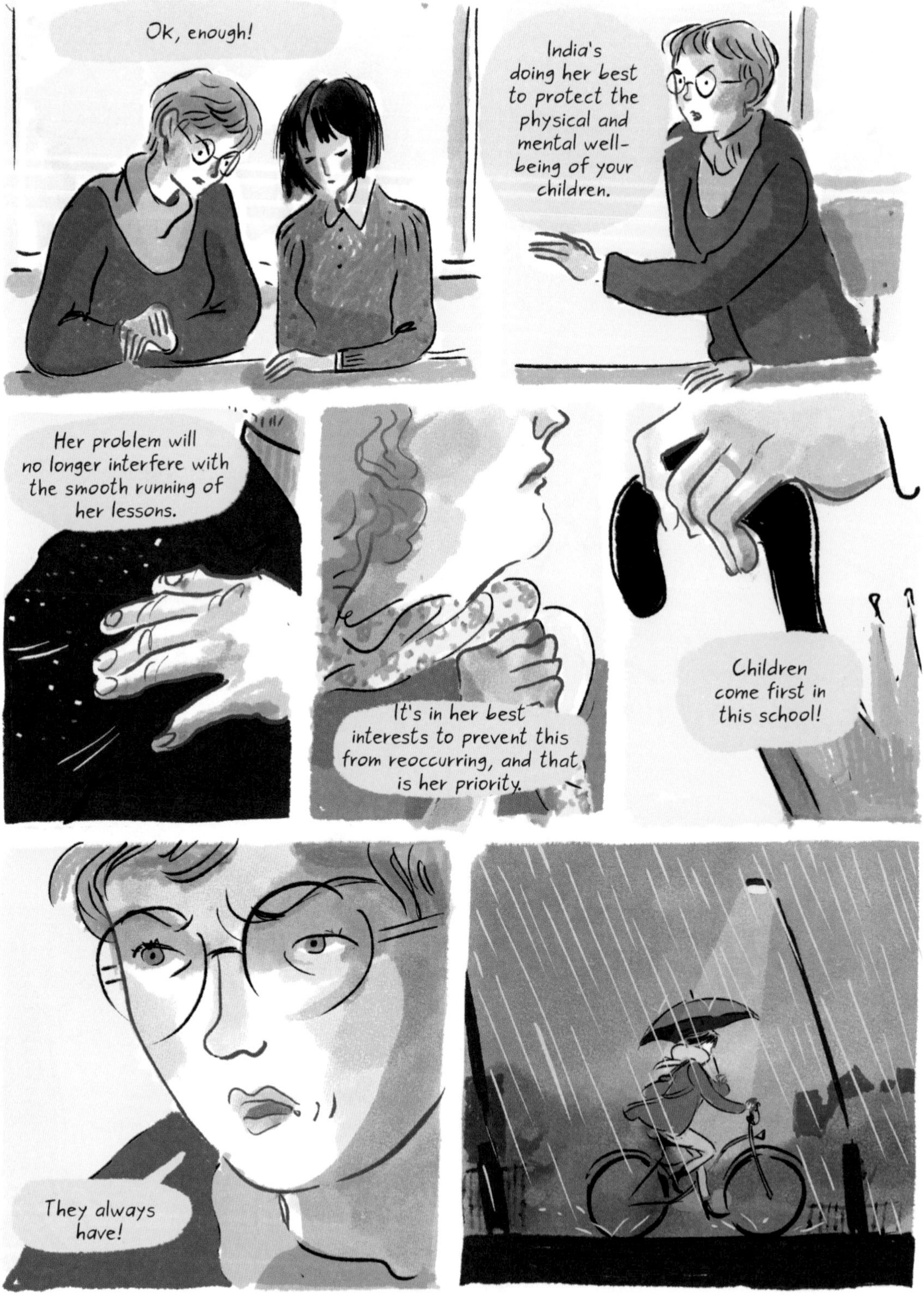
Ok, enough!
India's doing her best to protect the physical and mental well-being of your children.
Her problem will no longer interfere with the smooth running of her lessons.
It's in her best interests to prevent this from reoccurring, and that is her priority.
Children come first in this school!
They always have!

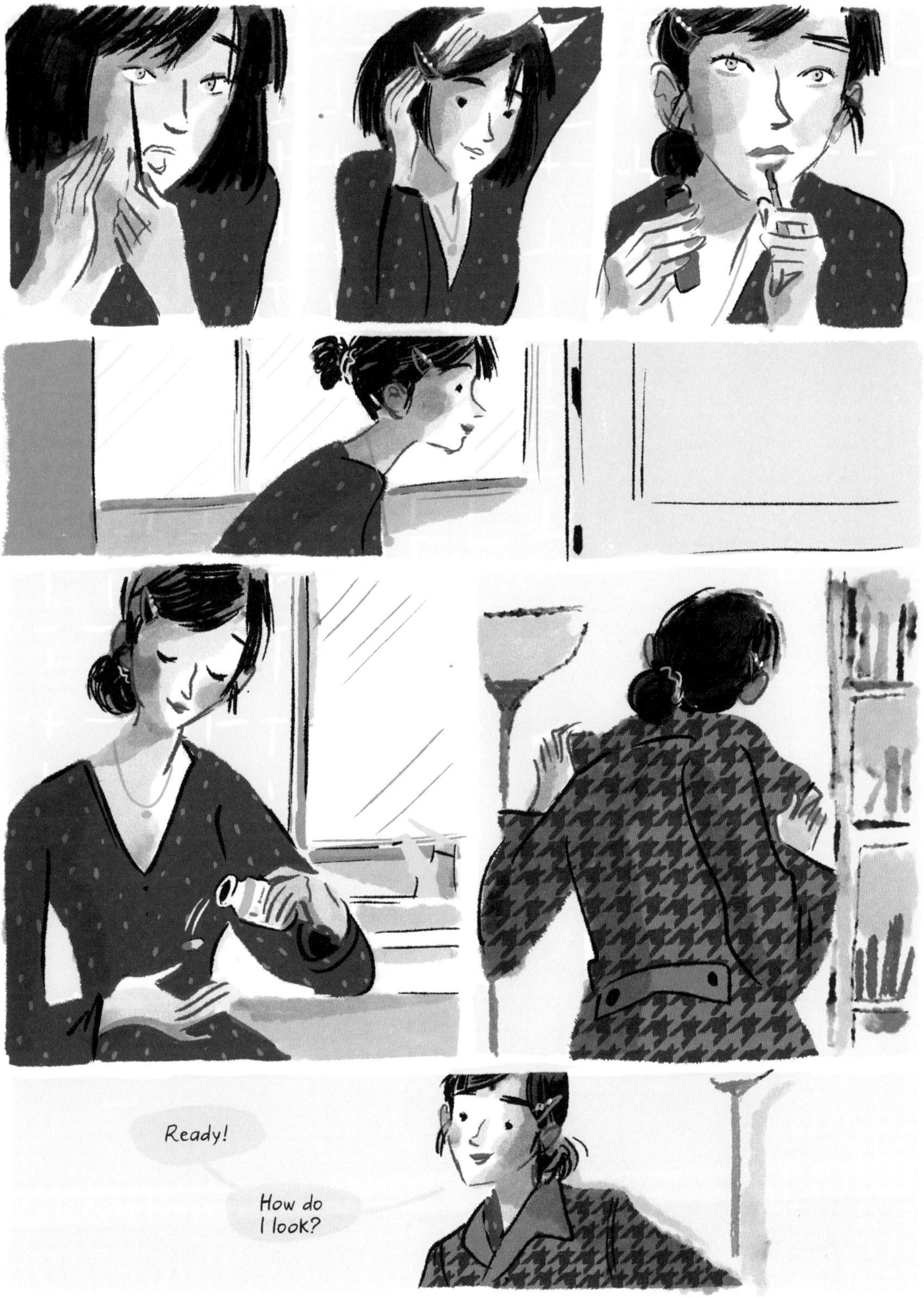
Ready!
How do
I look?

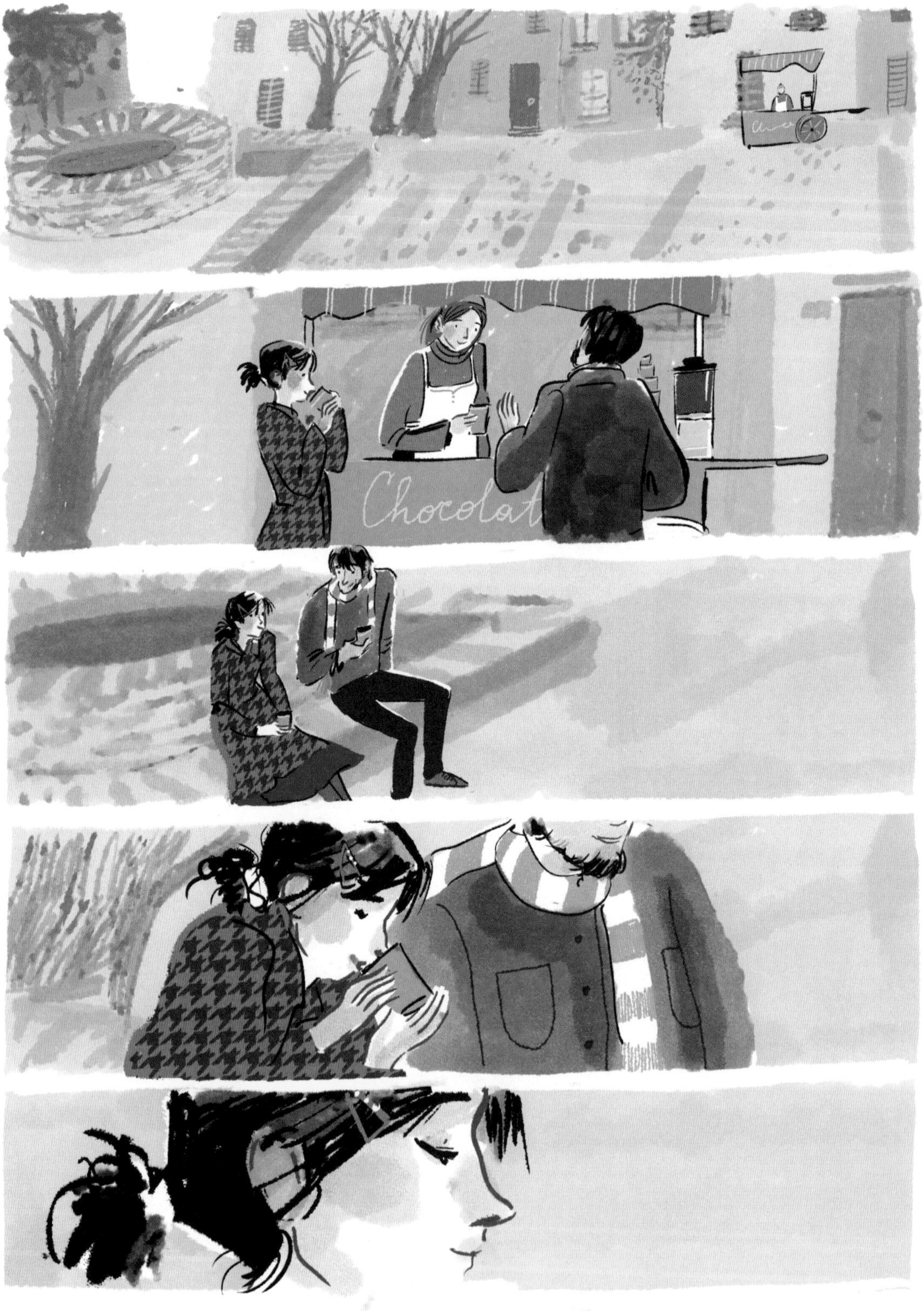
Chocolat

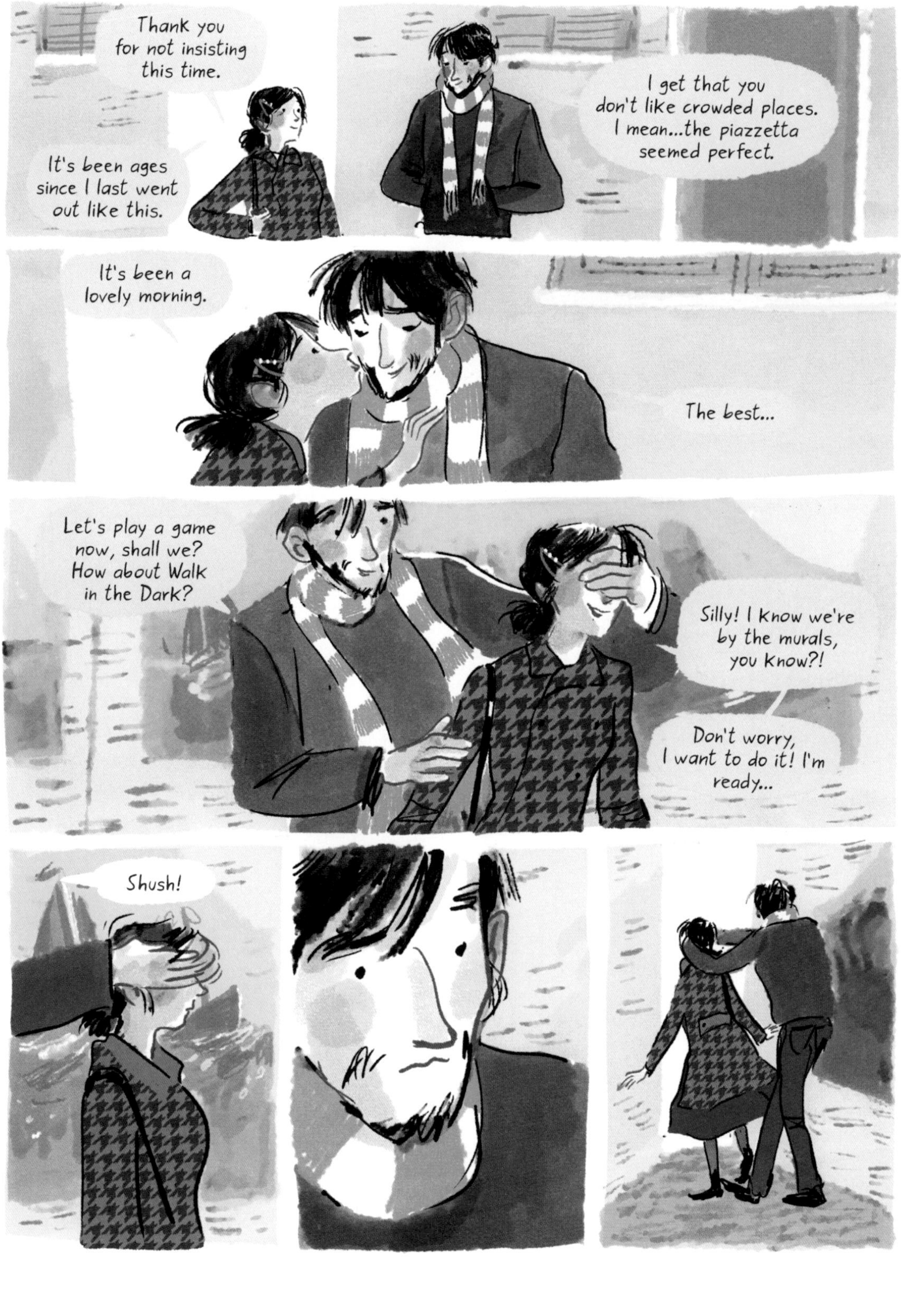
Thank you for not insisting this time.
It's been ages since I last went out like this.
I get that you don't like crowded places. I mean...the piazzetta seemed perfect.
It's been a lovely morning.
The best...
Let's play a game now, shall we? How about Walk in the Dark?
Silly! I know we're by the murals, you know?!
Don't worry, I want to do it! I'm ready...
Shush!

#01 - I DON'T TRAVEL ENOUGH

When I'm not traveling, a long filament of tension rises from the earth and tangles up inside my chest. I belong to the world that moves.
I would like to touch the poetry of Japan, the fiery maple trees of Canada, the eternal ice of Iceland, where man owns nothing.

#02 - I NEVER CALL GIADA

When we were kids, we'd speak every day. She moved away, but that's no excuse. I'm like a child losing a favorite toy. Or a best pal. They may forget, but the memory soon comes back to haunt them, taking away their sleep.

#03 - TURNING THIRTY

I'll turn that corner in a few months. Everyone's always telling me how thirty is a milestone for a woman, but what do they know about me, really? What if I'm not strong enough? What if I wasted more time than everyone else? What if yesterday's ambitions are too superficial today?

#04 - I READ VERY LITTLE

That's not true, I read a lot, but not as much as I'd like. I've yet to have a chat with Austen, Murakami, Zimmer Bradley...Not perusing enough pages leaves me with a sense of incompleteness and then I cannot think freely.

#05 - TEACHING

I love my job and couldn't live without it. Lately, however, the parents have become a real hassle and the children are ever so restless. I am no longer free to teach and address the children as I would like. What's the point then?

#06 - USELESSNESS

I look around and see dying oceans, desperate lives drowning in the hands of the smallest of men. What about me? Am I doing anything to stop this? Indifference and panic disorder are very similar: quiet and unnoticed, they creep up until they ask you to "foot the bill." Then it's too late.

#07 - NOISE

I'd like more quiet in my life. More still, yet constructive, moments. More moments FULL OF NOTHINGNESS. I'm tired of hearing the silence only when I'm in pain.

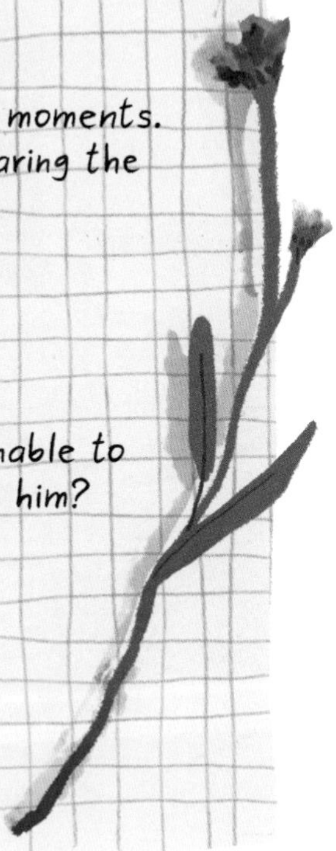

#08 - LEAVING

His leaving is an awareness that he still exists, but I'm unable to see him when I want. Does my self-confidence leave with him? Does it, really?

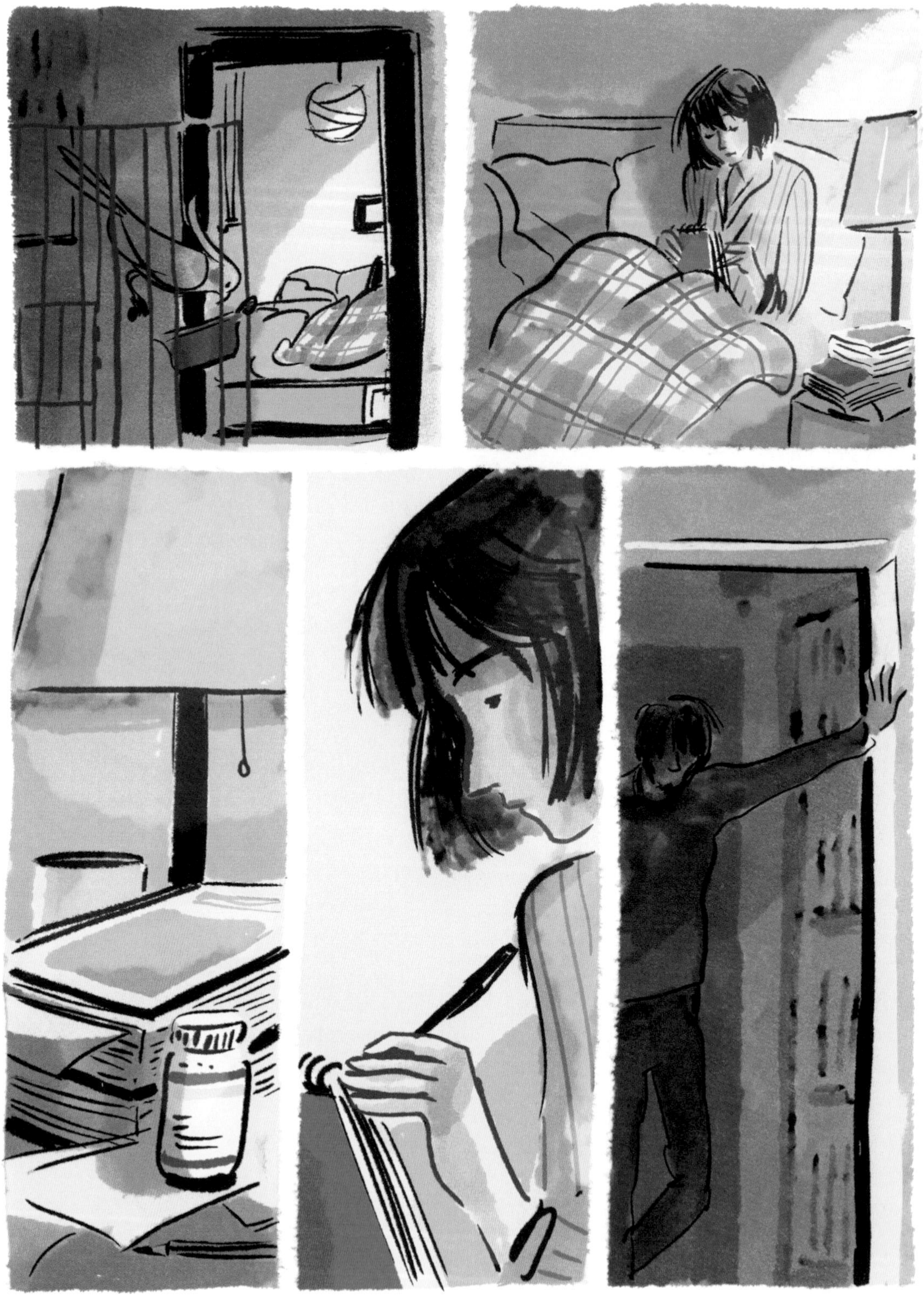

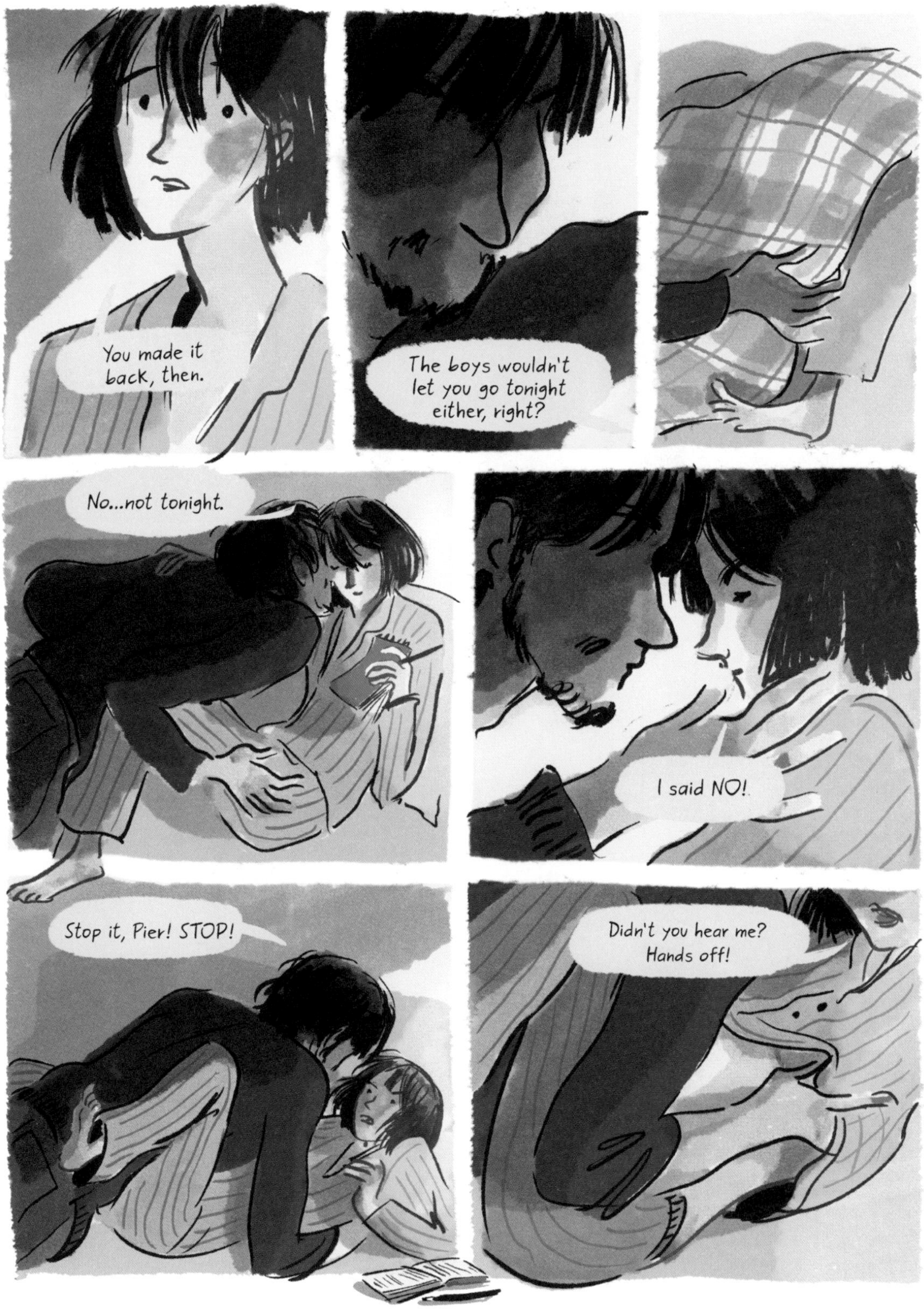
You made it back, then.
The boys wouldn't let you go tonight either, right?
No...not tonight.
I said NO!
Stop it, Pier! STOP!
Didn't you hear me? Hands off!

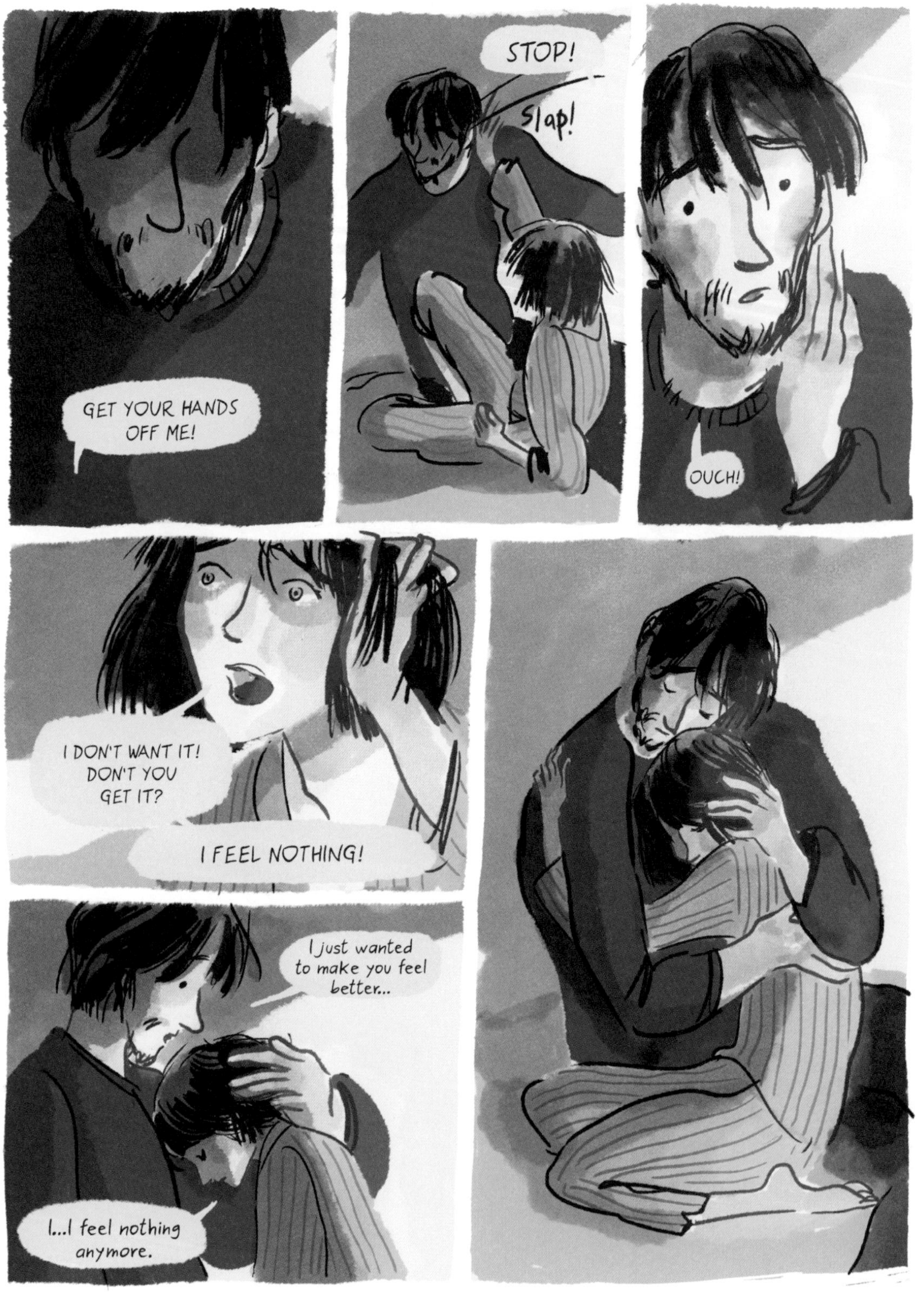
GET YOUR HANDS OFF ME!
STOP!
Slap!
OUCH!
I DON'T WANT IT! DON'T YOU GET IT?
I FEEL NOTHING!
I just wanted to make you feel better...
I...I feel nothing anymore.

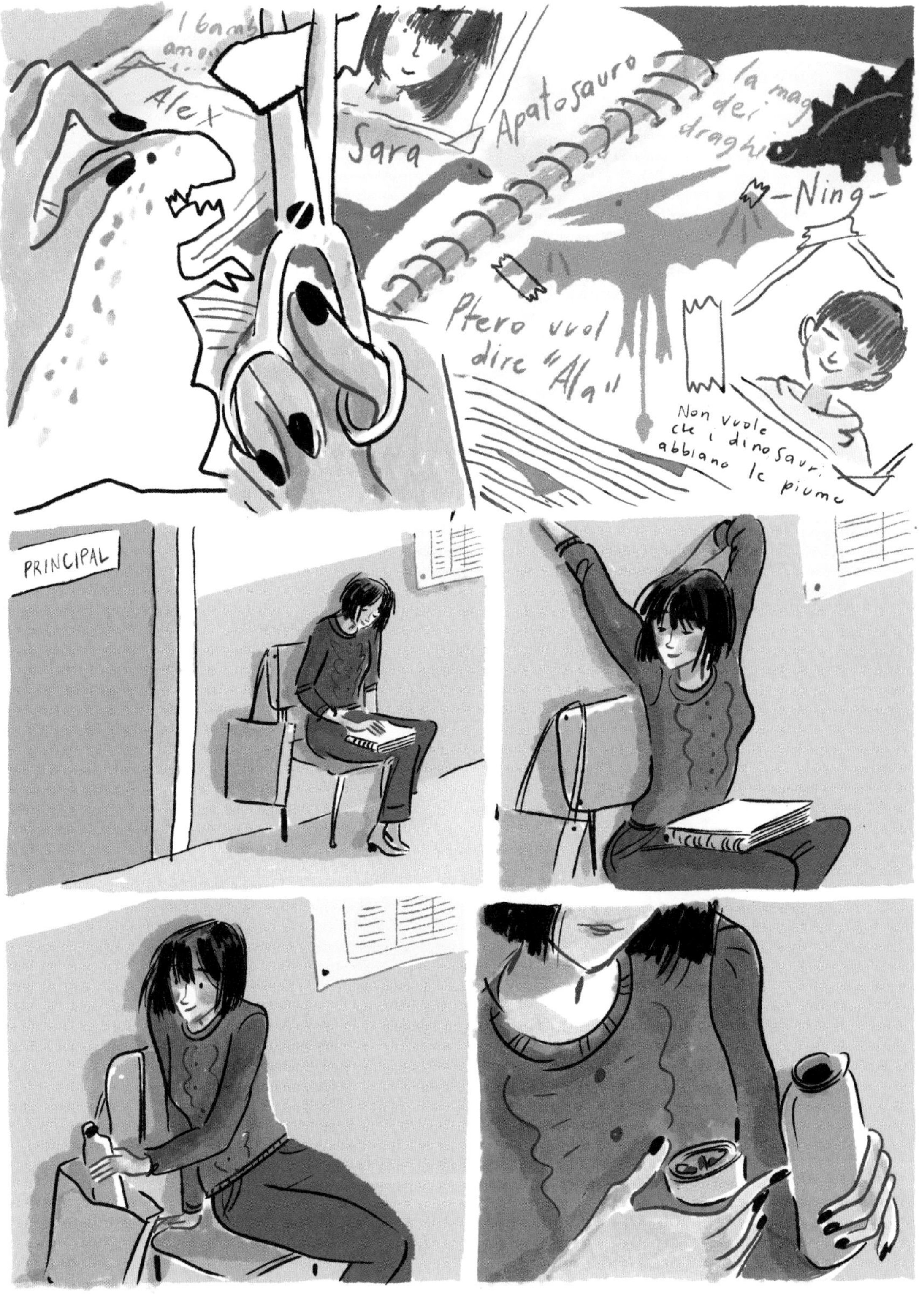
Alex
Sara
Apatosauro
dei
draghi
Ning
Ptero vuol dire "Ala"
Non vuole che i dinosauri abbiano le piume
PRINCIPAL

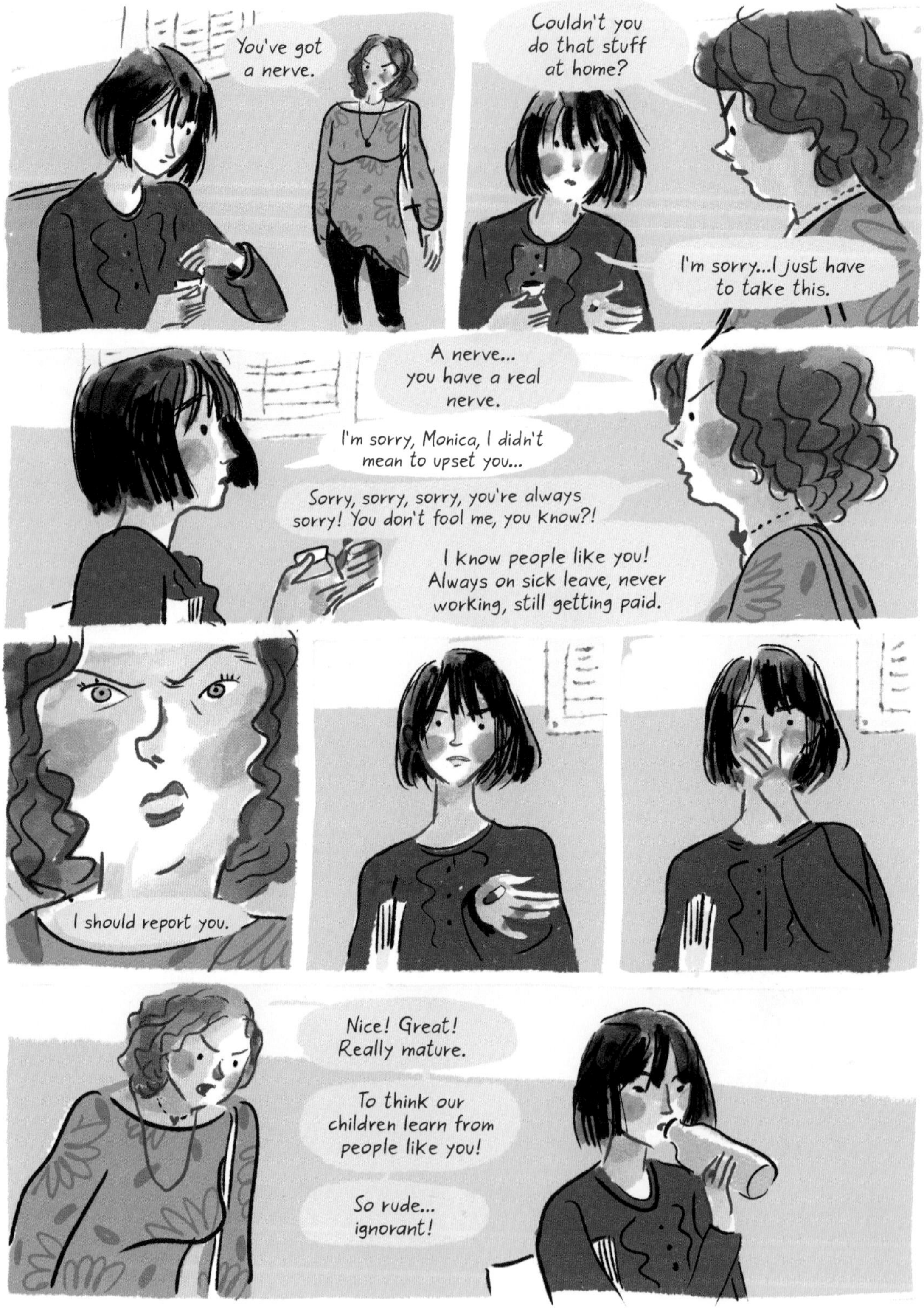
You've got a nerve.
Couldn't you do that stuff at home?
I'm sorry...I just have to take this.
A nerve... you have a real nerve.
I'm sorry, Monica, I didn't mean to upset you...
Sorry, sorry, sorry, you're always sorry! You don't fool me, you know?!
I know people like you! Always on sick leave, never working, still getting paid.
I should report you.
Nice! Great! Really mature.
To think our children learn from people like you!
So rude... ignorant!

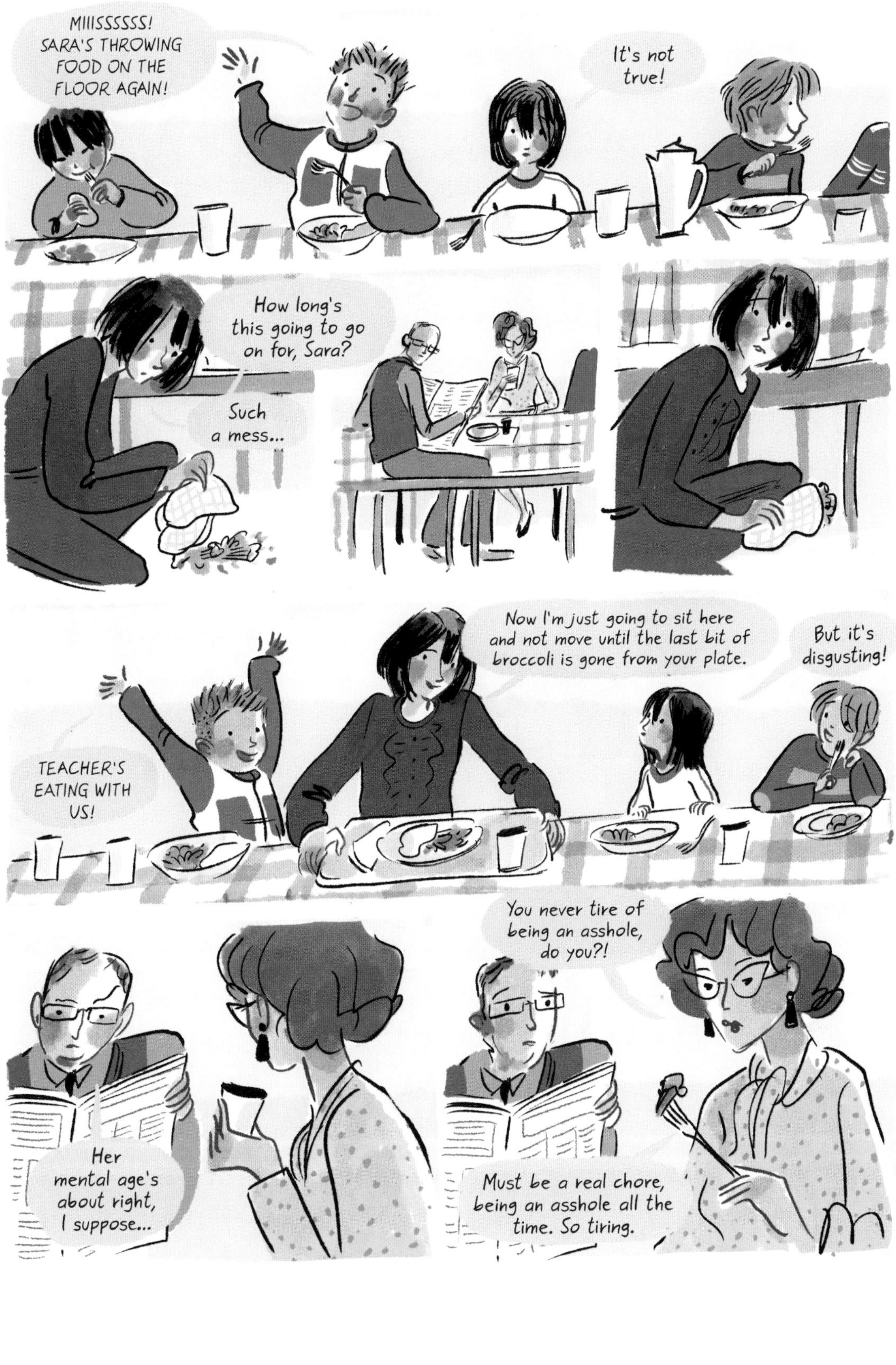
MIIISSSSSS! SARA'S THROWING FOOD ON THE FLOOR AGAIN!
It's not true!
How long's this going to go on for, Sara?
Such a mess...
Now I'm just going to sit here and not move until the last bit of broccoli is gone from your plate.
But it's disgusting!
TEACHER'S EATING WITH US!
Her mental age's about right, I suppose...
You never tire of being an asshole, do you?!
Must be a real chore, being an asshole all the time. So tiring.

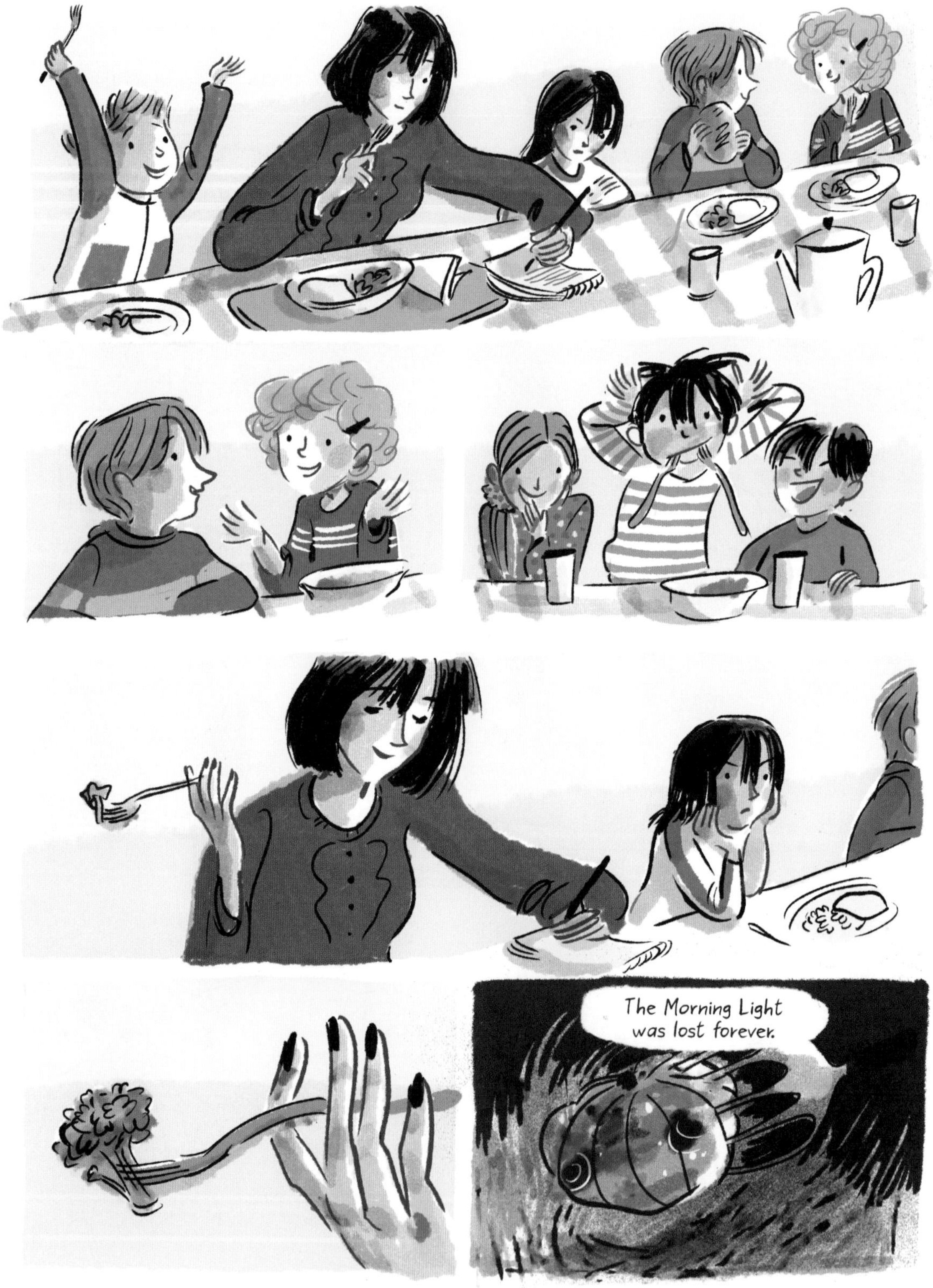
The Morning Light
was lost forever.

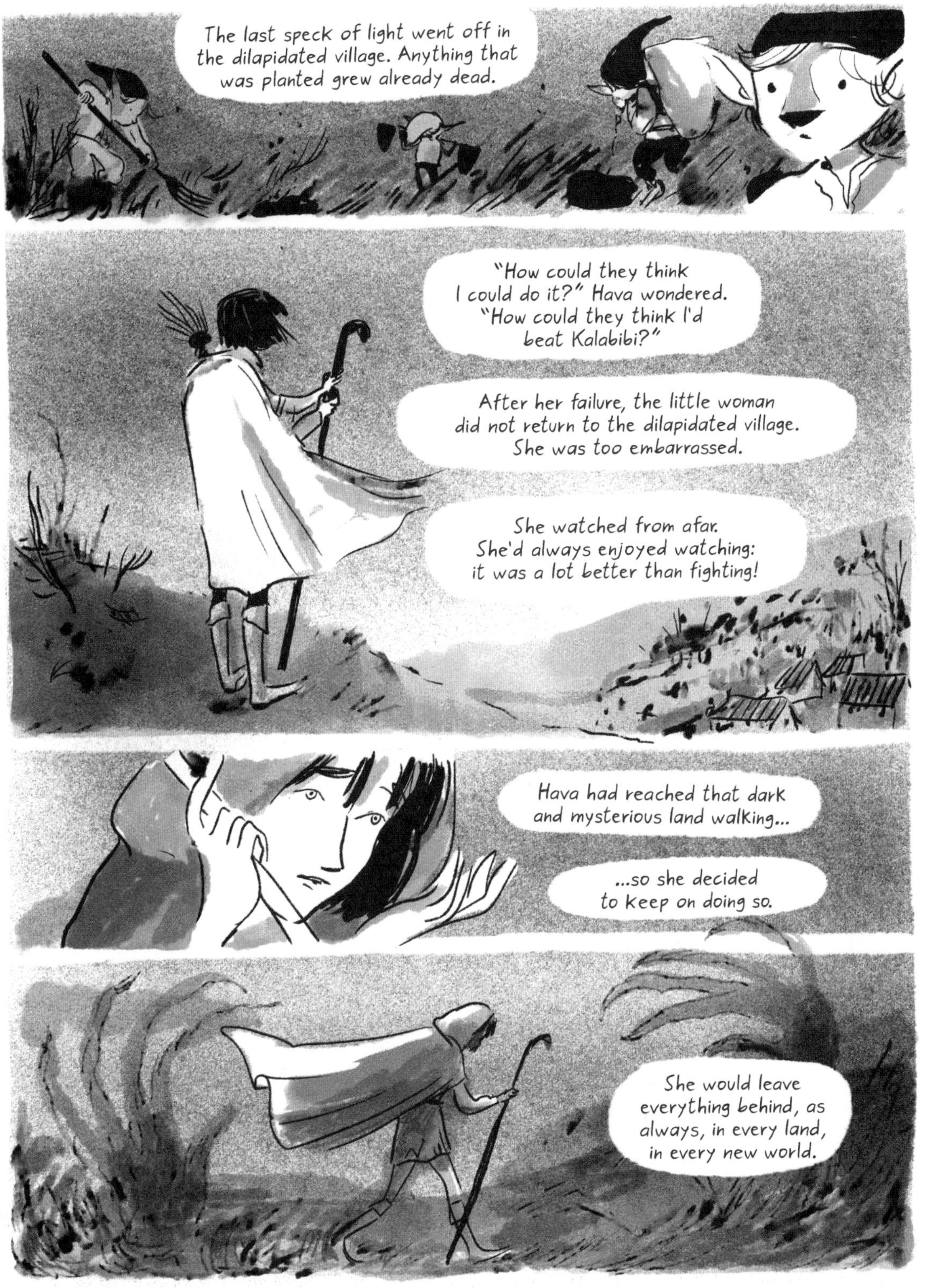
The last speck of light went off in the dilapidated village. Anything that was planted grew already dead.
"How could they think I could do it?" Hava wondered. "How could they think I'd beat Kalabibi?"
After her failure, the little woman did not return to the dilapidated village. She was too embarrassed.
She watched from afar. She'd always enjoyed watching: it was a lot better than fighting!
Hava had reached that dark and mysterious land walking...
...so she decided to keep on doing so.
She would leave everything behind, as always, in every land, in every new world.

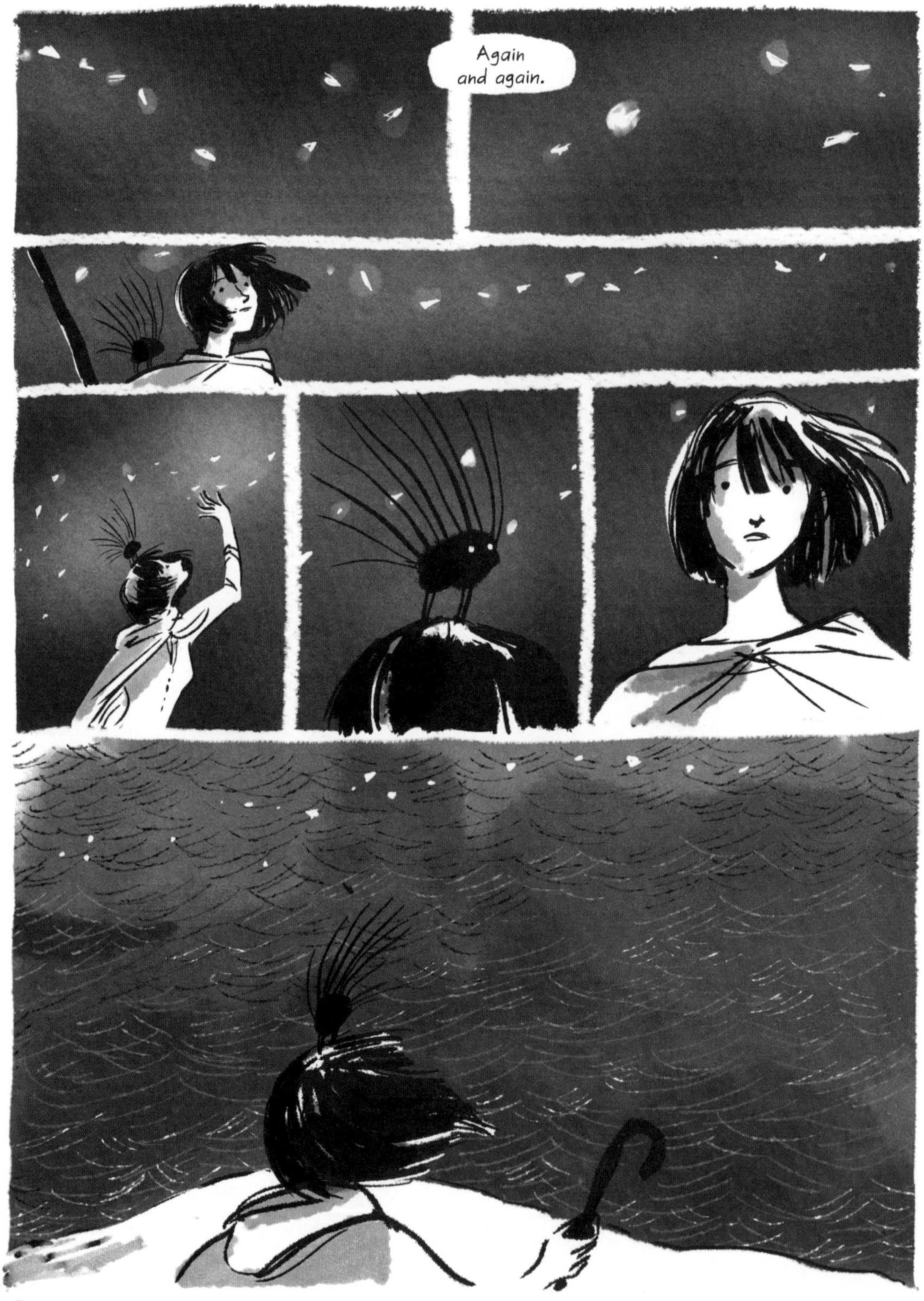
Again and again.

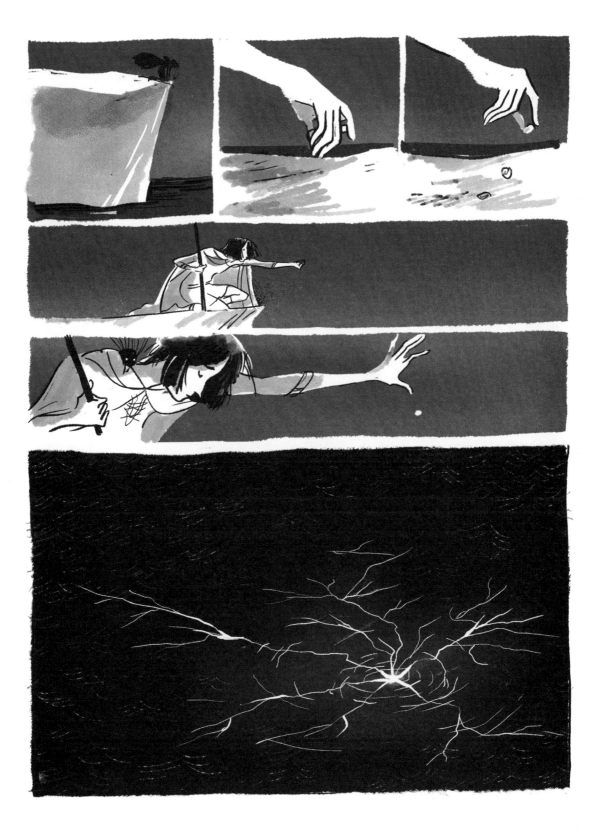

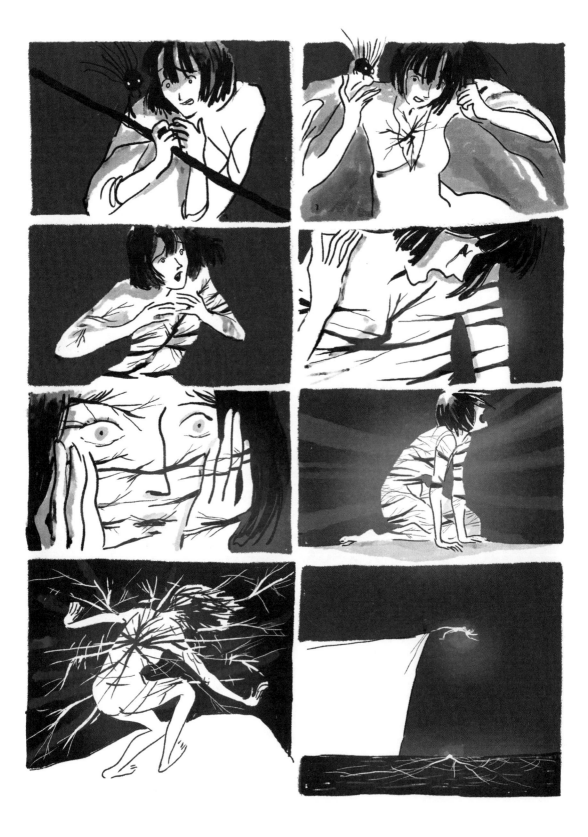

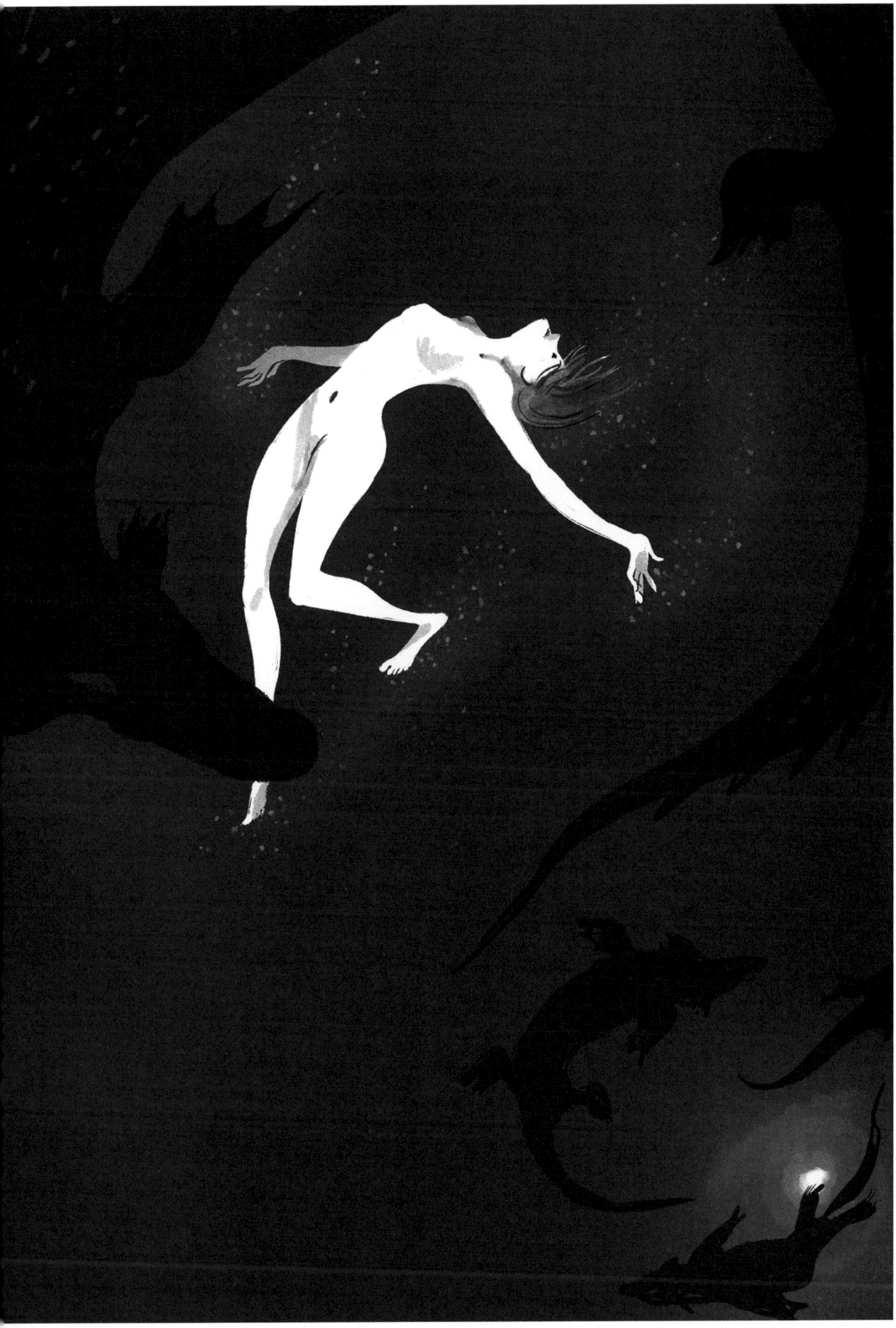

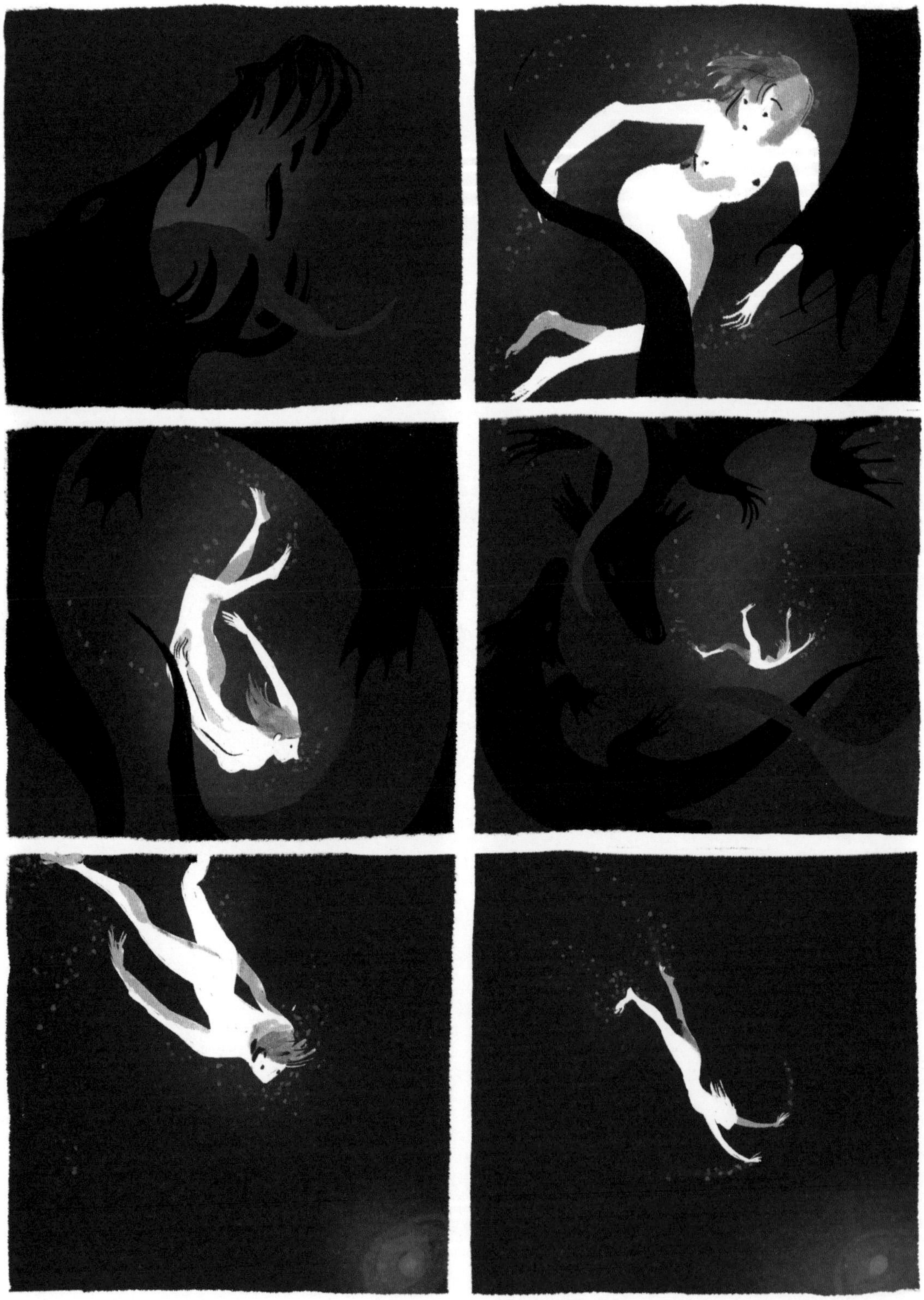

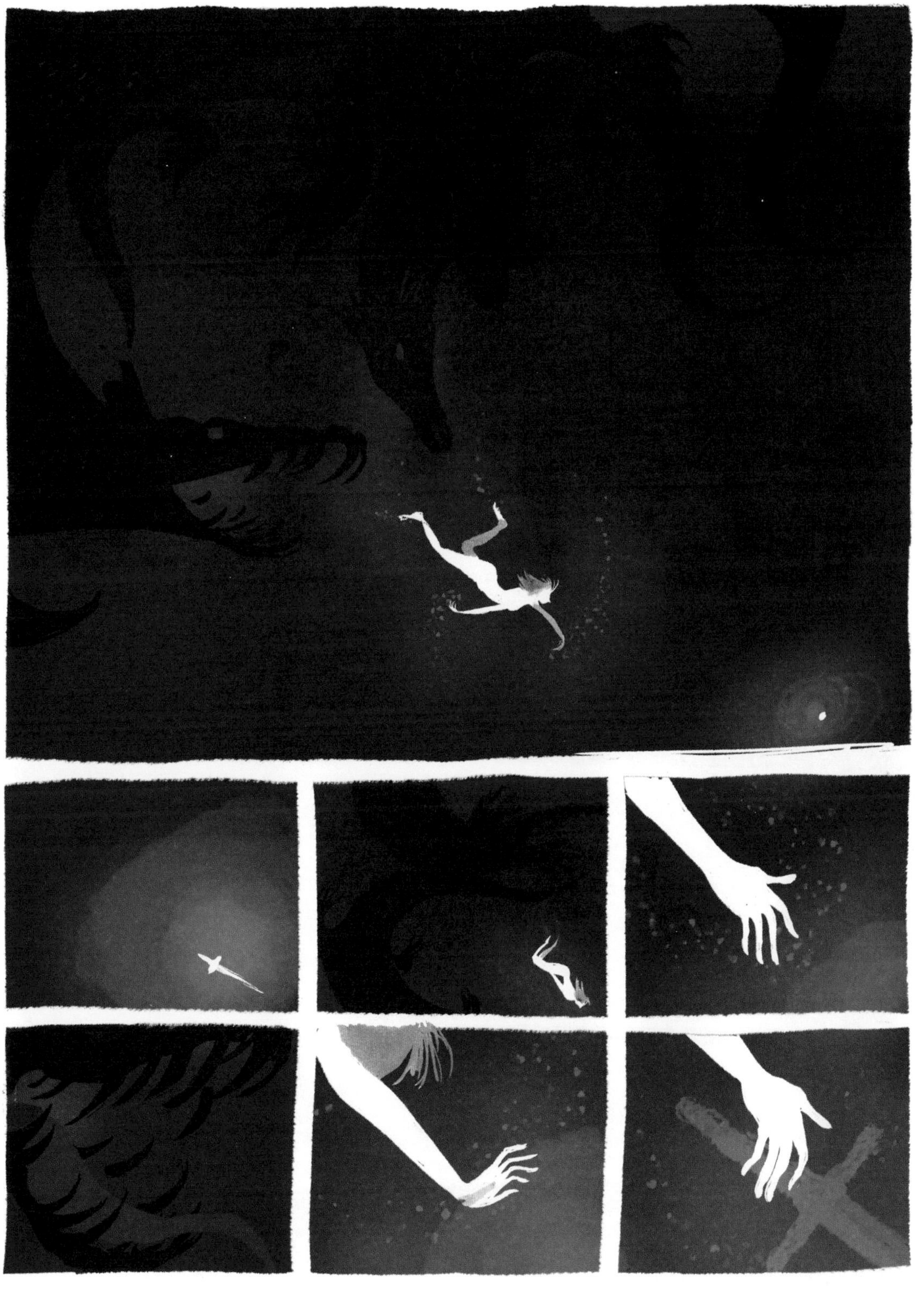

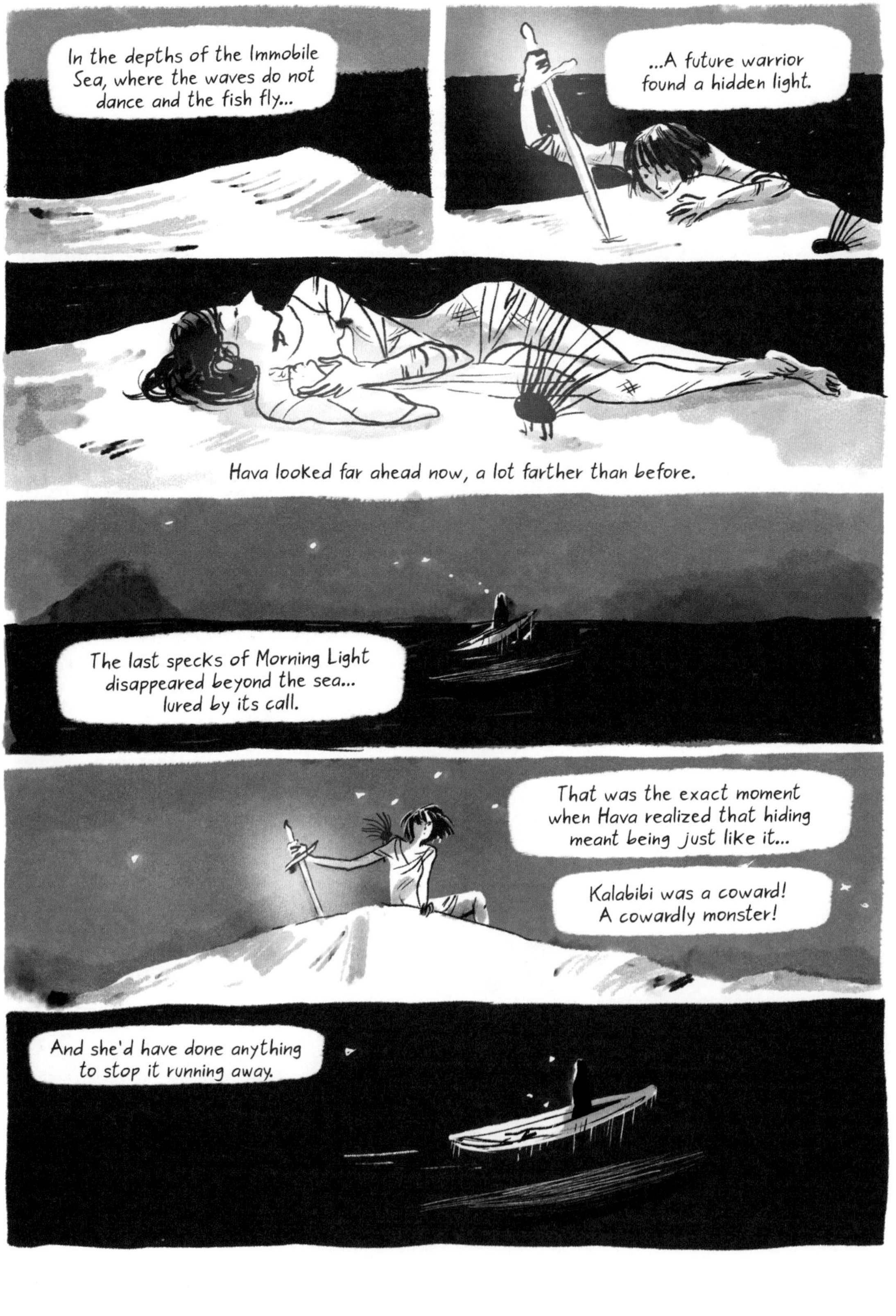
In the depths of the Immobile Sea, where the waves do not dance and the fish fly...
...A future warrior found a hidden light.
Hava looked far ahead now, a lot farther than before.
The last specks of Morning Light disappeared beyond the sea... lured by its call.
That was the exact moment when Hava realized that hiding meant being just like it...
Kalabibi was a coward! A cowardly monster!
And she'd have done anything to stop it running away.

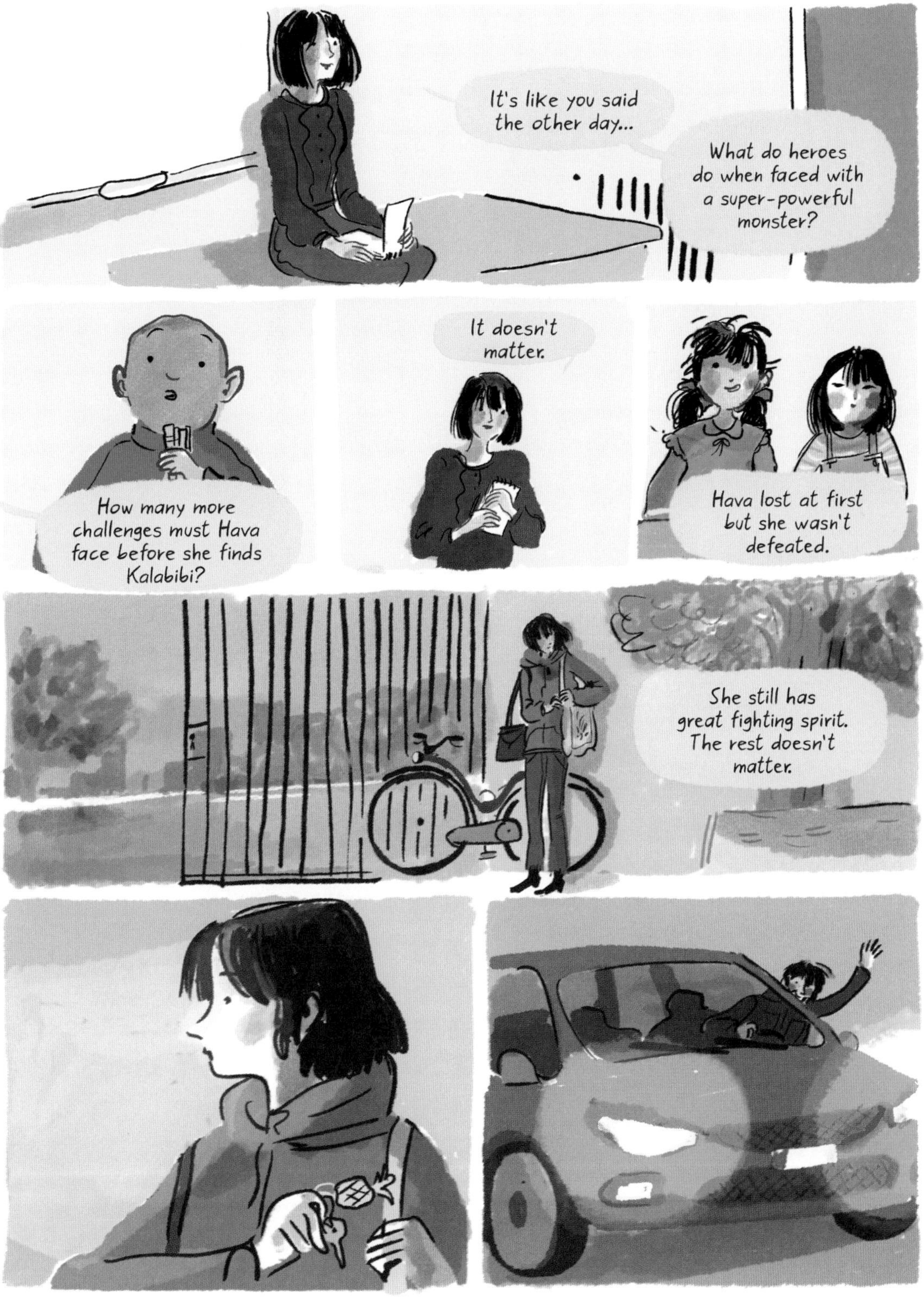
It's like you said the other day...
What do heroes do when faced with a super-powerful monster?
How many more challenges must Hava face before she finds Kalabibi?
It doesn't matter.
Hava lost at first but she wasn't defeated.
She still has great fighting spirit. The rest doesn't matter.

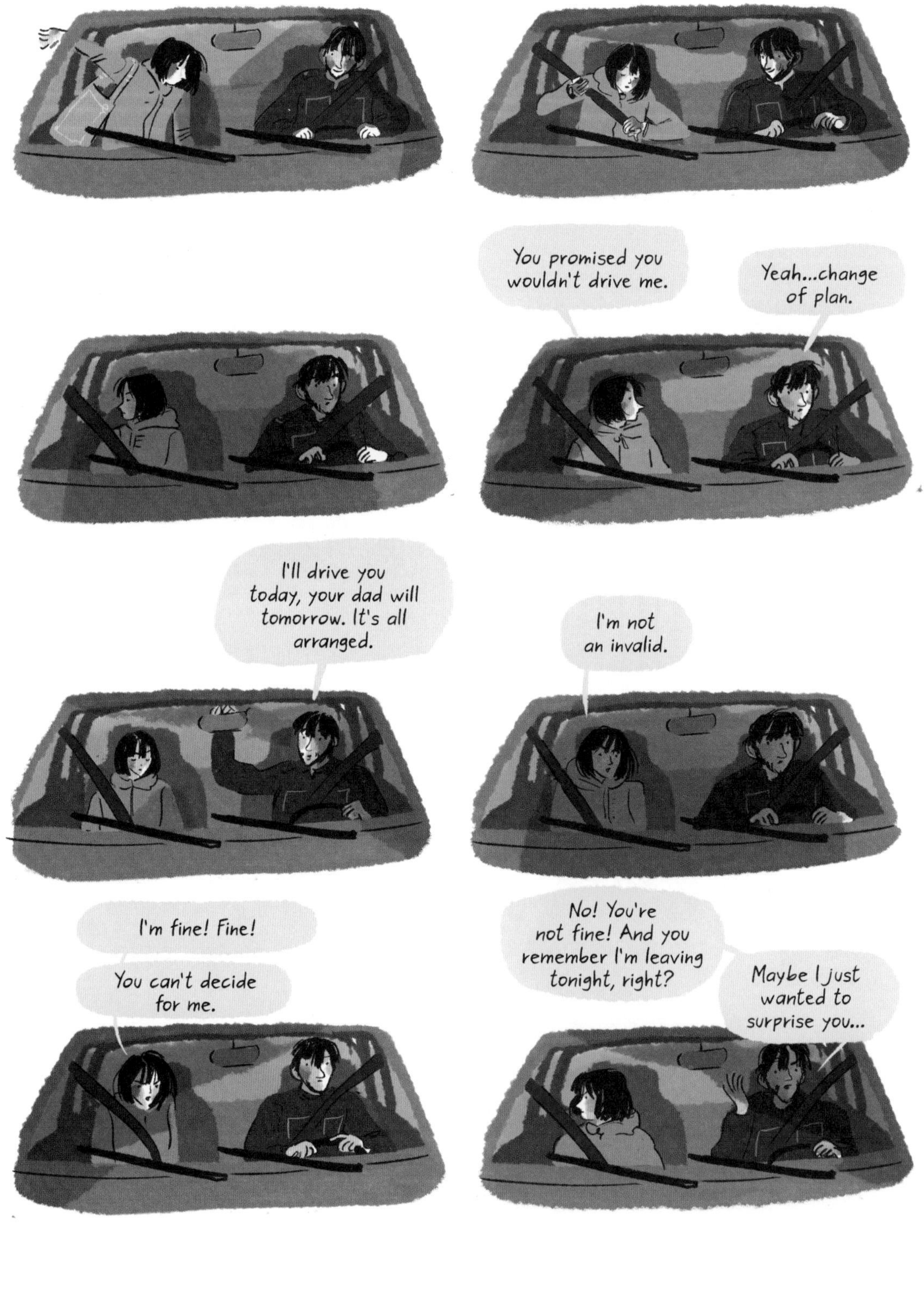
You promised you wouldn't drive me.
Yeah...change of plan.
I'll drive you today, your dad will tomorrow. It's all arranged.
I'm not an invalid.
I'm fine! Fine!
You can't decide for me.
No! You're not fine! And you remember I'm leaving tonight, right?
Maybe I just wanted to surprise you...

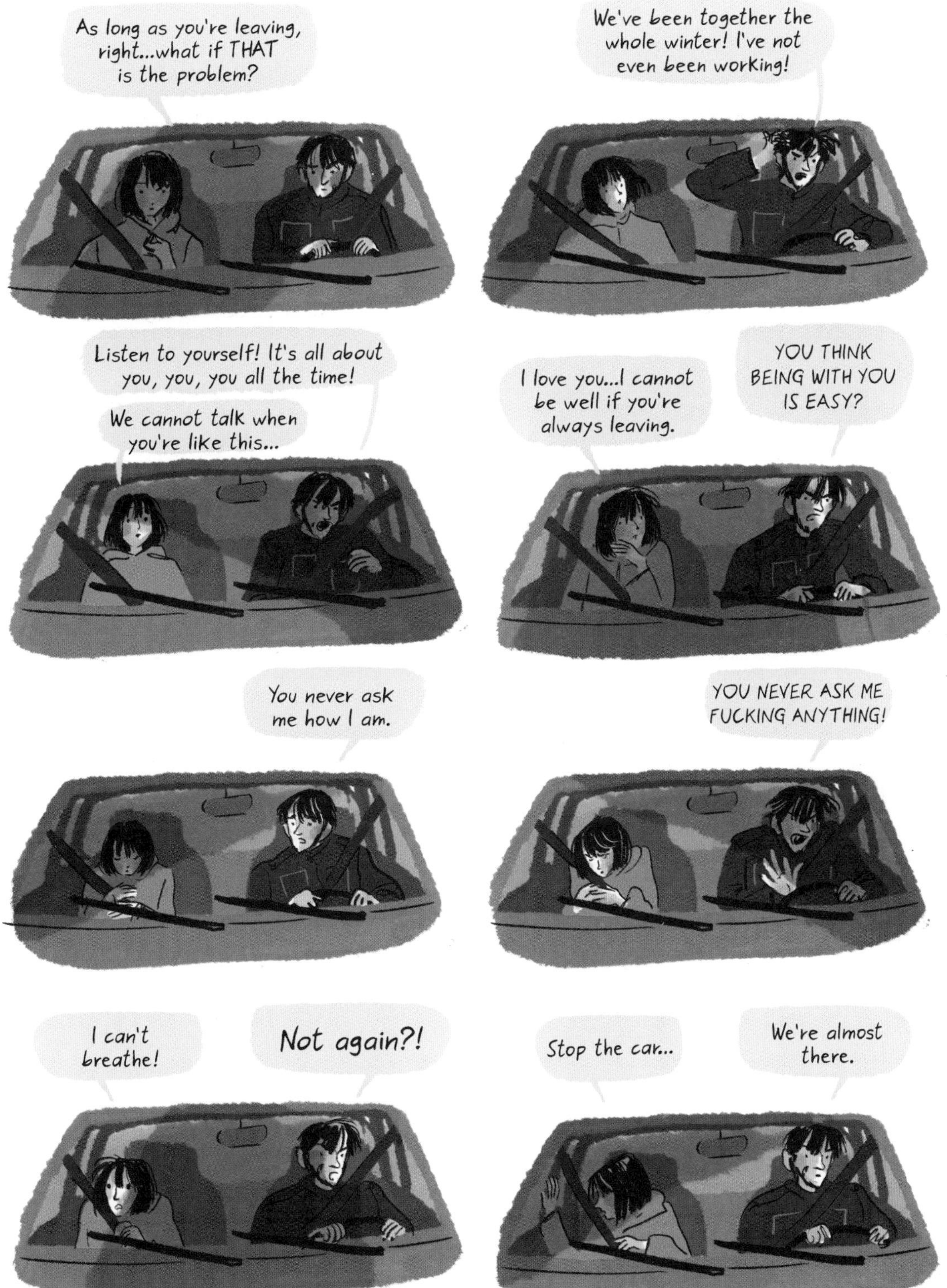
As long as you're leaving, right...what if THAT is the problem?
We've been together the whole winter! I've not even been working!
Listen to yourself! It's all about you, you, you all the time!
We cannot talk when you're like this...
I love you...I cannot be well if you're always leaving.
YOU THINK BEING WITH YOU IS EASY?
You never ask me how I am.
YOU NEVER ASK ME FUCKING ANYTHING!
I can't breathe!
Not again?!
Stop the car...
We're almost there.

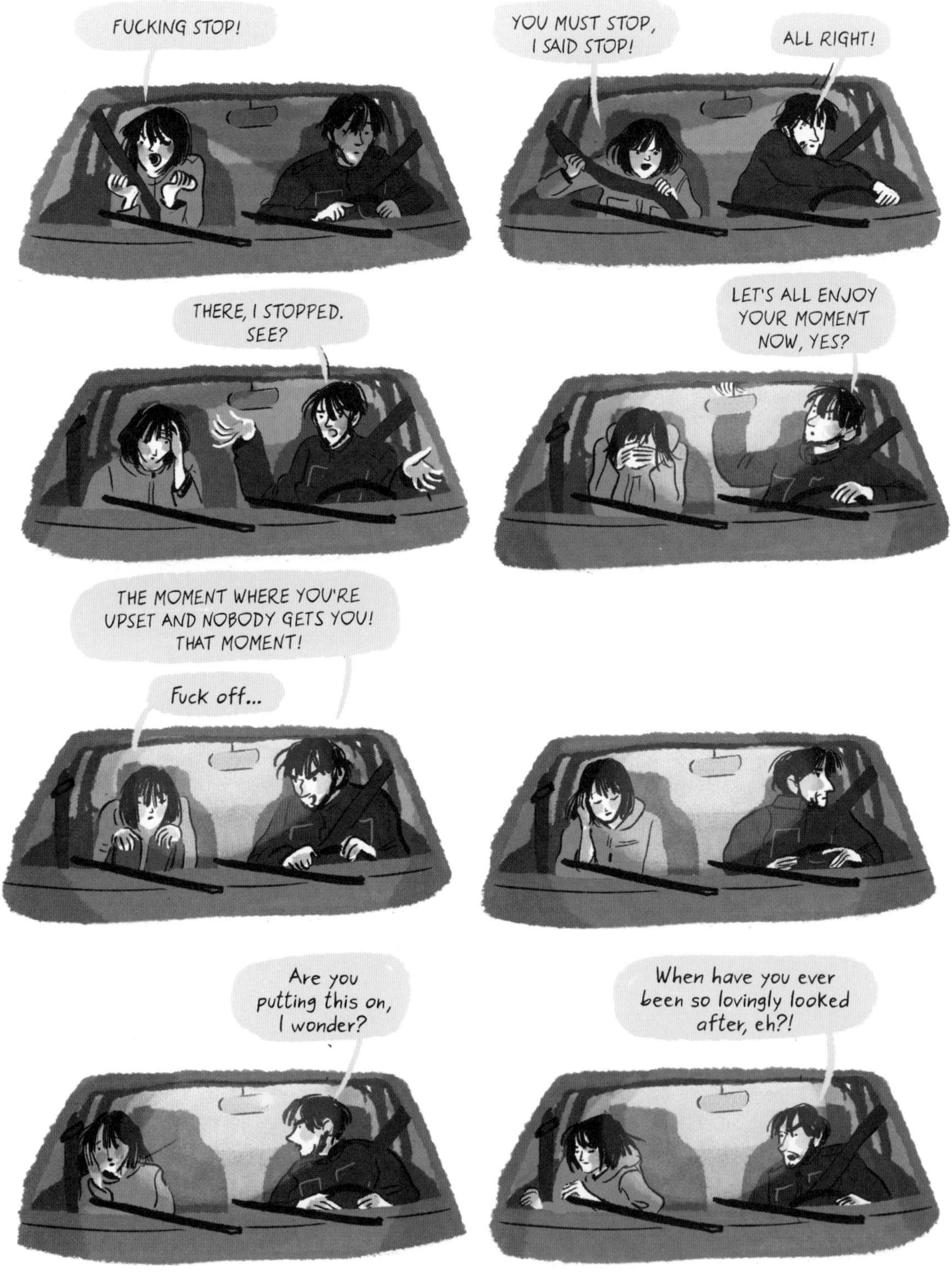
FUCKING STOP!
YOU MUST STOP, I SAID STOP!
ALL RIGHT!
THERE, I STOPPED. SEE?
LET'S ALL ENJOY YOUR MOMENT NOW, YES?
THE MOMENT WHERE YOU'RE UPSET AND NOBODY GETS YOU! THAT MOMENT!
Fuck off...
Are you putting this on, I wonder?
When have you ever been so lovingly looked after, eh?!

I BET YOU EVEN STOPPED TAKING YOUR MEDS, RIGHT?!
RIGHT?! YOU STOPPED TAKING THEM, DIDN'T YOU?!
Sbam!
FUCK!

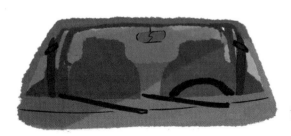

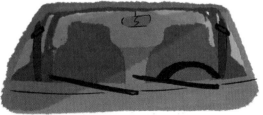

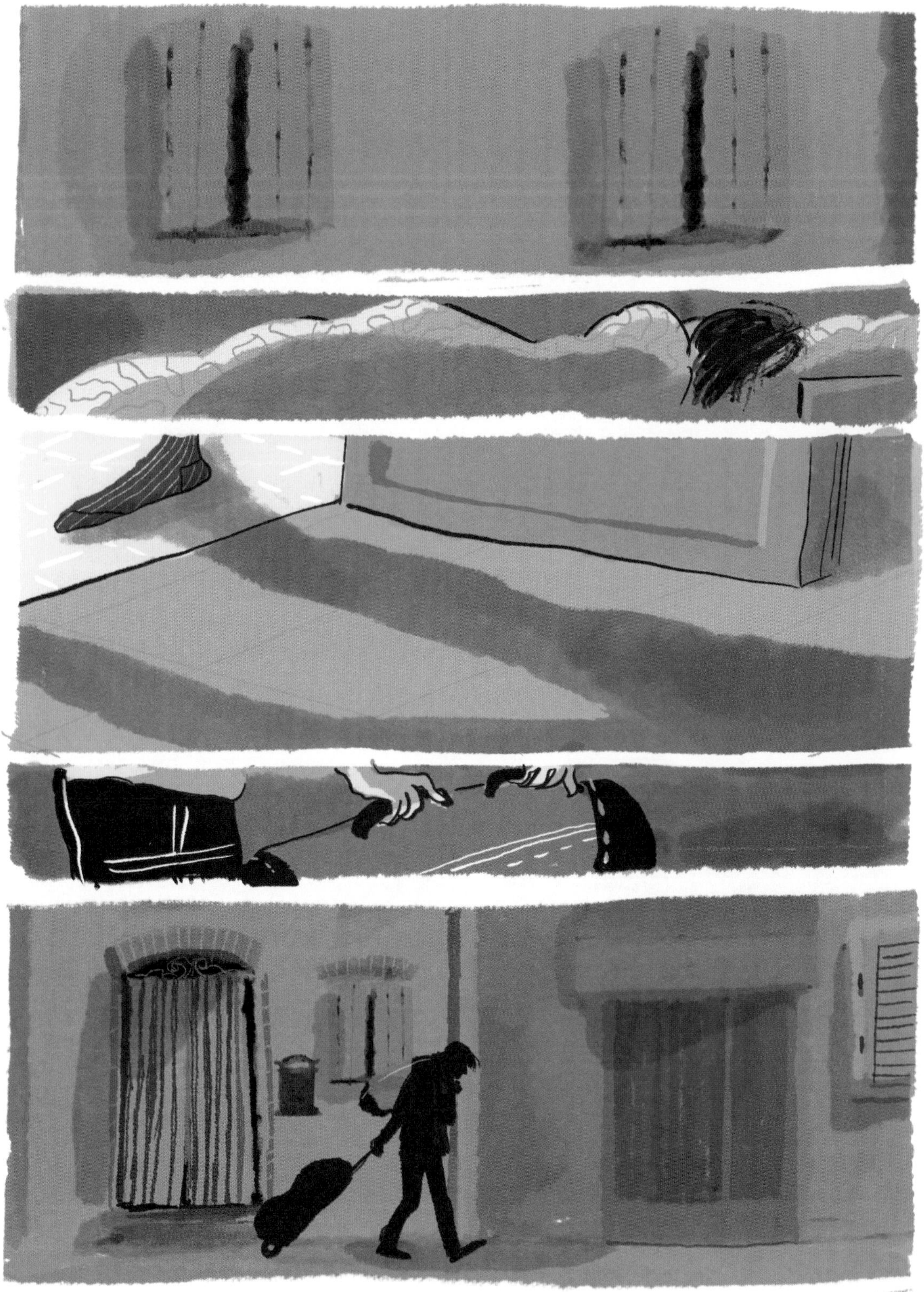

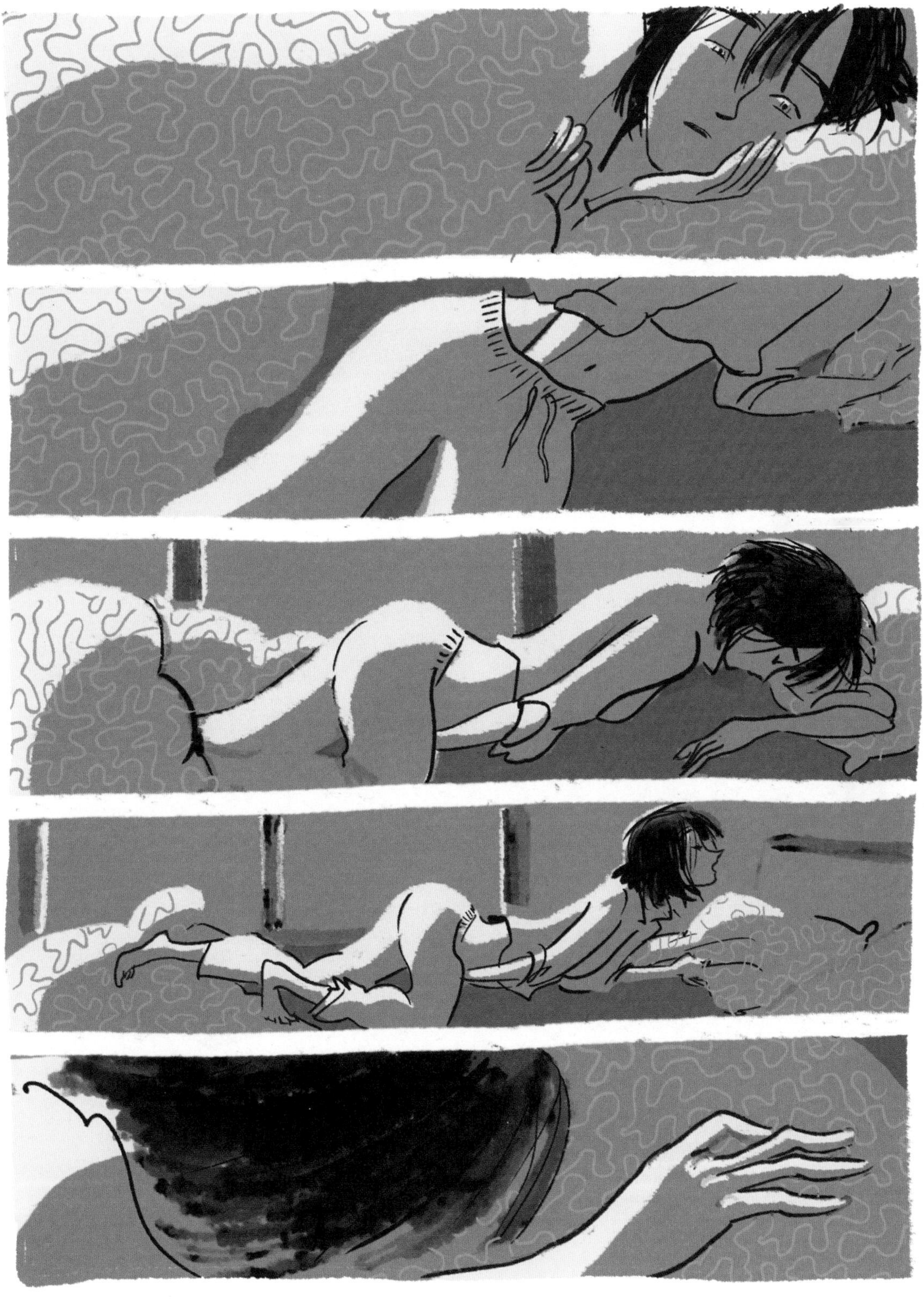

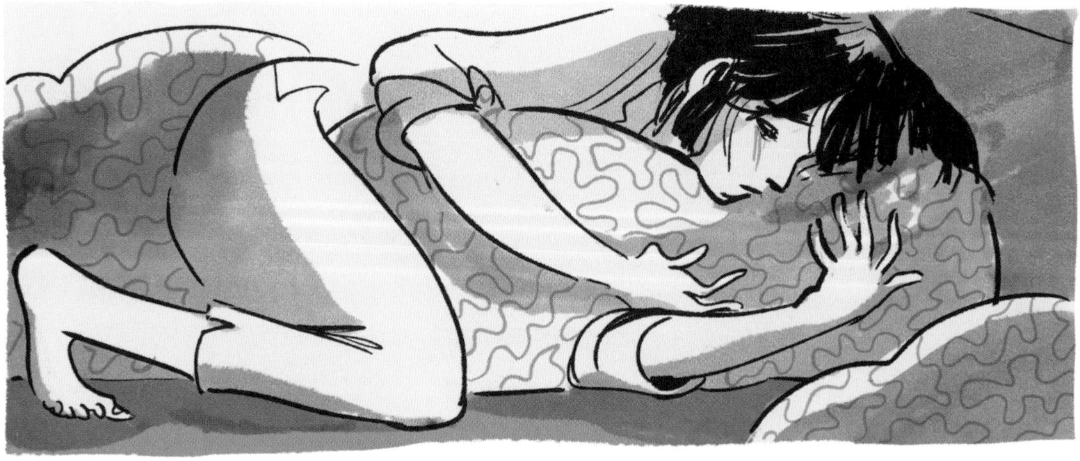

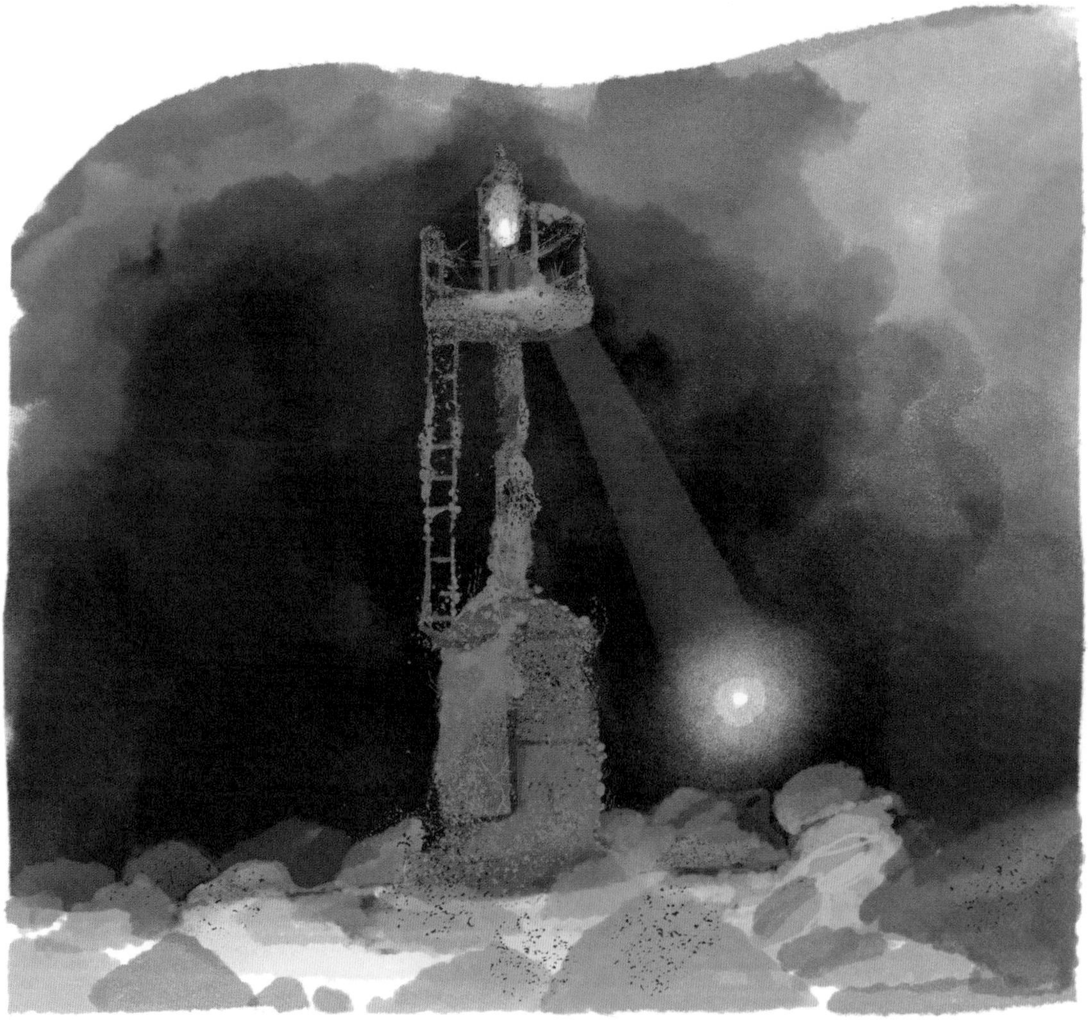

Chapter Four

Balance

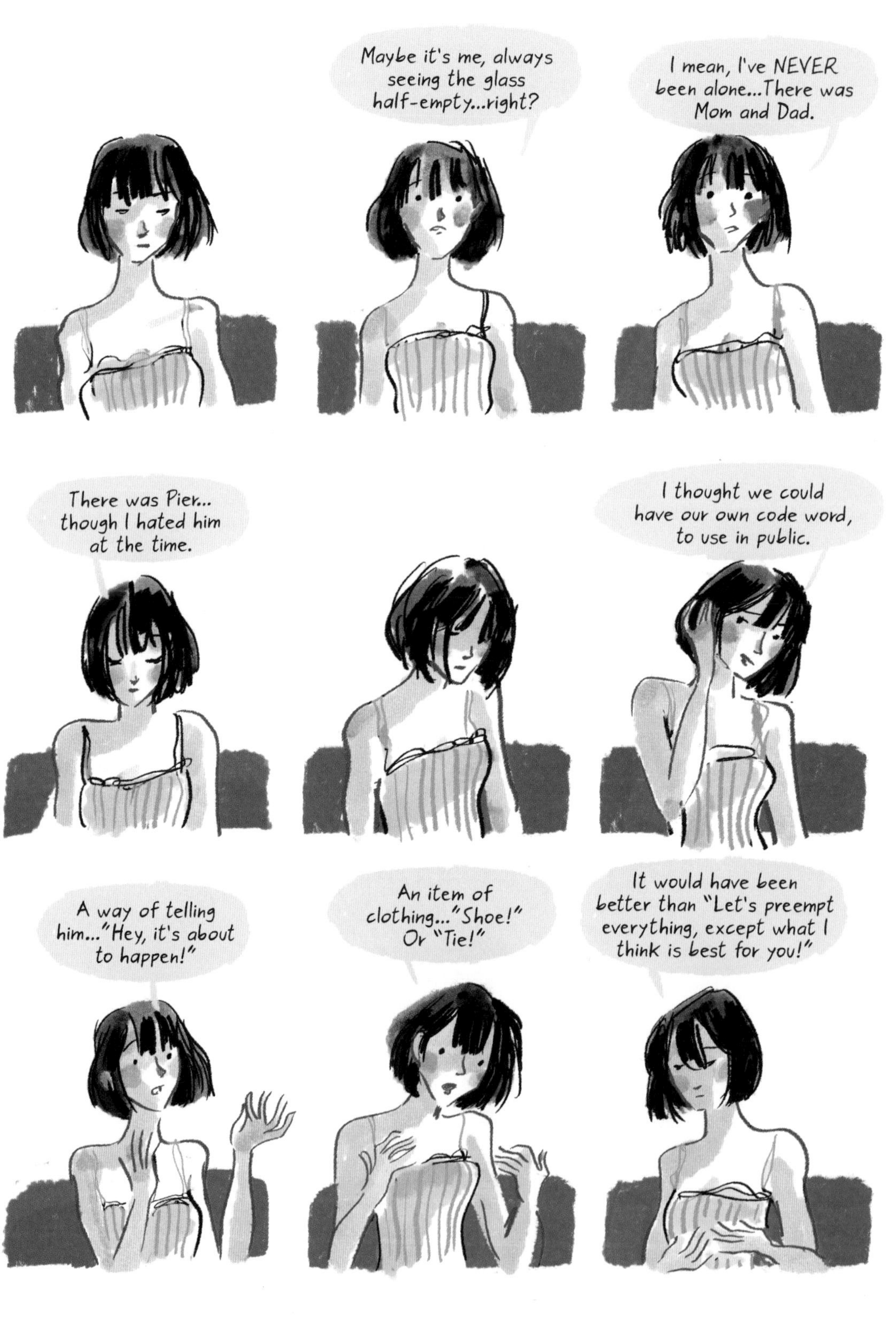
Maybe it's me, always seeing the glass half-empty...right?
I mean, I've NEVER been alone...There was Mom and Dad.
There was Pier... though I hated him at the time.
I thought we could have our own code word, to use in public.
A way of telling him..."Hey, it's about to happen!"
An item of clothing..."Shoe!" Or "Tie!"
It would have been better than "Let's preempt everything, except what I think is best for you!"

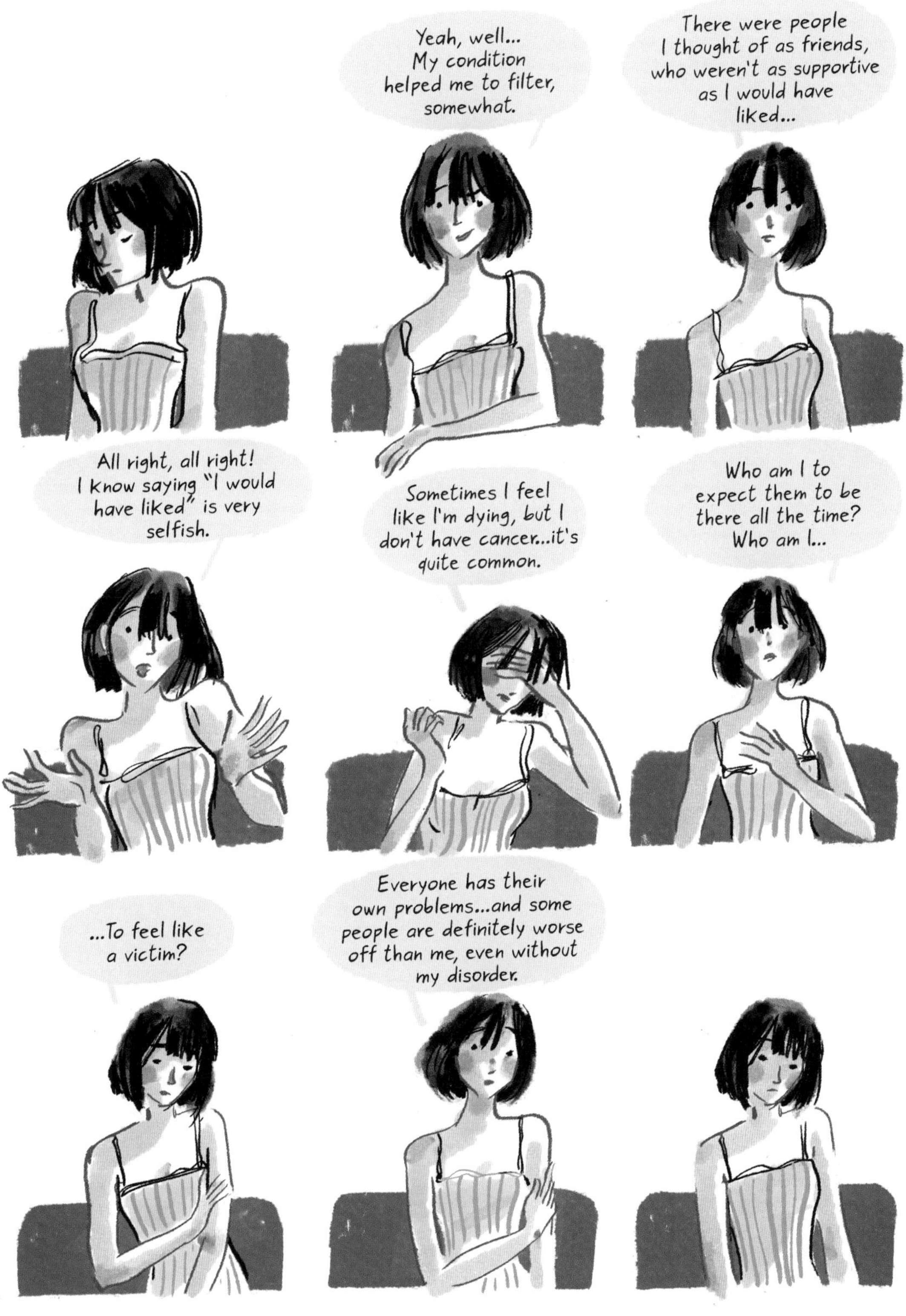
Yeah, well... My condition helped me to filter, somewhat.
There were people I thought of as friends, who weren't as supportive as I would have liked...
All right, all right! I know saying "I would have liked" is very selfish.
Sometimes I feel like I'm dying, but I don't have cancer...it's quite common.
Who am I to expect them to be there all the time? Who am I...
...To feel like a victim?
Everyone has their own problems...and some people are definitely worse off than me, even without my disorder.

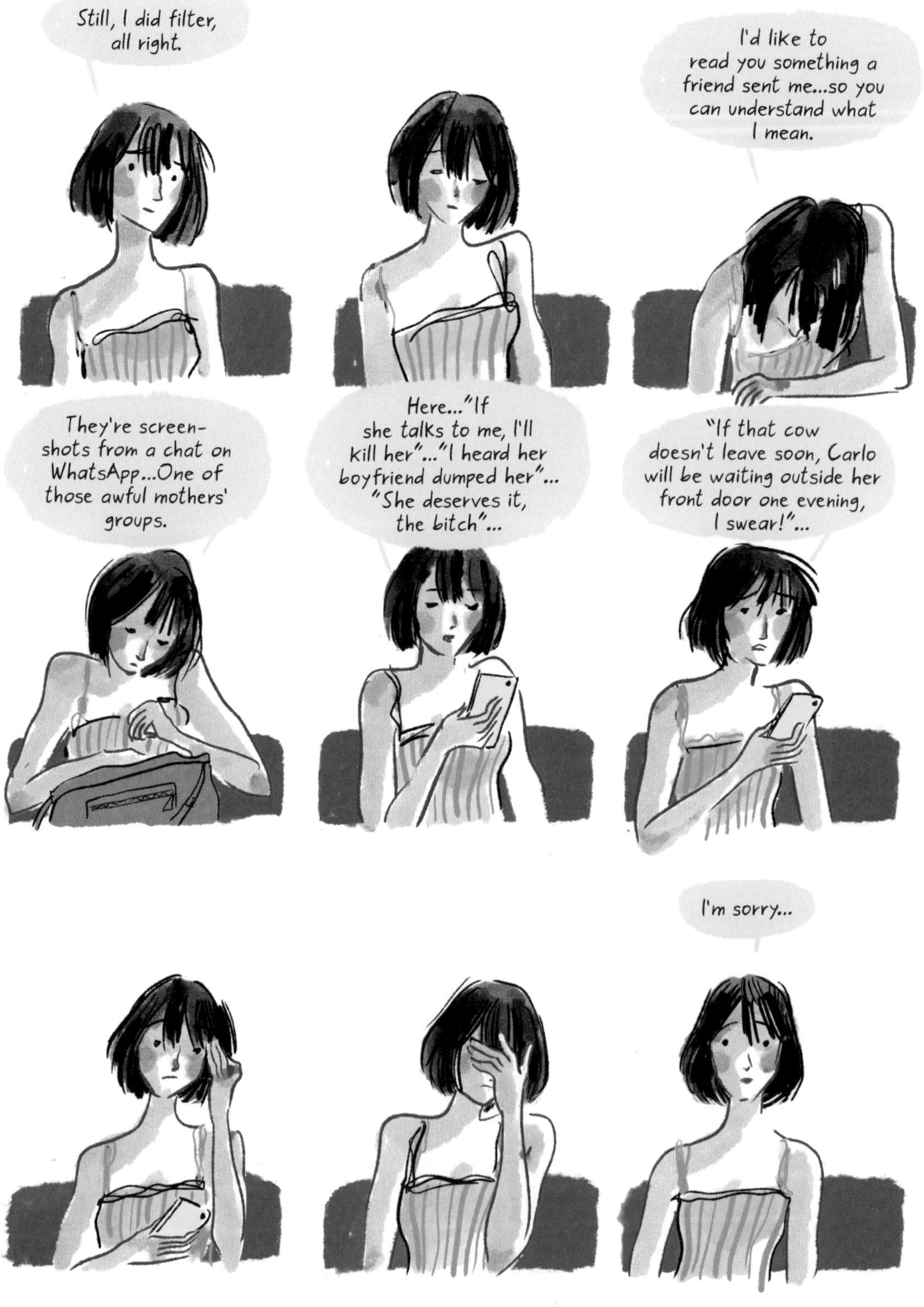
Still, I did filter, all right.
I'd like to read you something a friend sent me...so you can understand what I mean.
They're screen-shots from a chat on WhatsApp...One of those awful mothers' groups.
Here..."If she talks to me, I'll kill her"..."I heard her boyfriend dumped her"... "She deserves it, the bitch"...
"If that cow doesn't leave soon, Carlo will be waiting outside her front door one evening, I swear!"...
I'm sorry...

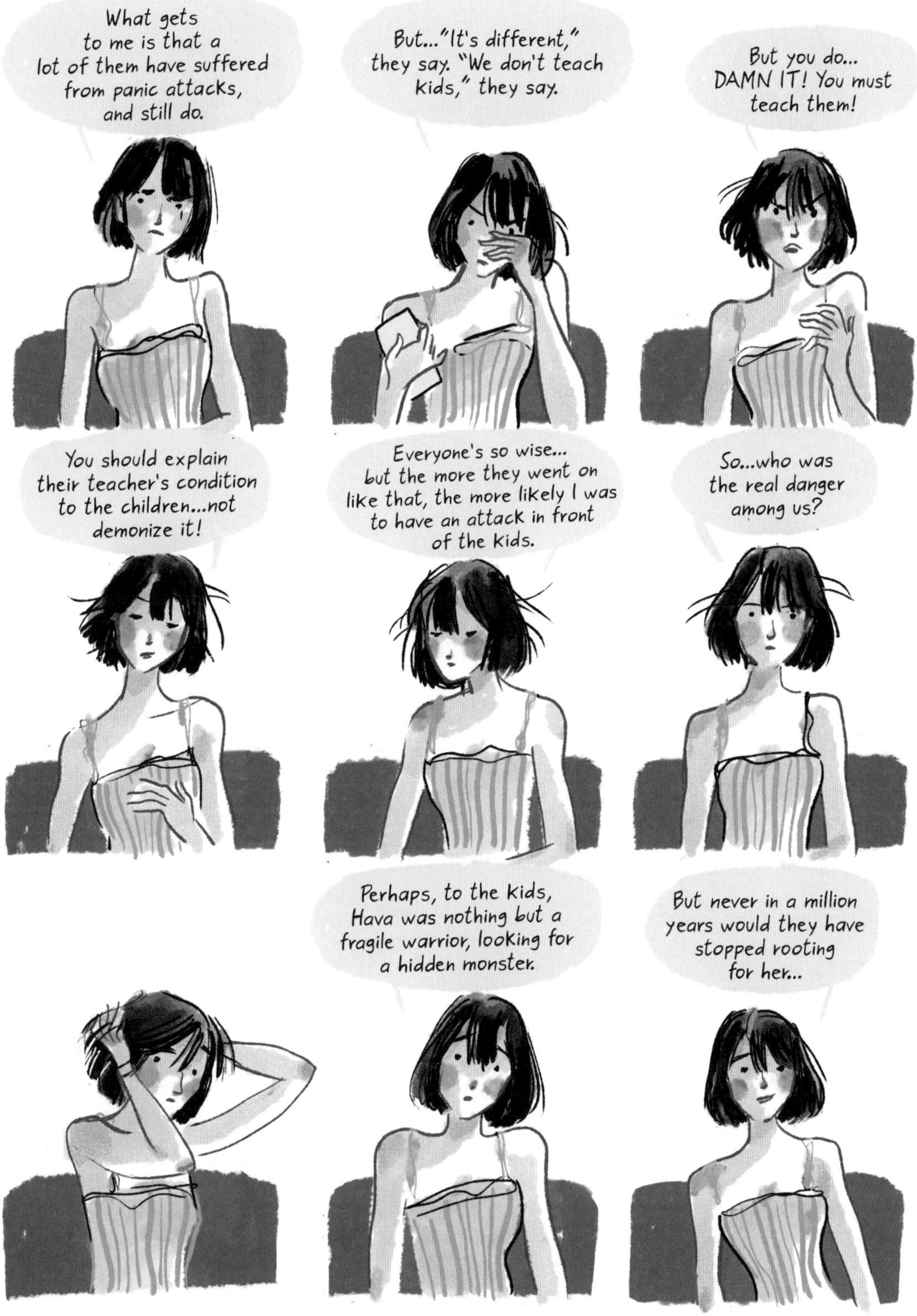
What gets to me is that a lot of them have suffered from panic attacks, and still do.
But..."It's different," they say. "We don't teach kids," they say.
But you do... DAMN IT! You must teach them!
You should explain their teacher's condition to the children...not demonize it!
Everyone's so wise... but the more they went on like that, the more likely I was to have an attack in front of the kids.
So...who was the real danger among us?
Perhaps, to the kids, Hava was nothing but a fragile warrior, looking for a hidden monster.
But never in a million years would they have stopped rooting for her...

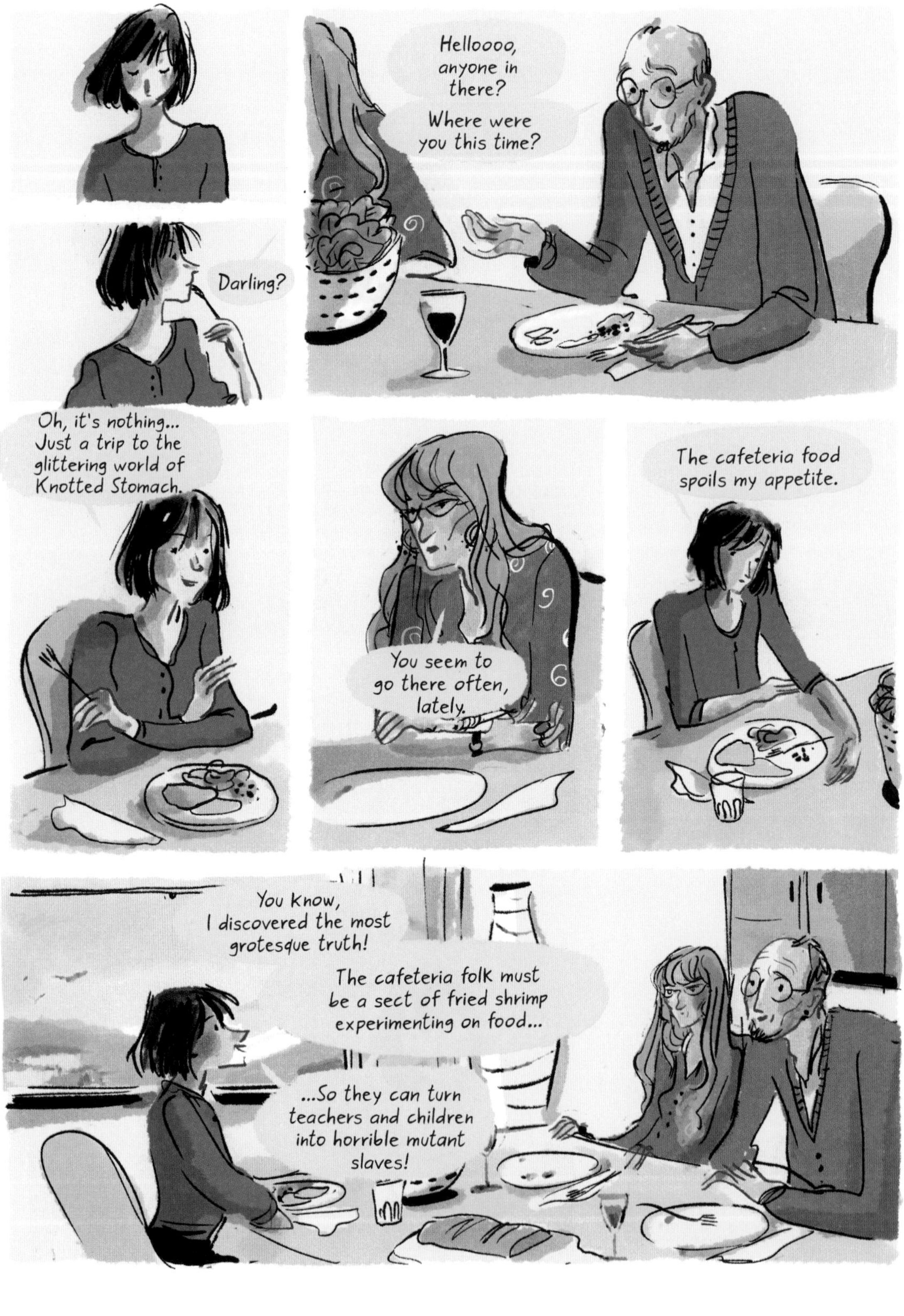
Helloooo, anyone in there?
Where were you this time?
Darling?
Oh, it's nothing... Just a trip to the glittering world of Knotted Stomach.
You seem to go there often, lately.
The cafeteria food spoils my appetite.
You know, I discovered the most grotesque truth!
The cafeteria folk must be a sect of fried shrimp experimenting on food...
...So they can turn teachers and children into horrible mutant slaves!

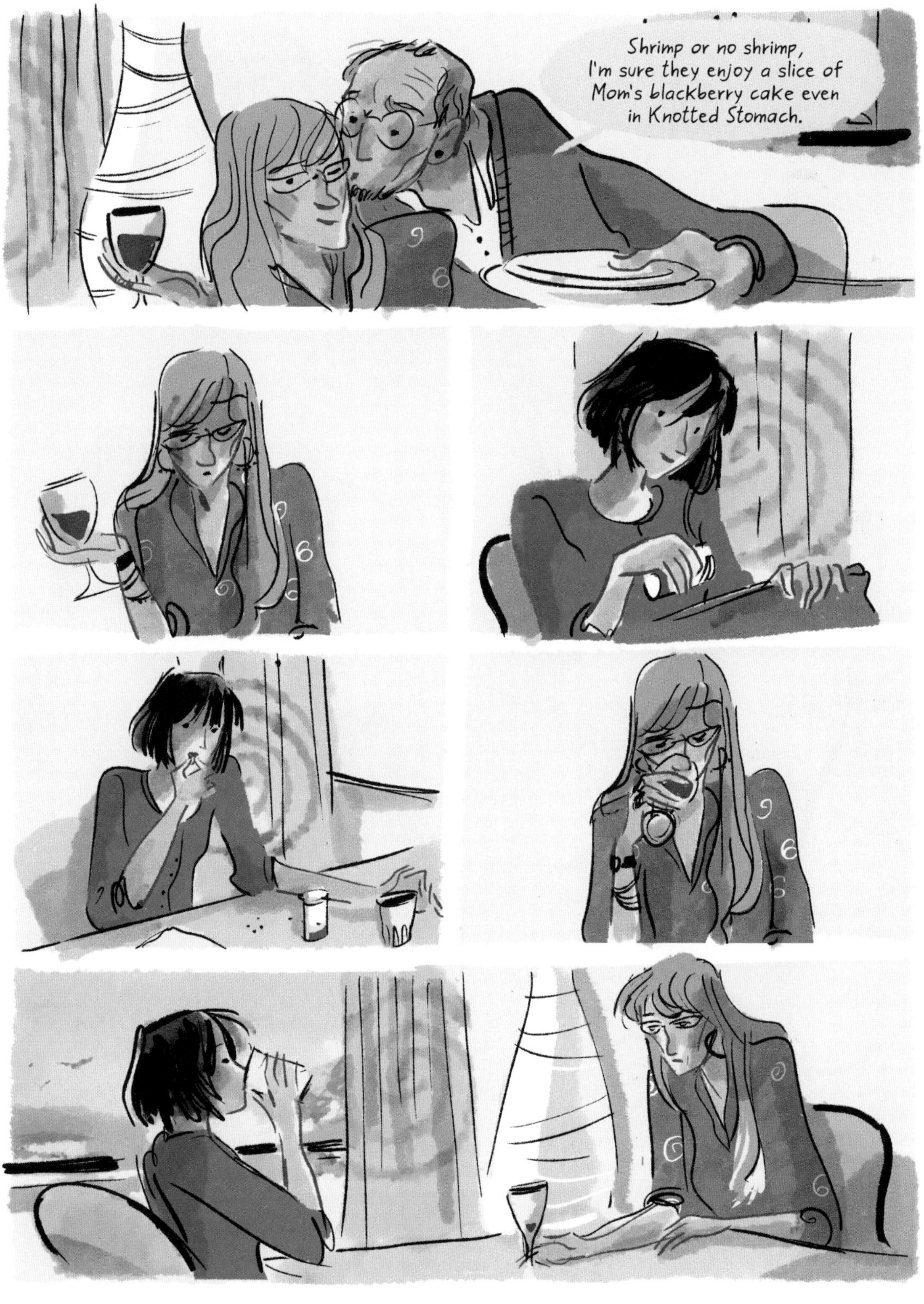
Shrimp or no shrimp, I'm sure they enjoy a slice of Mom's blackberry cake even in Knotted Stomach.

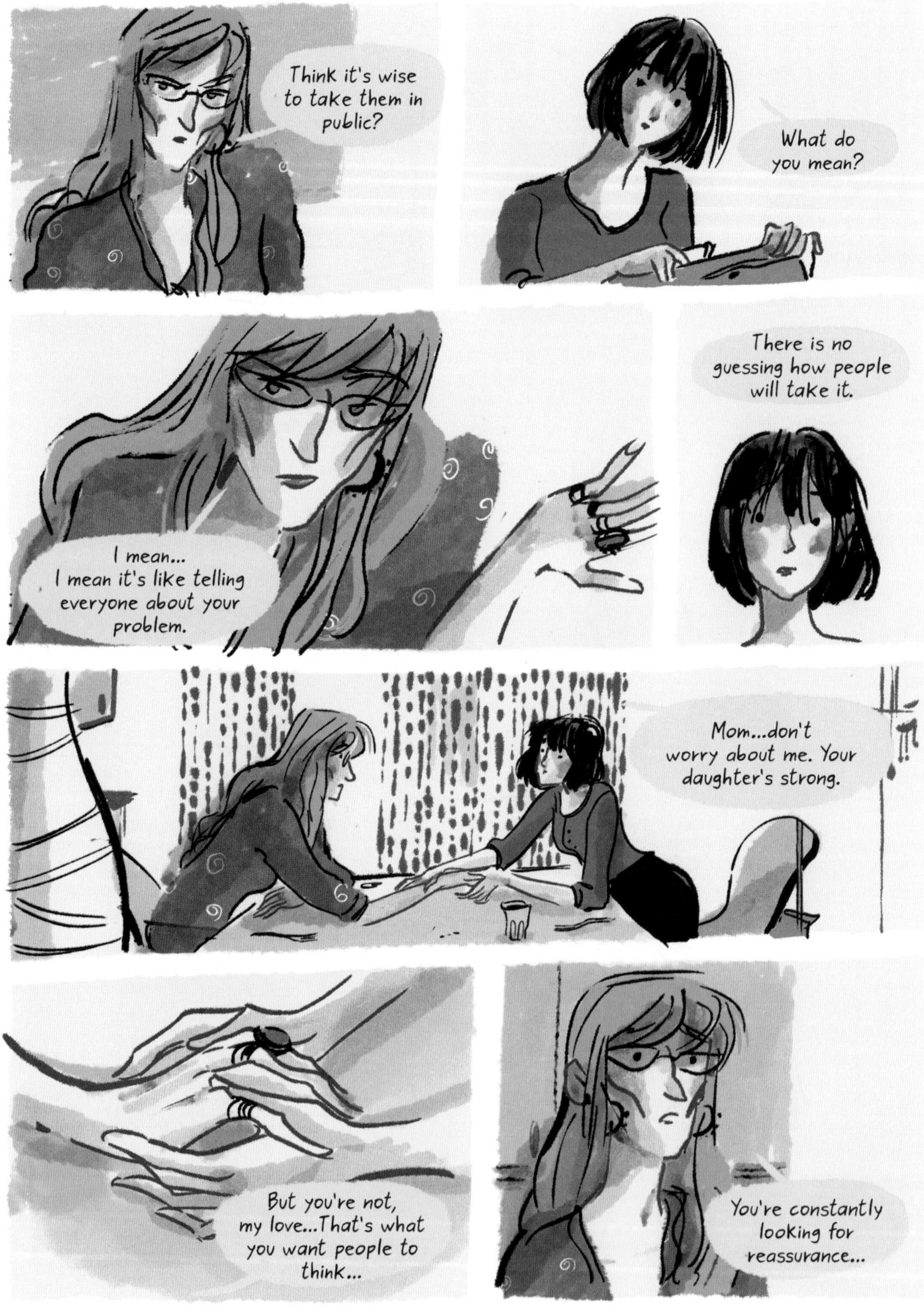
Think it's wise to take them in public?
What do you mean?
I mean...
I mean it's like telling everyone about your problem.
There is no guessing how people will take it.
Mom...don't worry about me. Your daughter's strong.
But you're not, my love...That's what you want people to think...
You're constantly looking for reassurance...

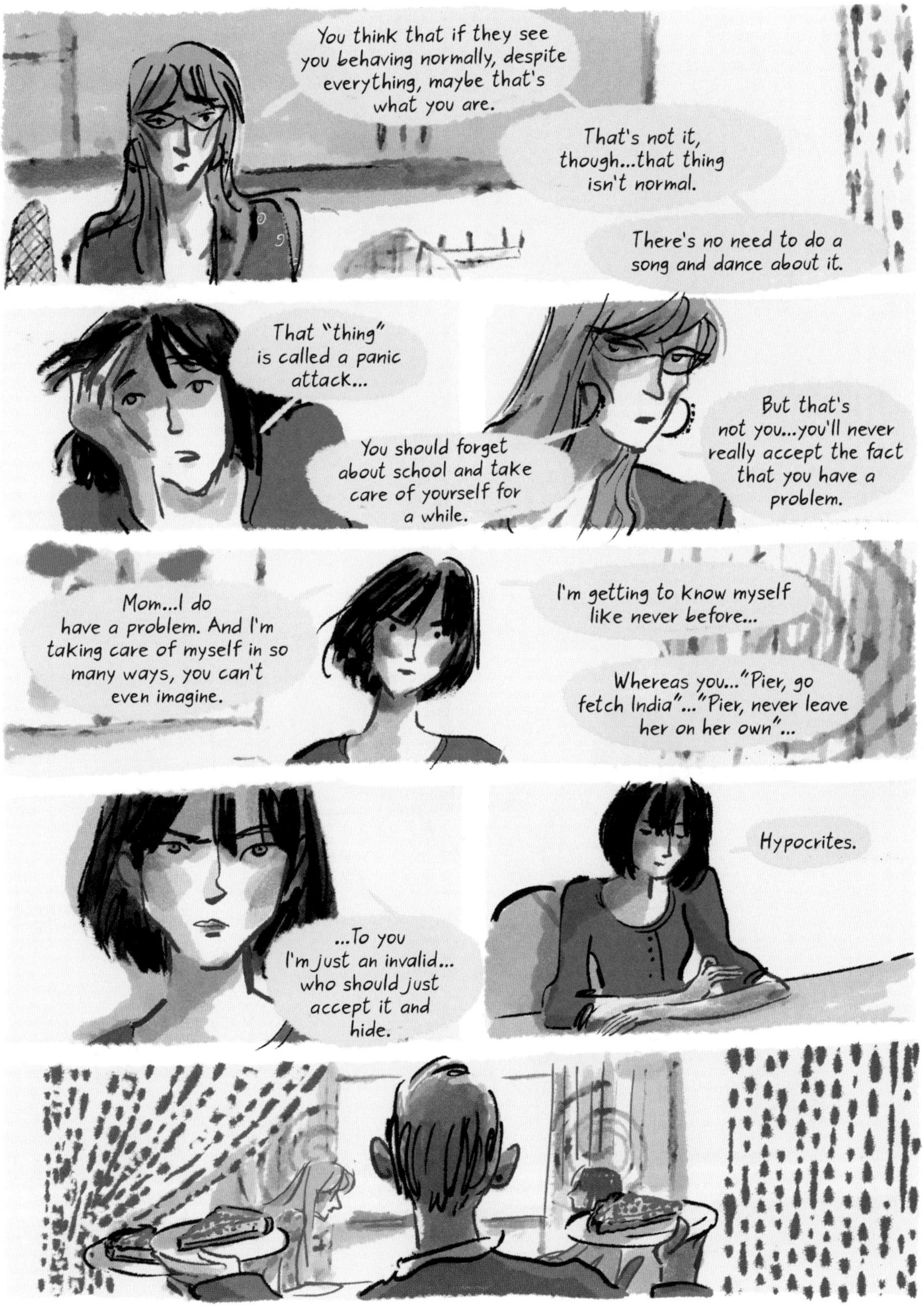
You think that if they see you behaving normally, despite everything, maybe that's what you are.
That's not it, though...that thing isn't normal.
There's no need to do a song and dance about it.
That "thing" is called a panic attack...
You should forget about school and take care of yourself for a while.
But that's not you...you'll never really accept the fact that you have a problem.
Mom...I do have a problem. And I'm taking care of myself in so many ways, you can't even imagine.
I'm getting to know myself like never before...
Whereas you..."Pier, go fetch India"..."Pier, never leave her on her own"...
...To you I'm just an invalid... who should just accept it and hide.
Hypocrites.

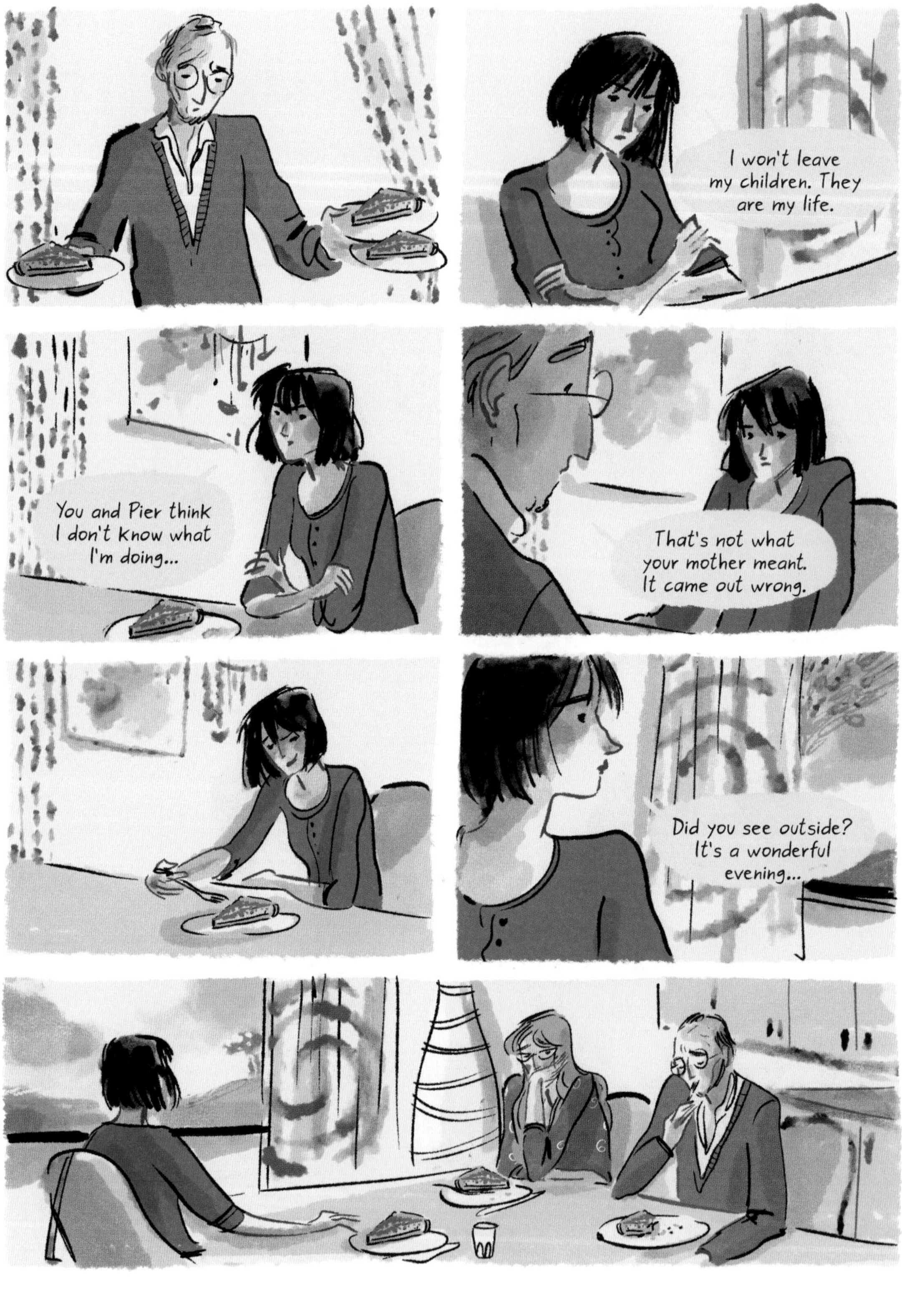
I won't leave my children. They are my life.
You and Pier think I don't know what I'm doing...
That's not what your mother meant. It came out wrong.
Did you see outside? It's a wonderful evening...

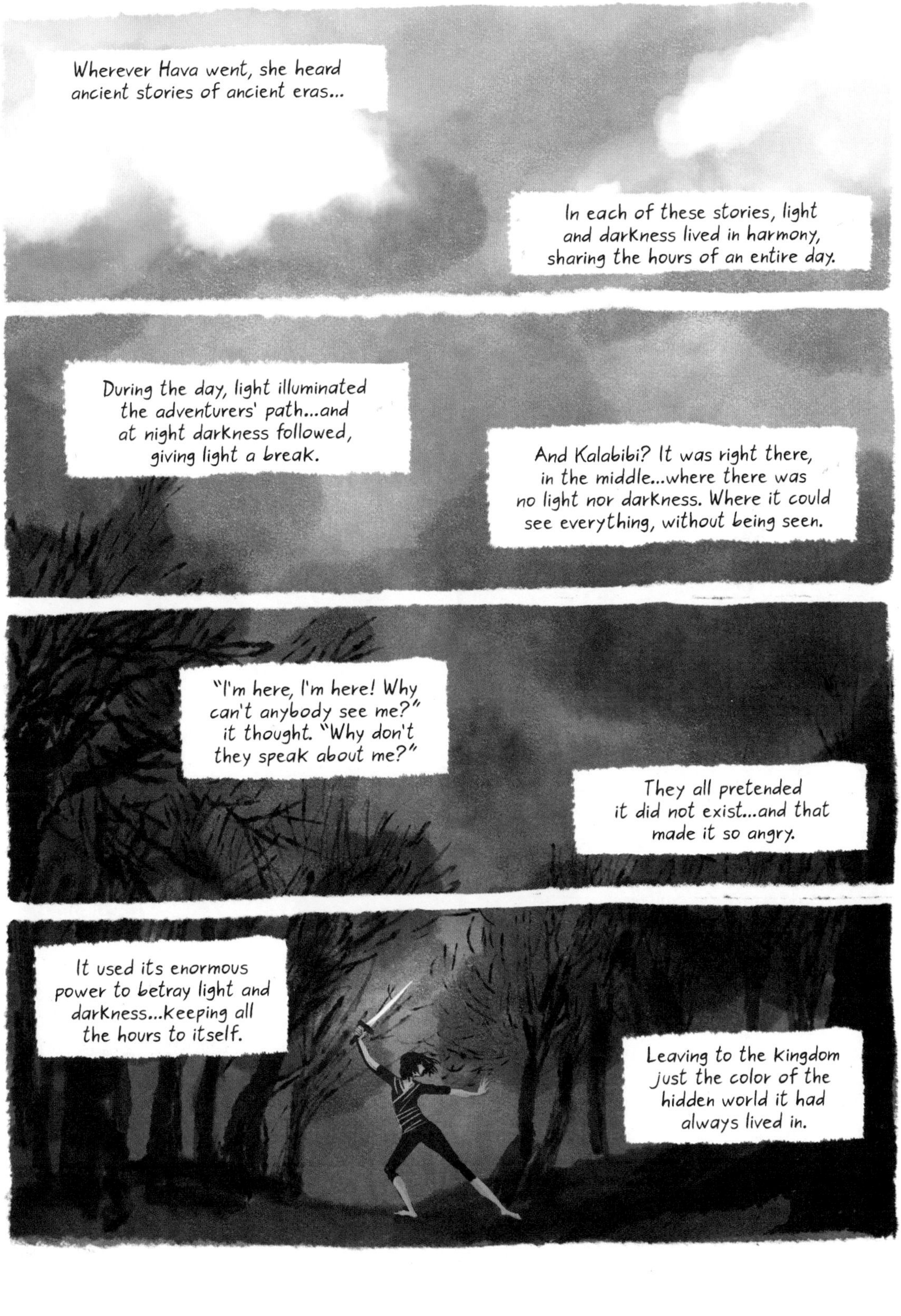
Wherever Hava went, she heard ancient stories of ancient eras...
In each of these stories, light and darkness lived in harmony, sharing the hours of an entire day.
During the day, light illuminated the adventurers' path...and at night darkness followed, giving light a break.
And Kalabibi? It was right there, in the middle...where there was no light nor darkness. Where it could see everything, without being seen.
"I'm here, I'm here! Why can't anybody see me?" it thought. "Why don't they speak about me?"
They all pretended it did not exist...and that made it so angry.
It used its enormous power to betray light and darkness...keeping all the hours to itself.
Leaving to the kingdom just the color of the hidden world it had always lived in.

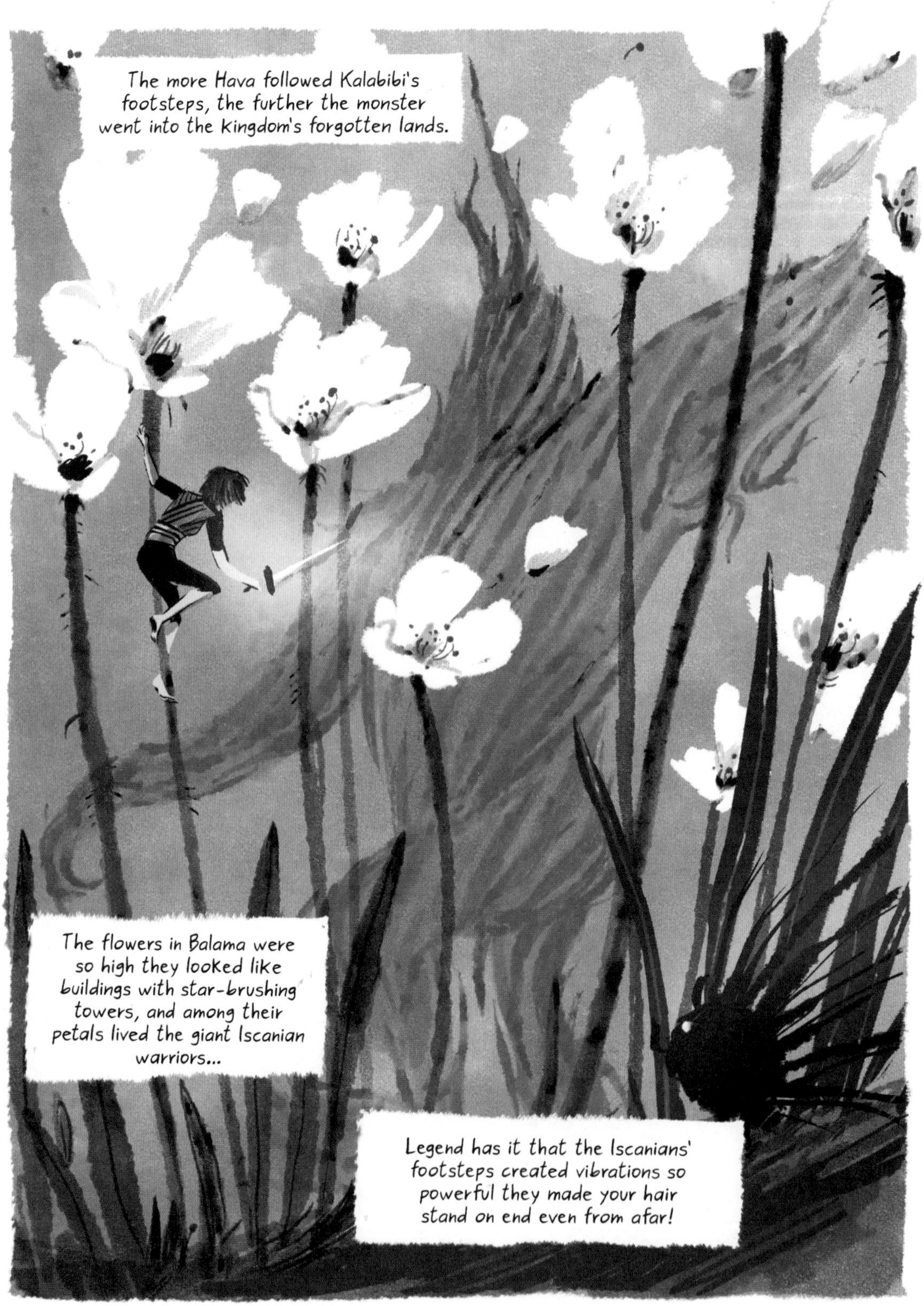
The more Hava followed Kalabibi's footsteps, the further the monster went into the kingdom's forgotten lands.
The flowers in Balama were so high they looked like buildings with star-brushing towers, and among their petals lived the giant Iscanian warriors...
Legend has it that the Iscanians' footsteps created vibrations so powerful they made your hair stand on end even from afar!

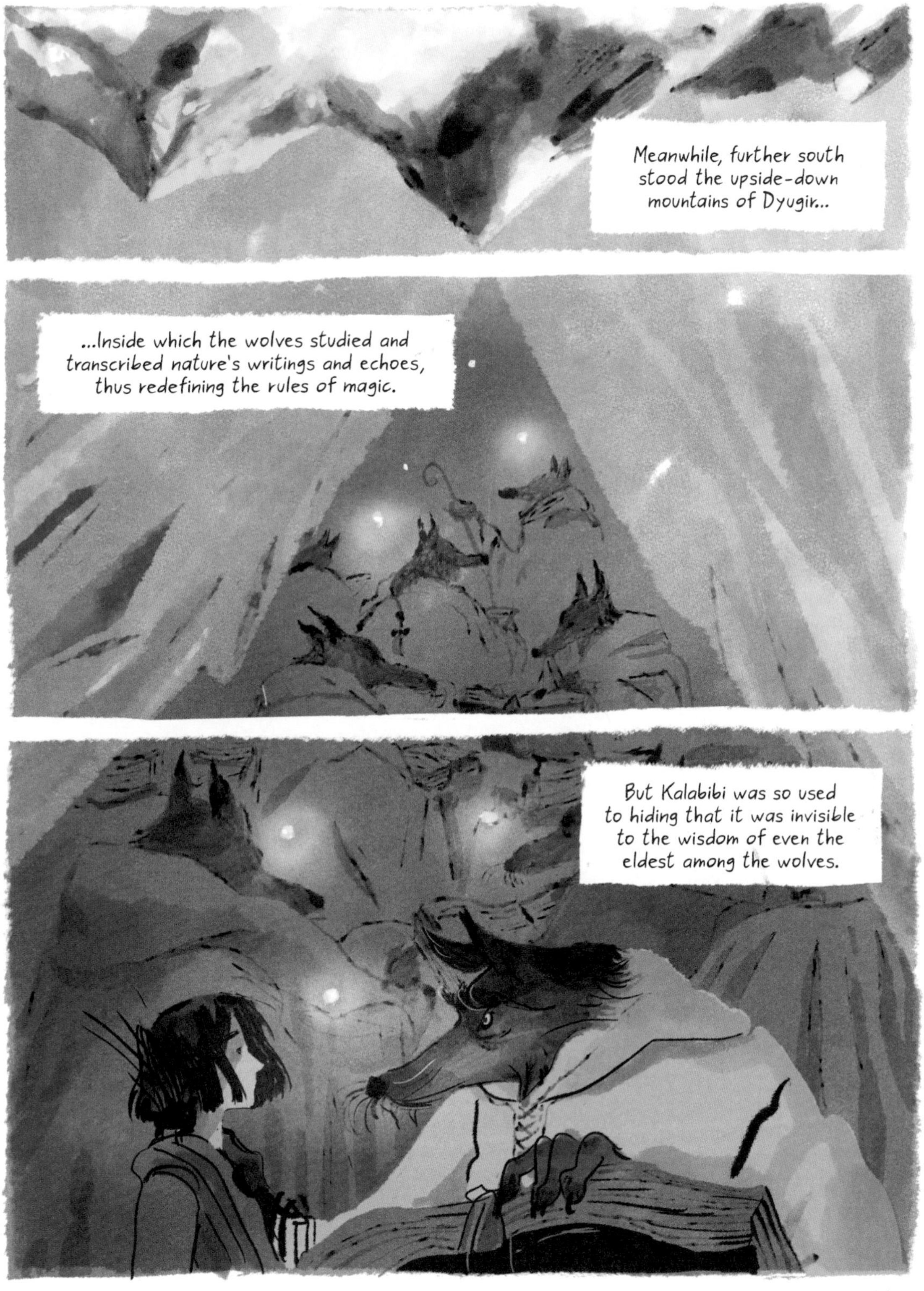
Meanwhile, further south stood the upside-down mountains of Dyugir...
...Inside which the wolves studied and transcribed nature's writings and echoes, thus redefining the rules of magic.
But Kalabibi was so used to hiding that it was invisible to the wisdom of even the eldest among the wolves.

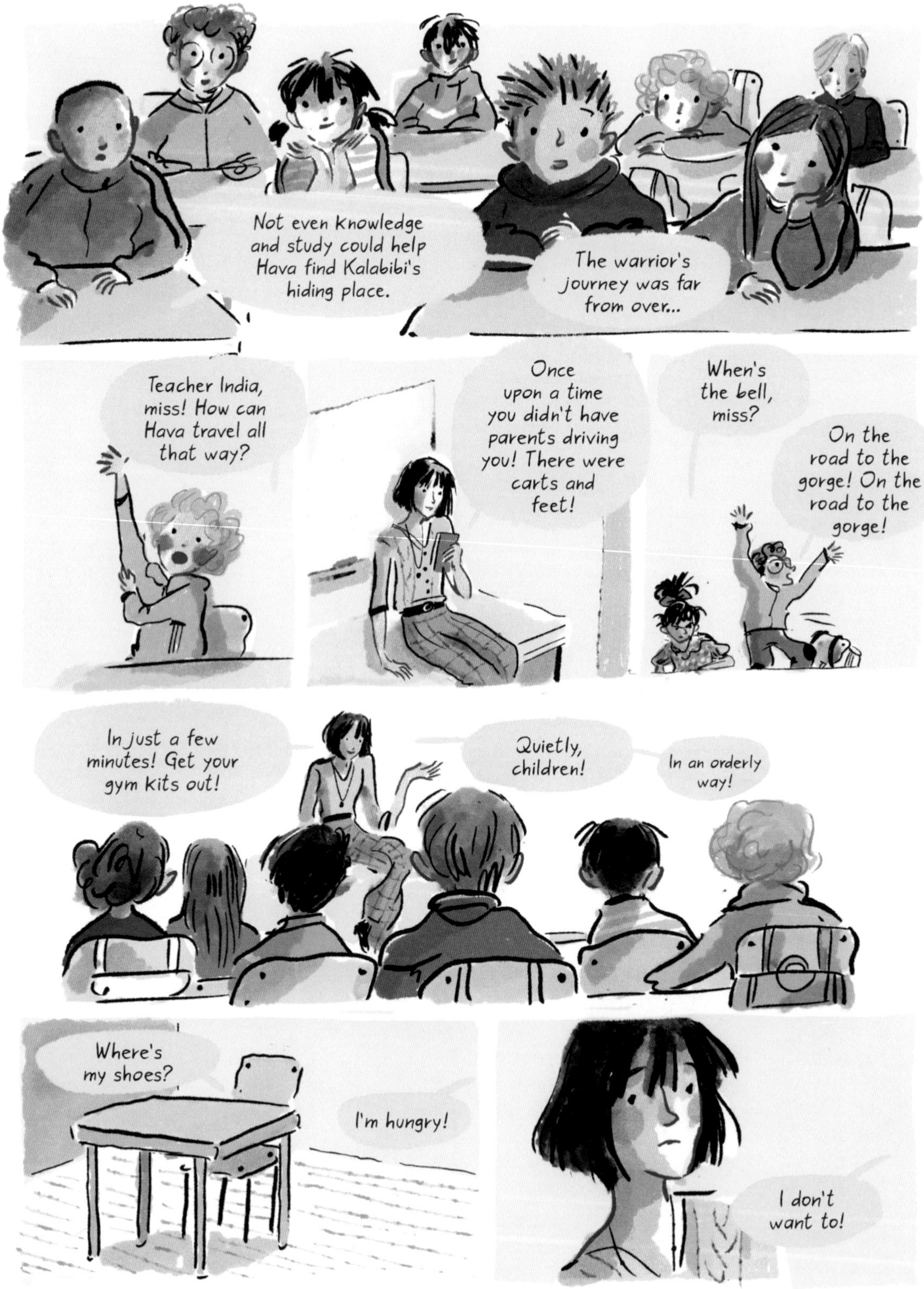
Not even knowledge and study could help Hava find Kalabibi's hiding place.
The warrior's journey was far from over...
Teacher India, miss! How can Hava travel all that way?
Once upon a time you didn't have parents driving you! There were carts and feet!
When's the bell, miss?
On the road to the gorge! On the road to the gorge!
In just a few minutes! Get your gym kits out!
Quietly, children!
In an orderly way!
Where's my shoes?
I'm hungry!
I don't want to!

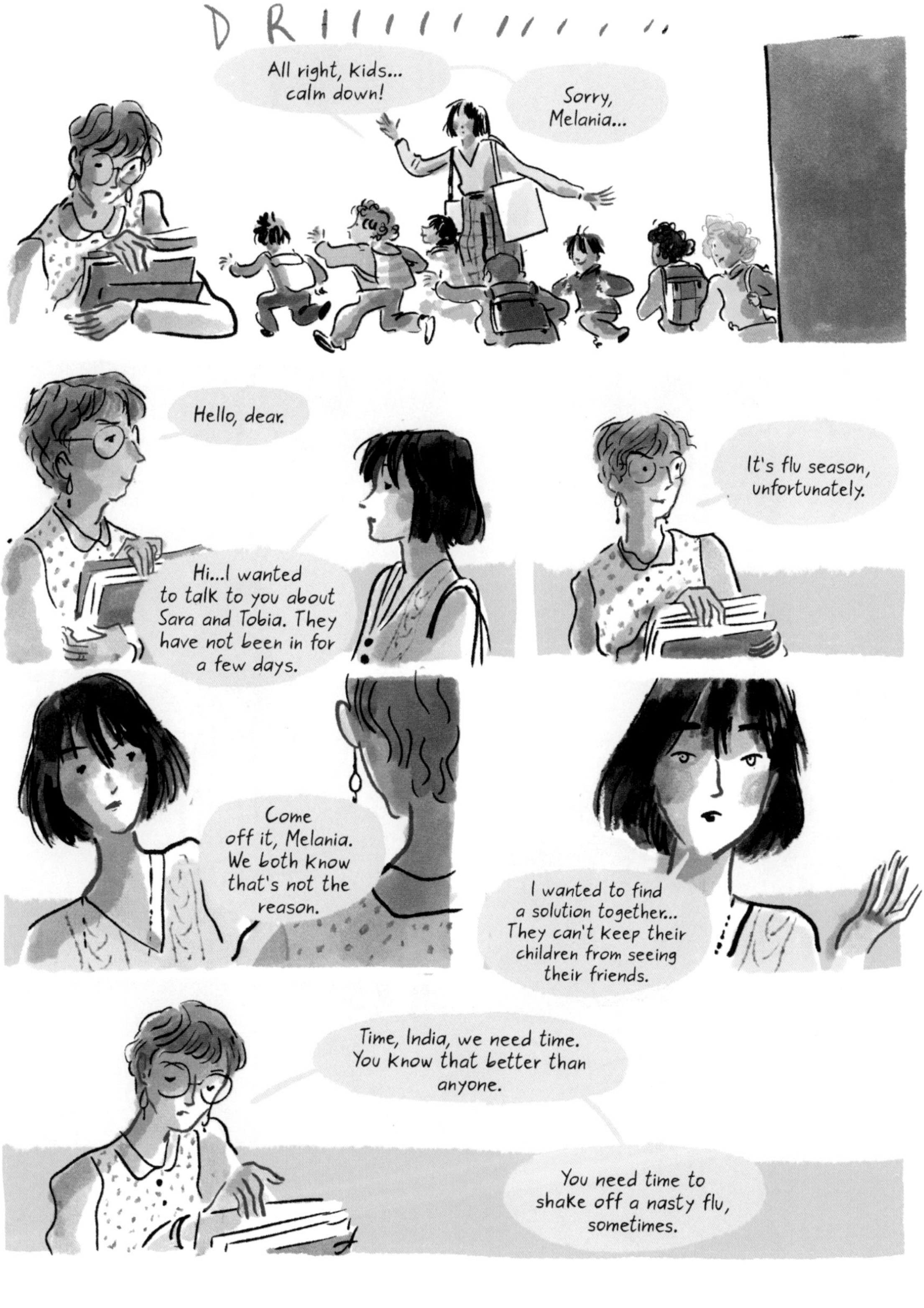

DRIIIIIIIII...
All right, kids... calm down!
Sorry, Melania...
Hello, dear.
Hi...I wanted to talk to you about Sara and Tobia. They have not been in for a few days.
It's flu season, unfortunately.
Come off it, Melania. We both know that's not the reason.
I wanted to find a solution together... They can't keep their children from seeing their friends.
Time, India, we need time. You know that better than anyone.
You need time to shake off a nasty flu, sometimes.

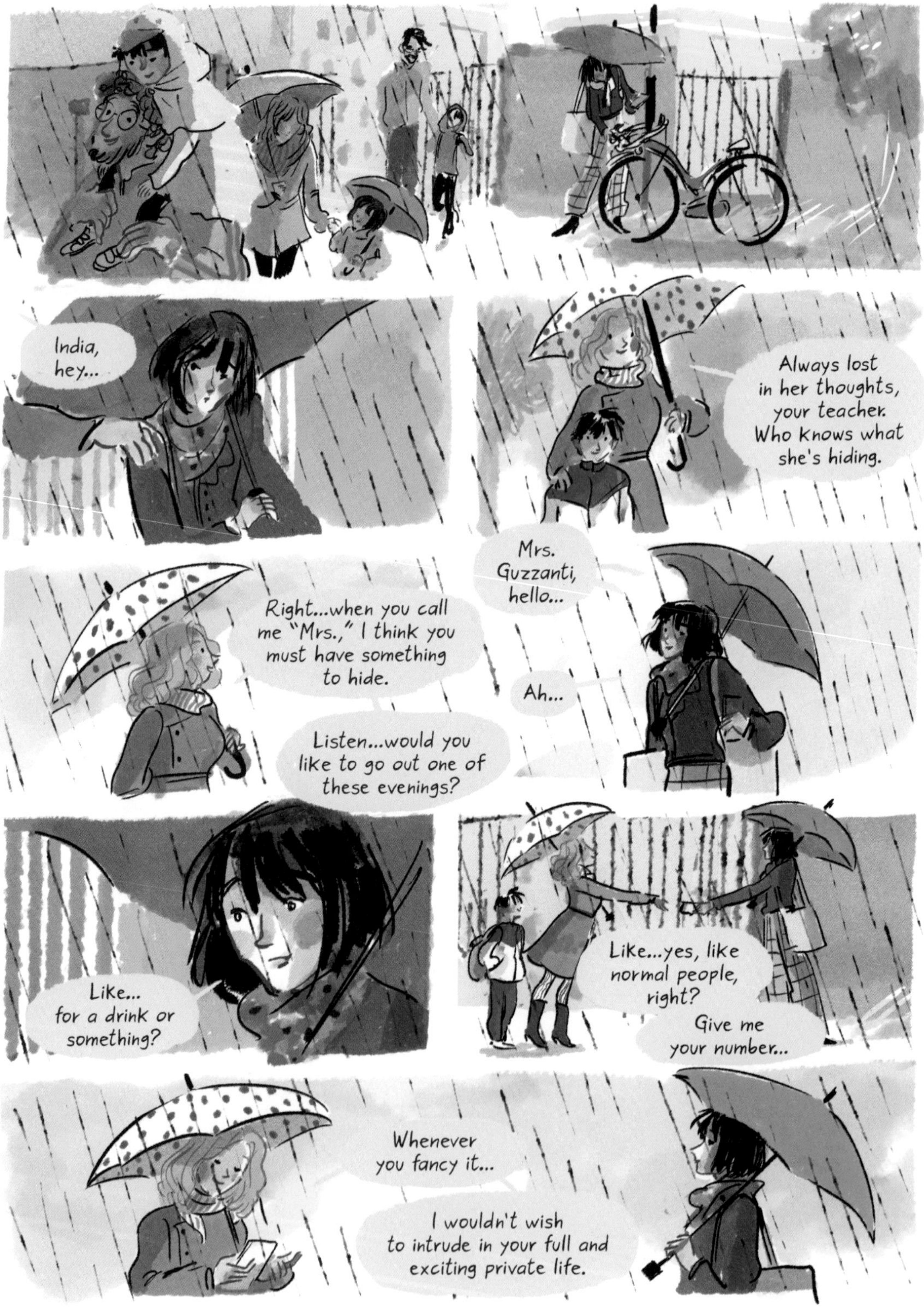
India, hey...
Always lost in her thoughts, your teacher. Who knows what she's hiding.
Mrs. Guzzanti, hello...
Right...when you call me "Mrs.," I think you must have something to hide.
Ah...
Listen...would you like to go out one of these evenings?
Like... for a drink or something?
Like...yes, like normal people, right?
Give me your number...
Whenever you fancy it...
I wouldn't wish to intrude in your full and exciting private life.

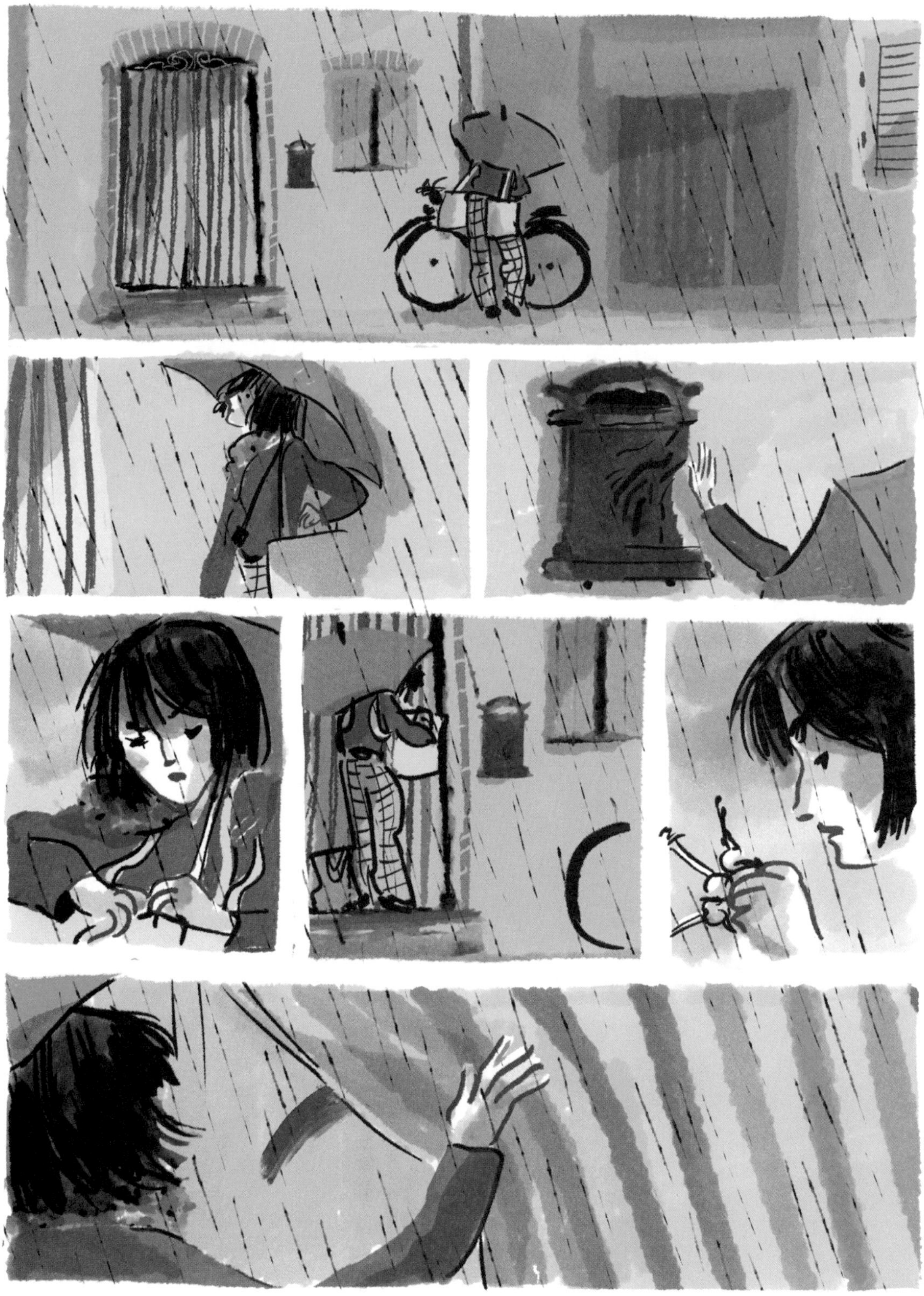

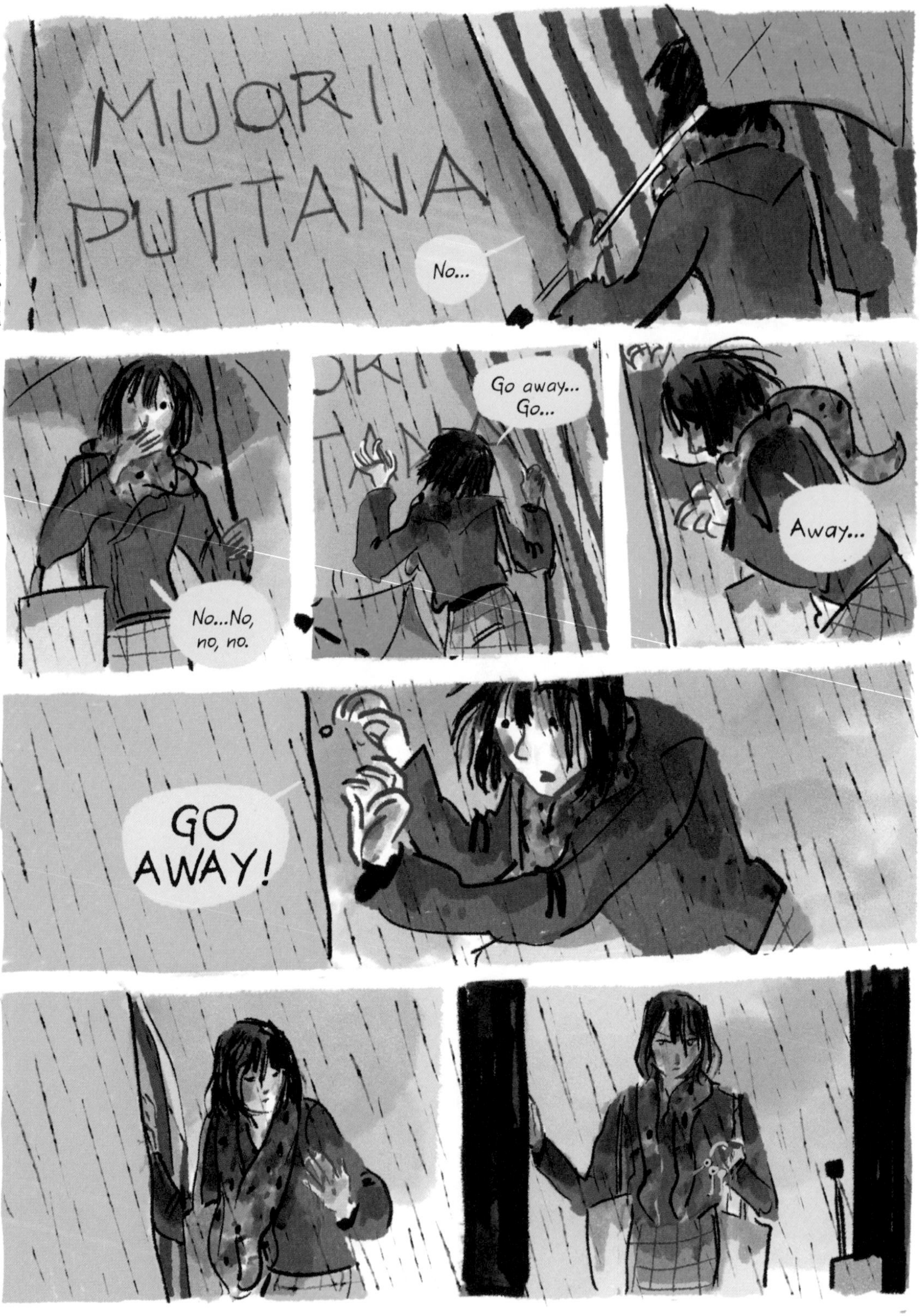
MUORI PUTTANA
No...
No...No, no, no.
Go away... Go...
Away...
GO AWAY!

*DIE BITCH

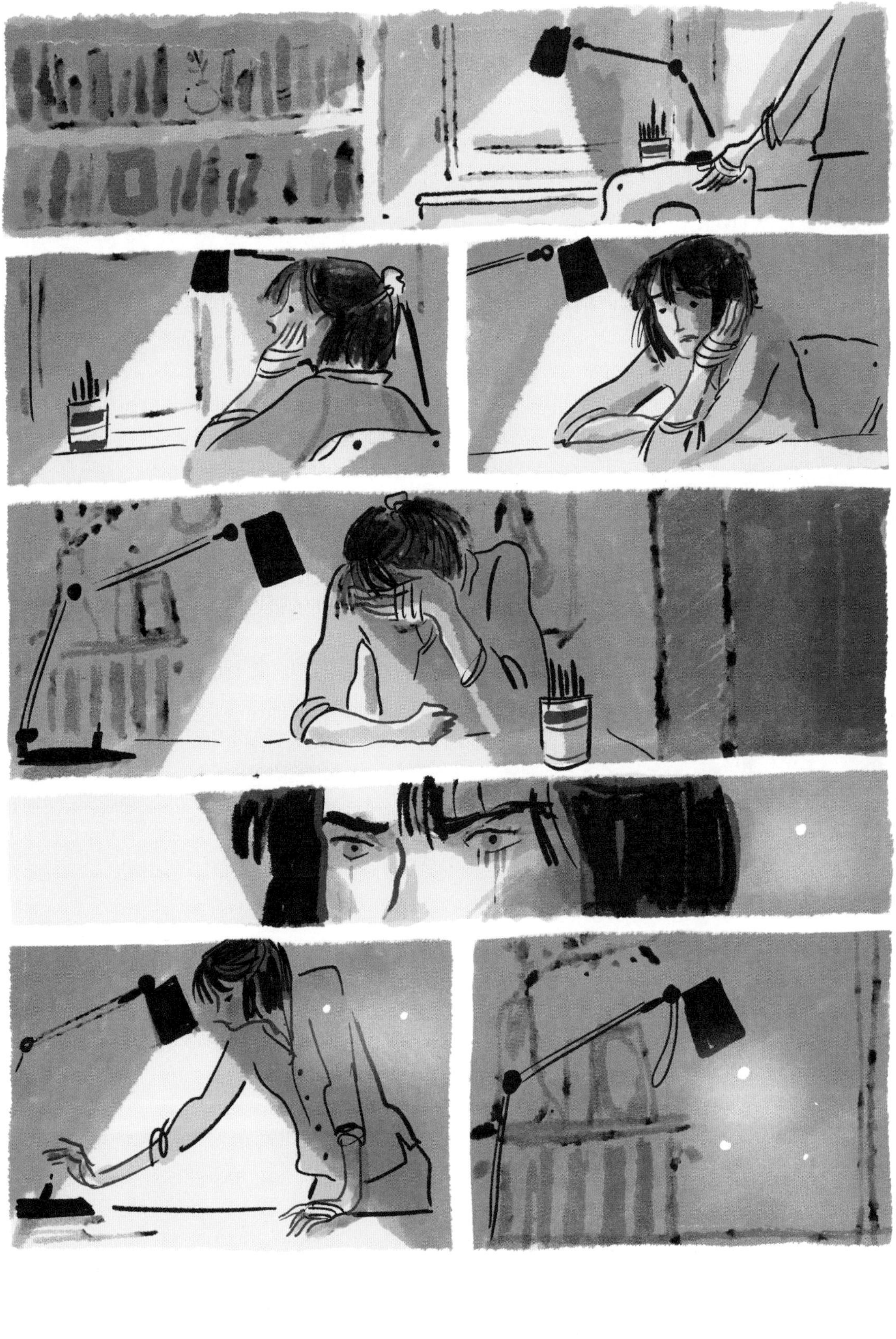

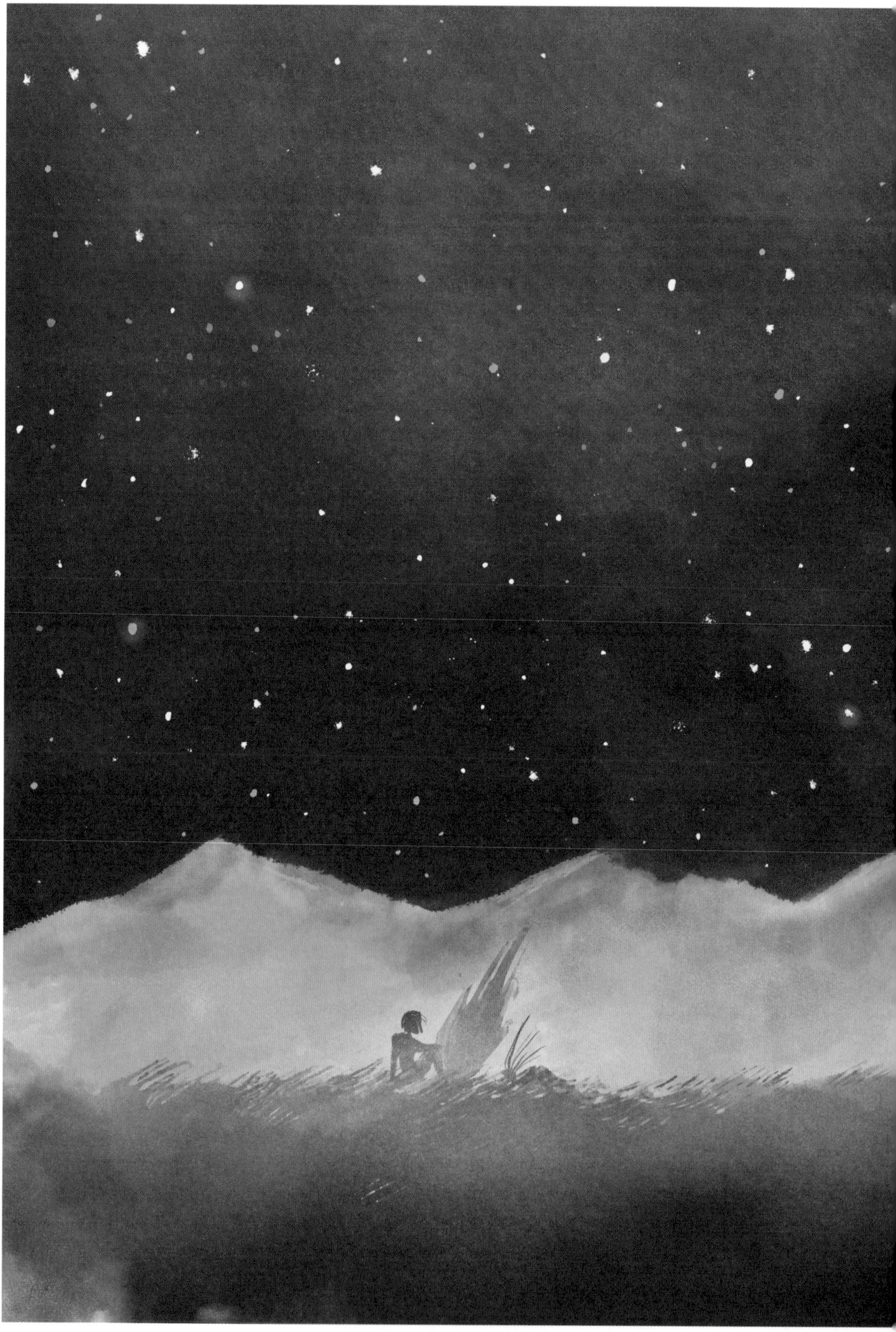

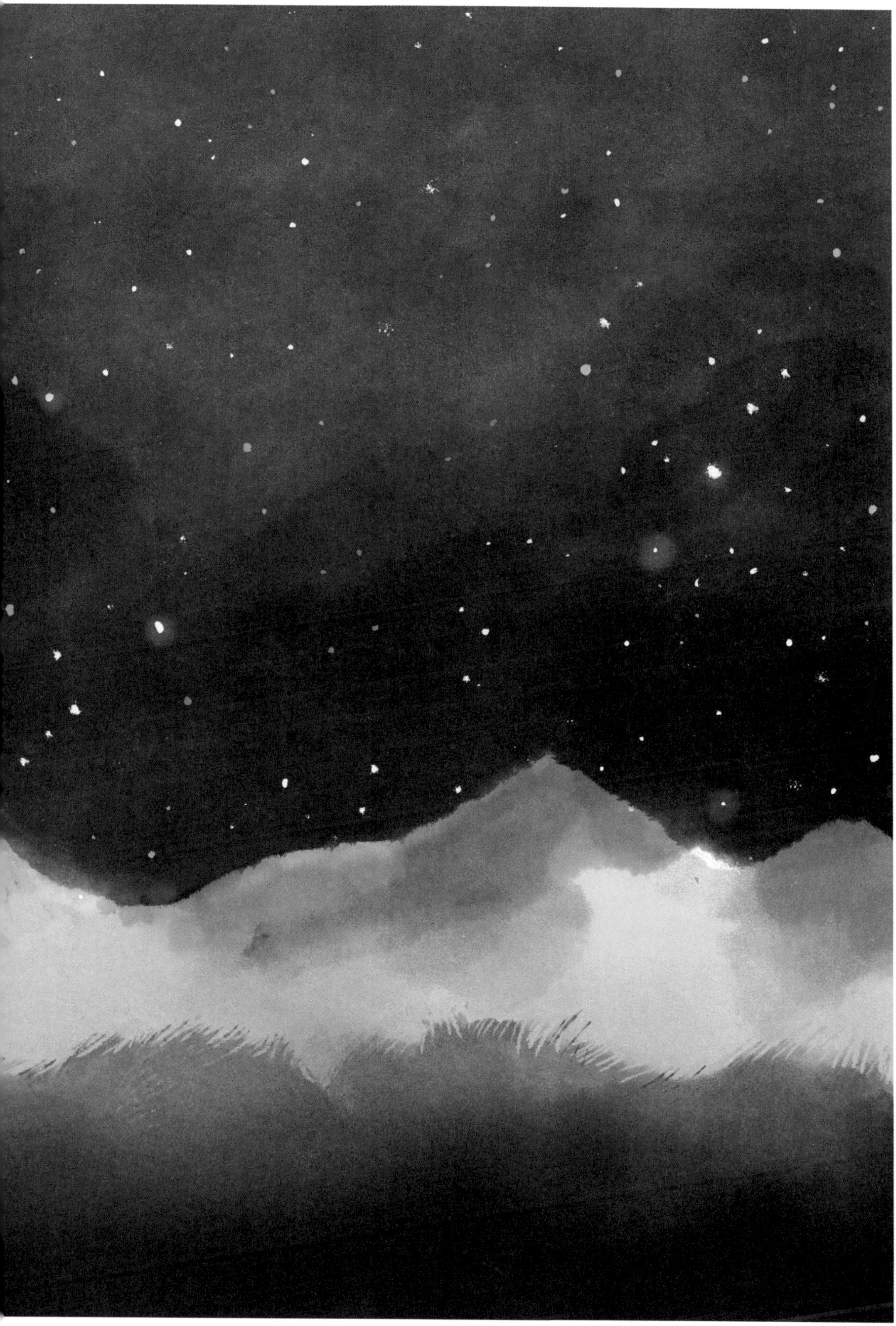

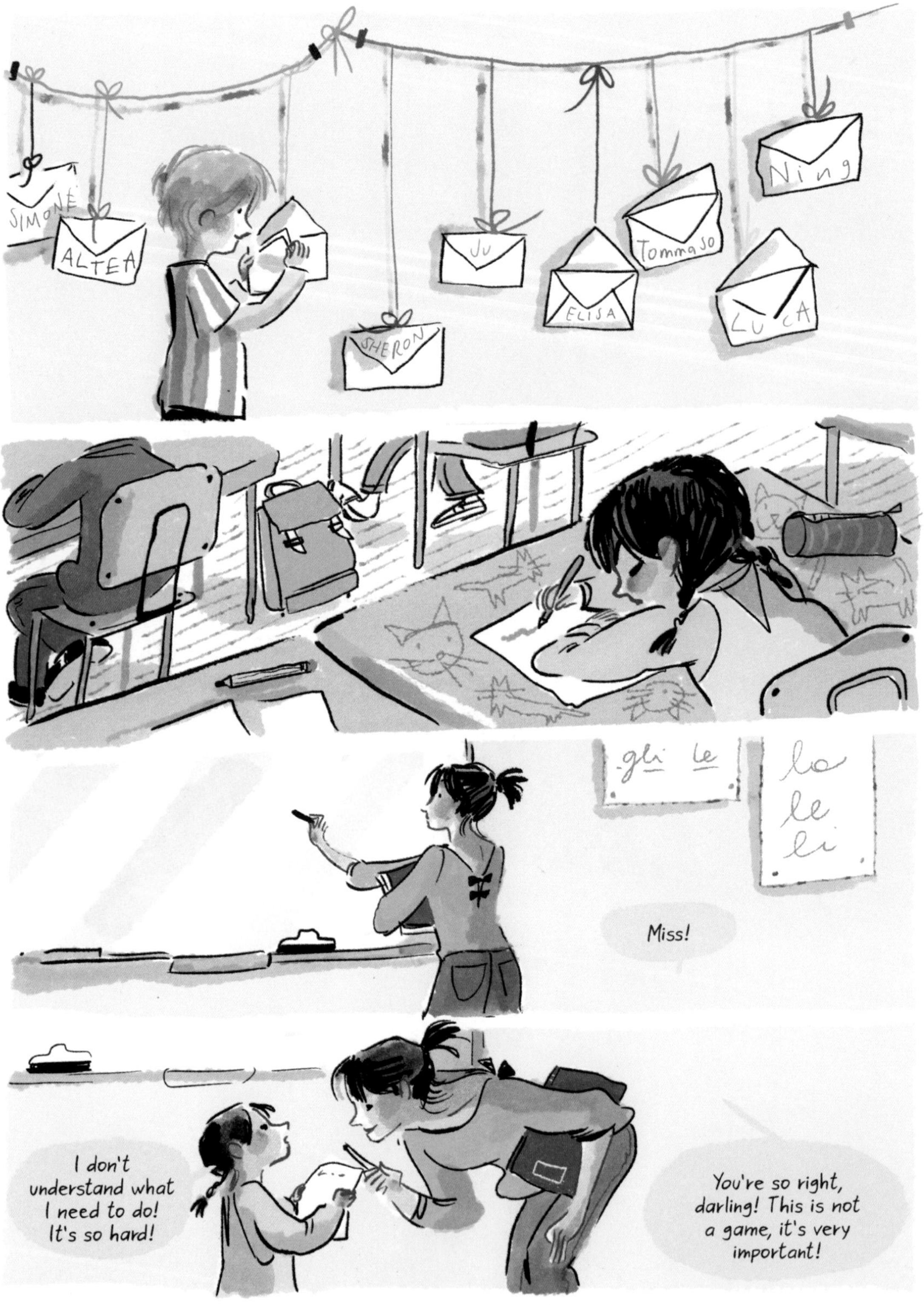
SIMONE
ALTEA
JU
SHERON
ELISA
TOMMASO
Ning
LUCA
gli le
la
le
li
Miss!
I don't understand what I need to do! It's so hard!
You're so right, darling! This is not a game, it's very important!

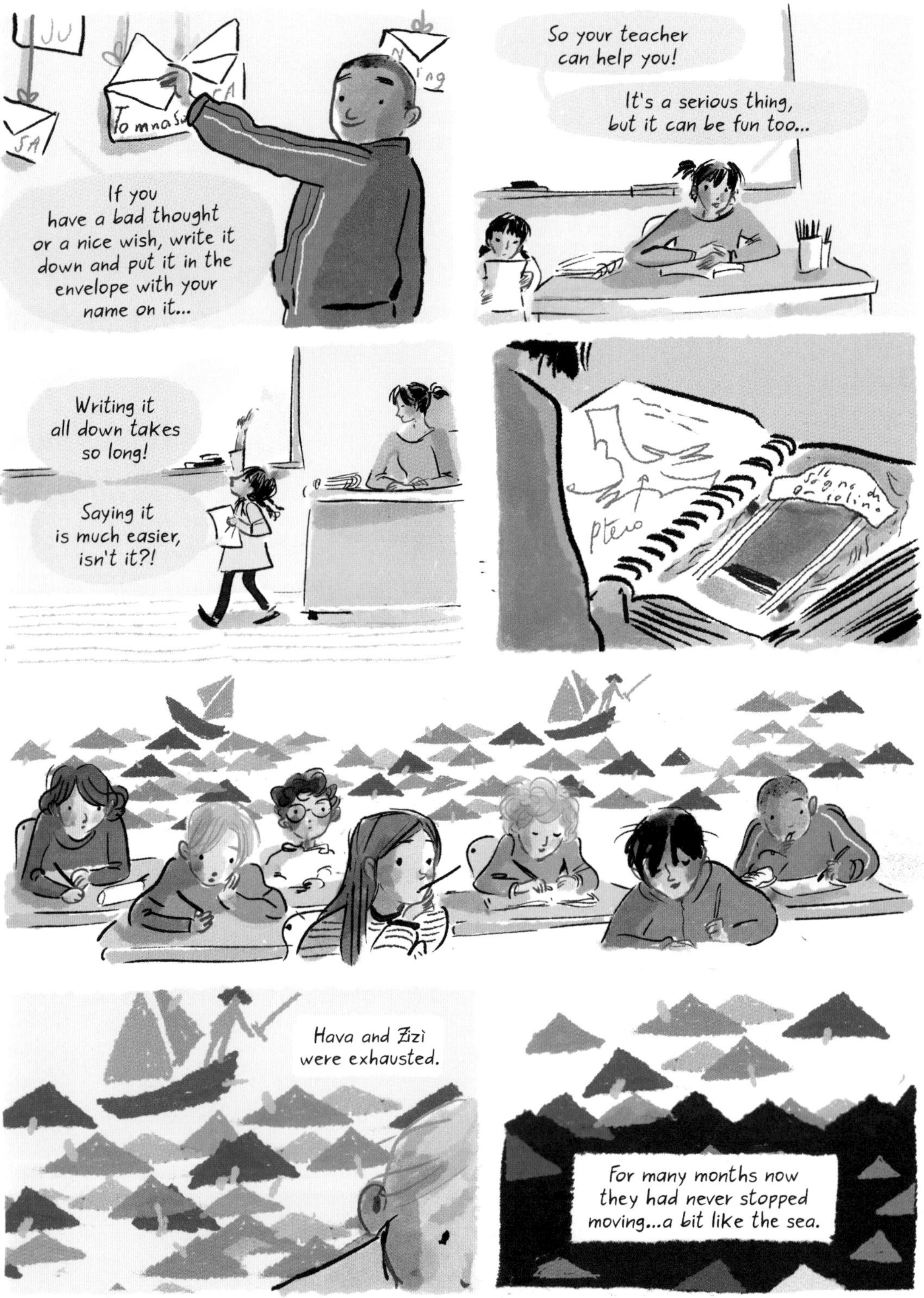
If you have a bad thought or a nice wish, write it down and put it in the envelope with your name on it...
So your teacher can help you!
It's a serious thing, but it can be fun too...
Writing it all down takes so long!
Saying it is much easier, isn't it?!
Hava and Zizì were exhausted.
For many months now they had never stopped moving...a bit like the sea.

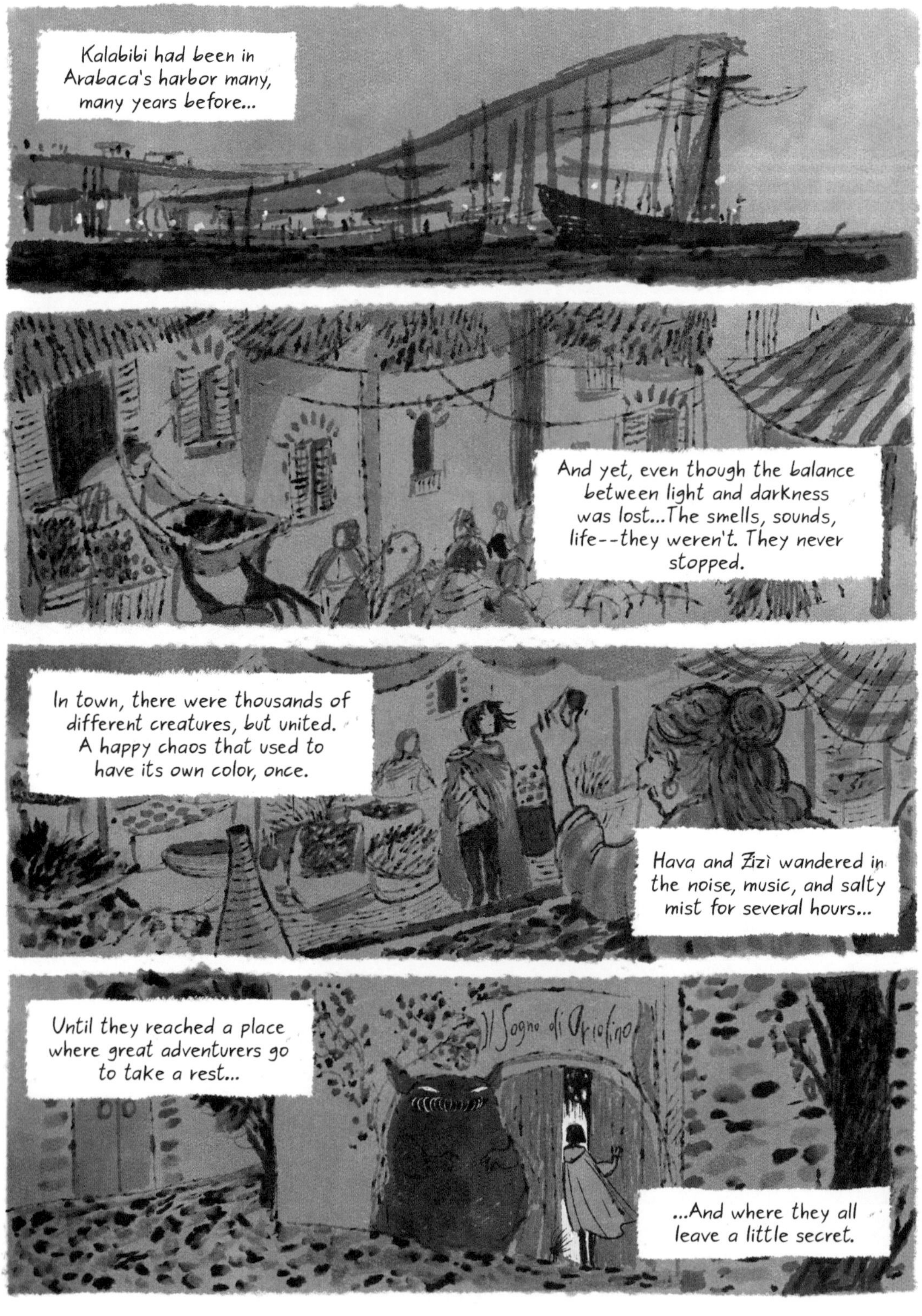
Kalabibi had been in Arabaca's harbor many, many years before...
And yet, even though the balance between light and darkness was lost...The smells, sounds, life--they weren't. They never stopped.
In town, there were thousands of different creatures, but united. A happy chaos that used to have its own color, once.
Hava and Zizi wandered in the noise, music, and salty mist for several hours...
Until they reached a place where great adventurers go to take a rest...
Il Sogno di Ariolino
...And where they all leave a little secret.

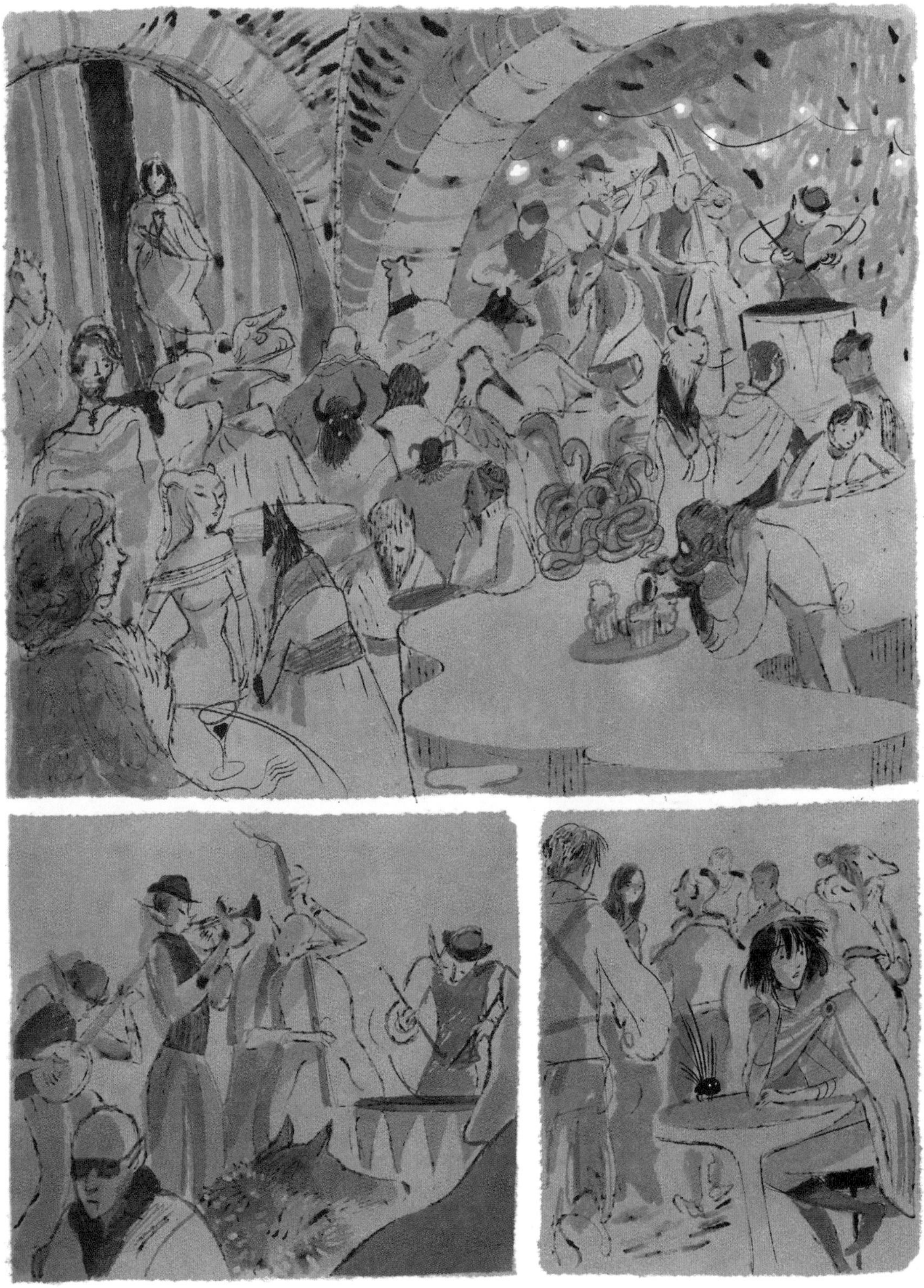

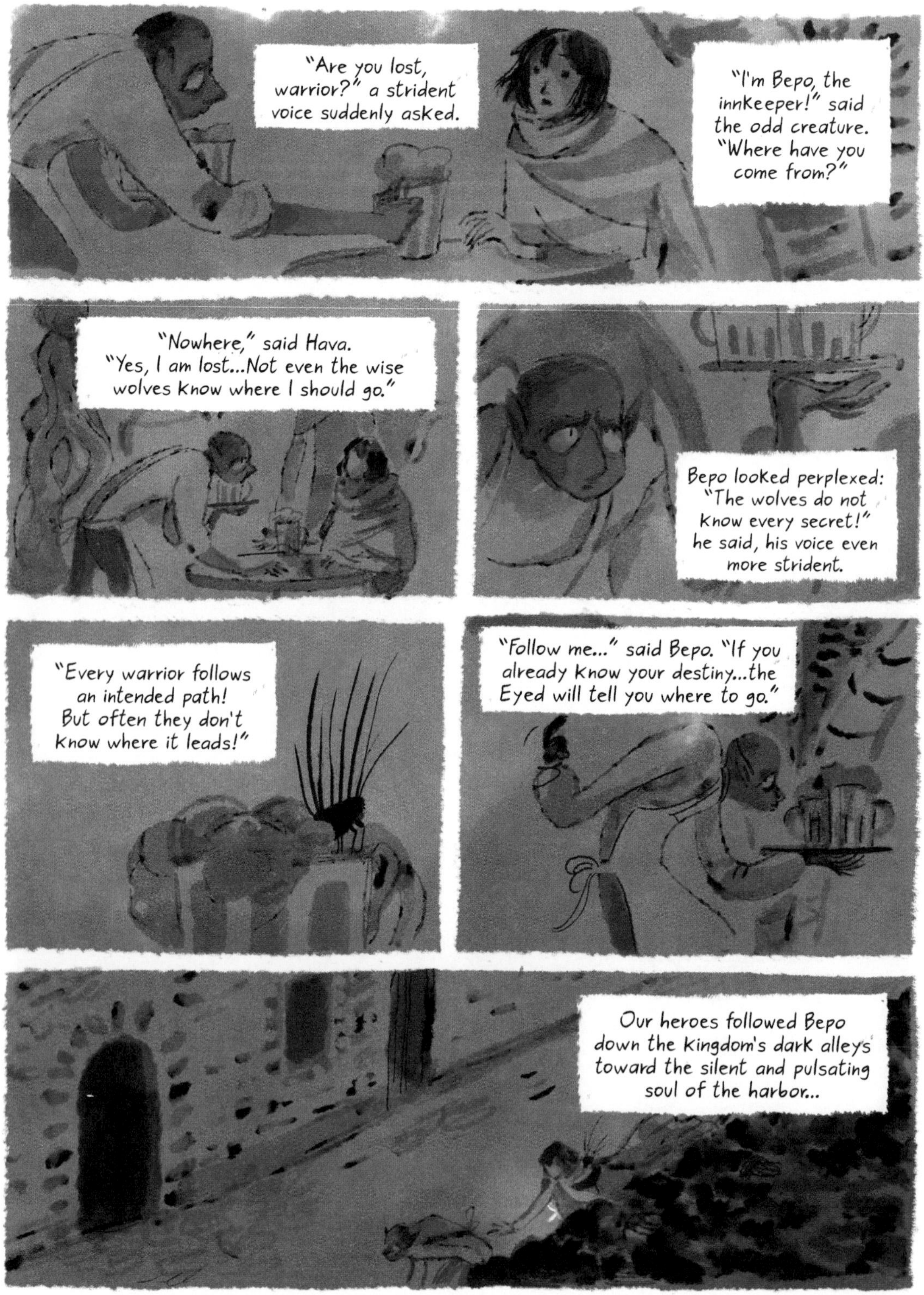
"Are you lost, warrior?" a strident voice suddenly asked.
"I'm Bepo, the innkeeper!" said the odd creature. "Where have you come from?"
"Nowhere," said Hava. "Yes, I am lost...Not even the wise wolves know where I should go."
Bepo looked perplexed: "The wolves do not know every secret!" he said, his voice even more strident.
"Every warrior follows an intended path! But often they don't know where it leads!"
"Follow me..." said Bepo. "If you already know your destiny...the Eyed will tell you where to go."
Our heroes followed Bepo down the kingdom's dark alleys toward the silent and pulsating soul of the harbor...

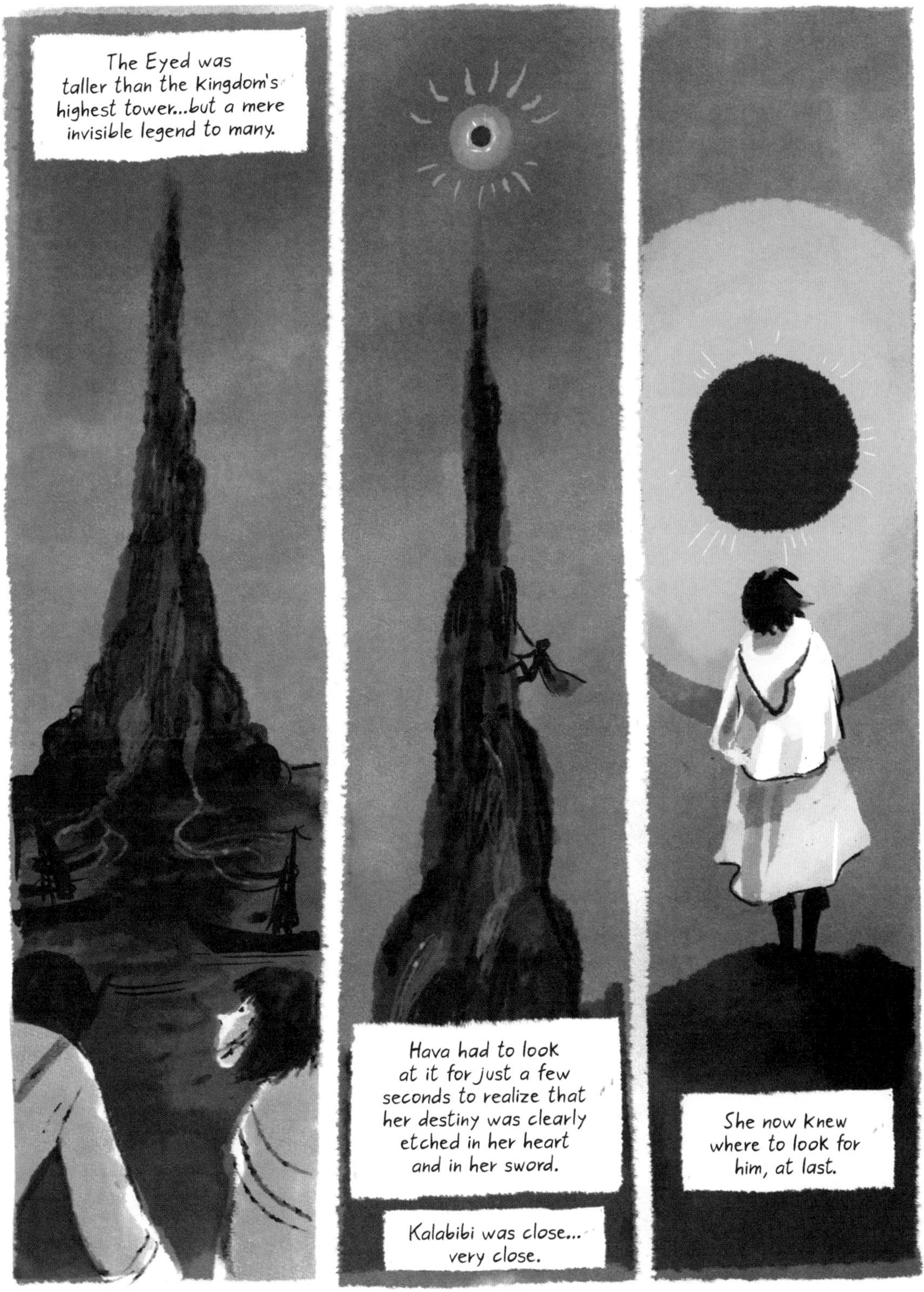
The Eyed was taller than the Kingdom's highest tower...but a mere invisible legend to many.
Hava had to look at it for just a few seconds to realize that her destiny was clearly etched in her heart and in her sword.
Kalabibi was close... very close.
She now knew where to look for him, at last.

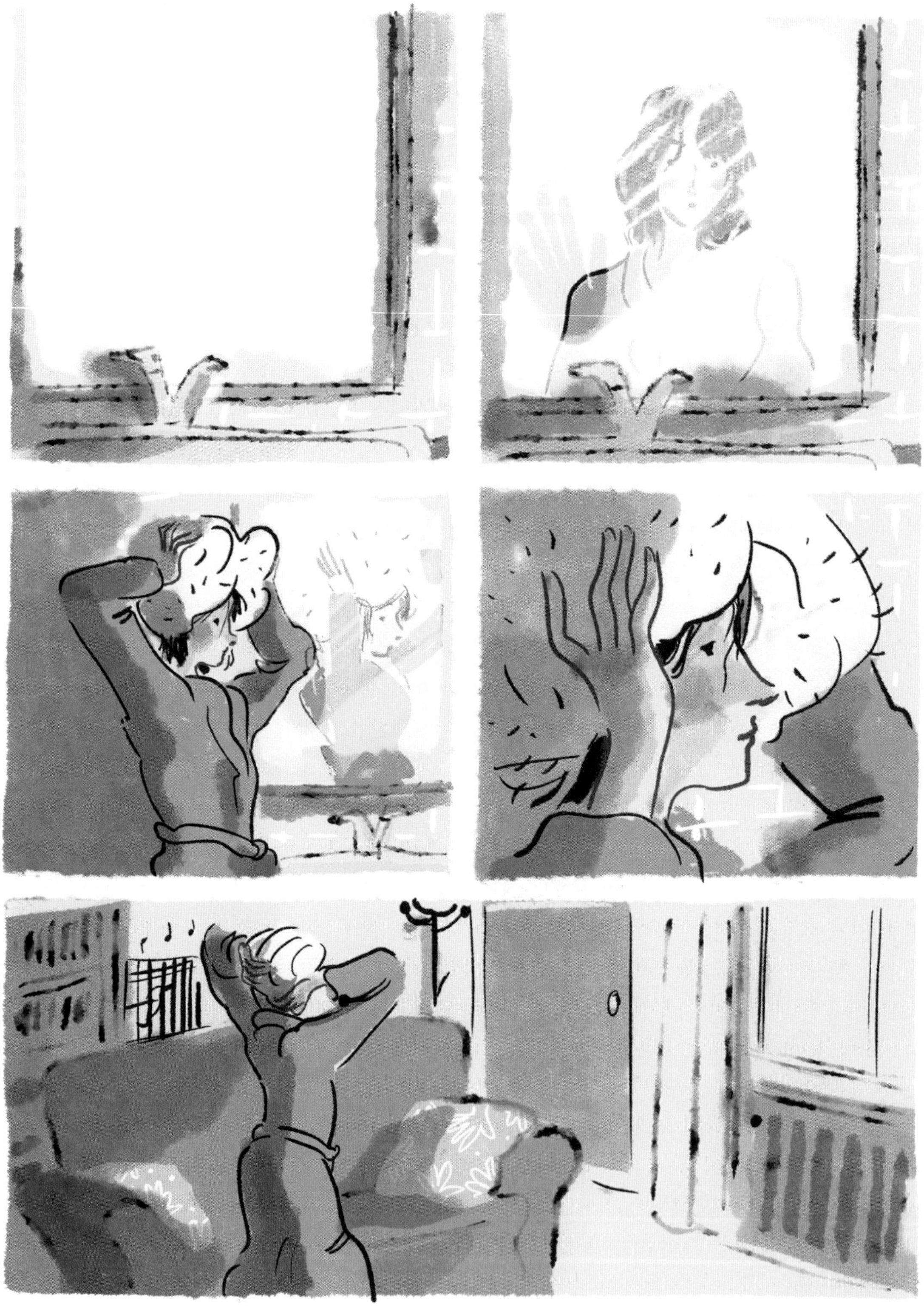

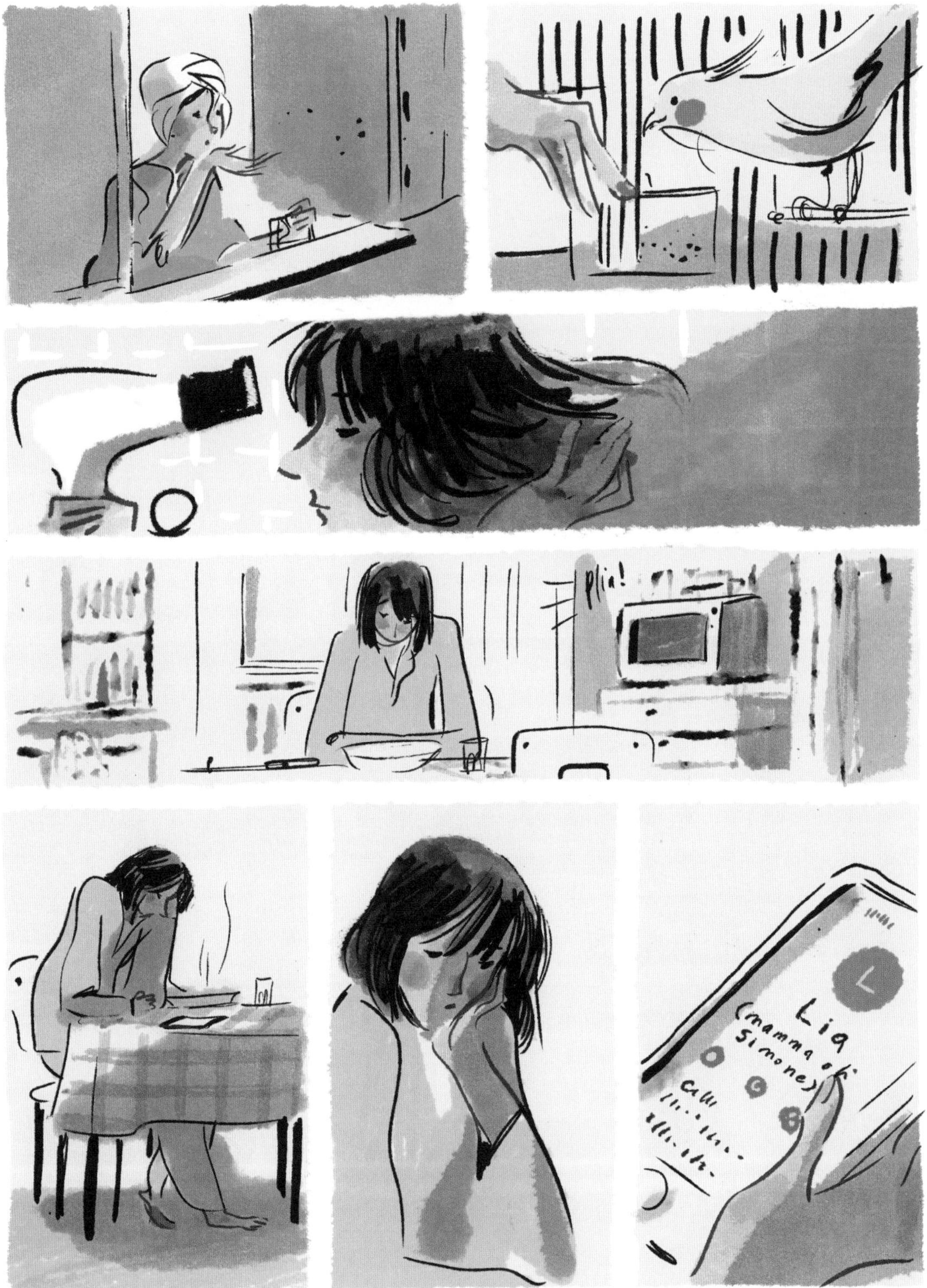
plia!
Lia (mamma di Simone)
Call

*Lia (Simon's mom)

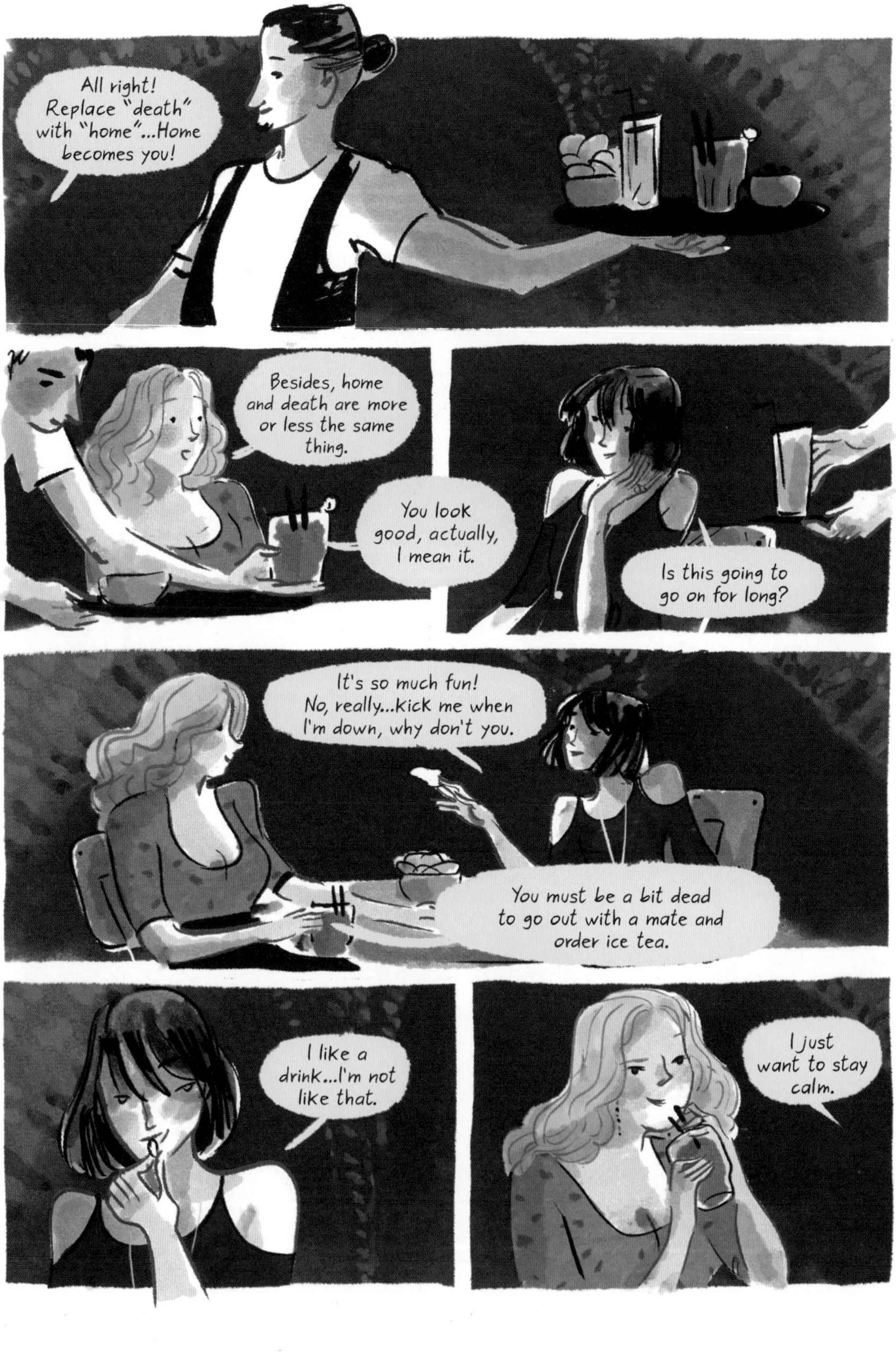
All right! Replace "death" with "home"...Home becomes you!
Besides, home and death are more or less the same thing.
You look good, actually, I mean it.
Is this going to go on for long?
It's so much fun! No, really...kick me when I'm down, why don't you.
You must be a bit dead to go out with a mate and order ice tea.
I like a drink...I'm not like that.
I just want to stay calm.

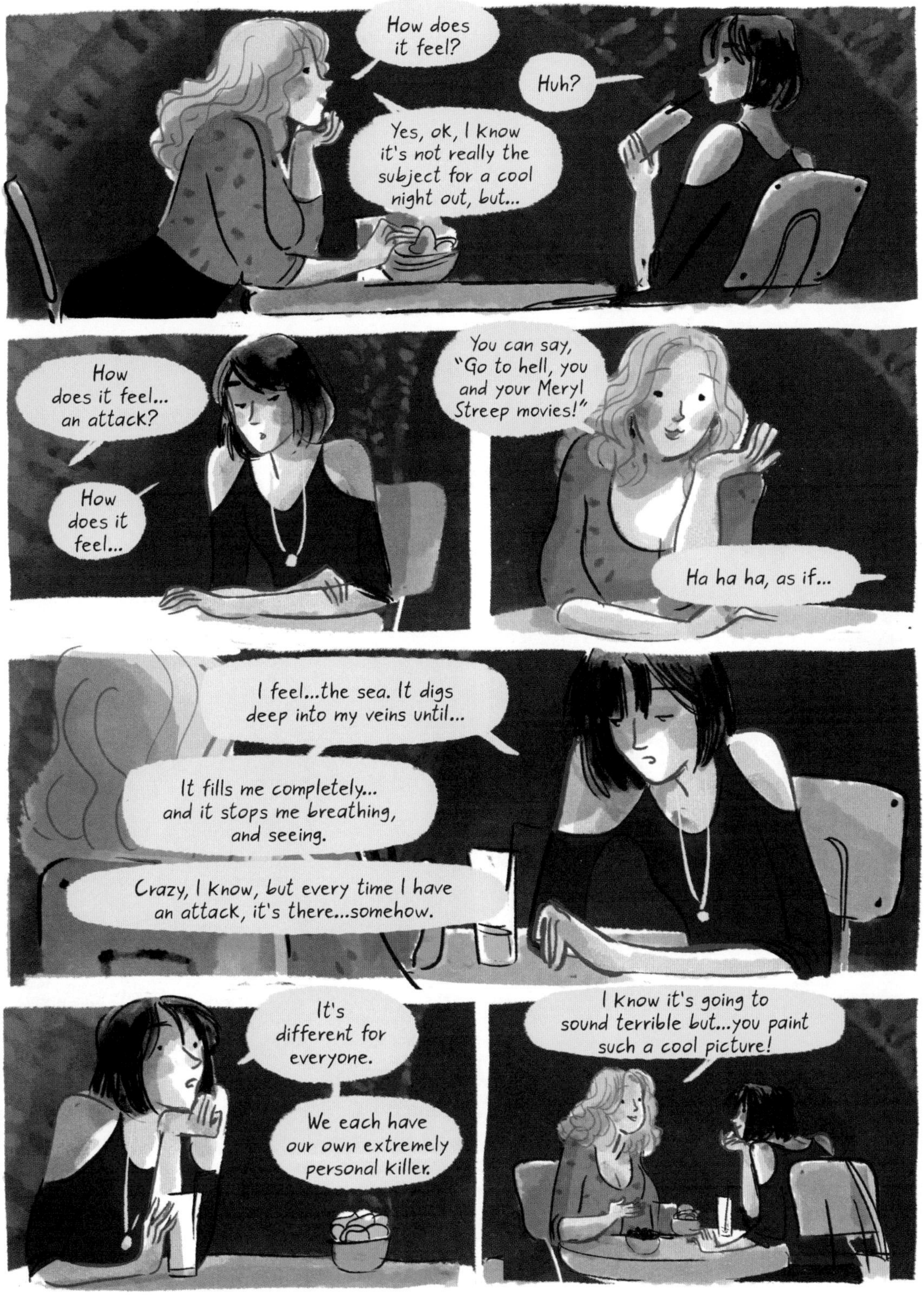
How does it feel?
Huh?
Yes, ok, I know it's not really the subject for a cool night out, but...
How does it feel... an attack?
How does it feel...
You can say, "Go to hell, you and your Meryl Streep movies!"
Ha ha ha, as if...
I feel...the sea. It digs deep into my veins until...
It fills me completely... and it stops me breathing, and seeing.
Crazy, I know, but every time I have an attack, it's there...somehow.
It's different for everyone.
We each have our own extremely personal killer.
I know it's going to sound terrible but...you paint such a cool picture!

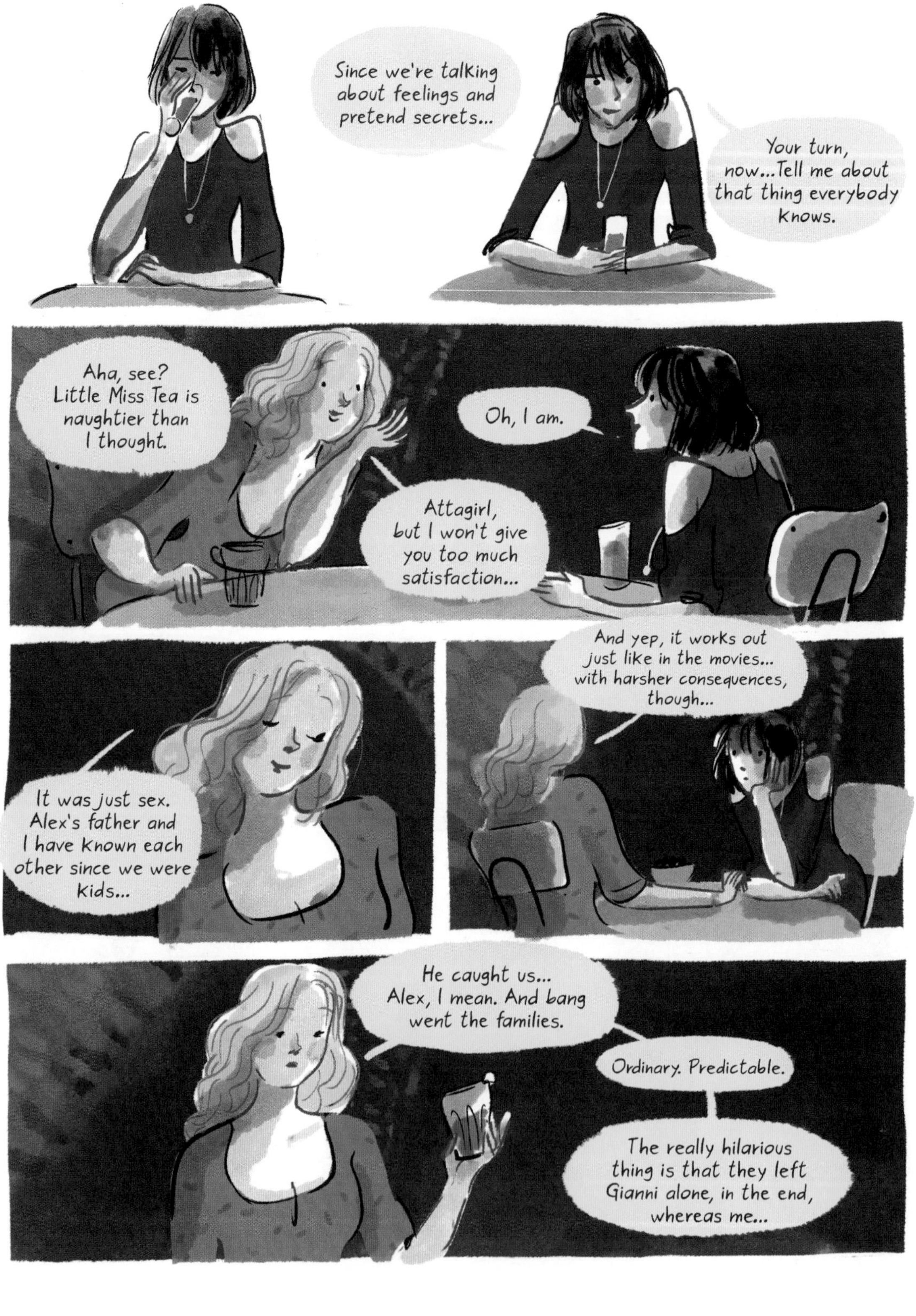
Since we're talking about feelings and pretend secrets...
Your turn, now...Tell me about that thing everybody knows.
Aha, see? Little Miss Tea is naughtier than I thought.
Oh, I am.
Attagirl, but I won't give you too much satisfaction...
It was just sex. Alex's father and I have known each other since we were kids...
And yep, it works out just like in the movies... with harsher consequences, though...
He caught us... Alex, I mean. And bang went the families.
Ordinary. Predictable.
The really hilarious thing is that they left Gianni alone, in the end, whereas me...

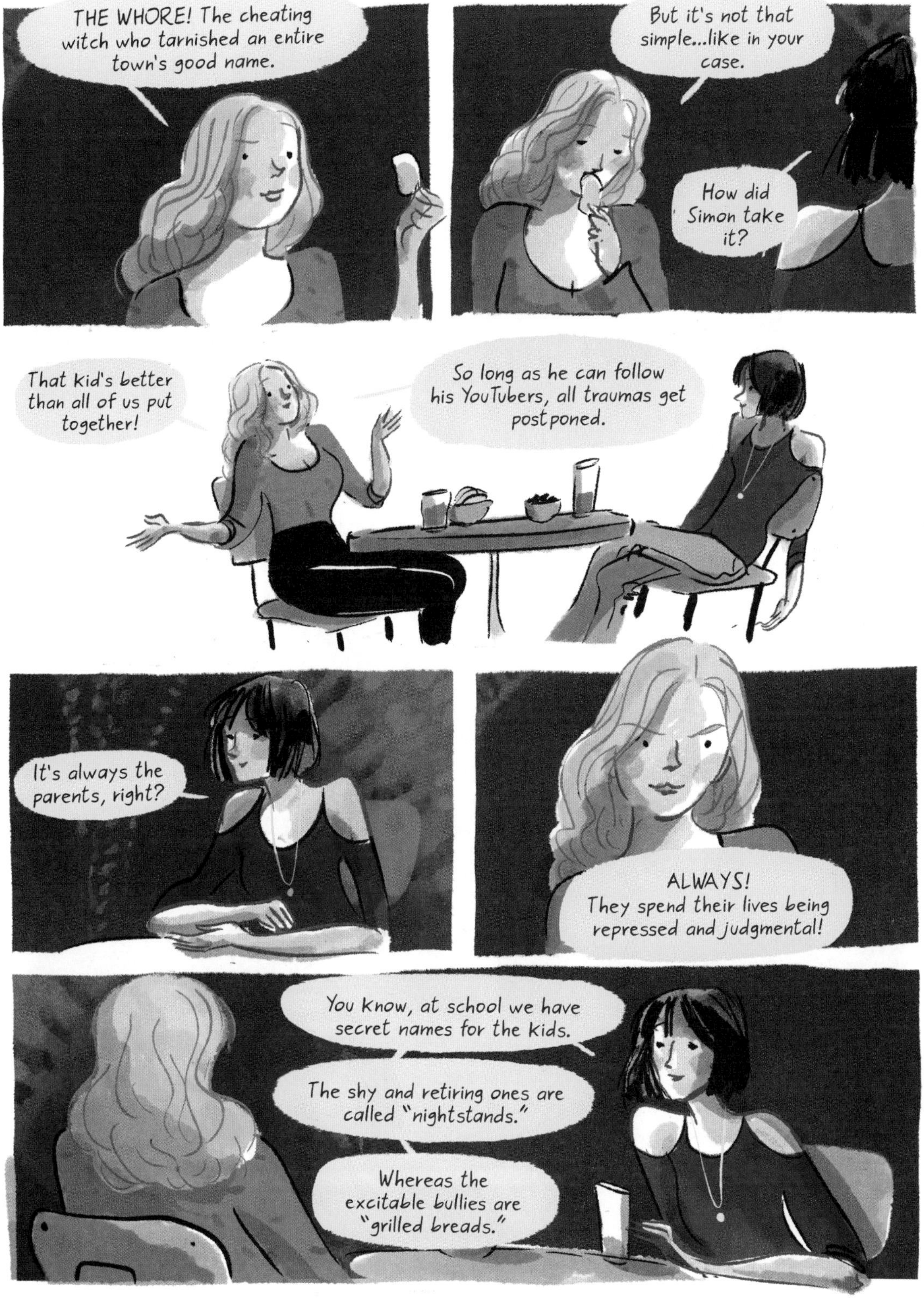
THE WHORE! The cheating witch who tarnished an entire town's good name.
But it's not that simple...like in your case.
How did Simon take it?
That kid's better than all of us put together!
So long as he can follow his YouTubers, all traumas get postponed.
It's always the parents, right?
ALWAYS! They spend their lives being repressed and judgmental!
You know, at school we have secret names for the kids.
The shy and retiring ones are called "nightstands."
Whereas the excitable bullies are "grilled breads."

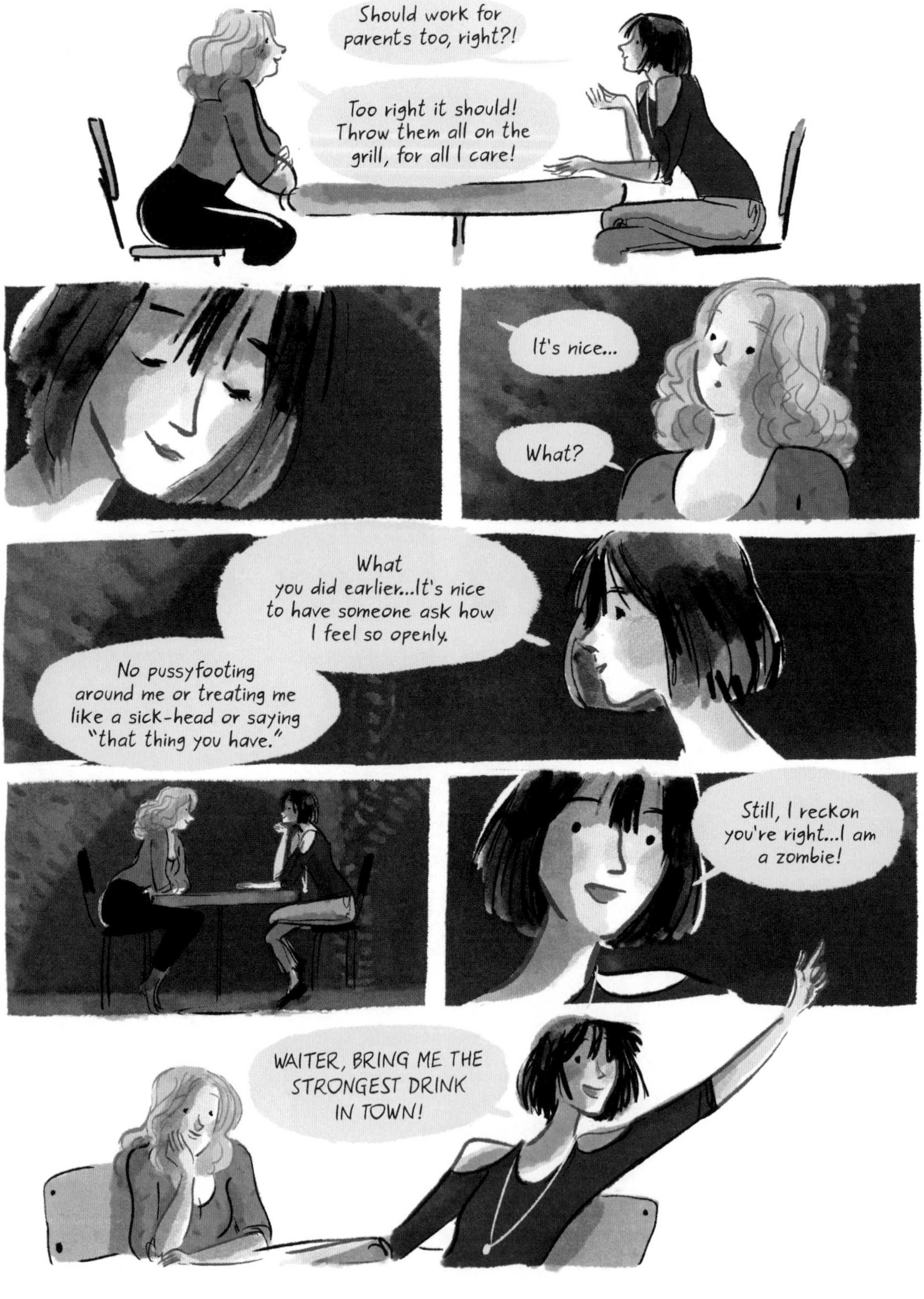
Should work for parents too, right?!
Too right it should! Throw them all on the grill, for all I care!
It's nice...
What?
What you did earlier...It's nice to have someone ask how I feel so openly.
No pussyfooting around me or treating me like a sick-head or saying "that thing you have."
Still, I reckon you're right...I am a zombie!
WAITER, BRING ME THE STRONGEST DRINK IN TOWN!

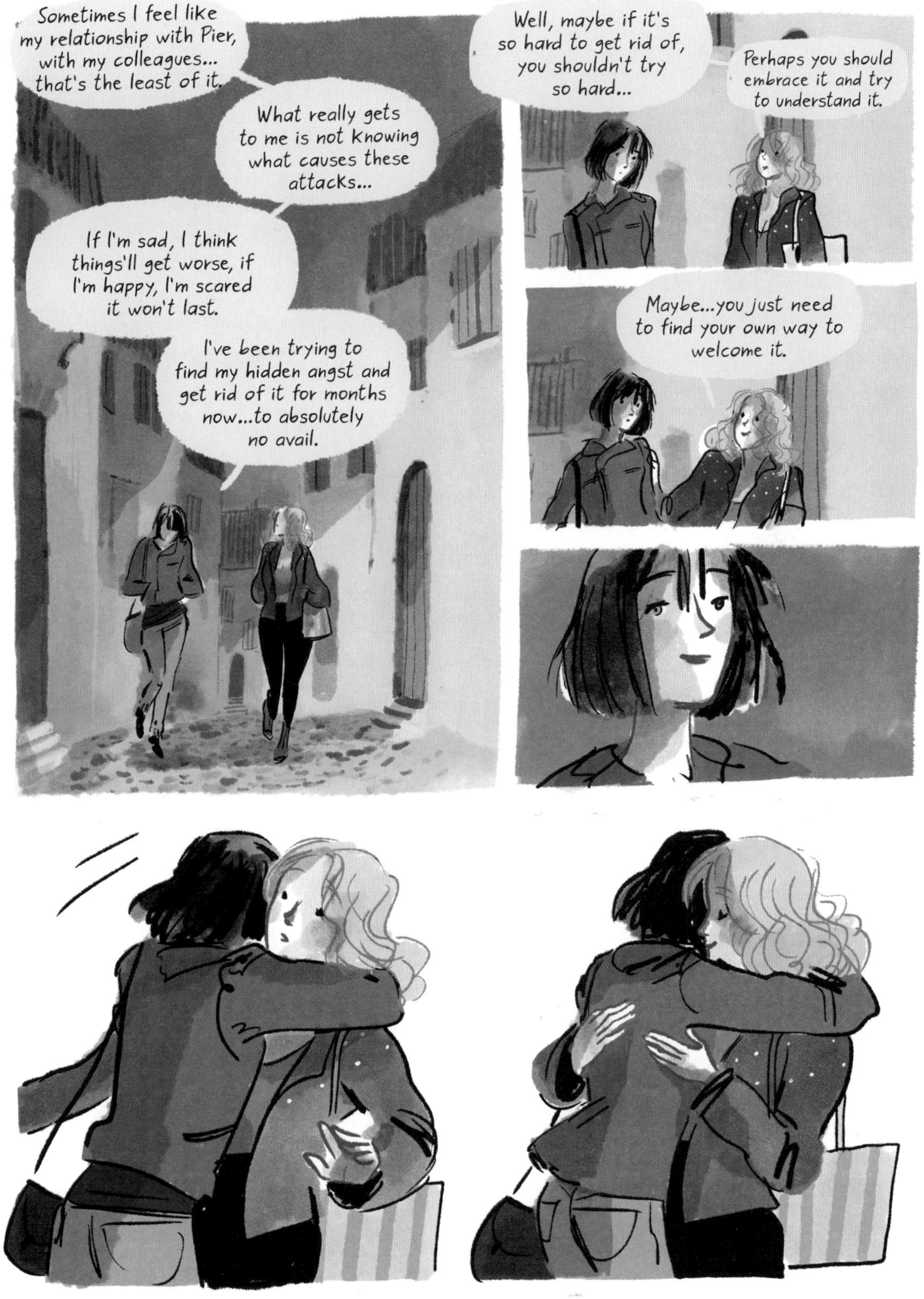
Sometimes I feel like my relationship with Pier, with my colleagues... that's the least of it.
What really gets to me is not knowing what causes these attacks...
If I'm sad, I think things'll get worse, if I'm happy, I'm scared it won't last.
I've been trying to find my hidden angst and get rid of it for months now...to absolutely no avail.
Well, maybe if it's so hard to get rid of, you shouldn't try so hard...
Perhaps you should embrace it and try to understand it.
Maybe...you just need to find your own way to welcome it.

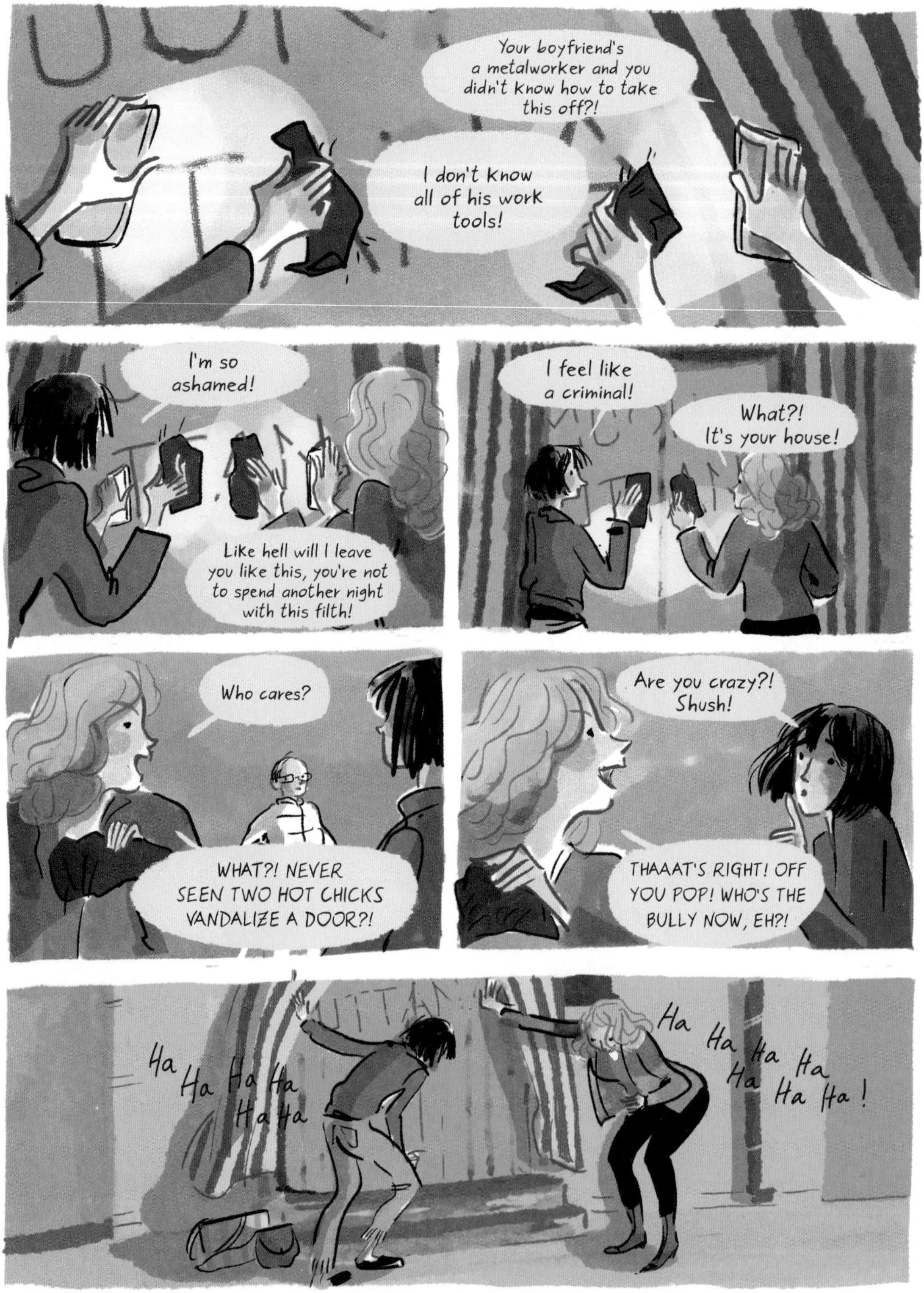
Your boyfriend's a metalworker and you didn't know how to take this off?!
I don't know all of his work tools!
I'm so ashamed!
Like hell will I leave you like this, you're not to spend another night with this filth!
I feel like a criminal!
What?! It's your house!
Who cares?
WHAT?! NEVER SEEN TWO HOT CHICKS VANDALIZE A DOOR?!
Are you crazy?! Shush!
THAAAT'S RIGHT! OFF YOU POP! WHO'S THE BULLY NOW, EH?!
Ha Ha Ha Ha Ha Ha
Ha Ha Ha Ha Ha Ha Ha!

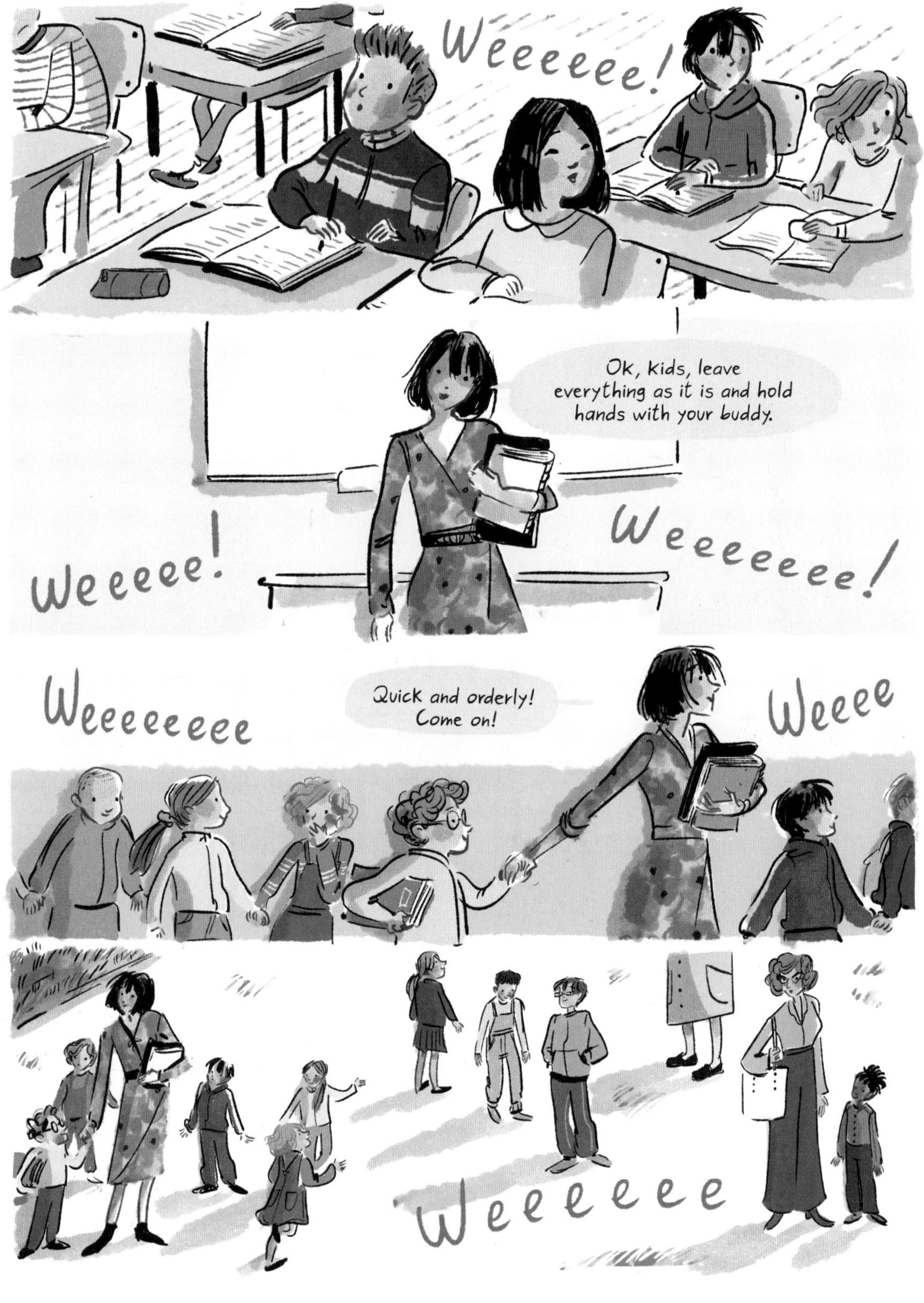

Weeeeee!
Ok, kids, leave everything as it is and hold hands with your buddy.
Weeeee!
Weeeeeeee!
Weeeeeeee
Quick and orderly! Come on!
Weeee
Weeeeee

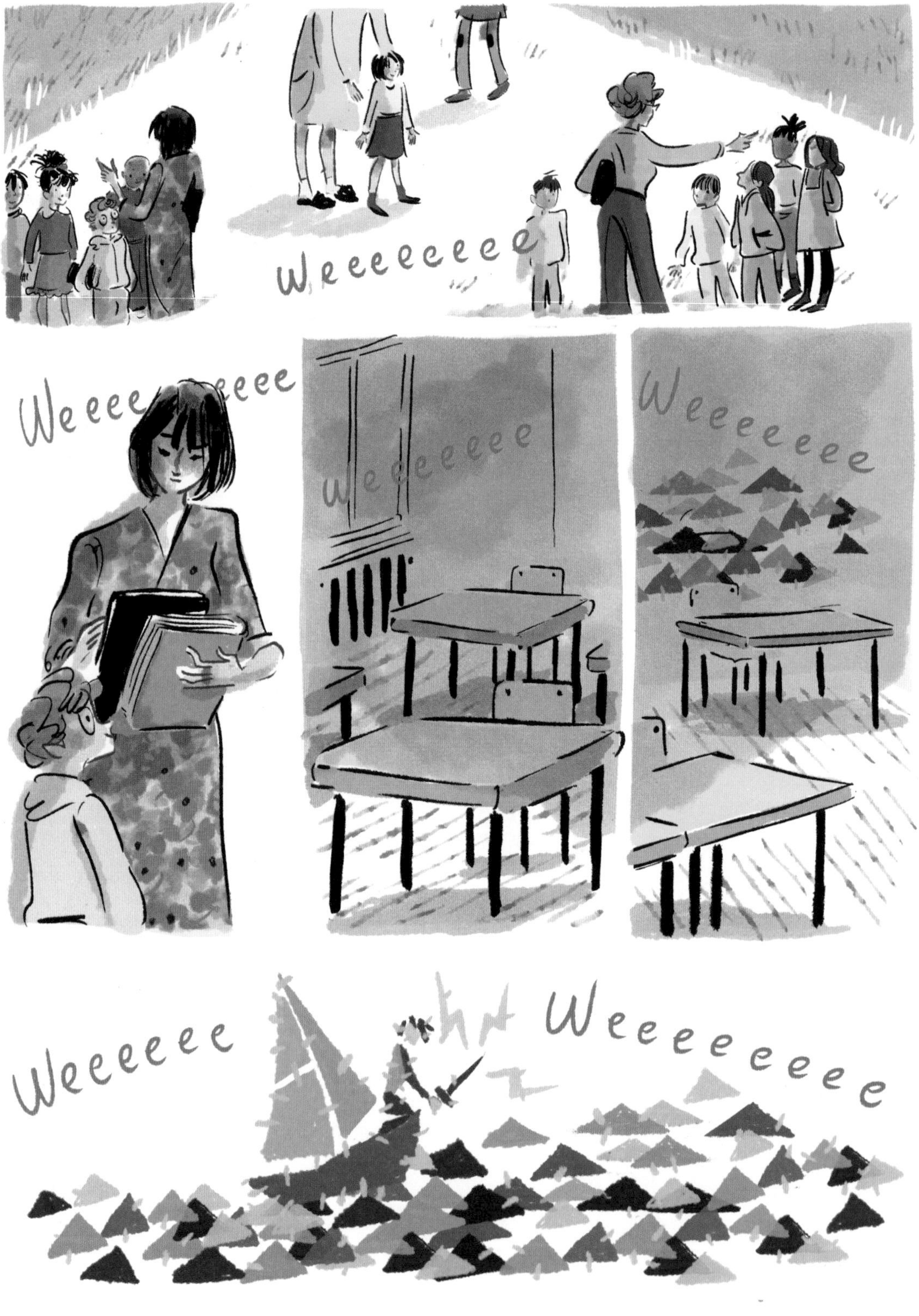
Weeeeeeee
Weeeeeeee
Weeeeeee
Weeeeeee
Weeeeee
Weeeeeeeee

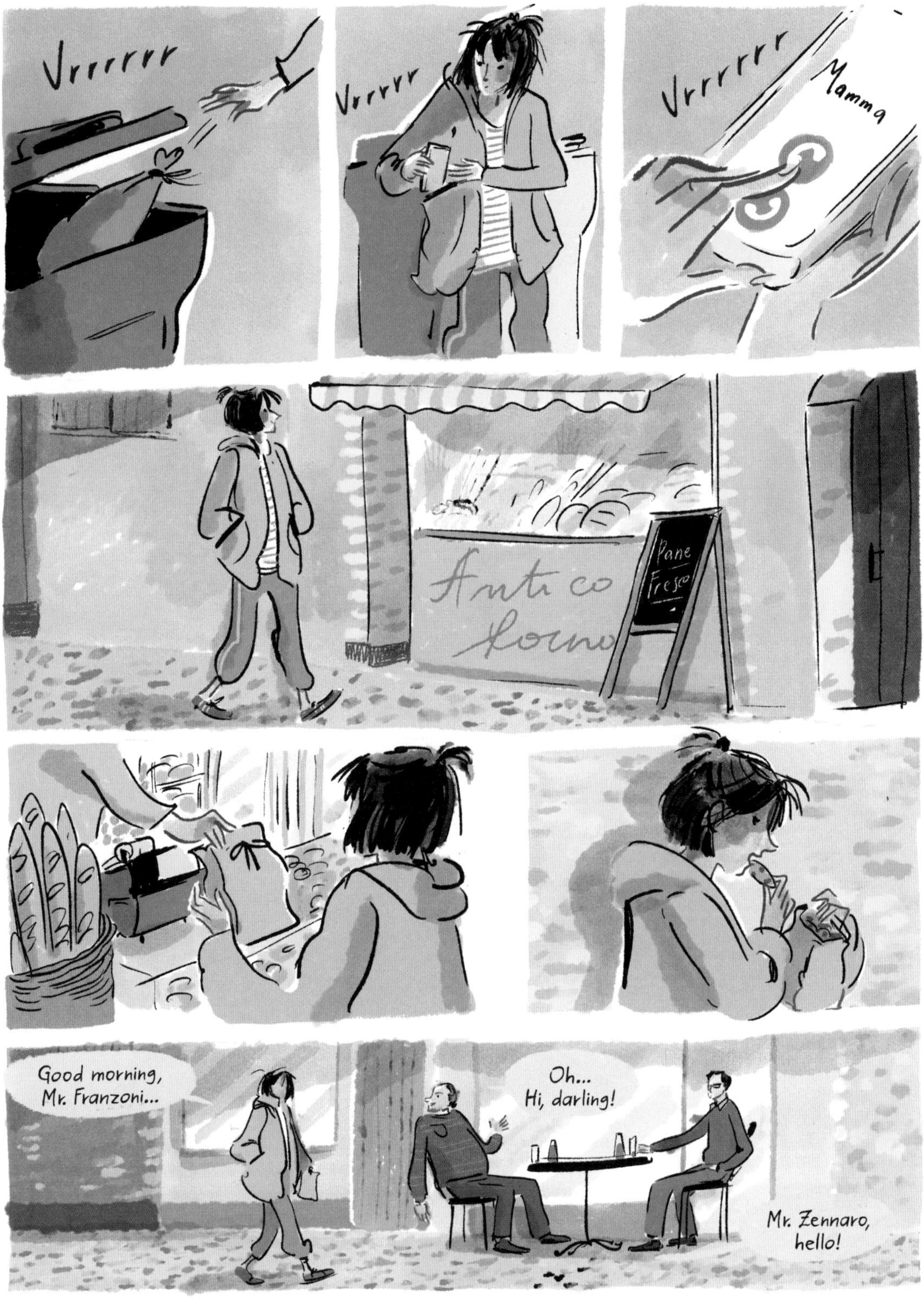
Vrrrrrr
Vrrrrr
Vrrrrrr
Mamma
Antico Forno
Pane Fresco
Good morning, Mr. Franzoni...
Oh... Hi, darling!
Mr. Zennaro, hello!

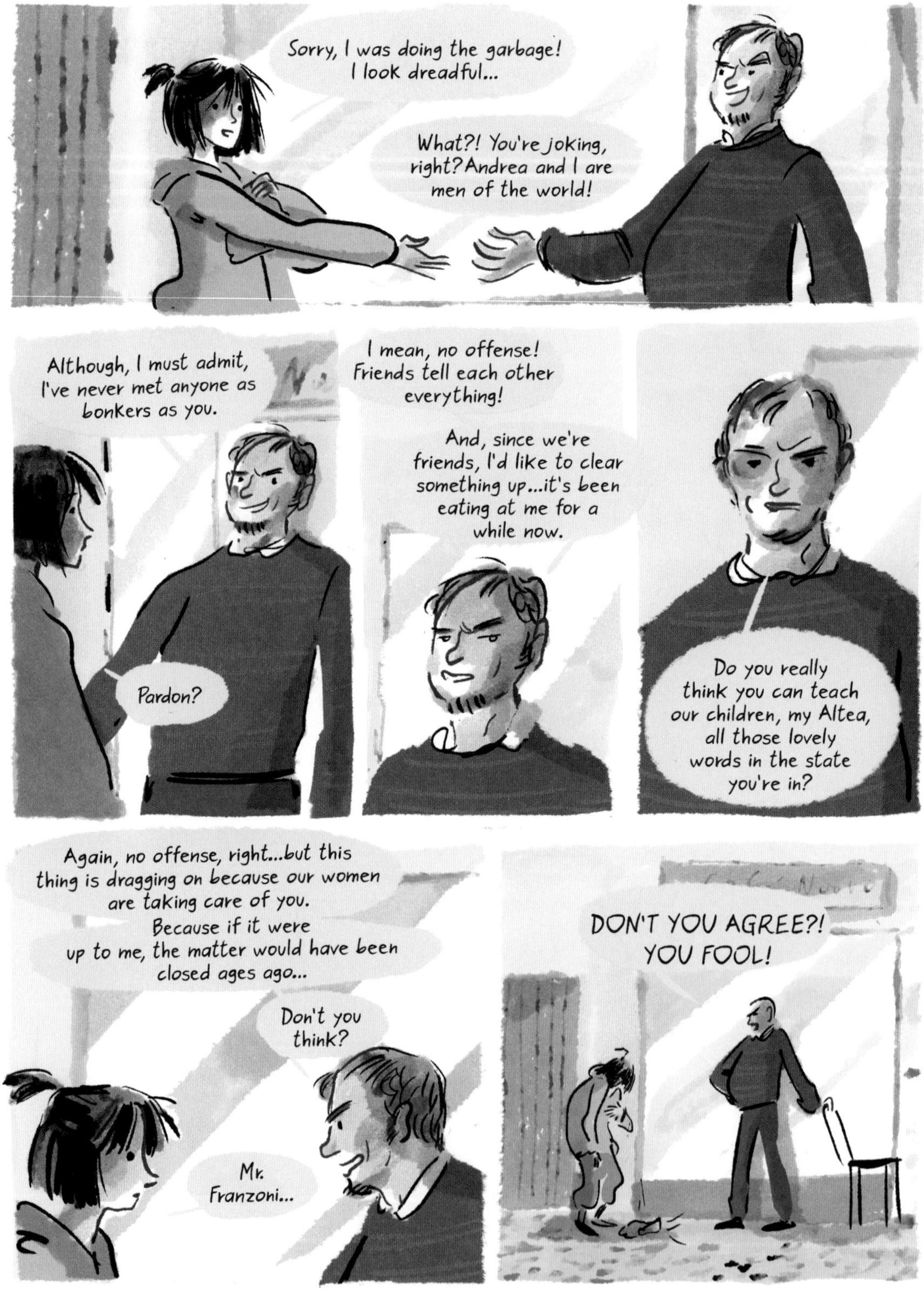
Sorry, I was doing the garbage! I look dreadful...
What?! You're joking, right? Andrea and I are men of the world!
Although, I must admit, I've never met anyone as bonkers as you.
Pardon?
I mean, no offense! Friends tell each other everything!
And, since we're friends, I'd like to clear something up...it's been eating at me for a while now.
Do you really think you can teach our children, my Altea, all those lovely words in the state you're in?
Again, no offense, right...but this thing is dragging on because our women are taking care of you.
Because if it were up to me, the matter would have been closed ages ago...
Don't you think?
Mr. Franzoni...
DON'T YOU AGREE?! YOU FOOL!

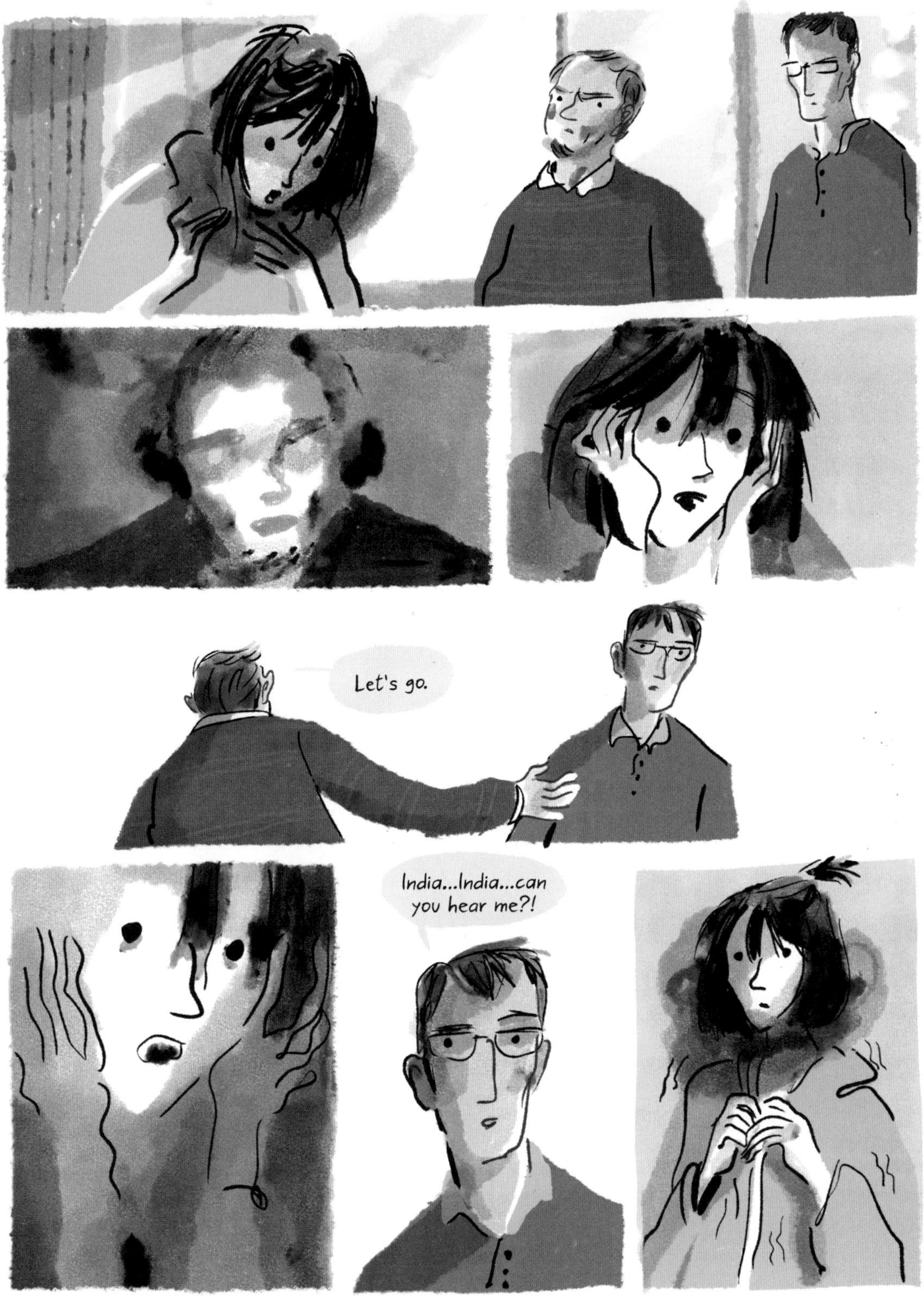
Let's go.
India...India...can you hear me?!

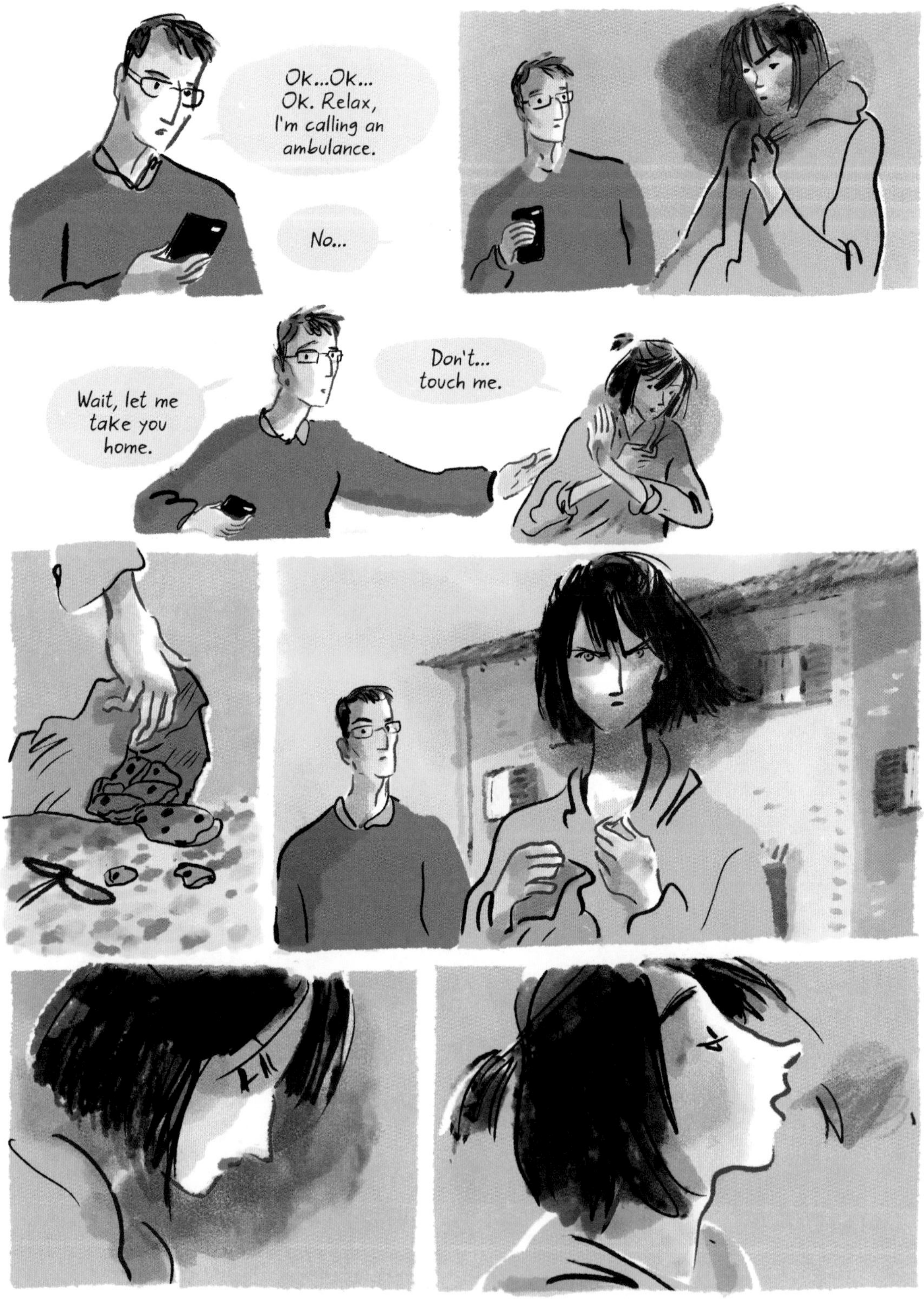

Ok...Ok... Ok. Relax, I'm calling an ambulance.
No...
Wait, let me take you home.
Don't... touch me.

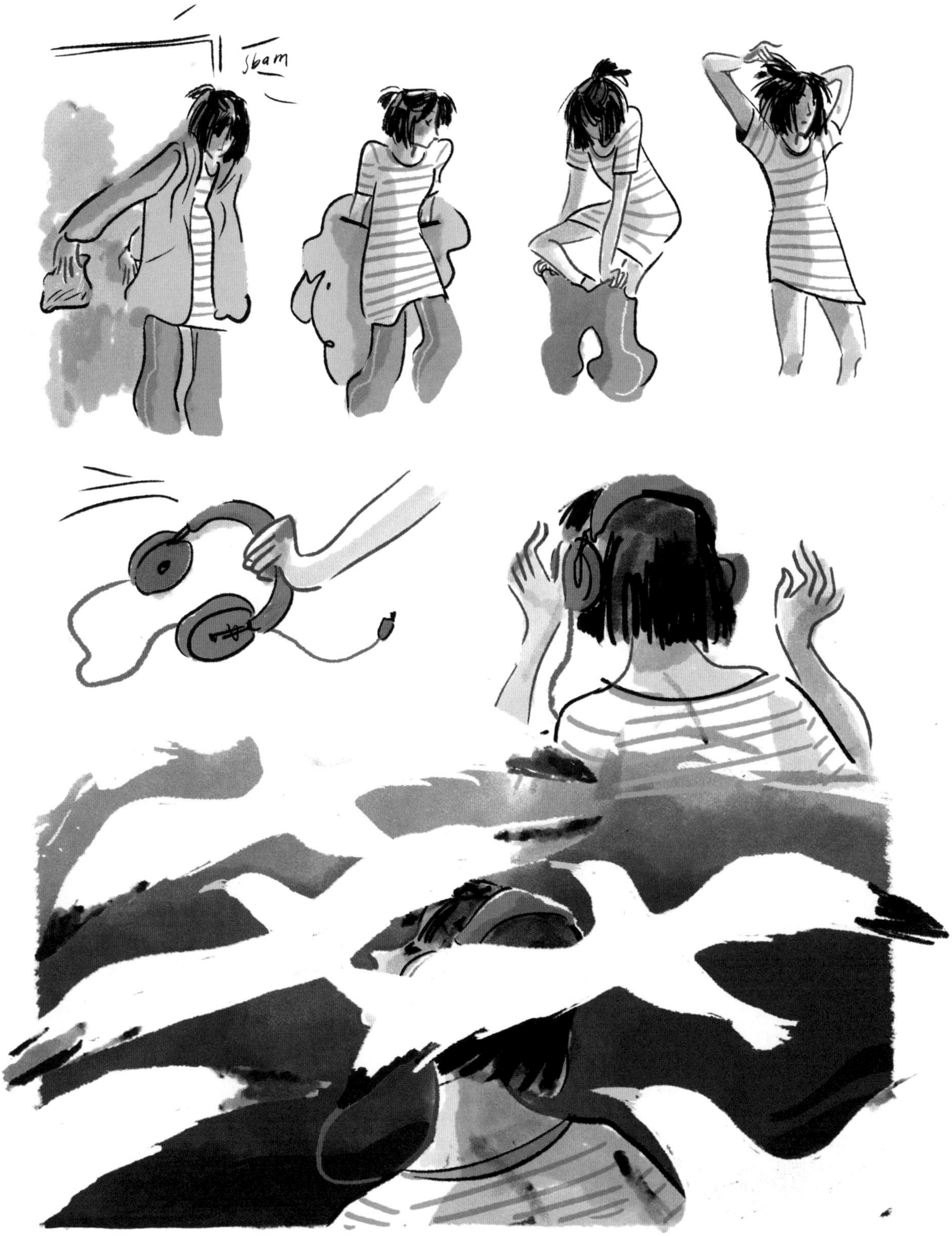
sbam

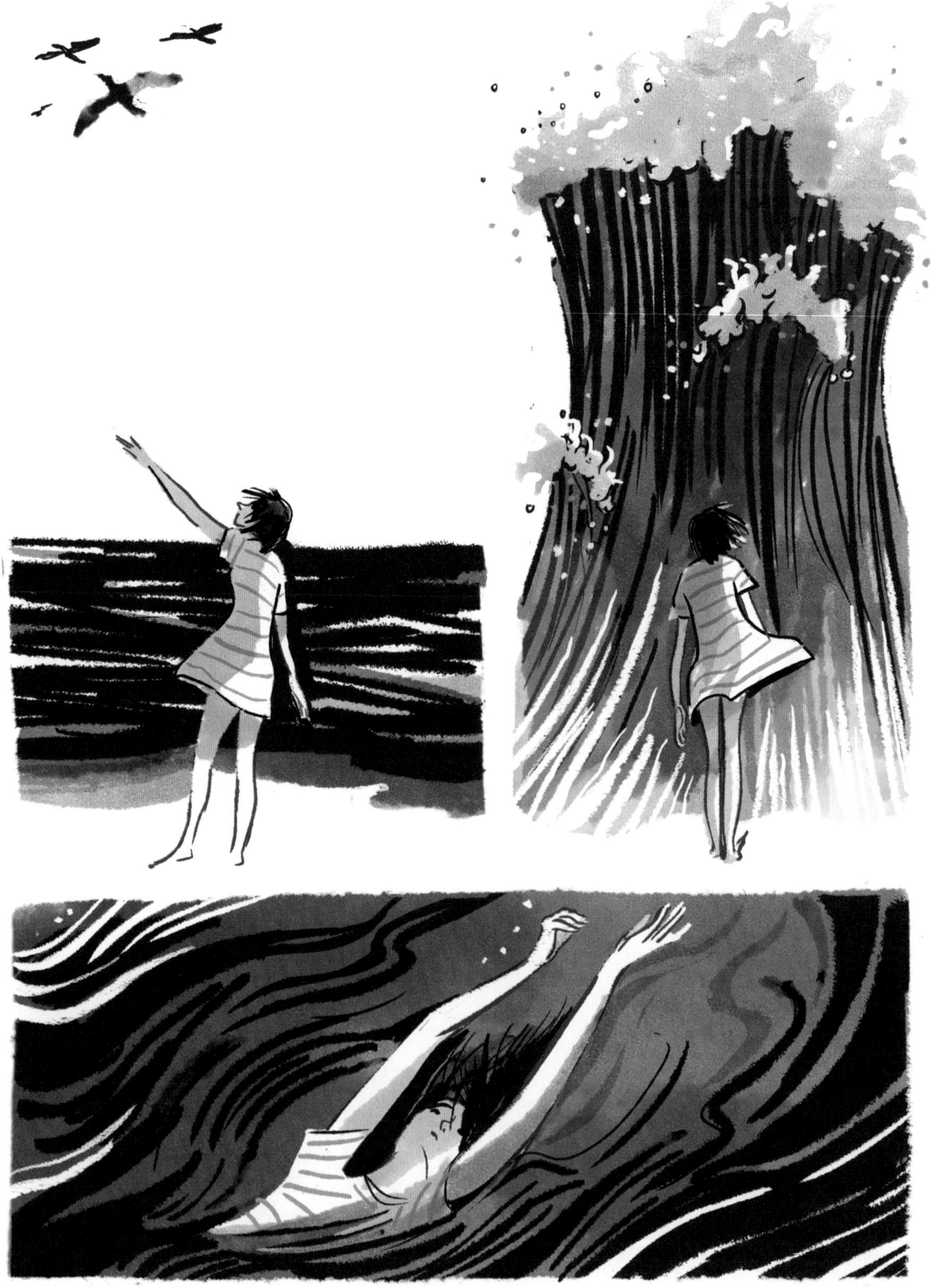

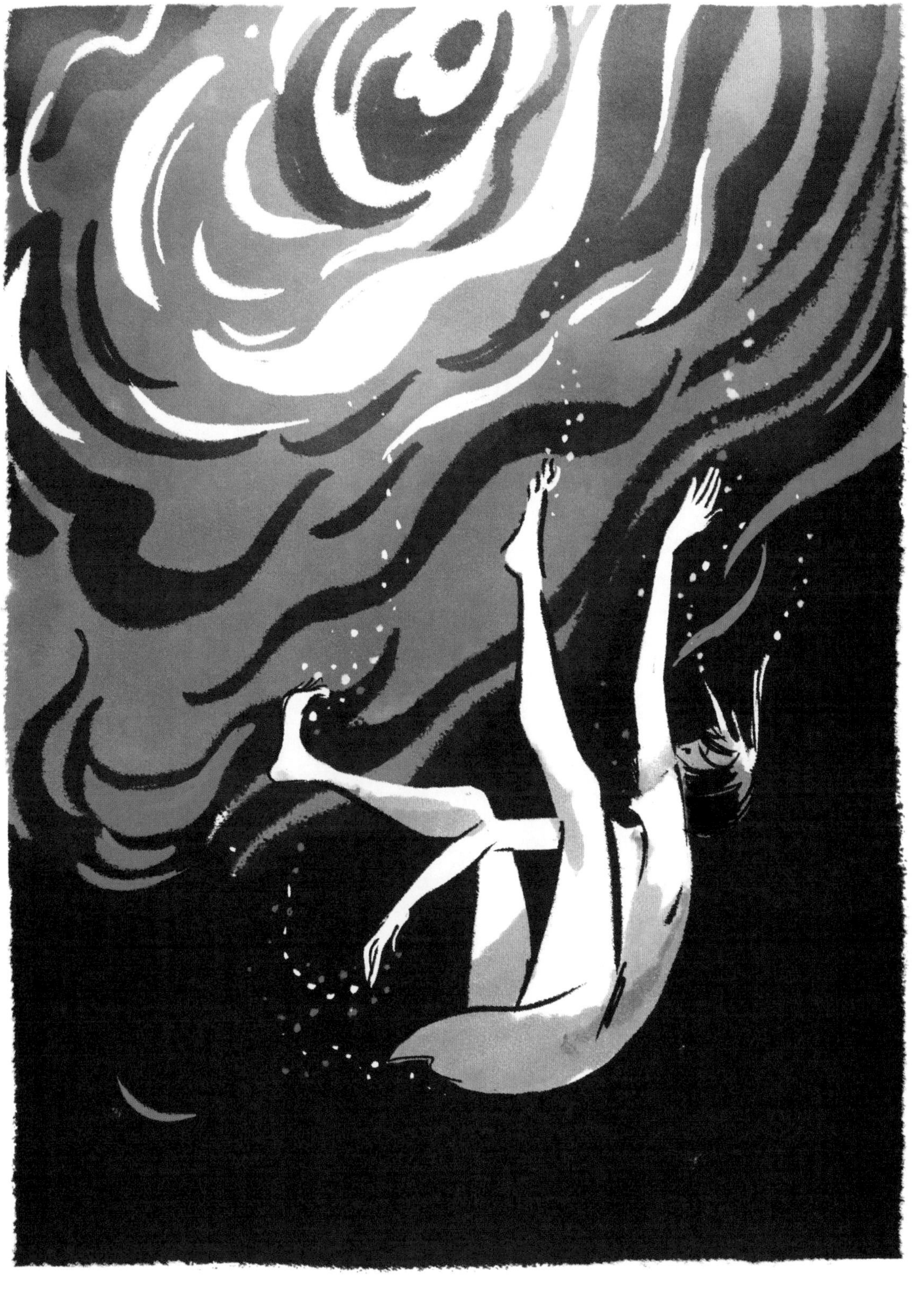

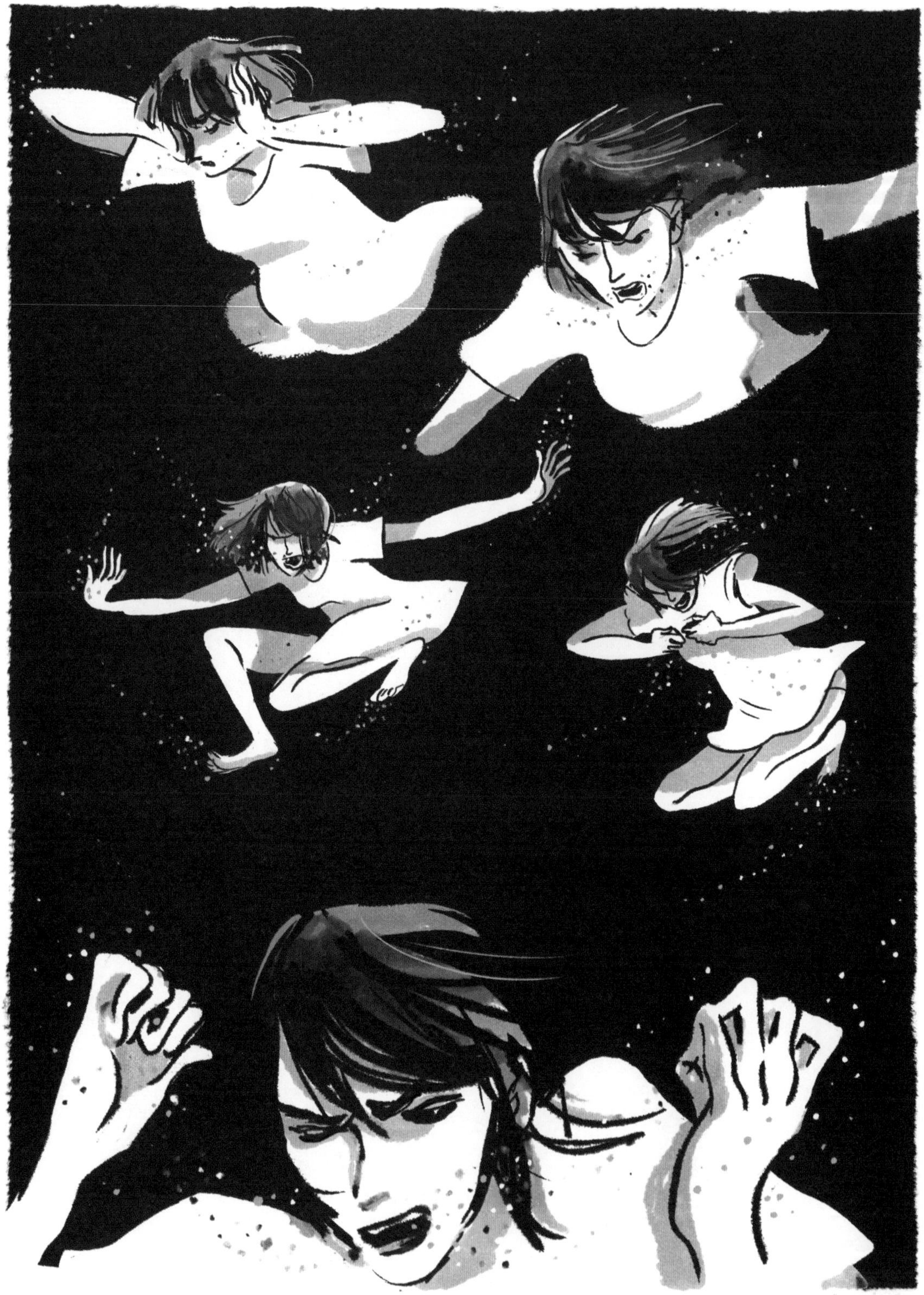

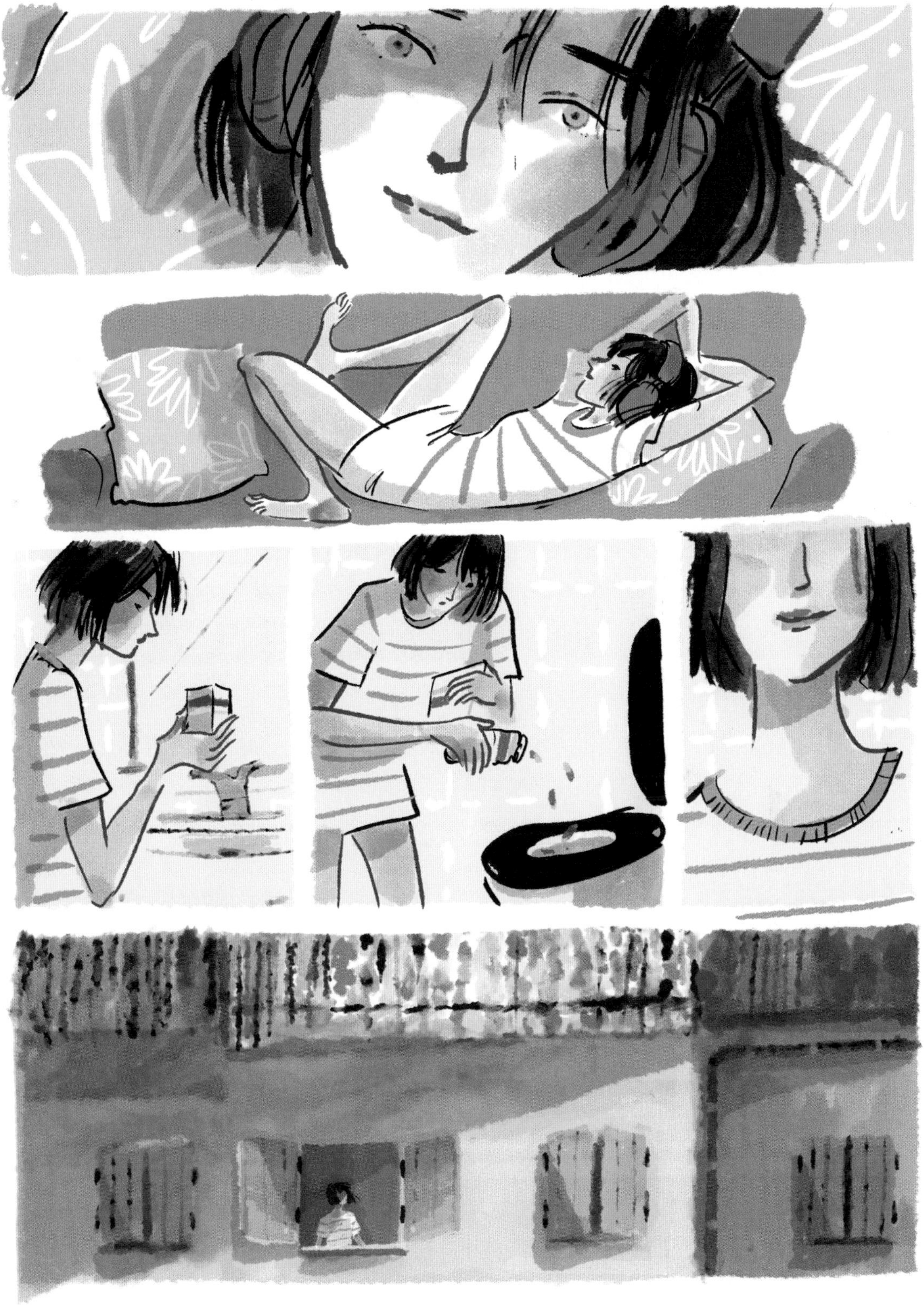

#01 - RED LIGHT/GREEN LIGHT PRACTICE!!! ☺ ☺ ☺

I take my index finger and my thumb and I draw semicircles on my fingertips. Enough? No way! I count to infinity. One, two, three, four, a thousand...until the attack gets bored and disappears. That is when I feel like I'm in a video game. I'm on my own. I manage my game. I lose and reboot...then lose and reboot again until I understand what to do. Then...victory!

#02 - HEY! WHO ARE YOU? IT'S ME! 💀💀🦴

I record my own voice on my mobile. My voice must be mellow, like that of someone I'd like to sleep with, like Morgan Freeman. Chilled, alone in a room. My arms and legs stretched out, palms facing down. I must tell myself to breathe slowly, focus on the eyelids, let them go, then my forehead, let it go, etc. I must listen to my breathing and understand it. Done? Great! Now I can play it back whenever I like, most likely in a darkened room.

Alternative--I describe some kind of wonder landscape to chill in.

#03 - POSITIVE THOUGHTS, COME TO ME! 💀

I think happy thoughts! I force myself to smile at least three times a day. I try to be aware of my thoughts as soon as I wake up and if I have negative thoughts I turn them upside down and try to "believe in them," although they seem like lies and I feel silly at first (indeed, I do).

#04 - I SING!!!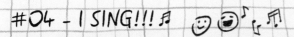

When I feel an attack a-knocking, I sing. I sing random words, whatever springs to mind..."Dog dog doo doo doo, cat cat doo doo doo..." until it's gone. Or I list the names of my entire family, all the way back to my great-great-grandparents. In a song, of course. I think and sing about everything, except my panic.

#05 - BRAIN, ARE YOU LISTENING?

Ok, this is weird. I take a glass of water, put it on my bedside table before going to sleep, I drink half of it, then I ask myself all these wonderful questions, like "What do I want?" "Where am I going?" "Should I leave everything?" and so on, also wondering how to fix the problem. I drink the other half in the morning and repeat the whole procedure, then I wait for evocative thoughts and visions to inspire me and stuff like that.

#06 - WHERE IS IT? I'M SURE IT WAS HERE! ☺

Every time I want to encourage myself and prevent an attack I jot a piece of advice down on a Post-it note, then leave it somewhere I'll completely forget about. Then again. And again. And again. When I stumble across one at random, I try to do as it says. And the others... well, I'll find them when I find them.

#07 - I'VE BEEN WAITING FOR YOU, YOU'RE LATE!

When I'm frightened and think of panic as my enemy, I let it do as it pleases, rather than facing it. I listen to it, rather than struggle against it. I don't put up any fight, I just try to understand why it came to me and ask it how it's doing. It's my guest, so I lay the table and make its favorite cake!

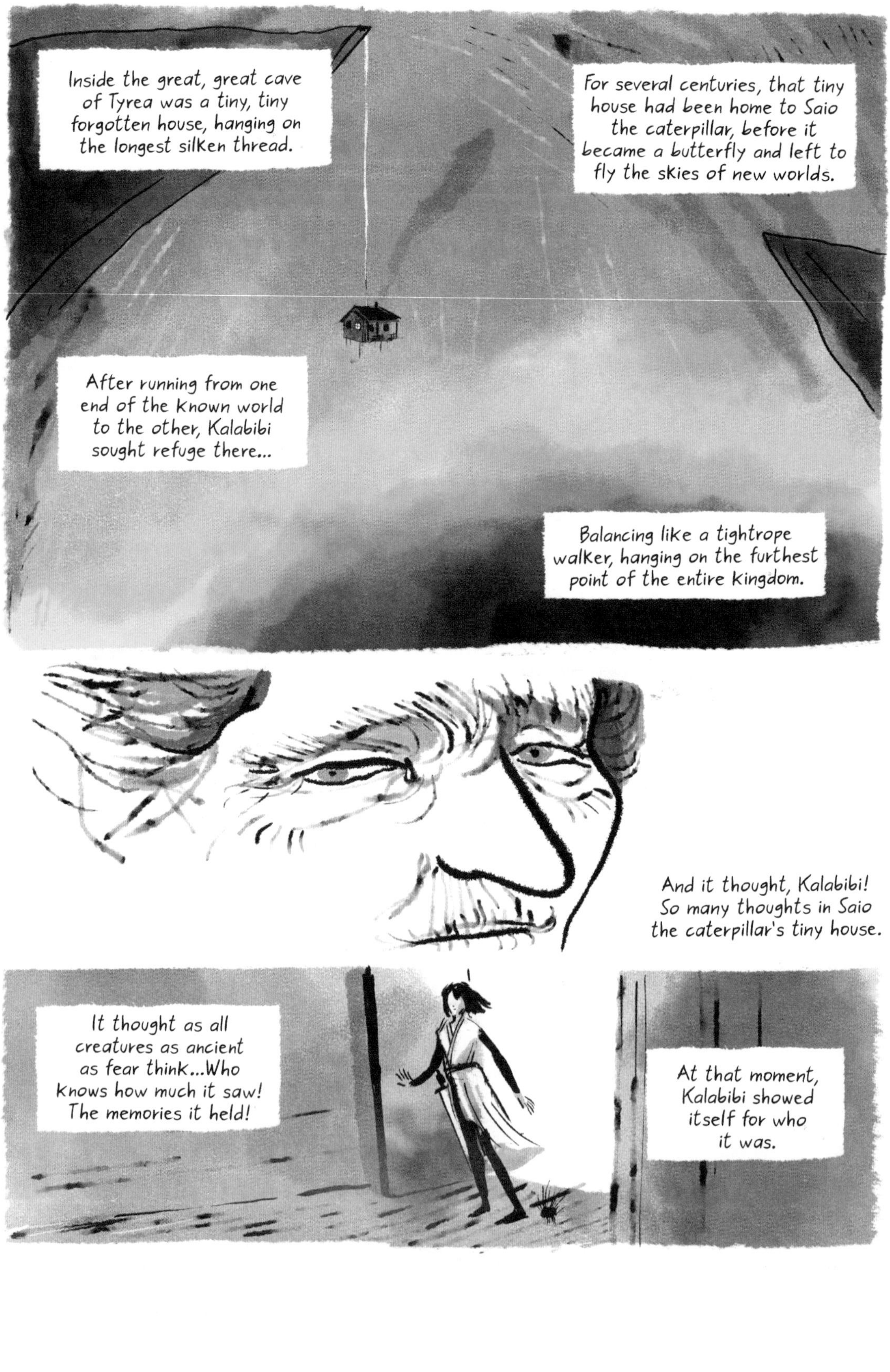
Inside the great, great cave of Tyrea was a tiny, tiny forgotten house, hanging on the longest silken thread.
For several centuries, that tiny house had been home to Saio the caterpillar, before it became a butterfly and left to fly the skies of new worlds.
After running from one end of the known world to the other, Kalabibi sought refuge there...
Balancing like a tightrope walker, hanging on the furthest point of the entire kingdom.
And it thought, Kalabibi! So many thoughts in Saio the caterpillar's tiny house.
It thought as all creatures as ancient as fear think...Who knows how much it saw! The memories it held!
At that moment, Kalabibi showed itself for who it was.

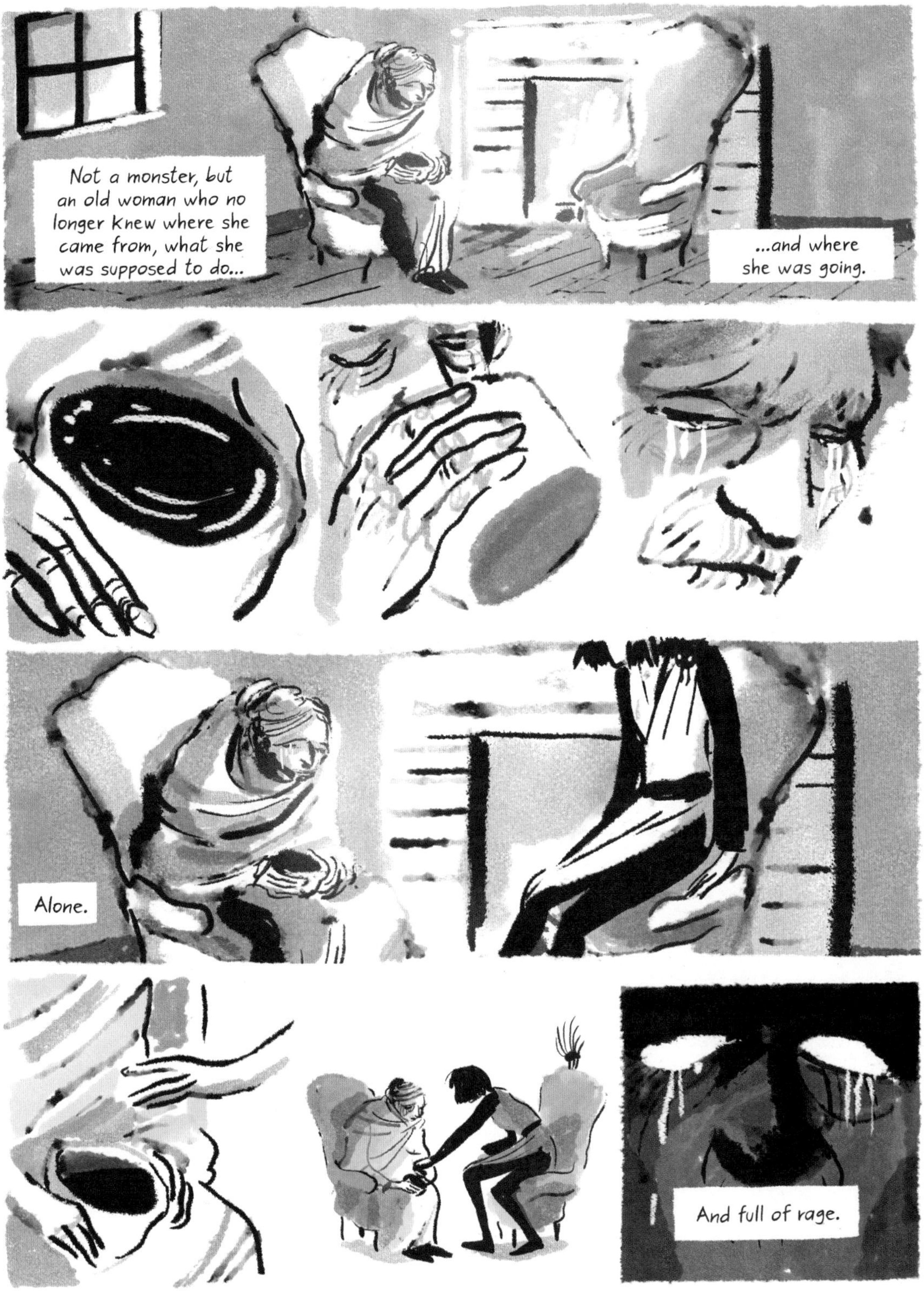
Not a monster, but an old woman who no longer knew where she came from, what she was supposed to do...
...and where she was going.
Alone.
And full of rage.

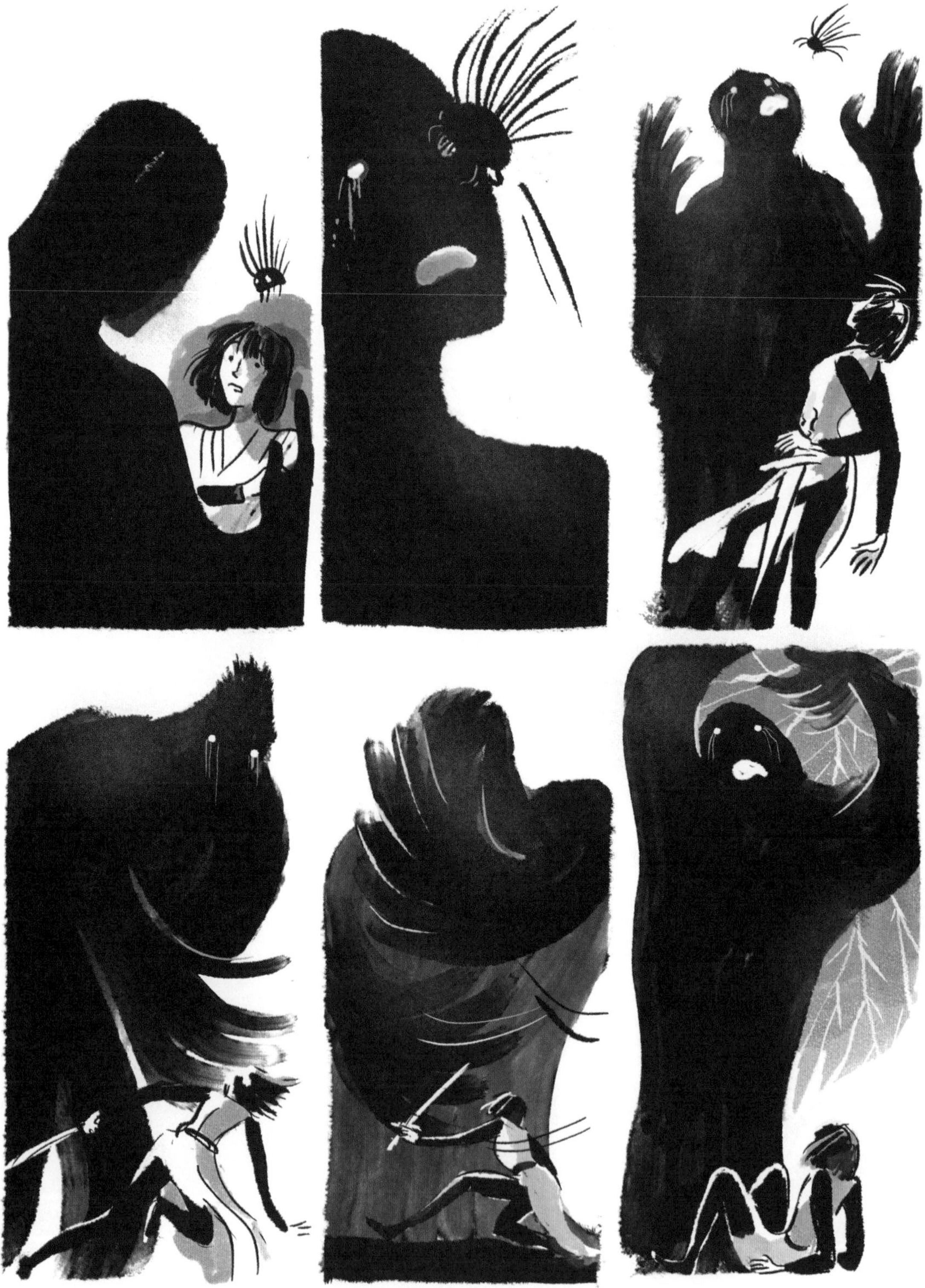

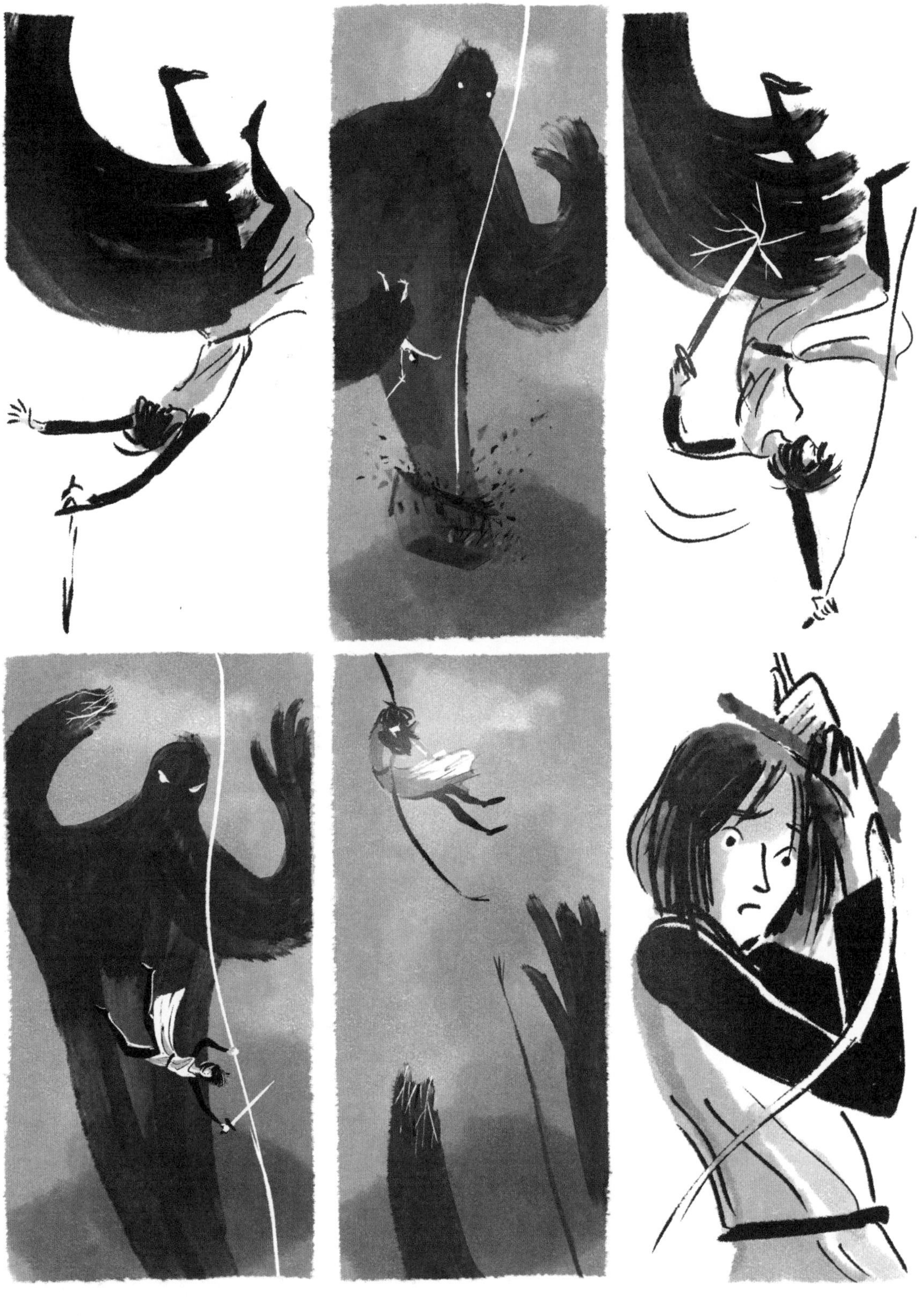

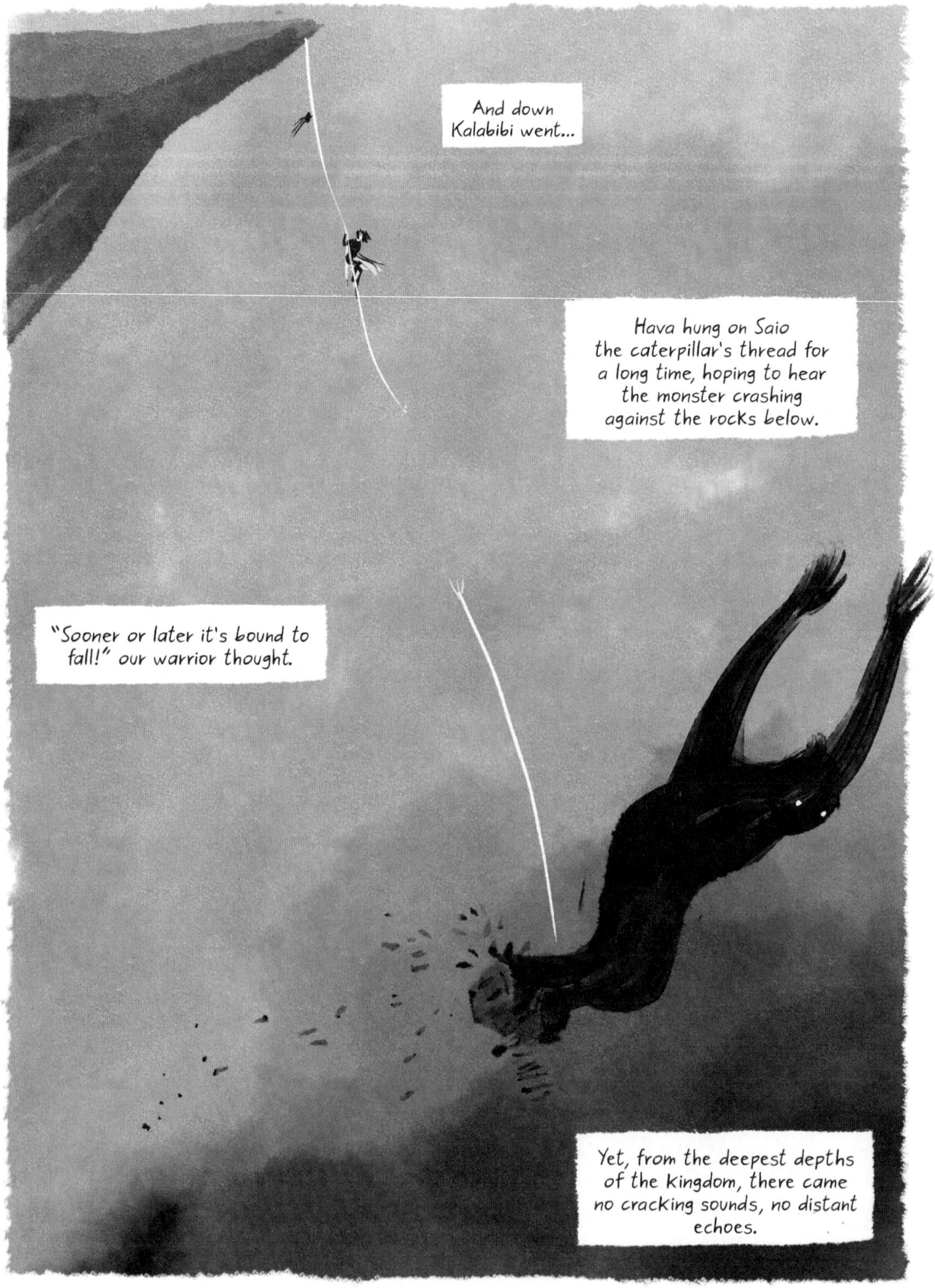
And down Kalabibi went...
Hava hung on Saio the caterpillar's thread for a long time, hoping to hear the monster crashing against the rocks below.
"Sooner or later it's bound to fall!" our warrior thought.
Yet, from the deepest depths of the kingdom, there came no cracking sounds, no distant echoes.

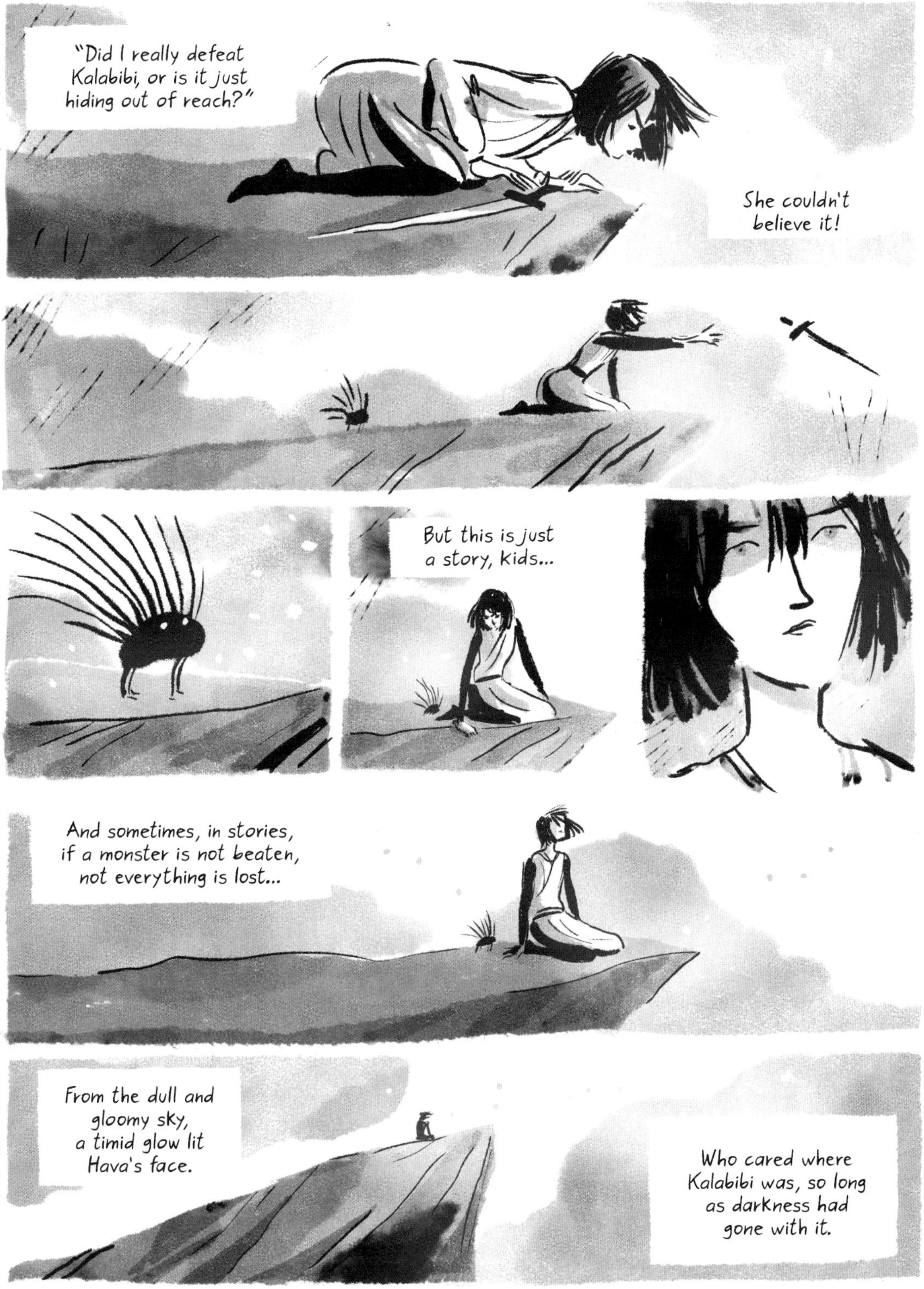
"Did I really defeat Kalabibi, or is it just hiding out of reach?"
She couldn't believe it!
But this is just a story, kids...
And sometimes, in stories, if a monster is not beaten, not everything is lost...
From the dull and gloomy sky, a timid glow lit Hava's face.
Who cared where Kalabibi was, so long as darkness had gone with it.

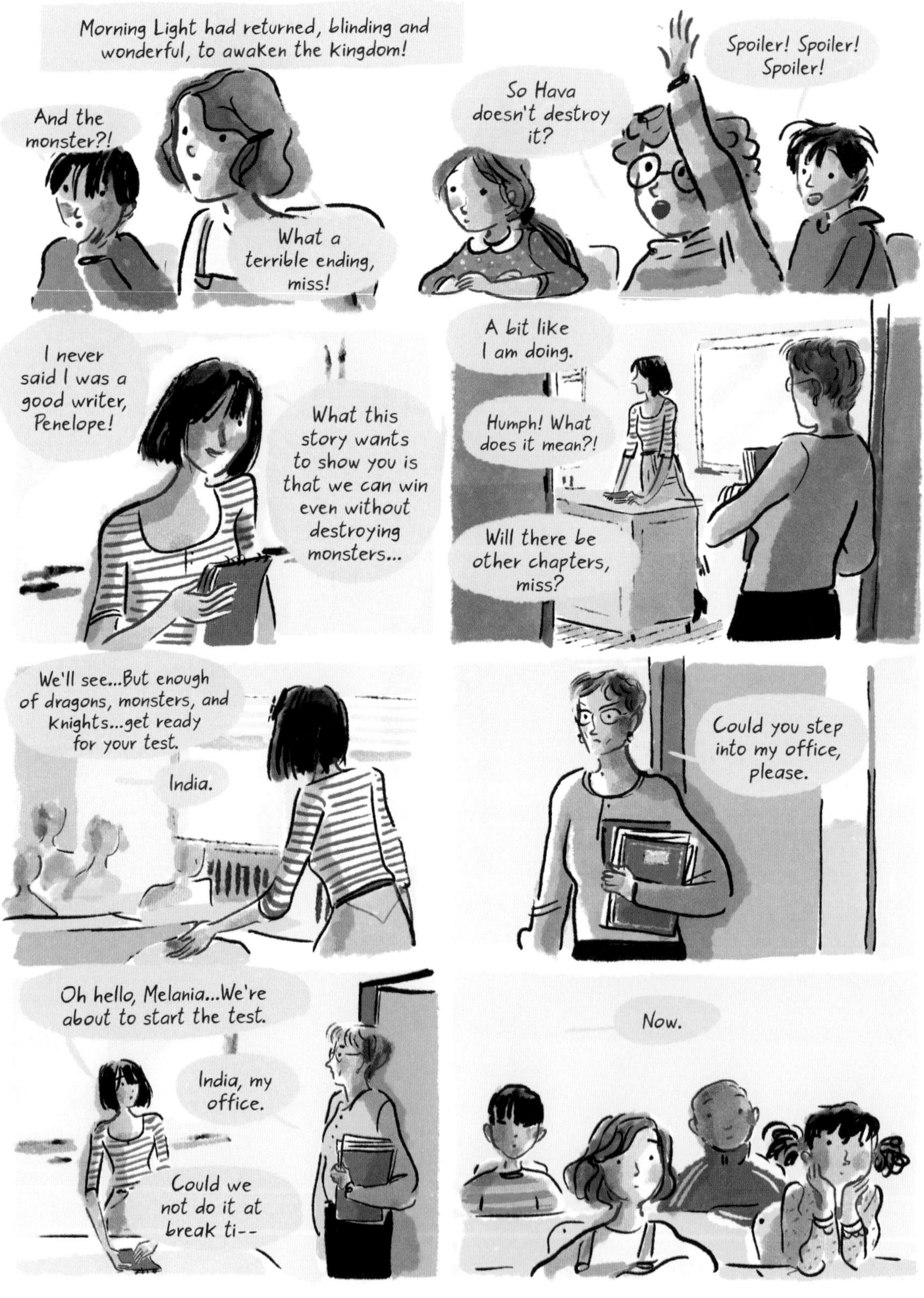
Morning Light had returned, blinding and wonderful, to awaken the kingdom!
And the monster?!
What a terrible ending, miss!
So Hava doesn't destroy it?
Spoiler! Spoiler! Spoiler!
I never said I was a good writer, Penelope!
What this story wants to show you is that we can win even without destroying monsters...
A bit like I am doing.
Humph! What does it mean?!
Will there be other chapters, miss?
We'll see...But enough of dragons, monsters, and knights...get ready for your test.
India.
Could you step into my office, please.
Oh hello, Melania...We're about to start the test.
India, my office.
Could we not do it at break ti--
Now.

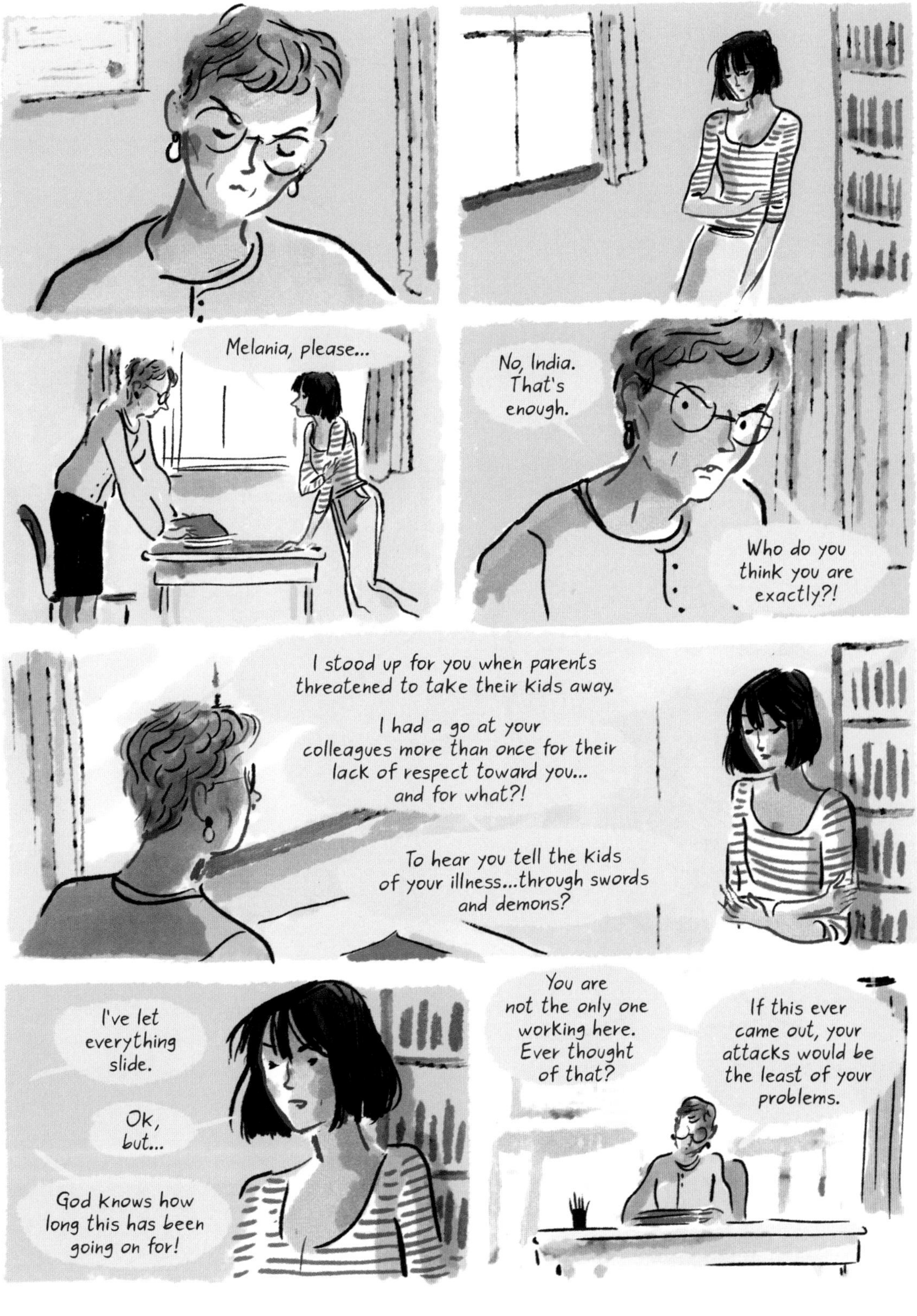

Melania, please...
No, India. That's enough.
Who do you think you are exactly?!
I stood up for you when parents threatened to take their kids away.
I had a go at your colleagues more than once for their lack of respect toward you... and for what?!
To hear you tell the kids of your illness...through swords and demons?
I've let everything slide.
Ok, but...
God knows how long this has been going on for!
You are not the only one working here. Ever thought of that?
If this ever came out, your attacks would be the least of your problems.

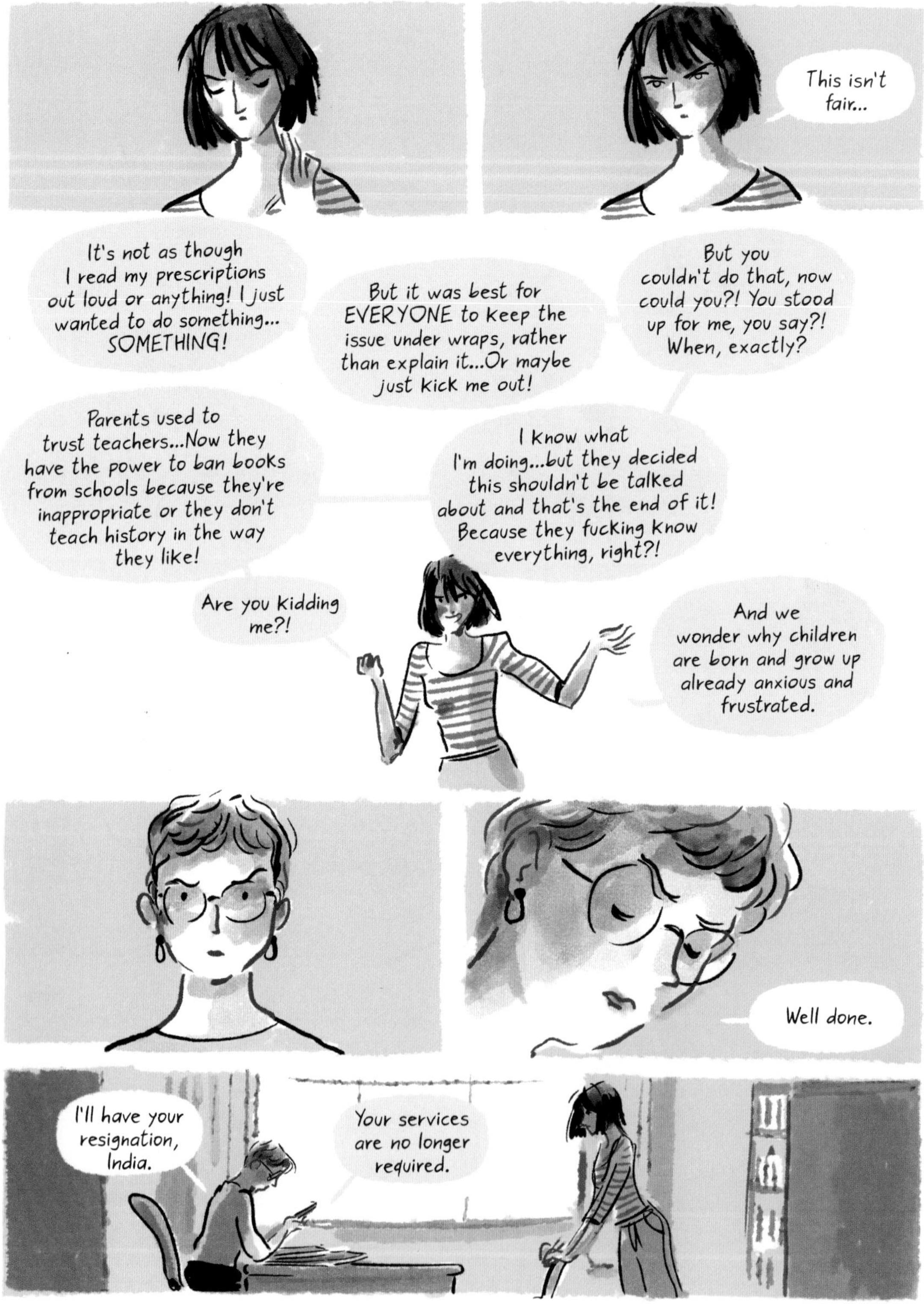
This isn't fair...
It's not as though I read my prescriptions out loud or anything! I just wanted to do something... SOMETHING!
But it was best for EVERYONE to keep the issue under wraps, rather than explain it...Or maybe just kick me out!
But you couldn't do that, now could you?! You stood up for me, you say?! When, exactly?
Parents used to trust teachers...Now they have the power to ban books from schools because they're inappropriate or they don't teach history in the way they like!
I know what I'm doing...but they decided this shouldn't be talked about and that's the end of it! Because they fucking know everything, right?!
Are you kidding me?!
And we wonder why children are born and grow up already anxious and frustrated.
Well done.
I'll have your resignation, India.
Your services are no longer required.

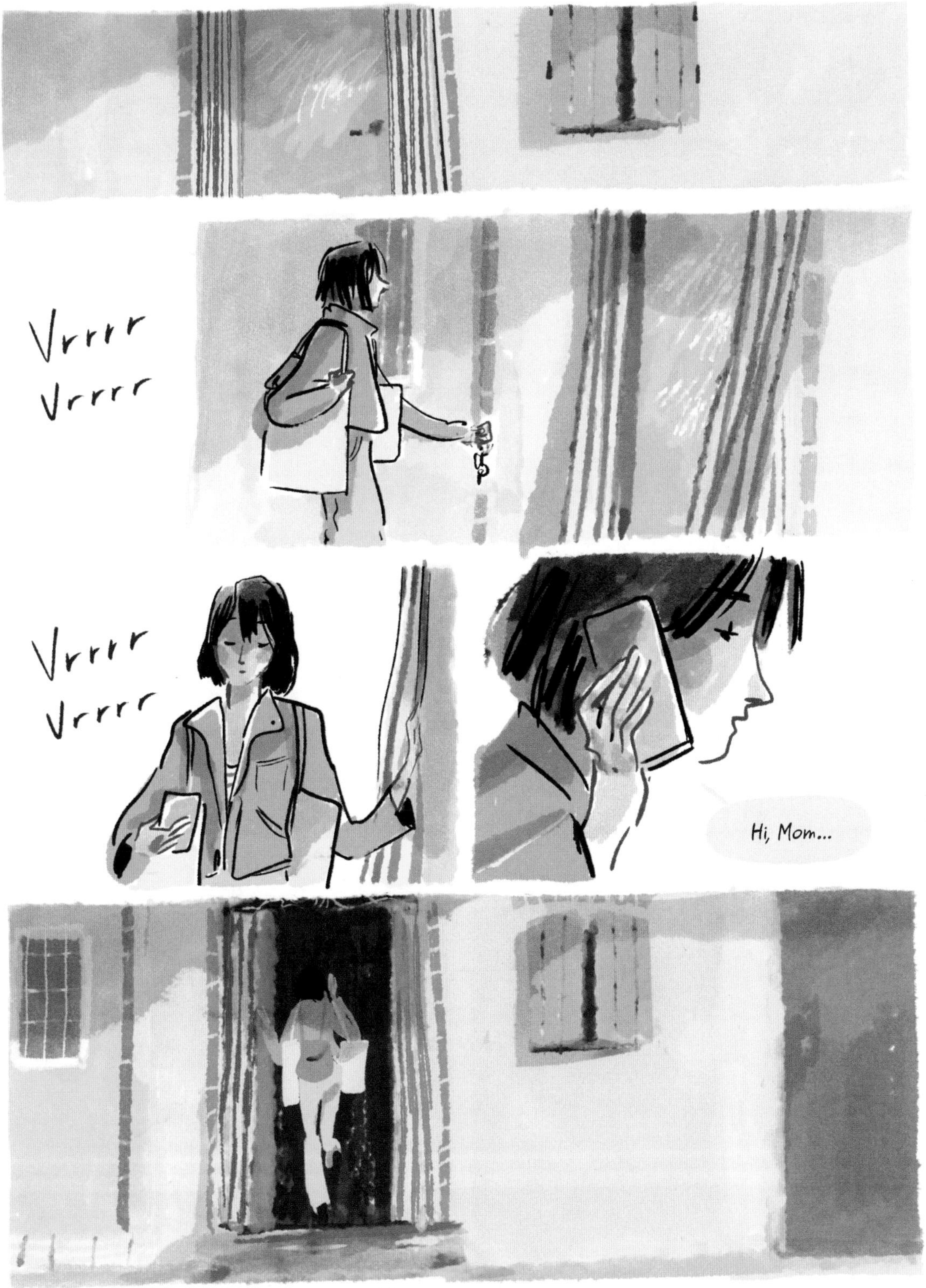
Vrrrr
Vrrrr
Vrrrr
Vrrrr
Hi, Mom...

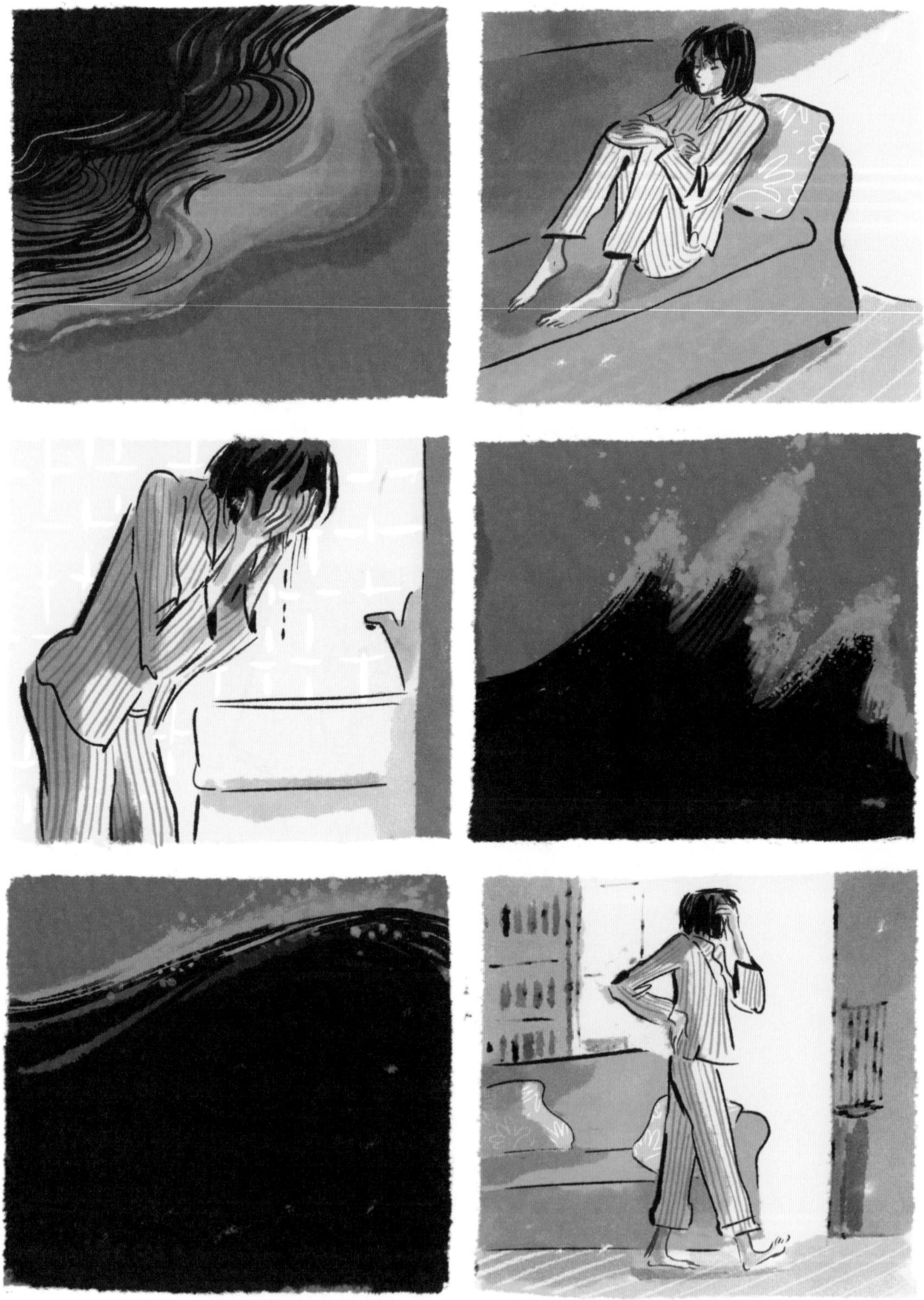

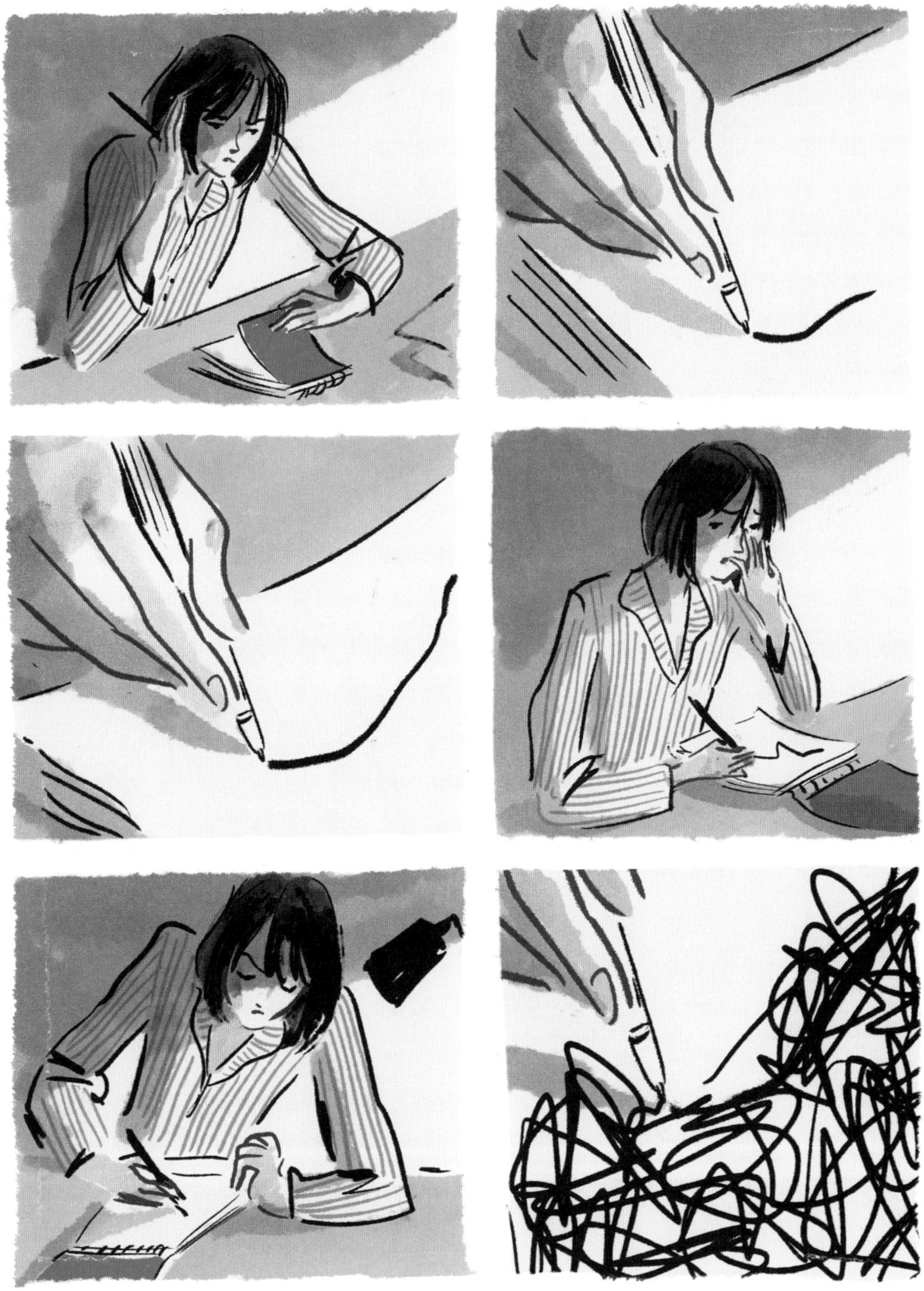

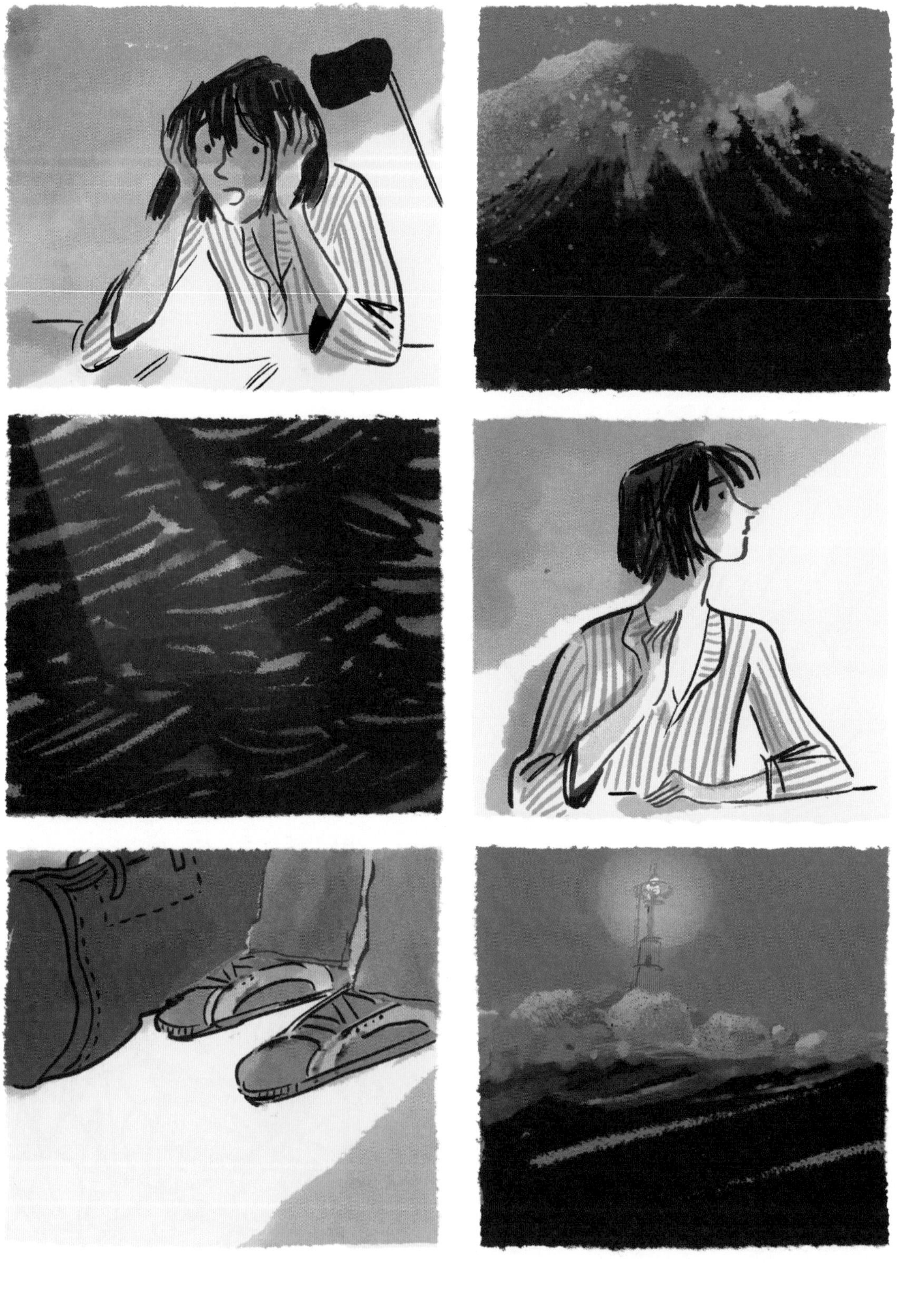

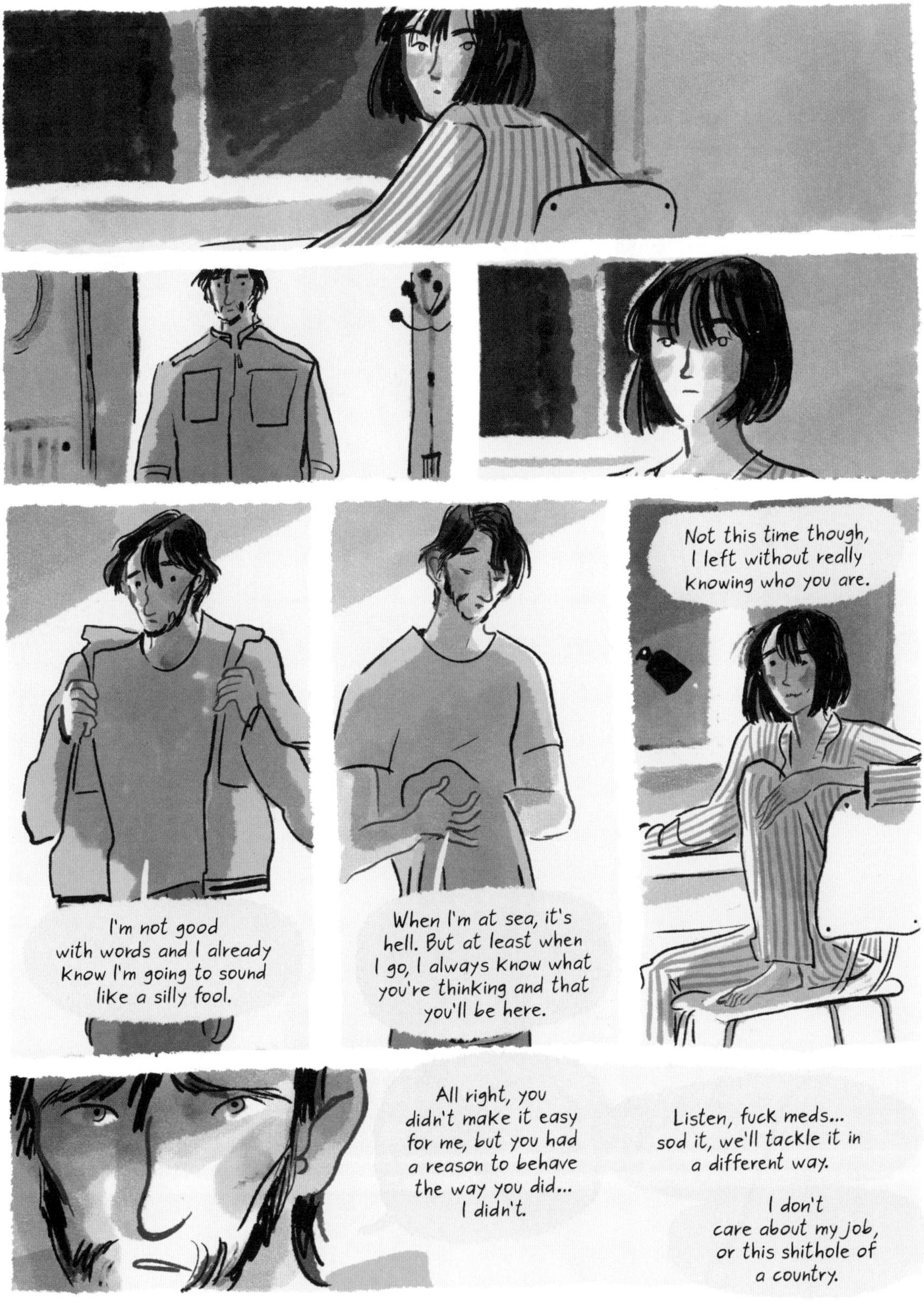
I'm not good with words and I already know I'm going to sound like a silly fool.
When I'm at sea, it's hell. But at least when I go, I always know what you're thinking and that you'll be here.
Not this time though, I left without really knowing who you are.
All right, you didn't make it easy for me, but you had a reason to behave the way you did... I didn't.
Listen, fuck meds... sod it, we'll tackle it in a different way.
I don't care about my job, or this shithole of a country.

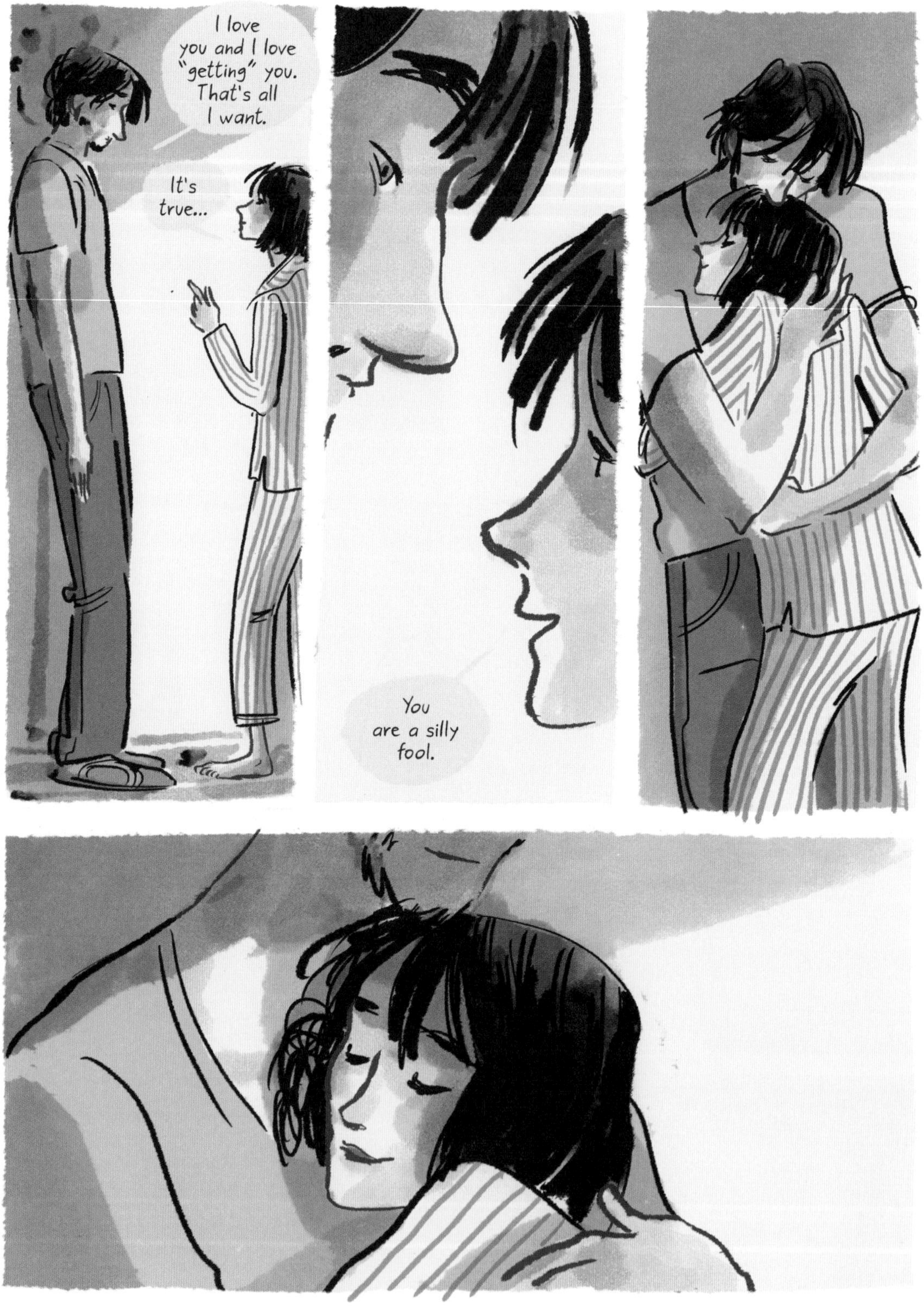
I love you and I love "getting" you. That's all I want.
It's true...
You are a silly fool.

Epilogue

The vertical sea

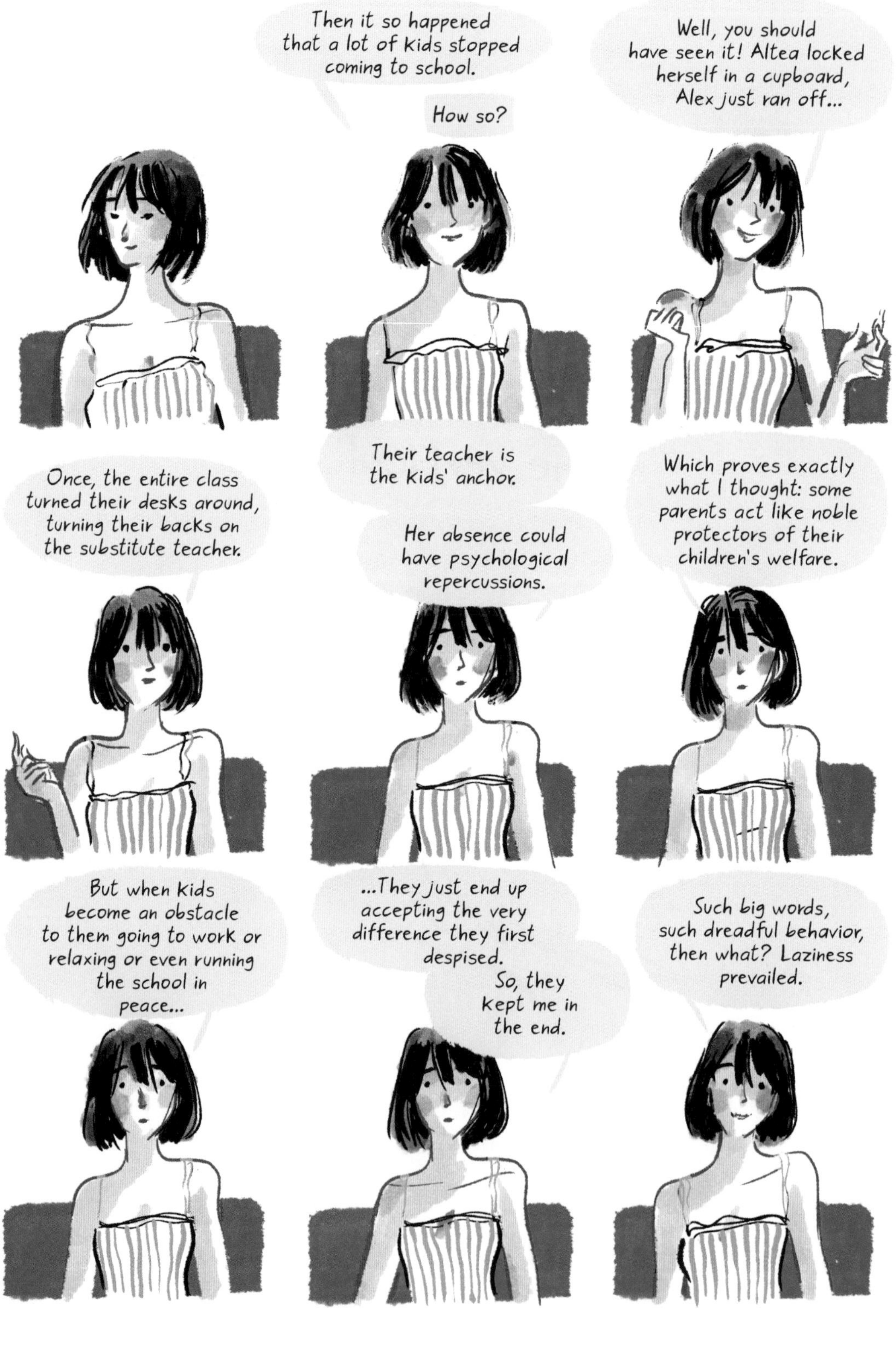
Then it so happened that a lot of kids stopped coming to school.
How so?
Well, you should have seen it! Altea locked herself in a cupboard, Alex just ran off...
Once, the entire class turned their desks around, turning their backs on the substitute teacher.
Their teacher is the kids' anchor.
Her absence could have psychological repercussions.
Which proves exactly what I thought: some parents act like noble protectors of their children's welfare.
But when kids become an obstacle to them going to work or relaxing or even running the school in peace...
...They just end up accepting the very difference they first despised.
So, they kept me in the end.
Such big words, such dreadful behavior, then what? Laziness prevailed.

Time's up, methinks.

Things cannot stay the same, India. You always said you love your life, your job...

Do you really think so?

But I've decided to stop looking for the great cure or the right path.

...And moments of discovery that'll help me control my fear.

...But your problem arose because there's a clash between your rational and your emotional side.

There's no potion that will heal me when I drink it, or magic words that'll keep panic at bay.

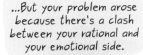

I don't want to face this thing as a warrior, as I know that what's inside me will never completely go away.

It would be like fighting against myself.

If this is not your path, your attacks will not spare you.

I simply realized that there are moments when every-thing seems clearer and easier.

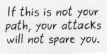

This newly acquired awareness may well be my ideal cure.

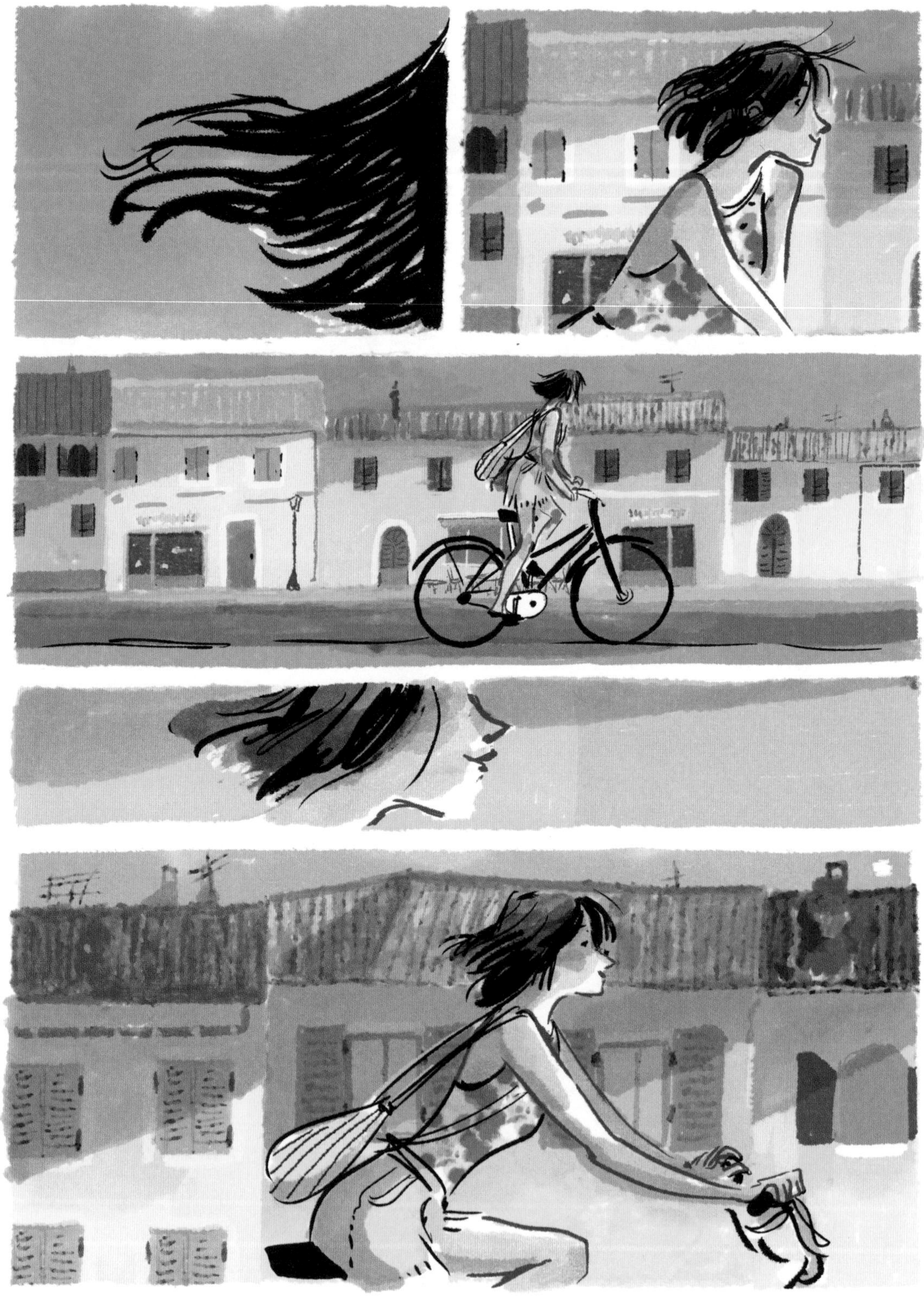

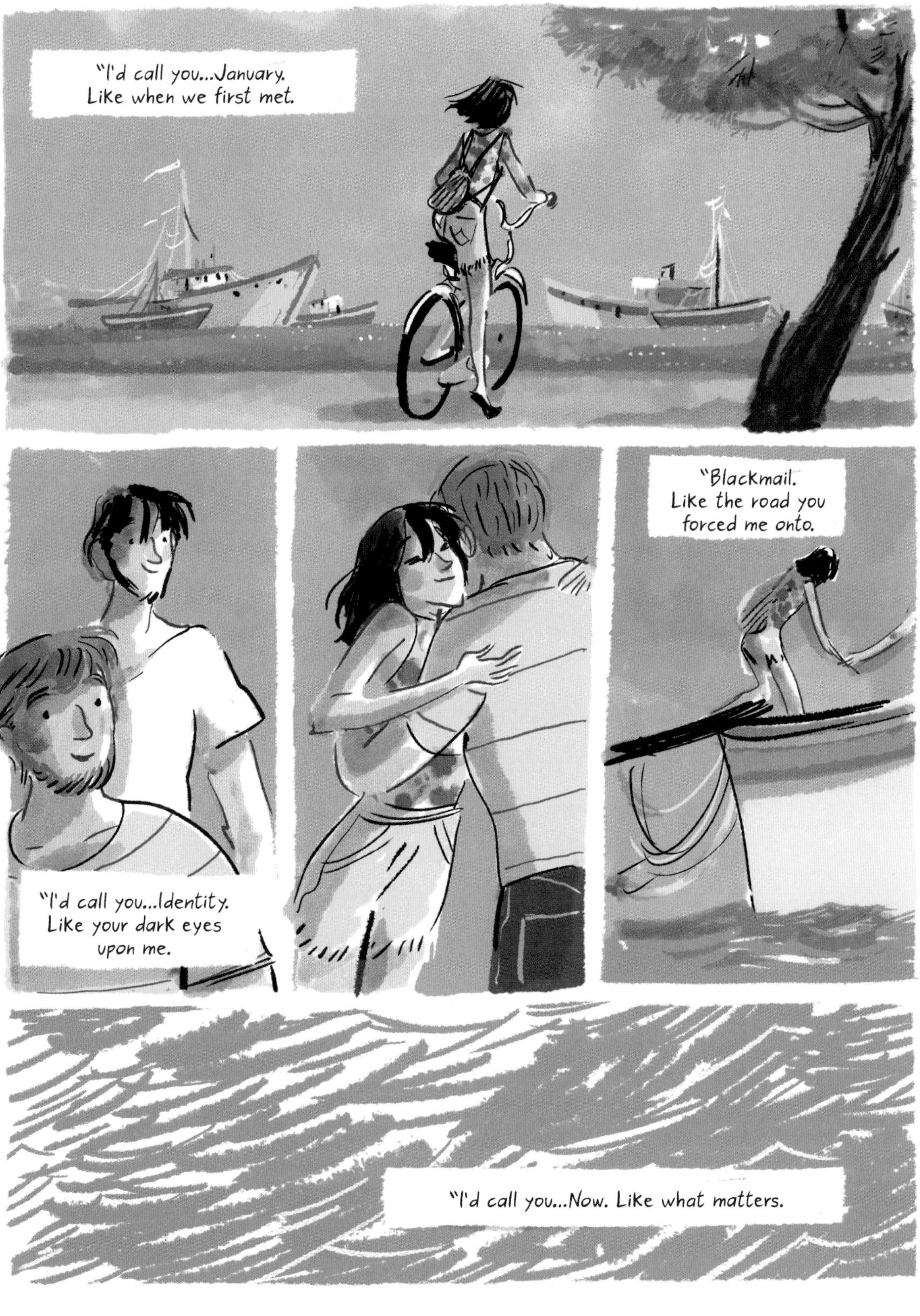
"I'd call you...January. Like when we first met.
"I'd call you...Identity. Like your dark eyes upon me.
"Blackmail. Like the road you forced me onto.
"I'd call you...Now. Like what matters.

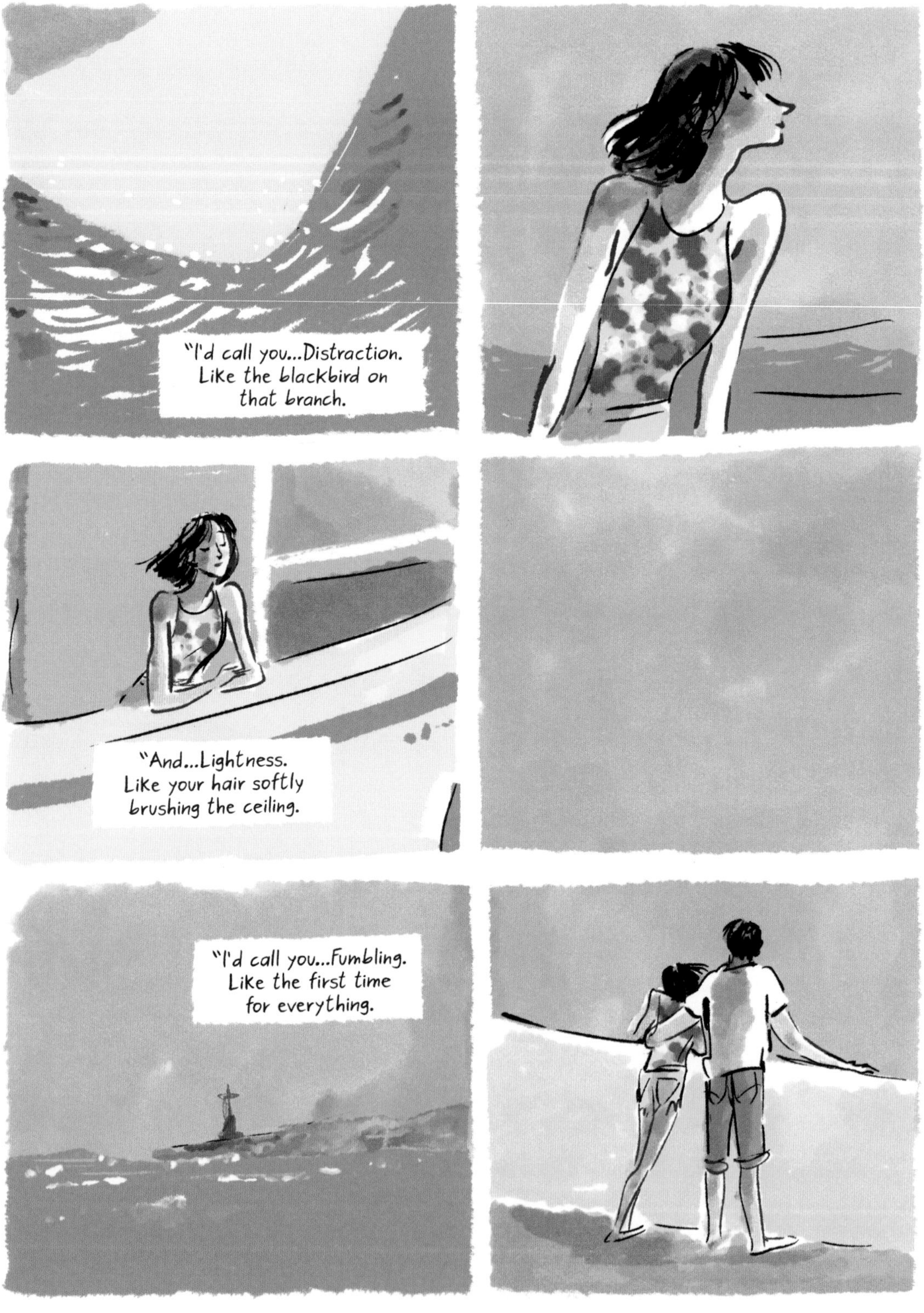
"I'd call you...Distraction. Like the blackbird on that branch.
"And...Lightness. Like your hair softly brushing the ceiling.
"I'd call you...Fumbling. Like the first time for everything.

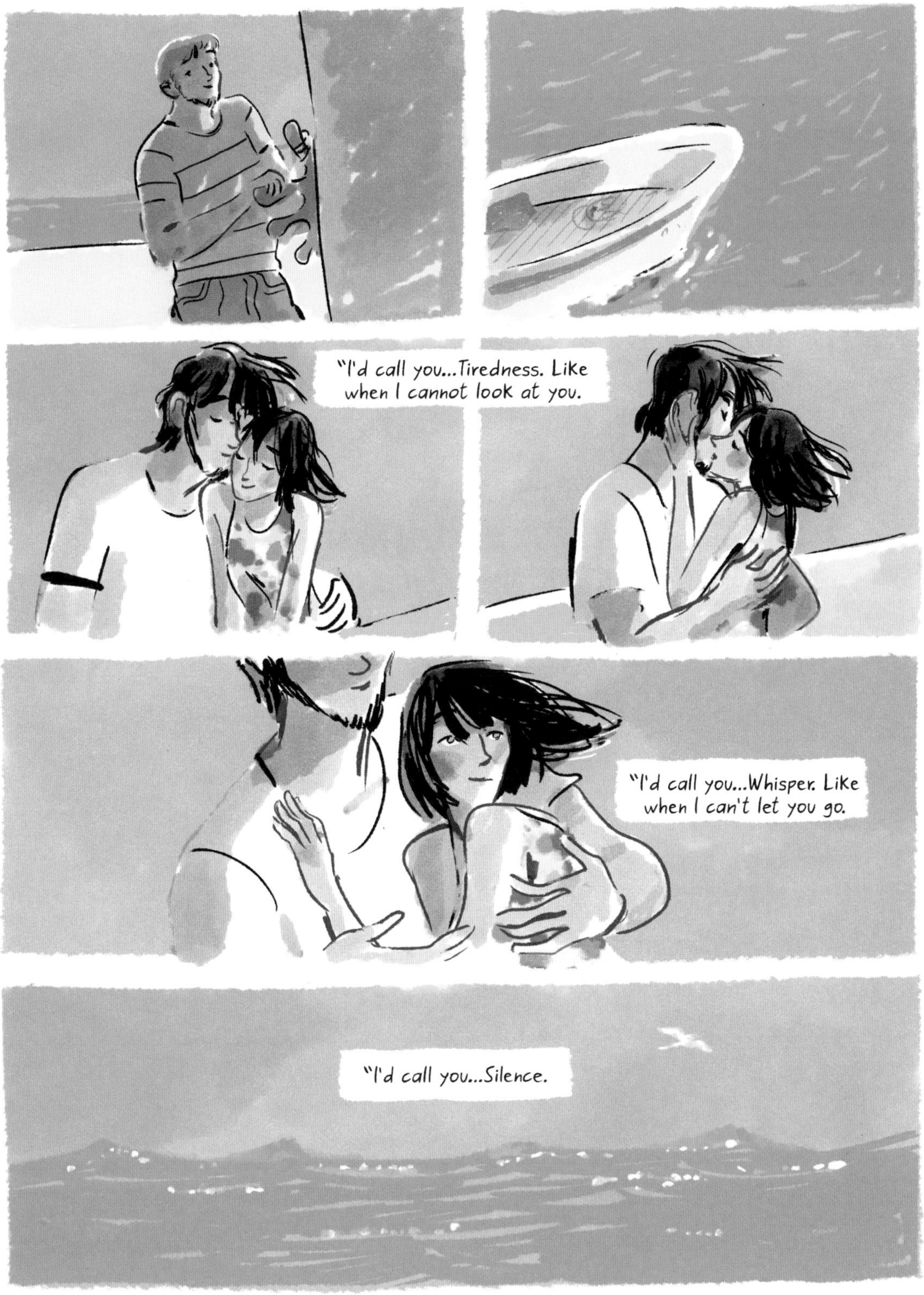
"I'd call you...Tiredness. Like when I cannot look at you.
"I'd call you...Whisper. Like when I can't let you go.
"I'd call you...Silence.

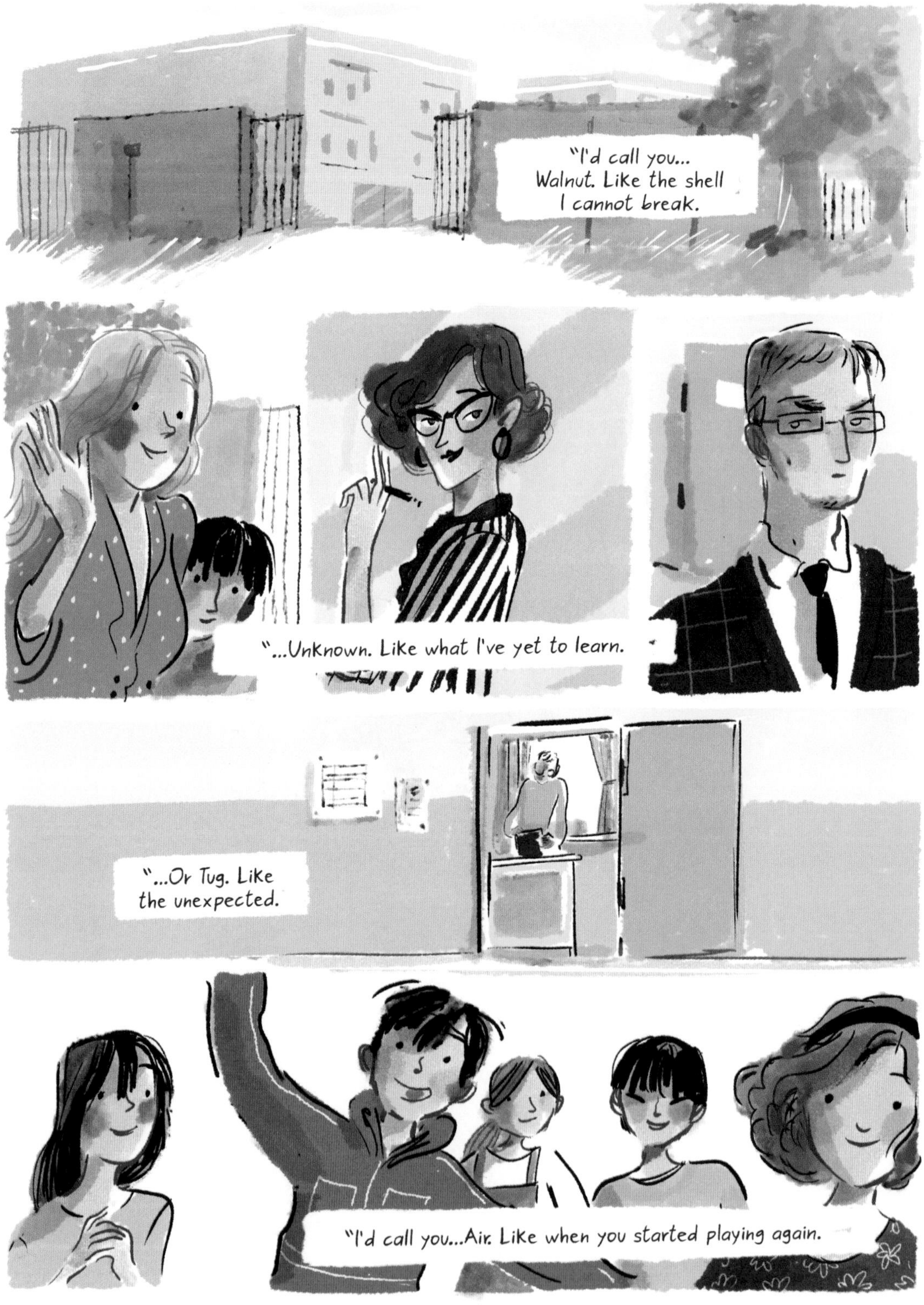
"I'd call you...
Walnut. Like the shell
I cannot break.
"...Unknown. Like what I've yet to learn.
"...Or Tug. Like
the unexpected.
"I'd call you...Air. Like when you started playing again.

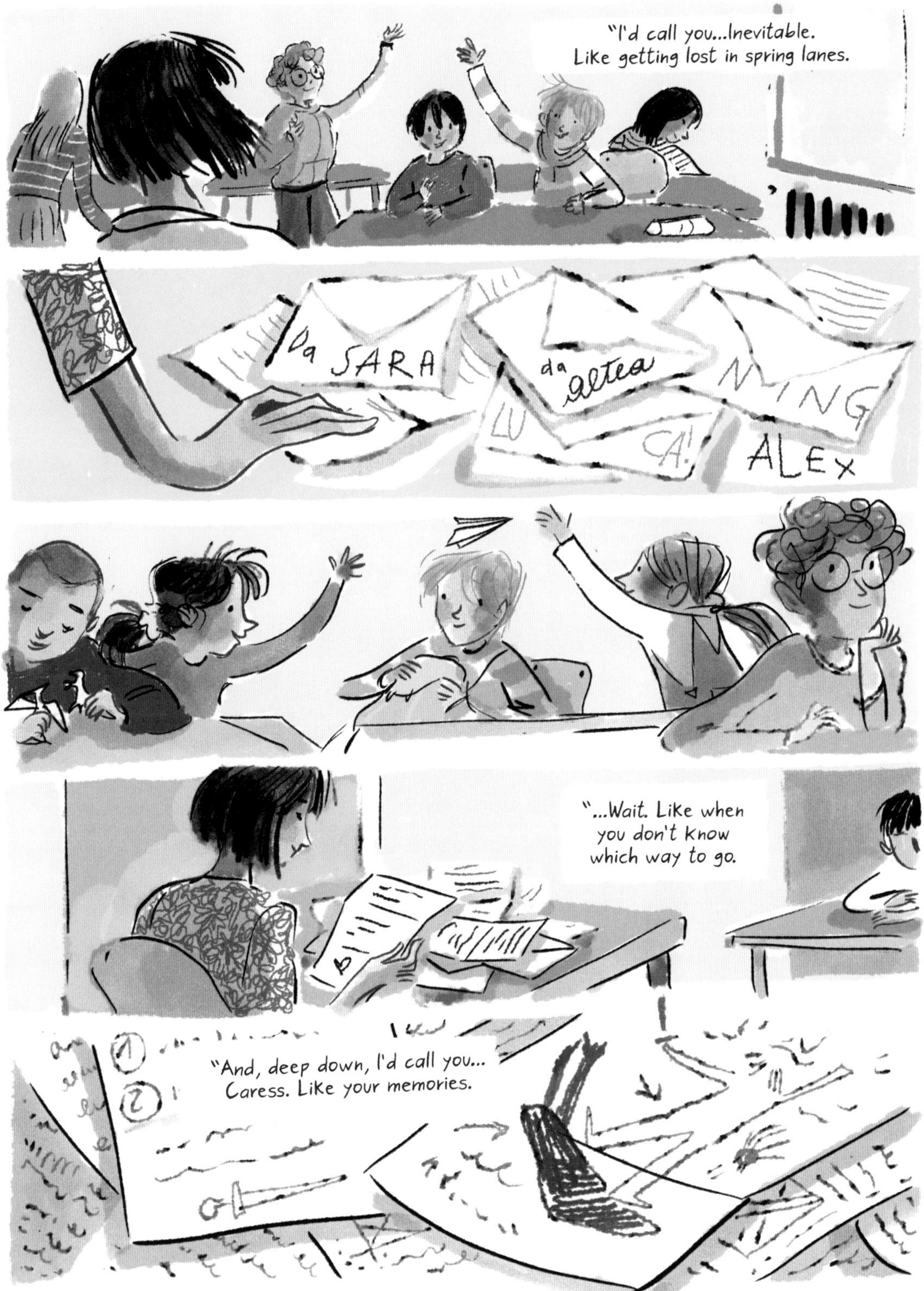
"I'd call you...Inevitable. Like getting lost in spring lanes.
Da SARA
da altea
NING
CA!
ALEX
"...Wait. Like when you don't know which way to go.
"And, deep down, I'd call you... Caress. Like your memories.

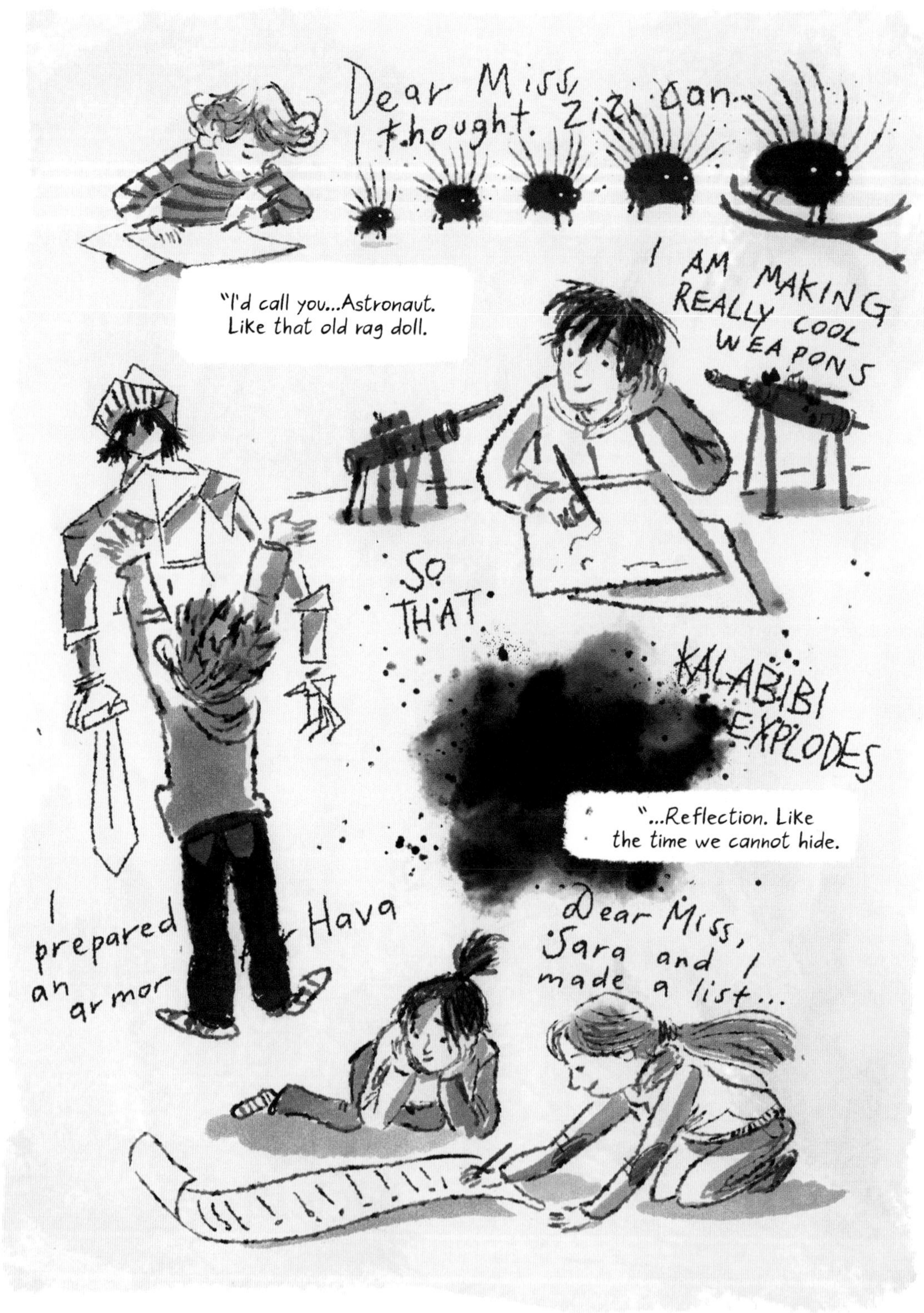
Dear Miss, I thought. Zizi can...
I AM MAKING REALLY COOL WEAPONS
"I'd call you...Astronaut. Like that old rag doll.
SO THAT
KALABIBI EXPLODES
"...Reflection. Like the time we cannot hide.
I prepared an armor for Hava
Dear Miss, Sara and I made a list...

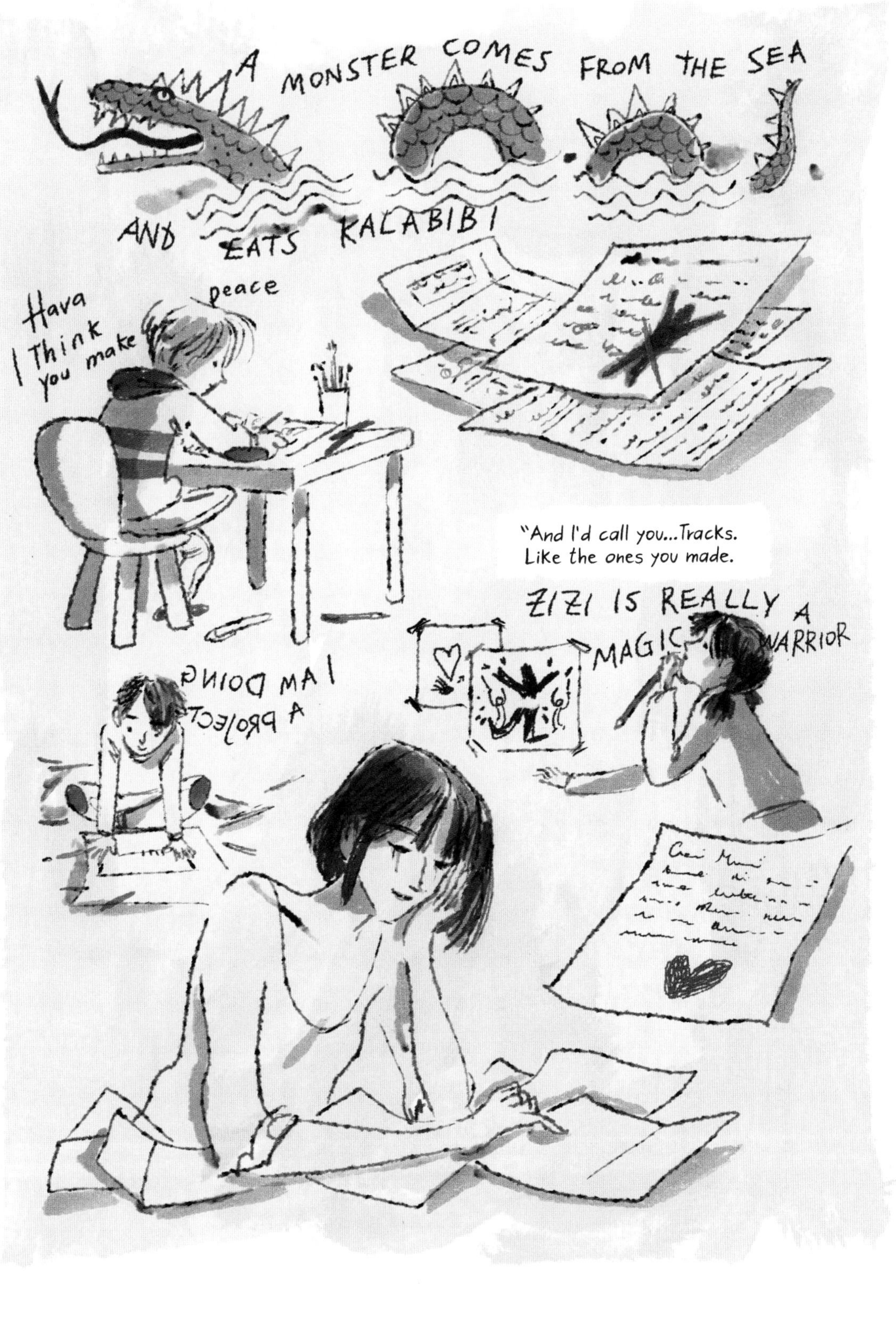
A MONSTER COMES FROM THE SEA
AND EATS KALABIBI
Hava I think you make peace
"And I'd call you...Tracks. Like the ones you made.
ZIZI IS REALLY A MAGIC WARRIOR
I AM DOING A PROJECT

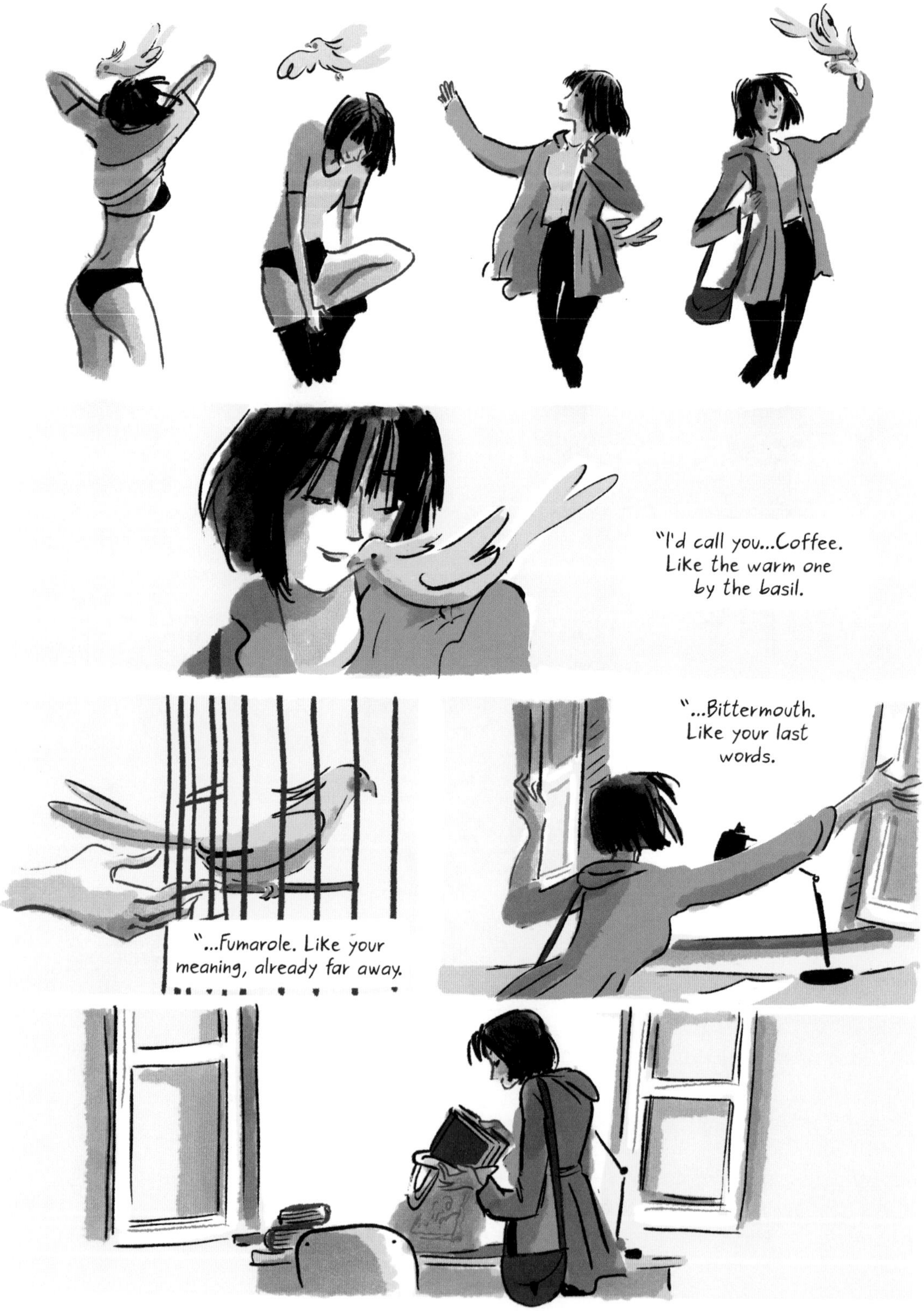
"I'd call you...Coffee. Like the warm one by the basil.
"...Fumarole. Like your meaning, already far away.
"...Bittermouth. Like your last words.

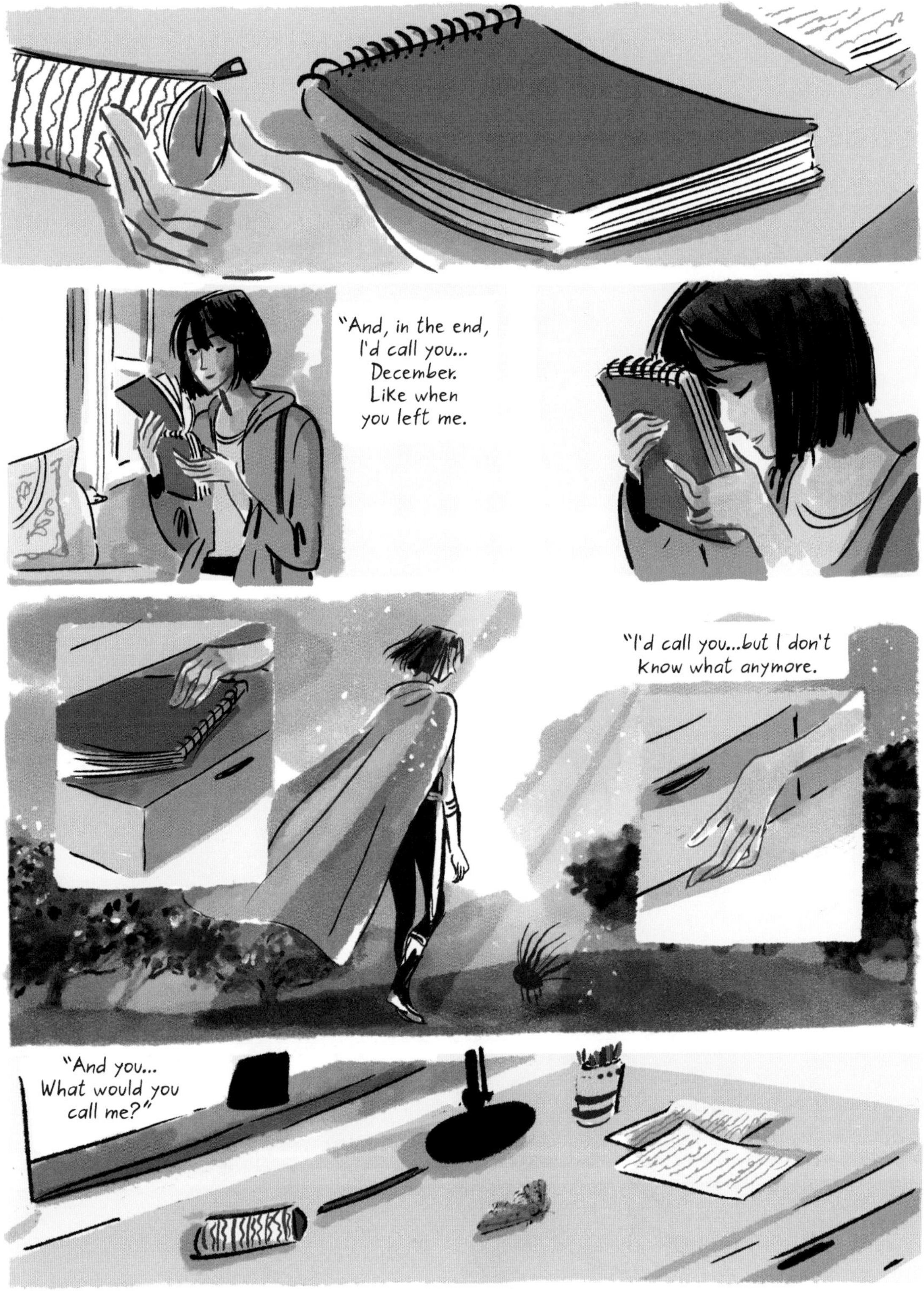
"And, in the end, I'd call you... December. Like when you left me.
"I'd call you...but I don't know what anymore.
"And you... What would you call me?"

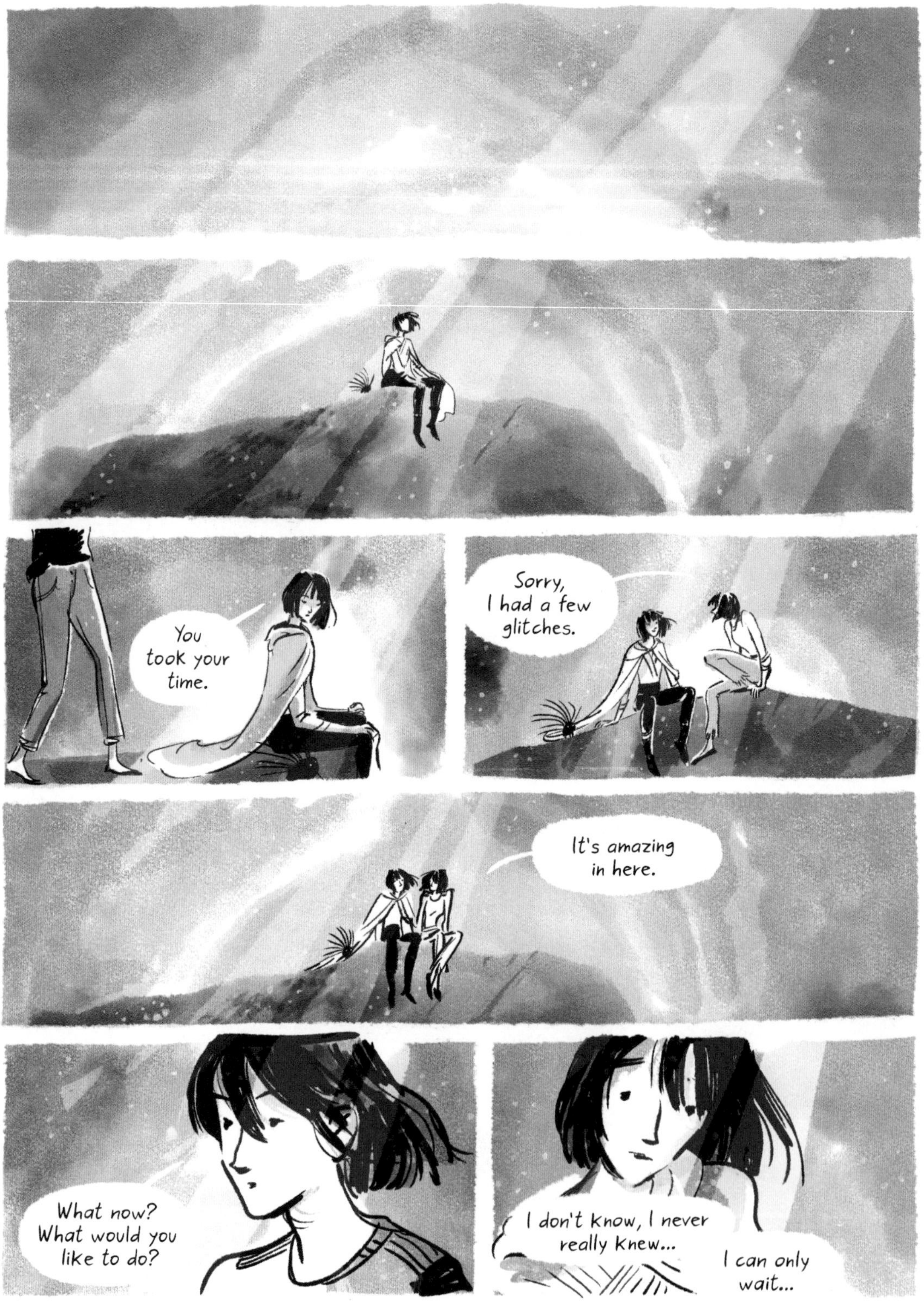
You took your time.
Sorry, I had a few glitches.
It's amazing in here.
What now? What would you like to do?
I don't know, I never really knew...
I can only wait...

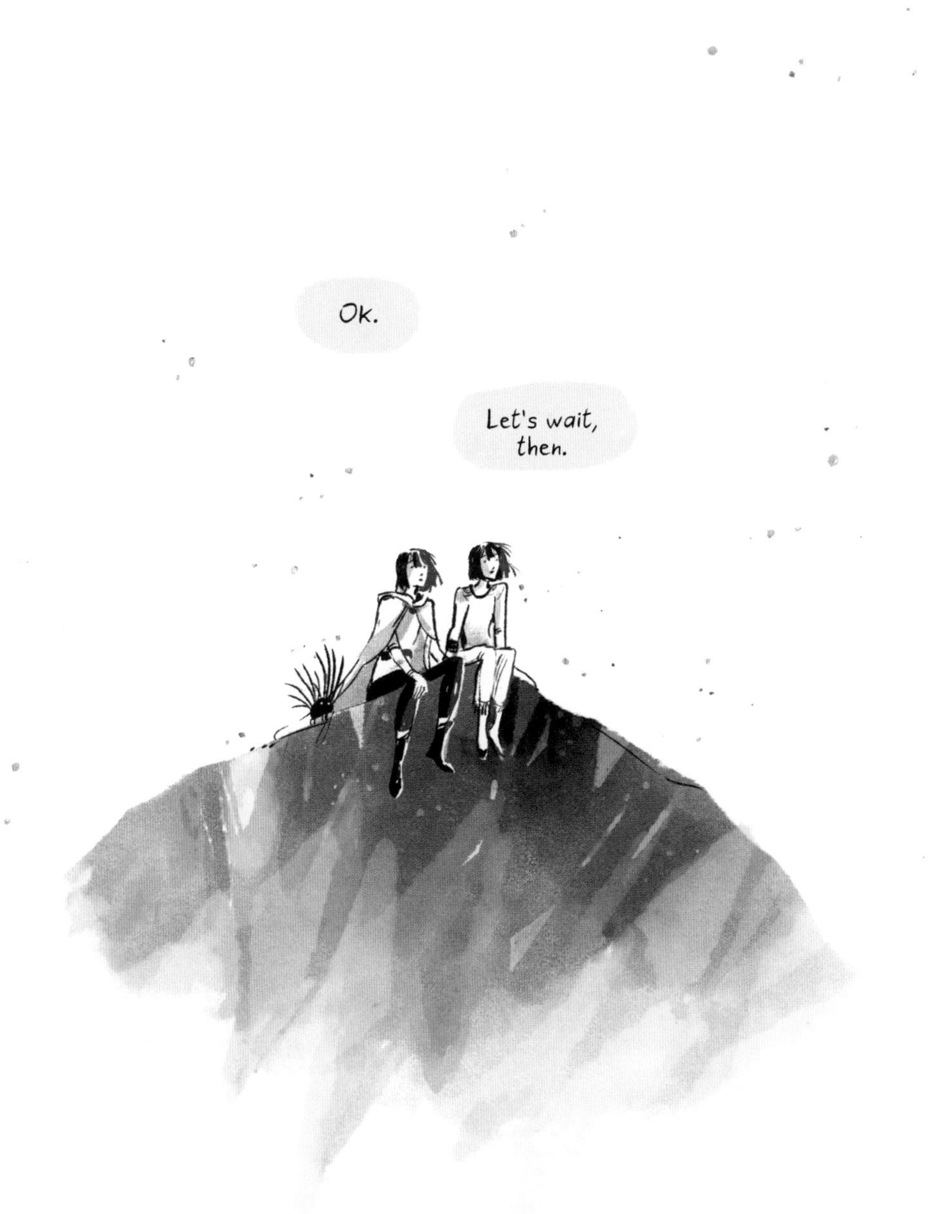
Ok.
Let's wait, then.

My thanks to my parents, for always being so supportive and patient.
To Elena, who was ever so patient during the making of this book.
My thanks also go to Michele, Caterina, Leonardo, Lorenz, and the entire BAO family for their relentless support in this extraordinary two-year journey.
Super thanks to Ilaria, for the passion, the hours-long phone calls, and the kind of working relationship that turns into an amazing friendship.
This story encapsulates her soul, too, and I could not have wished for anything better.
My thanks to Silvia for her precious advice and to all the voices that, whether they wanted to or not, contributed to form India's universe.

Brian

I've been creating this book in my mind for the longest time, and it is the result of a lot of luck, a few misadventures, and also some encounters that helped turn an idea into reality, which is always magic.

Thank you to Caterina and Michele, who, a few years ago, met this shy girl and gave her courage and confidence.
Thank you to Brian for the talent, the joy, and the sensitivity: I started working with a coauthor and finished the book with a friend who did an incredible job, filling it with personality and poetry.
Thank you to Lorenzo and Leonardo for their perfect work.
Thank you to Martina, who, by telling me her story with a mix of courage, honesty, and friendship, helped me understand India.
Thank you to Dr. Luisa Ortuso for her support, deep knowledge, and good humor.

Thank you to Davide, who pushed, supported, and encouraged me nonstop, dispelling dark clouds when necessary and making everything better.

Ilaria

BRIAN FRESCHI

Born in '93 among the Riviera beaches, he worked
with the Manticora collective, producing a number
of comics, and with numerous organizations such
as BAO Publishing, Smemoranda, Noise Press,
Attaccapanni Press, Out of the Box, and MaliEstremi.
In 2018 he began working as an author of books for
young adults with Sassi Junior, Pelledoca Editore,
Bacchilega Junior, and Giazira.

The Vertical Sea is his second book with BAO, after ***Gli
anni che restano*** (2017), illustrated by Davide Aurilia.

ILARIA URBINATI

Born in the mountains and a longtime Turinese, she is an illustrator and graphic novelist. She began to draw at about two years of age all over the house walls and decided she was never going to stop, which brought her to illustrate books for children and young adults for Italian and foreign publishers like Disney, Mondadori, DeAgostini, Il Castoro, Giunti, Erickson, and Little Bee Books. In the meantime, her drawings appeared in projects by McDonald's, *Science Magazine*, Barilla, and Unilever. For three years now she's been illustrating the Posta del Cuore in the daily newspaper *La Stampa*.

The Vertical Sea is her first book with BAO Publishing.

Cliff, the BAO Publishing logo,
as drawn by Ilaria Urbinati

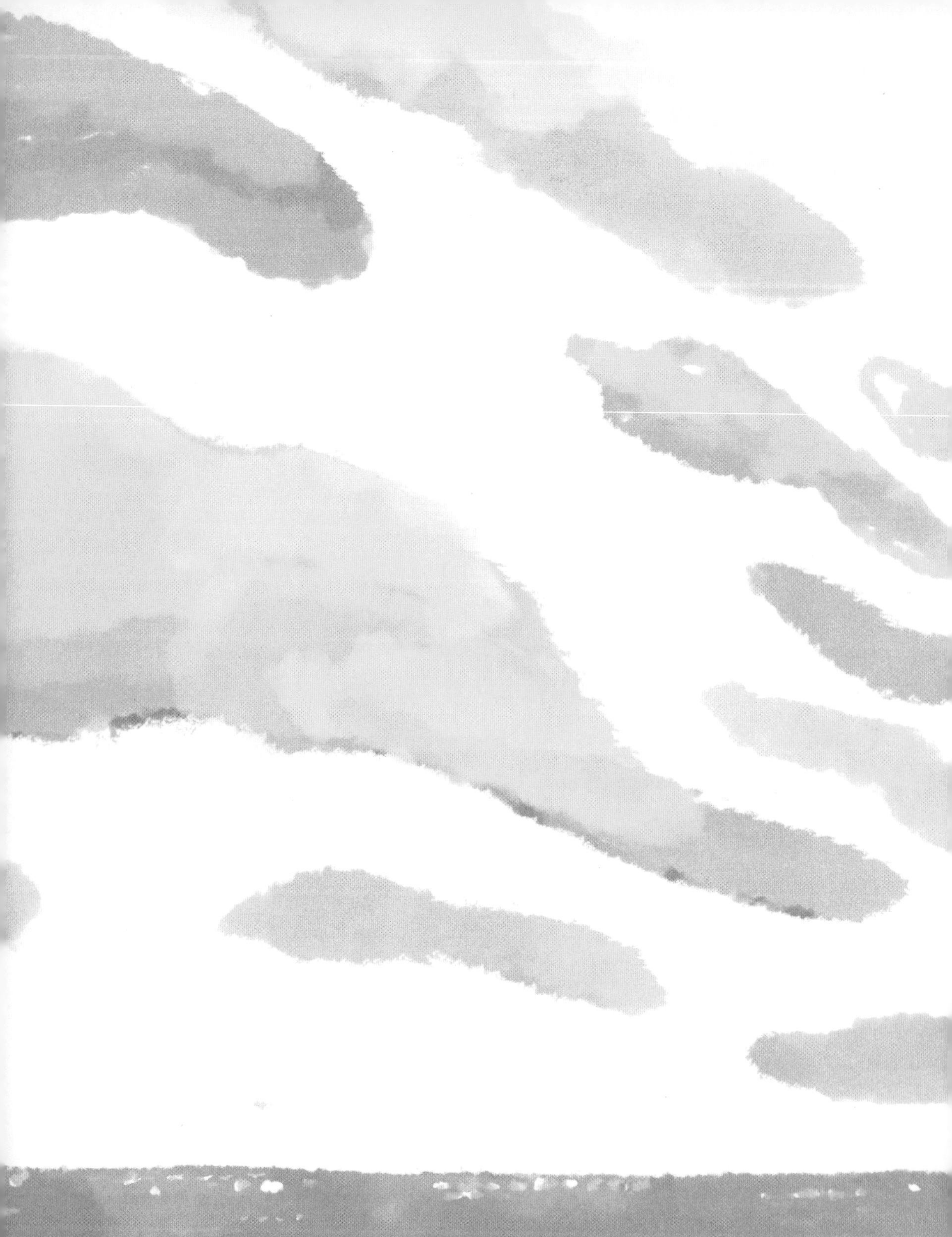